She could hear Pharaoh being lowered, his basket not coming down quite so lightly as her own, for it seemed to smack the walls. She looked toward the shaft, but the feet of Pharaoh did not appear. A great slab was being lowered on ropes. Renifer's torchlight showed it to be no beautiful painted object. Just rock.

Annie could make no sense of it.

When the huge stone had settled onto the bottom, the person above let go of the ropes. They fell into a coil of their own. Were she and Renifer meant to do something with those ropes?

A second stone was lowered onto the ropes from the first stone. Together, the two stones sealed the shaft. There was no longer an opening. Nobody else could come down.

Nobody could go back up, either.

A terrible racket began. It took Annie several moments to realize that rocks were being dropped down the shaft. Rocks that hit and ricocheted and echoed. Filling the shaft. Filling it for eternity.

Annie and Renifer were being buried alive.

ALSO AVAILABLE IN
DELL LAUREL-LEAF BOOKS

FOR ALL TIME

Caroline B. Cooney

Published by
Dell Laurel-Leaf
an imprint of
Random House Children's Books
a division of Random House, Inc.
New York

Visit us on the Web! www.randomhouse.com/teens

Educators and librarians, for a variety of teaching tools, visit us at www.randomhouse.com/teachers

---

ISBN: 0-440-22931-6

RL: 6.7

Reprinted by arrangement with Delacorte Press

Printed in the United States of America

July 2003

10 9 8 7 6 5 4 3 2 1

OPM

For my granddaughter

Elizabeth Anne

I

Time to Fight

ANNIE: 1999

When her parents finally got married again and left for their honeymoon, nobody was happier than Annie Lockwood.

She now had four days—precisely ninety-six hours—in which she would be unsupervised. Annie had convinced her parents that while they were gone, she would be responsible, trustworthy and dependable.

None of this was true. Every single promise to her mother and father she had no intention of keeping.

She was alone at last. The wedding guests were gone and her parents en route to Florida. Her brother was on a bus with his team, headed to basketball camp. The house was utterly quiet. Annie stood in the center of her bedroom, unaware of the clutter around her, and gathered her courage.

Opening her top desk drawer, Annie removed a small envelope and shook it until a scrap of newspaper fell out. It landed between a mug of pencils and a stack of CDs.

EGYPTIAN ART IN THE AGE OF THE PYRAMIDS
September 16, 1999—January 9, 2000

Metropolitan Museum of Art
New York, New York

Annie despised museums. Whenever there was a class trip to a museum, she tried to be sick and stay home for the day. If this failed, she slouched in the teacher's wake, wishing she could get pushed around in a wheelchair, because nothing was more tiring than standing in front of a painting.

But today was different. In a few hours, Annie would be standing in front of a photograph which had merited one brief mention in the newspaper article about the special exhibition. Taken one hundred years ago, this portrait showed every member of the original archaeology expedition.

And would the person she cared about most, the person she had known one hundred years ago, be in that photograph? How vividly Annie remembered Strat's moppy hair and broad shoulders, his casual grin and easy slouch. Every time she touched the newsprint, she felt Strat through the ink.

Strat was in Egypt, waiting for her.

She could feel him. She would cross Time and be with him again.

Four days lay ahead of her. Surely Time understood the urgency and would bring her to Strat.

Annie unzipped her bridesmaid dress. It was a fashion disaster in emergency room green, which indeed made Annie look as if she needed to be hospitalized. Why had Mom's college roommate agreed to put this dress on her body twenty years ago, when she was maid of honor? Why had this roommate saved the dress, so that Annie would have to wear it in public?

But in the end, wearing such a dress was a small sacrifice to celebrate that her mother and father were not getting divorced after all.

Dad's hobby for the last few years had been another woman. Annie and her brother hadn't expected their parents to have another anniversary, let alone another wedding. But not only did Mom and Dad seem truly back together, Mom had talked Dad into getting married a second time for their twentieth anniversary.

When Mom came down the aisle, as lovely as ever in her original white satin wedding gown, even Annie's cynical brother, Tod, was dabbing at tears. Annie chose to believe that Dad repeated his vows—broken once—with every intention of keeping them this time around.

The word *time* had swirled throughout every conversation of the second wedding day.

My parents loved and lost, thought Annie. Today, they swore to love again. I loved and lost. Today, I, too, will have a second chance.

She let the ghastly dress fall onto the carpet and stepped out of it. Annie was fond of floors, which were the best storage space. She kicked off her dyed-to-match satin shoes, peeled away her stockings and stood barefoot and happy in front of her closet. She had even bought clothing from an adventure catalog to wear for this museum trip.

She put on the long swirling skirt of khaki twill; the

full-sleeved silky white blouse; the jacket with bright buttons and many pockets. She tied a scarlet scarf loosely at her throat and pulled on footgear that was half army boot, half sneaker, and fully cool.

In the full-length mirror, with her pale complexion and sleek dark hair falling to her waist, she had a dated look, like a young schoolmarm from another time.

She drew some deep breaths, preparing herself, trying to still her racing heart and hopes. She had never gone into New York City alone. The kick of the city was going with friends. But if Annie was right about this, she would meet the friend she cared about most in the museum. He would be in the photograph, waiting.

She would climb through.

Strat: 1899

Strat was riding a camel.

He had expected a camel to be like a horse. He would become friends with his camel, which would trot to meet him in the morning and nuzzle him affectionately.

Camels, however, despised Strat. They spat and growled, they gave him dirty looks, they tried to bite and they never stopped making nasty noises.

Strat had had stepmothers like this camel.

His father had had two activities in life: money and marriage. Father had been extremely good at money, but not good at wives. But then, money was worth holding on to and wives were not. For this and other reasons, Strat hoped never to speak to, write to, or be in the same room with, his father again.

But once he mounted the camel (sitting on something more like a table than a saddle, with pillows and backrest, a carpet and a sunshade), the camel forgot Strat was there, as indeed Strat hoped Father had forgotten about him. Riding a camel was like sitting in a rocking chair that happened to progress toward the horizon. Strat could bring a picnic or a book, write a letter or take a nap.

Today, however, he was bringing two dead bodies into Cairo.

The bodies were wrapped in a canvas tent flap. The Egyptian servants had first draped the bodies over a donkey's back, but Egyptian donkeys were very small, so the bodies hung with their heads dangling in the dust on one side and their feet on the other. The loss of dignity was great. Strat had to bring them up onto the camel with him.

It was not as awful as he would have expected to have two dead bodies in his lap. In Egypt, who could fail to think of death? The land itself was death, blazing murderous desert encircling stone cities of the dead, occupied now by whole cities of archaeologists. Strat's archaelogist, Dr. Lightner, searched for death. It was Dr. Lightner's great hope to find a mummy in a royal tomb, untouched by Time or robbers.

Even Strat's camera was death. It recorded on paper what had existed a moment ago but would never exist in the same way again.

Strat had been dreaming of death. In the dream, he was buried alive. When a shaft leading to a long-lost tomb was opened, he, Strat, tumbled in and was forgotten, to be smothered by shovelsful of sand and bucketsful of stone as the shaft was filled in. The dream was so vivid that Strat would wake up with his fingers scrabbling at the low tent ceiling, trying to claw through canvas to get air.

He wondered what the two French campers had been dreaming of when they rolled over in their sleep.

The Egyptians had refused to deal with the bodies. The Pyramid, they said, was fine to climb by day, but by night, it belonged to the ghosts of the past. Persons on the Pyramid at night should expect to be accosted by the spirits of those who had gone before.

How Dr. Lightner scoffed. "You and I, of course," he said to Strat, as they packed the bodies, "have no such superstitious beliefs."

Dr. Lightner was incorrect. *Superstitious* meant believing in things inconsistent with the known laws of science. Strat had witnessed something inconsistent with the known laws of science. Father had imprisoned Strat in a lunatic asylum because of what Strat claimed. So Strat could not quite so easily dismiss the idea of ghosts from the past.

He had volunteered to go to the French embassy in Cairo because he could not bear to think of the families who would not know what had happened to their boys. Strat knew what it was like never to have answers about the fate of somebody you loved.

Everybody was delighted not to have to think of the dead tourists again and they were quite cheery as they waved good-bye to Strat.

Egypt was crammed with tourists. Boats overflowed with archaeologists; camels were top-heavy with dreamers; donkeys were laden with watercolor artists. Strat made all his spending money by taking photographs of elderly British maiden ladies and spry old Italian men, of sparkly uniformed British soldiers en route to conquer the Sudan and pipe-smoking German scholars who argued with Dr. Lightner's conclusions.

Tourists paid well, and the more money he made, the more he could send to Katie. Not that it was money Katie needed. In her letters, she assured Strat that she was proud of him and that was enough, he need send no dollars.

It was not enough, and Strat knew this utterly.

Katie wanted love, but Strat had given away the love he possessed. He had given love to his family, and in return, had been destroyed by his own father. He had given love to Harriett, and she had died. He had given love to Annie, and she was lost to another world.

Strat was still a nice person who knew his duty. But his heart was desiccated, like the hearts of mummies in tombs: a hard dry thing, without hope. And now he lurched on a camel with dead men whose hopes had ended.

Oh, Annie! he thought, staring at the burned gold of desert sand. Will I ever see you again?

Time was flying by. It was November of 1899. In six short weeks, Time would hurtle around a huge and magnificent corner, becoming another century.

Nineteen hundred.

If Strat did not cross Time now, he never would.

And so Strat decided that he, too, would spend the night on top of the Pyramid, in the hope that the Egyptians were correct and he would meet the spirits of those who had gone before.

He approached the French embassy in the belief that he had everything under control. He even spoke a little French, which was good, because Frenchmen felt that the English language—especially spoken with an American accent—was a poor way to communicate.

But after the spoken formalities were over, there were paper formalities. Forms to be filled out. Signatures.

Strat had not expected to need his name.

Everybody at the dig called him Strat and never asked for more. He was not one of the impressive young men, college boys from Yale or Princeton who were playing at archaeology for a few months before joining their fathers' law firms in Boston. He was merely the camera boy, practically a servant.

He should have come up with a false name long before, but he had been too dumb. He had thought thousands of miles would protect him from the name Hiram Stratton. Strat pasted a fake smile on his face and scribbled. "Archibald Lightner."

The French turned cold. He was no longer forgiven for being American. "You will sign your own name," they said sharply, "not your employer's."

"I'm not in charge," he protested.

They whipped out a fresh form. "You brought the bodies. You sign."

He could have chosen any name. John Strat. Strat Johnson. But he panicked and scribbled a meaningless squash of letters. He found himself with a cold and severe Frenchman.

Why was he reluctant to state his real name? the

attaché demanded. What made him volunteer to dispose of the bodies? Where had Strat been, at midnight, when the two boys supposedly rolled over and fell to their deaths?

The attaché pulled the ends of his mustache into thin cords, revealing thin lips tightened in suspicion. "How did these boys die?" asked the officer. "Did you push them?"

Annie: 1999

Annie climbed the Grand Staircase of the Metropolitan Museum, silently thanking every benefactor whose name was recorded on the marble panels on either side of her. New York would be less grand without this museum, and these were the men and women who had provided it.

Then she forgot everything except the special exhibition.

It was divided among rooms whose gray carpet went right up the walls, giving both exhibition and visitors a padded permanent look, as though they would be here forever, enclosed in cloudy gray. She was bumped by two very old ladies with museum headsets perched in their white curls. A girl in frayed black sweats sat cross-legged on the floor, sketching a statue whose eyes had been ripped out in antiquity. A middle-aged man read the translation of an ancient papyrus, while a tiny delicate woman studied a trinket box carved from hippopotamus ivory.

There were a number of photographs. Each one had a caption. LIGHTNER EXPEDITION. 1899.

The first one Annie studied was not framed, just tacked to splintered wood. It was black and white, yet full of glare and heat. It showed a woman caught in a whip of sand and dust, arm raised against her face so she could breathe, her long skirt billowing, and beyond her, the rising side of a vast pyramid.

Who was the woman? The placard did not say.

Maybe it's me, thought Annie Lockwood.

The contents of the next room had come from the tomb of a queen named Hetepheres, mother of King Khufu, who built the Great Pyramid.

The tomb of Hetepheres had been found entirely by accident when a cameraman employed by the archaeologists got clumsy. His heavy wooden tripod fell over, striking a patch of plaster that had hitherto concealed the entrance to the shaft.

The placard did not give the name of the cameraman.

Was it Strat?

If she could touch the photo, she'd know. She'd feel Strat through that paper. Or she wouldn't.

A museum guard, finely tuned to be aware of all ready-to-touch visitors, gave Annie the heavy-lidded look of authority.

She stumbled on.

In the third room was a small gold statue of Sekhmet, goddess of revenge, on a pedestal behind glass. And there, at eye level on the carpeted wall, was the photograph described in the newspaper article: every member of the dig that had uncovered the tomb of Hetepheres.

Museum visitors were standing in front of it and

blocking Annie's view. She peered around shoulders and between the straps of handbags.

The picture was large, with the quiet hazy look of early photographs. A dozen people had posed in two rows, shadowed by the brims of hats they had worn a hundred years ago to protect themselves from the Egyptian sun. They seemed to have been mummified as they waited for the picture to be taken.

Slowly the exhibition visitors rotated on. One boy was still half in Annie's way, but she couldn't wait any longer, even though she wanted to be alone with her photograph. She shouldered the boy away and carefully examined each tiny black-and-white face. This had to be her shaft through Time.

But Strat was not in the photograph.

Annie was just a silly girl in silly clothing, wearing her silly hopes. "Oh, Strat!" she said, heart bursting with grief.

The boy who was also still looking at the photograph said, "Yes?"

CAMILLA: 1899

Six months after the murder of her father, Camilla Mateusz decided to become a man, because men were paid more. She had read once that a Confederate girl pretended to be a soldier throughout the entire War Between the States and never got caught. So why couldn't Camilla be a man during the twelve working hours of the day—and never get caught?

Camilla possessed an advantage in such a masquerade. She towered over all ladies and most men.

A lady must be delicate, with white throat and narrow ankles. Not that anybody believed a Polish girl was within reach of being a lady, but Camilla Mateusz had an additional affliction. She was six feet tall in a generation where most girls were hardly more than five. When she was sitting, people thought her attractive, and praised the thick blond braids, rosy cheeks and blue eyes.

Eventually, however, Camilla had to stand up. Mill hand or shopkeeper, priest or policeman—everybody who saw Camilla unfold burst out laughing. Who would ever marry her?

Only once had her height been useful, in the wonderful new game called basketball. How grand to feel the joy men had always felt: throwing a ball.

Of course, girls did not play the same game as boys. Girls, for example, could not dribble, which was a skill far beyond their capacities. The court was only half as large, and in long skirts, girls did not move quickly. Last season, however, the girls had actually been permitted to play against another school's team. Oh, not without arguments. The community was outraged by this attack against feminine behavior. It was clear where this kind of thing would lead. Lovely sweet girls would be ruined.

They pointed to Camilla as proof, how unwomanly she was, with her attention to the ball and her desire to win.

Well, Camilla had lost the joy of basketball. She had lost her chance to win a high school diploma as well. But she had not lost her father's courage. He had crossed a terrible ocean, worked hard at a terrible job and died a terrible death. He had done this for his family and she could not do less.

What to do about the waist-length yellow hair of which she was so proud?

Since men wore caps or hats in the street, as a man, she could cover her hair to an extent, but caps were removed indoors. Camilla would have to have short hair. And so she gave herself a ragged haircut, put on Papa's clothing and Papa's cap. Low on her cheeks she rubbed a little soot from the kerosene lamp. Then she put on Papa's old reading glasses, smudging them a bit in hope of lessening the blue of her eyes.

Oh, Papa! He had had his heart set on seeing his

children finish school. *They* would not spend their lives in a mine or mill. *They* would go to an office, have clean jobs and wear white shirts with white collars.

The Mateusz family had but one photograph on their walls. It was large and quiet in its heavy brown frame. Mama was seated, Papa standing behind her, his hand resting on her shoulder. Mama wore the dress she had been married in and Papa his only suit—the one in which he had lately been buried. Seven children stood around them, solemn and proud to be in a portrait. Since then, the three oldest had had to drop out of school to work in the mills—or rather, the remaining mill; the one Mr. Hiram Stratton had *not* burned down; the one in which her father had *not* died.

This morning Mama had had no food to put in the lunch pails. Irena and Magdalena, Antony and Marya did not cry. They just looked a little more pinched as they set out for school. Stefan, age thirteen, shrugged and walked out to endure his twelve-hour day. But Jerzy paused for a moment, running his fingers over the pile of his abandoned schoolbooks, still stacked on the shelf by the door. He made a fist, hit the wall, apologized to his mother and went to the factory. Jerzy was fourteen.

Mr. Hiram Stratton, Sr., the man whose wealth and needs dictated all that happened in this city, had broken a strike by the simple expedient of burning down the factory. He had not checked to see if the factory was empty. He ordered his thugs to torch it, and they did. Michael Mateusz had been there. He had not gotten out.

Hiram Stratton was not accused of arson. He was not accused of murder. In fact, he was named the next police commissioner.

So Camilla left a note for her mother. "I've gone to get a good job. I will send money so the boys can return to school. Do not worry about me. I am strong."

Newspaper advertisements contained four possible jobs. The first three interviews went badly. She blushed when she pretended to be Cameron Matthews instead of Camilla Mateusz. She lowered her eyes demurely, forgetting to stare man to man. She did not remember to stride or swing her arms. Furthermore, she went in the morning, while sunlight streamed into each office. Nobody guessed that this very tall person could be a girl, but they were puzzled and uncertain and did not want to hire her.

The fourth interview was late in the afternoon. Camilla found herself at an office that did not yet have electric lights, and the single lamp in the little room scarcely illuminated the papers on the desk, never mind the stranger in the door. She paused for courage, reading the sign.

DUFFIE DETECTIVE AGENCY.
WE FOLLOW YOUR SPOUSE.
WE FIND YOUR MONEY.

Camilla's heart sank.

She could not be party to the sort of things that led to

divorce! Aside from the fact that the Church would disapprove, she might lose faith in the human race.

Although, given what Hiram Stratton had done, what faith had she in the human race anyway?

She raised her hand to cross herself, and keep away the evil of such practices as arson and divorce, when she was greeted by the man who must be Mr. Duffie. Just in time, Camilla remembered that her pretend self, Cameron Matthews, was probably not a good Catholic.

But Mr. Duffie thought she meant to shake hands, so he got halfway up from his desk, extending his hand over the wide wooden top. Luckily she had been doing this all day and knew to grip hard.

His black pomaded hair glistened on his head. He might, or might not, have brushed his teeth the week before. He handed her a form to fill out.

Cameron Matthews, she wrote, in big strong script.

High school diploma, she added, instead of *Eighth-grade graduate*.

Mr. Duffie held her paperwork close to the lamp and scanned the page quickly. "Matthews," he said approvingly. "A good English name. You don't know how many Poles and Czechs come in here, expecting to be hired, as if they were regular people."

Camilla spat into the tobacco stand to demonstrate her disgust at the current situation in America. This was a hard part of being a man. Why did men always have spit in their mouths? She certainly never had any spare spit in her mouth.

Mr. Duffie leaned back in a wooden swivel chair and

chewed the tip of a pipe. "What I need, Mr. Matthews," said Duffie, "is a man willing to masquerade as a woman. I know, I know. A shameful thing to ask. I have had men vomit at the suggestion of imitating a female. But in this line of work, there are situations into which a man cannot go. A female, however, could do so."

That would be interesting, thought Camilla. I'd be a woman pretending to be a man pretending to be a woman. "Why then," she asked, in her new deep voice, "do you not simply hire a female?"

Mr. Duffie laughed out loud. "Nobody would trust the evidence of a female. Who would hire my agency if it became known that I used female operatives? No, I need a man to disguise himself."

"You ask a great deal," said Camilla, accepting the offer of chewing tobacco.

"I pay a great deal, Mr. Matthews," said Mr. Duffie, writing the amount on a piece of paper and shoving it toward her.

Camilla nearly swallowed her tobacco. He told the truth. He paid a great deal. If she lived frugally, not only could Jerzy and Stefan return to school, lunch pails would be full! Mama could pay somebody else to do the laundry!

Camilla trembled with the desire to have all that money, but suppressed her shiver as unmanly.

"Well, Matthews?" demanded Duffie.

"I shall undertake the task, humiliating though it will be to act like a woman. You will call me Cameron as a man, and Camilla as a woman. You will give me an advance against my salary so that I may purchase female garments. Is this Camilla Matthews to be rich? Or some poor shopwoman? Is she to read and write? Should she talk with an accent? Describe her to me."

The detective was impressed. "You are going to be excellent, Mr. Matthews," he said. "Or should I say, Miss Matthews? You and I will make a great team."

And so it began.

The loneliest, strangest life Camilla could imagine. There could be no friends or family. There could not even be the Church. Tell a priest the sins she was daily committing? The sinful people she followed and watched? The sinful people from whom she accepted pay?

She lived in a boardinghouse, never going home, lest her family grasp the shameful, scandalous decision she had made. Were Jerzy and Stefan ever to understand the life their sister was leading, they would refuse her money, quit school again and go back to the mills. So Camilla mailed the money to her mother.

The boardinghouse was for men only, of course. Boardinghouses did not mix the sexes. She shared a bathroom with the other five boarders. This was an extraordinary difficulty. But she managed in part because the other five cared nothing for cleanliness.

At night, safe under rough sheets, Cameron-Camilla Matthews could be Camilla Mateusz again. She would smother her pain against the pillow, yearning to be back in school, studying history, increasing her math skills and translating her Latin.

But she was the man of the family now. When a man had a family to support, he must forget himself and his plans.

And so the months dragged on. Once, dressed as Cameron Matthews, she strolled past the grammar school to feast her eyes on Irena and Magdalena, Antony and Marya. The girls wore new dresses! Their cheeks were pink with good health. Antony had his own baseball bat.

Sitting on the stoop of a tenement, pretending to fix her bootlaces, Camilla saw Jerzy dash out of the adjacent high school, joyfully taking the steps two at a time, running across the paved playground to greet the little ones. She heard him laugh.

And so she went on with her masquerade. But she did not laugh.

At least she could let her hair grow out. When she had to be Cameron Matthews, she wore a cap, pinning her hair safely beneath it. But when she was Camilla, she could brush her hair and admire how yellow it was, buy a ribbon and try on hats.

She visited Duffie only at dusk, when the man was exhausted, ready to go to his own boardinghouse for dinner, wishing to spend as little time with her as possible. She had already ascertained that his eyesight was poor and his spectacles unhelpful. He saw only the tall gawky frame of Cameron Matthews, and unless she made a large blunder, Duffie would never realize the secret of her gender.

"Today, Mr. Matthews," said Duffie, "I have for you

an extraordinary assignment. You will have heard of the great gentleman, Hiram Stratton, Sr.—the railroad millionaire."

Camilla was almost sick with an evil hope. Perhaps Stratton's current wife was trying to divorce him. Perhaps Camilla was to have a chance to ruin the man. "I believe Hiram Stratton also owned a factory in the city at one time," said Camilla.

"Yes, it burned down. We're not involved with that. We're after the son. Hiram Stratton, Jr."

Camilla had not known there was a son. How dare Hiram Stratton, Sr., enjoy a son, while Michael Mateusz would never see his sons grow up?

"The son ran away," said Mr. Duffie. "It's a very sad story. He had to be punished for a serious dereliction of duty to his father. He was kept in a private asylum so that he might come to his senses. However, the boy fled from his captivity. Not only did he attack a doctor, but he kidnapped two fellow patients! He did it not for ransom, but for disguise, so that he might look like a family man. I cannot imagine how he pulled it off."

Disguise was overrated. If Camilla could trick the world, so could a sneaky sly son of a Stratton.

"How the great man dreams of a joyful reunion with his long-lost son," said Duffie.

Great man, indeed. Why was it that any man of wealth was great, no matter how he acquired his money or what he did with it? Camilla wanted to know.

"I was honored when the great man chose me to find the boy. I have been working on this, Mr. Matthews, and at last, have an avenue to follow. Stratton junior took his two victims to Spain, where he abandoned them. I am sending you to Spain to interview the female and obtain Junior's current address."

Spain! thought Camilla. Spain of bullfighters and flamenco dancers? Spain of a thousand castles? "Tell me about the kidnap victims," she said.

"Shocking," replied Duffie. "One was a young man with so small a brain he never learned how to talk; the other, a woman with a hideously deformed body. Naturally their parents put them away. We do not have the female's full name, since her family, of course, did not want the shame of admitting her existence. She wasn't identified by a last name even in the asylum records. But her first name is Katie. You will find her involved with some sort of hospital. St. Rafael. She seems to be a nurse now, rather than a patient."

Insane asylums were often kind enough to take in defectives, and perhaps the creature really had learned nursing skills. Camilla's heart broke for such a girl. What pain must she have met at the hands of Hiram Stratton, Jr.?

"But how will Mr. Stratton prevent a trial of young Stratton for the kidnappings?" asked Camilla. "Surely the parents of the two innocent victims will require justice."

"It is my understanding," said Duffie, "that the parents find it amusing. After all, they need no longer pay for care. No, do not concern yourself with them. As for a trial, naturally Mr. Stratton has paid everybody off. Such a low-class scandal must not be made public. No, we wish to accomplish the joyful reunion of father and son."

I cannot bring joy to a Stratton! thought Camilla.

Mr. Duffie pared his nails. He did this when he was lying. "For this task," he said casually, "you will be Camilla Matthews. You will offer comfort, real or false, whatever works. Promise the girl anything in order to get young Stratton's location. Mr. Stratton is providing a large expense account and you will spend whatever is necessary. You will cable me, of course, with every development."

Camilla was no saint, to walk away from assignments that paid well. And it might be that in Spain, she could arrange things to her own satisfaction: Destroy the father and ruin the son.

Camilla's heart raced in the ugly hot emotion of revenge. Oh, to have more power than Hiram Stratton! To shove in his face what he had shoved in hers! "I will go to Spain. I will need a large advance." She named an outrageous figure.

Duffie sputtered and refused.

She unfolded, her six feet casting a threatening shadow over his desk. "I could inform Mr. Stratton that you are already cutting corners."

They glared at each other and Duffie broke first. "Matthews, you are exactly right for this job. You shall have what you ask."

How wonderful were the long voyage and the days of female company. How she cherished being once more part of the conversations and laughter and kindness of women. What a delight to discuss hair and fashion, children and church.

And yet . . . being a woman again was not altogether satisfactory.

Camilla could no longer read a newspaper. She could no longer hold an opinion, nor be interested in sports and politics. As a man, she had commanded respect. As a woman, she was simply a creature too tall to be a dance partner.

Throughout the voyage, she studied Spanish, memorizing useful sentences, but once she arrived, as soon as she mentioned the name of the hospital—St. Rafael—every Spaniard melted away, saying nothing.

When, after several days, Camilla stumbled on St. Rafael, she knew why Mr. Stratton could get nobody else to interview Katie and why he did not go himself. She knew why Duffie had lied, pretending he was not aware of Katie's situation.

It was a leper hospital.

Dreaded since the beginning of time, lepers were shunned for good reason. Before leprosy killed the patient, it first killed the nose and lips and fingers and feet, which rotted and fell off. The image of Katie nauseated Camilla: deformed to start with—now a leper. She could not help imagining herself a leper. To interview Katie, not only must Camilla expose herself to this evil disease, she must lie to the nuns who ran St. Rafael.

For many hours, the twin desires for money and revenge were not enough to make her approach the lepers. At last, however, Camilla summoned her courage. "I am here," she said to the nun who kept the gate, "in hope of visiting your nurse Katie. I have been sent by Devonny Stratton, who seeks news of her dear brother, Strat." Camilla knew nothing of Devonny Stratton, except that the debutante had recently married a titled Englishman and was therefore also out of the country and her father's clutches. "Devonny prays that in spite of the suffering inflicted upon her, Katie will assist in this endeavor."

The nun said nothing.

Camilla remembered her instructions. Promise anything, whether you plan to do it or not. "Miss Stratton wishes to bring Katie home to America, and provide her with the means to live comfortably. Or should she prefer to stay here, to make a major donation to this very hospital."

Nobody was going to give Katie a penny and as for taking her out of the leper hospital, allowing the dreaded infection into society—absurd. Not for any number of dollars.

The nun inclined her head, and rustled away to deliver the message. There was a long wait, during which Camilla's courage dwindled. She fiddled with the lacy white cotton gloves that were part of her everyday clothing. Could mere gloves protect her from leprosy?

The nun returned. Katie would welcome Miss Matthews in her room.

Camilla was aghast. Go *inside*?

"Be not afraid," said the nun gently, in English, as if accustomed to fearful American girls. "It takes years of exposure to acquire leprosy. An hour will not put you at risk. You will find Katie a delight, and glad to speak with a friend of Devonny Stratton. Follow me."

Not at risk? Camilla thought. Of course I'm at risk! From time immemorial, people have known better than to get within rock-throwing distance of a leper.

She reminded herself of the money she would be paid. I'll stay only a minute, she promised herself. When I leave, I'll buy borax and scrub myself for hours.

Katie was heavily garbed in white, even more veiled than the nun. Only her eyes and hands were exposed. Katie offered a hand to be shaken. Camilla had no choice, but she would burn the glove later.

"I am not diseased, Miss Matthews," said Katie gently. "I wear this veil so you will not see my deformities. My mother and father gave me to an asylum for storage, just as lepers are stored here. A decent and good person saved me from that asylum. Here indeed I try to be an equally good and decent person to others."

"That's why I've come," said Camilla. "Devonny is so very very worried about her beloved brother. She has had no news. She fears for his fate, now that he has become a kidnapper."

Katie laughed behind the veil. "I was not kidnapped. I was saved from a life of torment in a house of cruelty. In decency and in honor Strat left behind that which he loved and brought me here."

Women! thought Camilla. How we fall for anything a man says. "Would you tell me what young Mr. Stratton did that could be called honorable? Because I must admit to you that others disagree."

When Katie turned and went to sit on a small stool, a table set for tea was revealed: two cups, sugar and lemons. Drink tea poured by the hand of a leper? Camilla gagged.

"Strat and I crossed the ocean together, pretending to be brother and sister," explained Katie. "When we arrived penniless in Spain, we stayed at a convent and pretended to be on a pilgrimage. I was awestruck by the work of the nuns and I embraced their holy lives. Strat chose adventure and sailed on."

That was one way to look at it. Another was that Junior, having dragged her across the ocean, now dropped her off to die among the lepers.

"And the second person young Mr. Stratton so generously brought along?" said Camilla.

"Poor Douglass was born with very little brain," said Katie. "His parents, like mine, stored him in the asylum. Strat brought both of us to safety. I have Douglass with me here. He is happy. All is well, Miss Matthews."

All is well? Such sainthood made Camilla want to race out into the streets and do something wicked.

"And young Mr. Stratton?" she said carefully. "Is *he* safe? Is *he* happy? His dear sister misses him painfully and hopes for communication."

From a tin box on a rickety wooden table by her narrow bed, Katie removed a packet of letters. She cradled them in her two hands like a bouquet, drinking in their scent.

Camilla tried to see the return address on the envelopes.

"Strat is a true gentleman," said Katie softly. "A fine athlete and a splendid conversationalist. Generous of heart."

Claptrap. The Stratton fellow would be his father's son, gross and sweating. Wax on his mustache and gaudy rings denting his thick fingers. But then, how could poor Katie judge a man? All the men of her acquaintance had been born deformed, become criminal or decayed from disease.

Camilla made a decision. She drank her tea. "How refreshing," she lied. "Is young Mr. Stratton yet in Spain? Does he visit you?"

Katie shook her head. "I had fine jewels, which a friend of Strat's gave me when we were fleeing. We sold them, and with the proceeds, Strat was able to buy passage to Egypt."

But not *your* passage, thought Camilla. "Egypt!" she cried, as if it were wonderful, and not the end of the earth. When young Stratton abandoned somebody, he really completed the job.

Accepting tea had been ever so wise. For now Katie was bursting with truth. "The coming war attracted Strat," she said, leaning forward in excitement. "British troops are even now sailing up the Nile to attack rebels in Khartoum. Lord Kitchener asked for volunteers. Strat hoped to join a camel corps or help build the first desert railway on earth. But! Passing through Spain was the very famous Dr. Archibald Lightner. Of course you have heard of Dr. Lightner's archaeological research."

Camilla had hardly even heard of archaeology.

"Strat managed to make the great man's acquaintance! Dr. Lightner had never had a staff photographer, as he was suspicious of the machinery, but had always used a watercolor artist. When Strat said he would become Dr. Lightner's photographer for no pay, the great man accepted."

Who would accept the gross and disgusting son of Hiram Stratton? Dr. Lightner had probably found out the family connection and was hoping for money. An expedition to chop open a sphinx or a blast into a pyramid must be costly.

Her heart broke watching Katie, who had only death and letters to live for.

"Strat writes often with the details of his adventures," said Katie, fingering the letters as if they were treasure. "He sends me all he earns."

Not likely, thought Camilla, reading the address upside down.

H. Stratton
c/o Dr. Archibald Lightner
Road to the Pyramids
Giza

Katie lifted the letters to her lips and kissed them through the veil. And Camilla knew then that Katie loved Strat the way any girl loves a boy. With all her heart.

RENIFER:
IN THE TWENTIETH YEAR OF THE REIGN OF KHUFU, LORD OF THE TWO LANDS

Renifer paused to gaze at the row of bodies staked on poles along the edge of the desert.

The three tomb robbers caught last week had finally died. The priests liked to spear prisoners so the stake traveled all the way up the inside of the body, but did not instantly kill. In this case, the tomb robbers had lived many hours, and one for days. Jackals crept out from the desert by night to chew on the dead men and had not minded eating the feet and thighs of one still alive.

Renifer gave a prayer of thanks that the tomb robbers had been so thoroughly punished.

Then she looked reverently at the just-completed Great Pyramid. How splendid it was, a mountain of shining limestone.

Everybody who lived on the Nile had been part of the Pyramid's creation.

Farmers and potters, fishermen and papyrus makers had the privilege of working on it. They cut and loaded stone, poled barges, dug out the sacred lake, paved the causeway. They baked bread to feed ten thousand workers and sun-dried a million bricks for their houses. They constructed a slideway and ramps to move the massive rocks. They polished the limestone casing, brought flowers for offerings and carried away the sand, one basket at a time. They painted the walls of chapels and the columns of courtyards with a hundred times a hundred portraits of gods, especially their own God. Pharaoh Himself.

The celebrations for the finished Pyramid had lasted for months.

Every man and woman with the strength to greet the morning sun came. They came from Upper Egypt and Lower Egypt, from Lebanon and Punt. They came if they were rich and they came if they were poor. They brought their children and their offerings and their prayers.

They rejoiced at the glory that was Pharaoh, and knelt at His passage when He was borne on His sedan chair, wearing His two crowns.

Twice, Renifer herself had attended Princess Mere-sankh, Pharaoh's daughter, when the princess brought food to her dead grandmother the queen. Together, royal princess and handmaiden prostrated themselves on the blistering hot silver-faced pavement in front of the queen's chapel.

"Mother of the King," Renifer sang, "follower of Horus, O gracious one, whose every utterance is done for her, daughter of the God's body, Hetepheres, we honor thee."

Afterward, Princess Meresankh actually *spoke* to Renifer, saying how well she sang the chants.

And then the festivities ended, and all Egypt went home.

Pharaoh's barge went back to His palace in Memphis. Shopkeepers sold linen; bakers sold bread. Boys learned to read; girls tended geese. Mothers nursed babies; farmers dug fields.

And tomb robbers, she thought, robbed tombs.

Renifer walked slowly, because it was very hot, one servant girl carrying the fruit they had bought at the market and the other fanning Renifer. Renifer was soon to have her own household and must become experienced in shopping.

Renifer was the envy of every girl she knew. Pankh was strong shouldered and brave. His skin, burnt so dark by the remorseless sun, was like black gold. He was the most handsome and the youngest supervisor of a royal wharf.

Eternal life was fine, and waiting on the princess was fine, but what Renifer cared about was having her own husband, her own house, and as soon as possible, her own children. She was fourteen and it was time.

The doorkeeper opened the big wooden entry set deep in the mud-brick wall. Inside, date palms kept the courtyard cool and shady. Father was reclining under the yellow-and-white-striped awning on the rooftop and Renifer went up the steep ladder to join him. Servants brought bread fresh from the oven and dates still hot from the lowering sun.

Soon the distant sand would turn red and purple with shadow and Pharaoh Himself would be praying for the sun's return in the morning. She would not repeat her own prayers in front of Father, who found religion amusing. Even the Pyramid meant little to Father, who just shook his head when he happened to notice it.

"You look especially lovely today," said her father, "and I think it time to discuss your marriage."

"Oh, yes, Father!" cried Renifer. "Pankh will be here soon. He's taking me to a concert on the wharf."

The days were so hot and glaring that the best entertainments occurred after dark. She helped herself to olives, planning what to wear. She owned much gold jewelry, but neither Father nor Pankh liked her to wear it in public. Sometimes Renifer pouted over that rule.

"Perhaps," said Father, "you should not marry Pankh after all. I can find a more prestigious match, now that you are in Princess Meresankh's favor."

She said dizzily, "But Father! Pankh is ready to bring me home."

Father shrugged. "Why settle for Pankh when you could do better? My grandsons could have noble blood."

Renifer cared more about hot blood, and from what Pankh said and did when they were alone, he could give her all the sons she might want. She tried to dispel her father's hopes. "The princess barely noticed me. She picked me out of a row of girls. Any soprano would do."

"No. The princess has requested you to attend her again next week. Furthermore, Daughter, the princess ordered you to meet her *within the palace walls,* not on the plaza where the musicians gather. You, my daughter, will be in the presence of Khufu, Lord of the Two Lands. The princess wishes you to sing for Him."

Pharaoh Himself would hear her sing?

It was too great an honor. She was not good enough.

And she was not sure she wanted the honor. She wanted to think about having a household, and folding bed linens freshly pressed, and of course making babies. If she had to sing for Pharaoh, she might get scared, and sing badly, and receive punishment, for the Living God must have the best and the first in all things.

She wanted to put Pankh first in all things. That was part of the wedding vow, and she could hardly wait to tell him yet again that he was first in all things.

"Tonight you will stay home with your mother," said her father in the voice that brooked no discussion. "Nor will you be in the presence of Pankh. Tonight or any other night. You can do better. I shall end the engagement."

"I must have misunderstood that statement," said Pankh in a slow deep voice, startling them badly. He was standing on the rim of the roof, hands on hips, feet apart, looming in the dusk like a temple god. His white kilt was bright as moonlight and the gold bands on his arms as thick as jawbones. "Surely, Pen-Meru, you are not thinking of taking your daughter away from me."

"It is not an official agreement, as you recall," said Father dismissively. "Merely a discussion we had. A discussion I will now have with others as well."

Pankh lifted from its pedestal the beautiful small

statue Father had recently acquired of the goddess Sekhmet.

Sekhmet was portrayed as a seated lion goddess; her powers were many and terrifying. She could escort Pharaoh in war, but also sweep the country with disease. She was both love and hatred; both revenge and protection.

This Sekhmet was pure gold and fit for a Pharaoh.

Now Pankh lifted the goddess by her back, as a cat lifts her kittens. He tapped an insolent rhythm on her lion mane.

Father sat very still.

"Renifer is mine," said Pankh softly, "and you, too, Pen-Meru, are mine." He tightened his grip on Sekhmet, as a killer holds the rock with which he will break the skull.

Renifer felt Sekhmet's anger like a spider's web. The goddess's fury was enveloping them all, as when irrigation canals open, and water turns the world into a web of water, and none can pass.

Her father caught his breath. "I was mistaken, Pankh," he said hoarsely. "Of course Renifer is yours. Whenever you wish her."

Renifer could hear the slap of oars on the water of the Nile, the laughter of children playing in the neighbors' courtyards, the rustle of palm leaves in the wind. Her father—Pen-Meru—afraid?

Servants bustled up with torches to be set in their niches, plates of meat and bread and cheese, bowls of stew with barley and chickpeas. Renifer's little sister and brothers, having spent the day playing naked in the sun, came shrieking and giggling for dinner, their nurses running alongside to put robes on them as the air grew chilly.

"Come, Renifer," said Pankh. "The night is beautiful. We will return when it pleases me. Your father will not be talking to other suitors."

Her father was no longer in charge. She might have said her marriage vows already, because Pankh was the one whose permission she needed.

In the streets of Memphis they walked. They said good evening to friends, bought sweets from vendors, listened to a band of flutes, and sat on a bench above the Nile, watching parties on pleasure boats.

"You look lovely in that shawl," said Pankh.

"Father is always coming home with some extraordinary gift," she said nervously. "Pankh? Up on the rooftop? It almost sounded as if you were threatening Father."

"Silly goose," said Pankh. "I just reminded him that I always get what I want."

Renifer was horrified. He was begging a god to lash out and prove him wrong. Or a goddess. "But you treated Sekhmet as a weapon," she whispered. She felt herself at the top of something as high as the Pyramid, and as steep; felt herself falling, and falling with her was a shape so terrible she must keep her eyes closed and her thoughts protected.

"A weapon?" Pankh laughed. "I was just juggling it around." He snapped his fingers to show how little he cared for the goddess. "If I need a weapon, I have a knife."

"But Pankh—"

"I have reached the end of my patience," said Pankh sharply. "I do not care for a wife who questions my decisions."

What decisions? thought Renifer. I don't even know what we're talking about.

"I'm sorry," she said humbly, but she was afraid.

Her father and her beloved were hiding something, using a goddess who would gladly destroy them with one swipe of her immortal paw.

Evil was coming, and Renifer was powerless to get out of its way.

II

Time to Fall

ANNIE: 1999

Suddenly the special Egyptian exhibition exploded with schoolchildren. Seventh graders, possibly eighth. Filled with the noisy excitement of a field trip, they had not the slightest intention of learning anything. They rattled around the exhibition while their teacher read aloud from placards.

So she was not going to change centuries.

Strat had done that for her. He was here. In her time.

Annie wanted to touch Strat as tenderly as they had touched a hundred years ago. How perfect he still looked. He wore cargo pants and a navy sweater heavily knitted in braids and whorls. He could have been a young sailor from some Irish island, whose sister or mother had been knitting all winter to create this masterpiece. Strat's hair was the same moppy annoying badly cut hair she had known a hundred years ago. He had worn a cute little cap then, the kind men wore when they drove automobiles with open tops and running boards.

Annie had a moment of regret. Other times were so much more exciting and romantic. Neither word could ever be used to describe the suburbs of New York City. She had bought the adventure outfit not to travel into New York, but to travel into 1899. And now she wouldn't get to go.

A yelling knot of boys jostled them, and then an elbowing cluster of girls. Their teacher raised her voice and loudly proclaimed her views of ancient Egyptian art. The class scattered in all directions.

The boy Strat was paying more attention to the photograph than to Annie. Finally he said to Annie, "I think you're right." He smiled in a friendly bland way, only half looking at her. A shock wave went through Annie Lockwood.

He did not know her. She was going to have to introduce herself to a boy whose smile and hair and kiss she remembered so well. "What am I right about?" she said weakly. "I don't see Strat in the picture."

"Stratton was the photographer, remember, so he isn't in any of the pictures. But I'm curious. How do you know about Stratton?"

Annie never thought of him as Stratton. To her, he had always been Strat. To a boy who did not remember her, however, she could hardly say, "I used to date you, a hundred years ago." So she said, "I read that Strat left his home in America and went to Egypt."

"Where did you read that?" asked the boy excitedly. "Because our family has tried to find out more about him. You see, Stratton was my great-grandmother's brother. His full name was Hiram Stratton, Jr."

That's what you think, thought Annie Lockwood. *You* are Hiram Stratton, Jr.

Then his words sank in. This boy's great-grandmother was the *sister* of Strat. That would be Devonny. So he wasn't Annie's Strat at all. He had not come through Time. He was nothing but the descendant of a sister. Some distant cousin killing time in a museum. Oh, surely not! Time wouldn't do that to her.

"We have other photos that Stratton took, also in Egypt," said the boy, "but he didn't leave many trails for us to follow. We don't know what happened to him later. What book did you read it in?"

She hadn't read it anywhere. She'd been there. "What is your name again?" she asked.

"They call me Strat. But my real name is Lockwood Stratton."

Annie Lockwood nearly fell over. He possessed *her* last name as *his* first name? That could not be coincidence.

Eighth-grade boys swarmed like hornets around the gold Sekhmet, bumping into Strat's knees and Annie's back.

"We can't concentrate on the exhibition until this class has moved on," said Annie. "Want to go to the museum cafeteria and have a dessert with me? I'd love to hear about your family. You see"—she considered a reasonable lie—"I think we have a photograph of Strat's too."

"You talk as if you know him," teased the boy. "He died a hundred years ago, you know."

"He lived a hundred years ago," Annie corrected him.

They walked down the magnificent stairs, which made Annie feel like a princess in a palace. The boy tapped one of the names incised on the walls: *Hiram Stratton, Sr*. "My great-great-grandfather," he said.

A man Annie had encountered another time. The cruelest man she had ever met. A man who had sworn to destroy his own son—and had. A man who had sworn to destroy the mother of his own children—and had. A man who . . .

Annie's head swam. A veil came between her and the names of the donors. The letters fell off the walls and onto her face like hail, pelting her with memory.

Time opened like a cellar door, for her to fall into blackness.

Hiram Stratton even now was planning to destroy . . . *something . . . someone . . .*

Her feet slipped on the marble steps.

It had been this way before. A first falling, then a second. Then, at last, the step through Time. Scudding across the years like a ship in a high wind.

A guard leaned his face into hers. How antique his features, how dark and wind-beaten his glance. For a moment, the guard stood on the far side of Time. But then he was just a museum employee. Had she skipped breakfast? he wanted to know. He didn't want her to faint and fall on the stone steps and hurt herself.

"I caught her," said the boy, putting his arm around her. Annie knew that hand. The hand on Annie's shoulder was Strat's hand. "She's fine," he told the guard.

"We're on our way to the cafeteria anyway. I'll see she has something to eat."

He pulled Annie to her feet and they walked on together, not touching. Not touching him made her ache. She had known the ache before, too. This was Strat. The real thing. Not a distant cousin.

Time! she called silently. Strat's here. Forget what I asked for. I don't want to change centuries after all. I don't need to anymore. You can leave.

But she had called upon Time too strongly.

Time, having listened, would answer.

Katie: 1899

Katie washed out the teacups, which she had borrowed from Mother Superior when she found she had a guest. A guest who offered to save her, bring her home and even provide her with an income!

But with what speed Miss Camilla Matthews had departed. Having squinted at Strat's letters, she was done. She did not care about seeing Douglass, nor did she wish a tour of the hospital.

I trusted her, thought Katie. Here among nuns, I let myself believe that being a woman makes a person good. I, with my childhood! I know that gender does not predict goodness.

Katie beat her fists on the tiny tea table. Then she ripped off her veil and sobbed into her hands. At St. Rafael, she was usually at peace with the Lord and the cruelly formed body into which He had placed her. Now she felt assaulted. This woman—girl, really, hardly older than Katie herself—had connived and lied and encouraged Katie to expose the thoughts of her heart.

It wouldn't be Devonny trying to find Strat. If Strat

wished to communicate with Devonny, he could do so—and probably had.

It was Hiram Stratton, Sr., who had enough money and interest to send a woman across the ocean to ply Katie with falsehoods.

Hiram Stratton, Sr., could not tolerate defeat. He did not care who had to be crushed as long as he was the victor. Not only had his one and only son talked back and offered unusual opinions, but then the boy refused to marry Harriett, whose hand Mr. Stratton had chosen for Strat. First among virtues in a son was absolute obedience. When Strat failed to display it, Mr. Stratton put him in an asylum so that his will would be broken.

Katie herself had heard the asylum doctor read aloud the letters he wrote to Mr. Stratton, describing how Strat whimpered and cringed like a kicked dog. But Mr. Stratton had not won, in the end, for by fair means or foul, Strat had defeated both the asylum and his father.

What destruction might come to Strat now, at the hands of this Camilla Matthews?

Katie composed a cable, telegrams being a marvel of technology. Why, this cable would arrive in Egypt long before Miss Matthews could even find a ship! Truly, the nineteenth century was a magnificent time. Katie trembled to think of the twentieth, only weeks away, and what might be invented in those decades.

STRAT. DANGER. MY FAULT. IMMEDIATELY LEAVE EGYPT. YOUR FATHER IN PURSUIT. HIS

AGENT A WOMAN, CAMILLA MATTHEWS. LETTER FOLLOWS. LOVE KATIE.

She took the carefully printed telegram and more than enough money to cover the cost of sending it to Cairo and went to the gate of the hospital. The gate was not to keep patients in, but to warn strangers away.

She had not left since the day Strat sailed. His letters were her only door to the world. And now, stepping beyond the pale, she remembered the world!

The profile of a Moorish castle and a row of green cedars. An ancient Roman aqueduct against a blue sky and a street market down the hill, full of children and laughter. The clop of horses' hoofs and the clatter of wagon wheels called her name.

What temptation to give up her cause and walk away from her patients into sunshine and safety. Beyond the beautiful city lay a gleaming sea. She herself could carry the warning to Strat. He had been a true friend, such a few on earth ever have.

But if Katie went to him, she would be a burden. Strat would have to figure out what to do with her . . . when there was nothing to do with her.

Katie prayed. The Lord strengthened her.

Then she called out to a friendly-looking passerby. She spoke in Spanish, of course, having learned it easily. She was proud of her accent. "Will you deliver a cable to the telegram office, please? Here is plenty of money, and a good tip as well."

The man pointed to the ground halfway between

them. Katie set down her precious warning, piling coins on top so the wind would not blow the page away. She gave the man God's blessing and returned to the enclosure.

When she had shut the gate behind her, tears assaulted her: for herself and for all ruined lives. And while she prayed for calmness of heart, the man in the street walked on without pausing. Nothing would make him handle what a leper had touched.

A wagon passed by. The wheels sent the coins flying into the dust and tore the cable in half. Later a child found one of the coins and bought food.

Archibald Lightner: 1899

Archibald Lightner was furious. He had enough to do without having to go into Cairo and rescue his foolish photographer. "I've half a mind to fire you," he said when he finally stomped into the French embassy. "You can't even do a decent watercolor."

"I'm the photographer," the boy protested. "I never said I could paint."

"Well, then, you should be more versatile," snapped Archibald Lightner. His dig was full of stupid people. Of course, he was of the opinion that most people were stupid, but one always hoped to avoid them. Or at least not hire them.

"Actually," said the boy, "you aren't paying me anything."

Dr. Lightner remembered now. Something to do with a leper colony. The boy certainly looked healthy. In fact, he looked perfect. Archibald, who was beaky, gawky and gaunt, had always wanted to look like this young man. Bronze and strong, like a Greek statue. Archibald resembled a heron.

"What is your full name, anyway?" he said irritably. He had searched the boy's possessions, hoping to find a passport, but paperwork was not required at most borders, and it did not look as if the boy possessed any. In fact, other than love letters from a girl named Katie, the boy possessed virtually nothing.

I don't know a thing about him, thought Dr. Lightner. Perhaps I should request that he move on. If I give him money, he will be eager to do so. On the other hand, I pay him nothing, and in exchange he gives me fine photographs.

"I cannot lie to you, sir," said the boy, his cheeks turning red. "I must tell you my full name, although I beg that you not use it. I am Hiram Stratton, Jr."

"Your father is Hiram Stratton?" Archibald Lightner was astonished. He had perceived the camera boy as a servant, just above the natives who toted rubble. Hiram Stratton was one of those astonishing Americans who had achieved inconceivable wealth, and now, bored by wives and mansions, was giving it away. People were lined up, hoping their museum or hospital or library might be handed a vast sum.

Archibald Lightner considered how he might spend a vast sum. Quickly and enjoyably, he decided.

"How is it that the son of Hiram Stratton has no possessions except a change of clothing and a camera?" asked Dr. Lightner. "Are you being fully honest in this matter?"

"My father and I are estranged," said the boy stiffly. "I

do not possess a dime of his, nor do I anticipate a return to his household."

"You will pardon the insult implied by my next remark, Mr. Stratton." (For he could not continue to address the youth as if he were mere staff.) "But when a young son is so deeply estranged, one must wonder if the son committed misdeeds so great that he dare not return to the bosom of his family."

The French, who were always committing misdeeds so great that they dare not return to the bosom of their families, liked Strat better now.

Strat flushed deeply. "I ask you, sir. Is it not possible that the misdeeds were committed by the father? Perhaps the son has chosen a life in which he and his father's misdeeds will not collide."

The French were satisfied. Not only was the young man from a fine family, he cast off wealth as if it mattered not. He was morally above his own parent, refusing to be stained by his father. It was worthy of an opera.

The attaché said, "We accept, *monsieur,* that our two citizens were careless and caused their own deaths. We regret this unfortunate episode here in Cairo, Mr. Stratton." There was bowing and nodding and stroking of mustaches.

They patted the Stratton heir on the shoulder as he left.

Dr. Lightner was not so quick to believe in the boy. All America knew that Hiram Stratton, Sr., had done evil things en route to becoming rich.

The apple, thought Archibald Lightner, does not fall far from the tree. Hiram Stratton, Jr., might travel halfway around the world to escape being his father's son, but he is still his father's son. And that means he has the capacity for evil.

ANNIE: 1999

In the center of each table in the museum restaurant were folding paper pyramids describing the exhibit. Annie yearned to keep one. Should she ask the waitress and risk being refused, or just quietly fold it up and slip it into her purse?

The tables were jammed next to one another. Inches away, an elderly couple argued hotly about the same problem. "Fine," said the husband testily, "steal one."

His wife glared at him and tucked the paper pyramid into her purse. "It isn't stealing, Albert. It's a souvenir. Besides, lunch was expensive."

"It's stealing," said the husband, as if he might summon New York's Finest, arrest his wife, and be done with it.

The boy was laughing. "That's the thing about marriage," he whispered to Annie. "The decades pile up and so do tempers."

"Tell me about it," said Annie. "But sometimes they rescue themselves. My parents left today on their second honeymoon."

"Really? How nice. Did they get married again and everything?"

Annie nodded. "My mother went on a killer diet so she could fit into her wedding gown again, and Dad into his same tux. My brother was best man and I was maid of honor. We even had the same guests. It was fun in an embarrassing kind of way." She skipped the part about the affair her father had promised to abandon. Who knew whether to believe him? But Mom believed, and it was her marriage.

She said, "I remember that Hiram Stratton, Sr., made a fortune in railroads. I never knew he was a philanthropist." If I could touch your hair, she thought, I would know whether you are my Strat.

But they were sitting opposite each other in a public place and he thought they were strangers. "The family legend is that Hiram Stratton, Sr., disowned Hiram Stratton, Jr., because Junior went insane. Junior took up gentle Victorian activities like watercolors and eventually went to Egypt for a rest cure. He took a few photographs for the Lightner dig and then—who knows?"

They called him Strat, not Junior, thought Annie. And he wasn't insane. He loved me. Of course, my brother, Tod, would call that insane. "So you're Devonny's great-grandchild," she said instead.

"You make it sound as if you and Grandmother Devonny met," he said, laughing.

We did, thought Annie. She sent me on a mission, to save Strat from the asylum. But it went wrong in the end, and we had to part.

"Devonny Stratton married an Englishman," he explained. "They had two children. The older son became an earl or something, but the younger son came back to America and called himself Lockwood Stratton. His son, my father, was plain old Bill Stratton, and now I'm Lockwood Stratton again. Ridiculous British-type name, huh?"

No. Lockwood was not a ridiculous British-type name.

It was a ridiculous American-type name. Annie's.

Annie folded and unfolded the paper pyramid to distract herself. She swallowed her latte. She loved the puffy creaminess and the soft sugar at the bottom. "I'm a Lockwood myself. My name is Annie Lockwood. It would be," she said carefully, "somebody in my family that Devonny got the name from." Because I tried to save Strat, she thought. And maybe I did. I've never really known.

"That is so terrific! Then we're related, in a nonrelated kind of way."

He had Strat's smile. The one that said, This is the best day and you are the best person to spend it with.

The second falling came.

She gripped the tiny restaurant table and did not fall completely. It was more the dizziness that hits anyone from time to time: a skidding of the mind, the tires of your thoughts on black ice. She could not quite see the boy's face, and could not quite remember Strat's, and then it was over, and Lockwood Stratton was studying the bill.

"What's my share?" said Annie thickly.

"Please let me pay. I'm getting a kick out of this. I love that we're both Lockwoods."

RENIFER: IN THE TWENTIETH YEAR OF THE REIGN OF KHUFU, LORD OF THE TWO LANDS

The great torches along the polished causeway had been lit. The avenue past the temples and up to the Pyramid gleamed in the night. The wind off the desert grew cold.

The tomb robbers held no grudge against Hetepheres. They hoped she would have eternal life. They assumed, however, that she would be fine without her jewels.

They had been robbing her tomb for several nights now, having chipped away the plaster that hid the entrance. Her little mortuary chapel had potted palms and ferns, watered by temple servants. Now there were many more, watered by tomb robbers, which after their night's work, the thieves slid over the stones to hide the forced entry.

They had taken from the tomb most of the smaller items and were now considering how to take the larger ones.

Using levers, they tipped up the lid of the great stone sarcophagus. In it would rest the finest jewels, lying next to and on top of the mummy. The queen's *ka* would be flying around, frantic and angry, but they had been robbing tombs for generations. No man yet had been hurt by a *ka*—only by priests who thought they were above bribery.

It took some time to maneuver the two-ton stone lid out of the way. They balanced it crosswise on the rim of the sarcophagus and hoisted out the light wooden coffin. They removed an immense gold pectoral of vulture's wings, solid with jasper and lapis lazuli. Somebody's wife or daughter would look magnificent in the morning.

Of course, she would have to look magnificent in private, until the gold was melted down and molded into something that could not be recognized. But melting down stolen gold was a daily activity, like baking bread or netting fish.

If Pharaoh caught them, He would have them impaled. But the robbers merely found this exciting. They did not expect Pharaoh to be told. Sufficient bribes had been paid for many nights of privacy. The guardians of the City of the Dead were always happy to receive gold. The priests who served the dead queen her daily meals were also satisfied by gold.

That was the thing about gold. Everybody wanted it and everybody was satisfied by it.

Except when they wanted more.

ANNIE: 1999

The third falling was hideous and wrong.

Even as it was happening, Annie knew that only bad things could come of this. She would suffer—and worse, she would cause others to suffer.

She saw the boy's eyes open wide, saw his puzzlement.

She tried to call to him, but Time peeled them apart.

Decades ripped at her hair and years tore her skin. She gained velocity. Passing years heaved around her like earthquakes. Annie was screaming, but her voice was torn from her throat by the wind of Time. Her fingertips scraped along centuries, her body bruised by millennia.

Stop, begged Annie. *You're taking me too far. If Strat is out there, he's in 1899.*

But she was merely mortal and had no weapons.

Time possessed them all.

Hiram Stratton, Sr.: 1899

"Ah, Mr. Stratton," said the museum trustee, "such a delight to lunch with you."

Actually, he found Hiram Stratton appalling. The man had grown so obese from fine food and liquor that his belly jutted into a room like the prow of a tugboat. The immense mustache was groomed and waxed, the teeth yellow from nicotine, and the pipe clenched in the jaw gave off a noxious odor. The eyes were too small for the lumpy face, and blinked too seldom, as with a shark. Below the small beard, the starched white collar was crushed by the weight of jowls and chin.

The museum had opened an American Wing, which embarrassed the trustee, since Americans were not capable of producing art. The museum should contain only *actual* art—Italian oil paintings or Greek statues. Perhaps Mr. Stratton had been coaxed into believing in the existence of American art.

No doubt the man wanted his name on a plaque or a door. The trustee shuddered to think of his beloved museum stained by the name of this family. Must I have anything to do with this revolting person? thought the trustee, resenting his assignment.

"I am thinking," said Hiram Stratton, Sr., "of giving several million dollars to the Egyptian collection."

The trustee was passionate about the Egyptian collection. He loved pyramids and the Nile, papyrus and tombs. He found he didn't care as much about the Stratton name as he had a moment ago. "Archaeology is expensive, dear sir. One must have quite a staff. We, of course, sponsor Dr. Archibald Lightner, who even now is working at the foot of the Great Pyramid. Naturally you have read his gripping books."

Personally the trustee didn't think Mr. Stratton could read. But the man could count. Millions at a time. What that money could do for the Egyptian collection!

And it was imperative to remove antiquities from Egypt swiftly, because the country was making noises about wanting to keep them for itself! Absurd. To think of leaving such treasures with mere Egyptians!

"I wish," said Mr. Stratton, "to visit the excavation prior to making my gift."

The trustee imagined Mr. Stratton flattening little Egyptian donkeys. "How thrilled Dr. Lightner will be to have a man of your stature visit," he lied.

Mr. Stratton had a peculiar request. He did not wish his name used. Dr. Archibald Lightner was merely to know that an important donor was arriving. In fact, Hiram Stratton would arrange his visit through another group entirely. "My dear sir," said the trustee, confused, for there was but one reason to give money—to be applauded by one's friends—"surely you want your name in the papers."

"When one has wealth, one is forced to take precautions," said Hiram Stratton.

In other words, thought the trustee, the factory fire haunts you. Somebody out there would like to cut you to pieces. "It is a sorrowful world," he said, "when gentlemen such as yourself must deal with an ungrateful public."

CAMILLA: 1899

Camilla was astonished to find that Egypt was overrun by tourists.

She met hunters eager to bag a crocodile, collectors of mummies, explorers of rivers and invalids in sedan chairs hoping to bake themselves healthy. Hordes of British officers were exploring Cairo and Giza and Saqqara before joining the attack at Khartoum.

Camilla pretended that a handsome British officer—no, a *titled* handsome British officer—would fall in love with her and beg for her hand in marriage.

But the British were even shorter than the Americans. Camilla towered over every man in sight.

She had come as a newspaperwoman, Duffie having obtained a fake assignment for Miss Camilla Matthews. Camilla, with a mass of other tourists, approached the Pyramids. The donkey she rode was small and plump and hung with tassels. She had to hold her feet up so they did not scrape the ground.

Nothing had prepared her for the sight of the Pyramids.

She knew there were two million two-ton rocks in

Khufu's Pyramid, but to see them! To gaze up and up and up, stunned by the actual accumulation of all those stones, and each its own color of gold; the Egyptian sun beating down until every angle and corner burned with fire.

Oh, thought Camilla, to have known the man—or god—who thought to build this monument.

The Pyramid was clustered with climbers: two or three natives in billowing white robes vaulting easily from stone to stone, and then reaching out long brown hands to haul up an exhausted and sweating tourist. In every language came their cries of encouragement: *"Allez-y doucement!" "Dem halben-weg!" "Pazienza, signora!"*

The wind lifted sand and flung it in her face, leaving her skin raw and stung. Just so had Camilla flung lies at Katie. Camilla felt as sick in her gut as if she had been drinking from the Nile. Far worse, she had drunk from the example of Hiram Stratton.

She, Camilla Mateusz, had trespassed on a saint.

Life had already used Katie so badly. What right had Camilla to use her?

I had to! Camilla told herself. It was necessary to find the son, and through the son punish the father! I must shrug about it.

But she knew herself to be infected, from her rage toward the father and her daily practice of lying and cheating and conniving for Mr. Duffie.

Camilla strode on. The walking was difficult. The Giza plateau was nothing but sand and stone broken by centuries of weather and feet and by decades of excavation. Her chestnut leather boots were scratched by shards and rubble. Fine clothing was a good thing, but better was a clean heart, she thought.

Quarrying had taken place everywhere, giving the plateau an odd geometry, with so many squares cut away over the millennia. The passage of so much time allowed Camilla to shrug. Who cared about a clean heart? She cared about money, and if it was dirty, so be it. It would still feed her brothers and sisters.

Several hundred feet beyond the Pyramids and the Sphinx was a tent city: headquarters of Dr. Lightner's dig. Fenced off by posts and a single frayed rope, it was guarded by an Egyptian in a long swirling robe of chocolate brown. He was armed—a rifle on his shoulder, a pistol at his waist and a knife literally in his teeth. Camilla loved him. He was treasure and greed, adventure and attack.

Her letter of introduction to Dr. Archibald Lightner—her false letter, designed by Hiram Stratton himself—moved Camilla past the barricade.

The great man sat under an awning and behind a table littered with shards of rock and pottery. He looked at her with dislike, read the letter and sighed. "Miss Matthews, I prefer not to deal with females. Their educations are poor and their presence distracting."

Camilla, whose education was indeed poor, and who planned to be a major distraction, could not argue.

In spite of his opinion of females, however, Archibald Lightner obeyed the rules of courtesy and got to his feet.

And now the word great was appropriate. Archibald Lightner was six-and-a-half-feet tall.

Camilla made an instant decision to marry him.

Plenty of women married for money. It couldn't be worse to choose a husband by height. Of course, age was a problem. He had to be twenty years older than Camilla. Possibly thirty. But who cared? He was taller. "I have never been accused of being low to the ground, sir. And I shall not be a nuisance. I shall be the best publicity you can buy. My article will generate large donations. An archaeologist can never have too much money."

Dr. Lightner laughed. It was a rusty sound, as one who rarely encounters anything comic. Making him laugh was how she would accomplish his proposal of marriage. Camilla gave herself a deadline, as if he were a newspaper article. Three weeks, she said to herself, and he will ask for my hand. She looked *up* into his eyes: the first time in her life that a man's eyes were above her own.

"Miss Matthews," he said reluctantly, "how may I begin your instruction?"

She pointed to the Pyramids. "I want desperately to ascend. I spent the voyage reading about Egypt and have yearned for this moment. Must I hire assistance like other tourists? I am strong and accustomed to playing ball games. Might I climb alone?"

He was puzzled, as if she were a hieroglyph not yet deciphered. "No, madam. A lady mustn't attempt the ascent alone. She might grow fatigued from heat or lose her balance and topple."

Camilla had never lost her balance and toppled; not when her father died; not when she masqueraded as a man; not when she visited a leper hospital. She did not plan to topple from a Pyramid either. But women did not contradict great men, nor receive marriage proposals by being strong.

"I will take you," he said suddenly, surprising her; perhaps surprising himself; definitely surprising his staff, who took a second glance at the female in their midst.

They approached the base of the Pyramid. Camilla touched one of the great yellowing stones. She swayed from the impact of such antiquity. She felt she almost knew the men who had piled these stones. Knew their wives and children, their gods and dreams.

"Are you faint already?" demanded the great man irritably.

"I am overcome not by heat, but by history. Not by weakness, but by strength." Camilla caught Dr. Lightner's arm. "Tell me how the stones were quarried and moved. Tell me who was here. Tell me how they lived."

He stared at her as if she were an artifact. "Put your hat back on," he said gruffly. "Fasten the scarf. You must be shaded from the glare." He tightened the chin strap on his own stiff, wide-brimmed hat and took her hand to help her up. She did need help, as her skirt proved confining. Dr. Lightner could vault easily up to the next level, from whence he would reach down to grip her hand, and lean backward. Up the tautness of his body she would scramble. She felt her arm would be pulled from its socket with every yank. She bruised her shin and banged her elbow, but gave no sign, unwilling to ask for rest.

"From the top, Miss Matthews, you will see for miles because the land is flat and the air so clear. You will comprehend this area as one vast graveyard. You will see the floor plan, so to speak: the causeway, the quadrangles of lesser tombs and the remains of minor pyramids."

Twice he dusted her off, apologizing for the intimacy of this act. Once Camilla dusted him off. She was thorough. She did not apologize.

"Tell me," said Dr. Lightner. "What reading did you do to prepare for this article you will write about me?"

"I began of course with your own three books," said Camilla, having purchased them from American tourists who didn't care if they ever heard another word about Egypt again. "My favorite is volume two, in which you discourse about the current events in Egypt as compared to the upheavals of Egypt's magnificent past."

He said casually, as one to whom the topic is of minor interest, "I am preparing volume four."

"Dr. Lightner! What an honor it would be were I permitted to gaze at your first draft."

They reached the summit. Two or three stones of the

final tier remained, creating shade and seating. It might have been designed for tired ladies and handsome men to rest and eat an orange. Dr. Lightner had a tin canteen hanging at his waist, and they shared sips of water. Her lips rested where his had been and now when their eyes met, his dropped first.

In the distance was Cairo with minarets and towers. Closer were farms of emerald green, split by canals, dotted with camels and donkeys moving down dusty lanes.

Peace descended over Camilla.

It was not possible to think of revenge and rage. Perhaps rage and revenge had once occurred in Egypt, but today it was serene and Camilla was part of the eternally repeating life of that eternal river.

"This is the stage of a great theater, isn't it?" Camilla said softly. "Cairo is the audience. A million people are crammed into the auditorium that is Egypt."

"How beautifully you expressed that." Dr. Lightner pointed to a line as sharp as an edge of paper that divided the green fields from the yellow desert. "Look there. Fields and sand are not friends," he told her. "They march up to each other and neither will surrender. That sand extends from the Nile to Morocco! To the Atlantic Ocean itself."

"I should like to travel from oasis to oasis with my camel train," said Camilla, "and meet the Bedouin."

"Yes! And write an article about it! I will help you arrange it." He took her hand for a different purpose than hauling her upward. He took it, she thought, from excitement. From looking forward to her company. He held her hand flat between both of his, as in Egyptian wall paintings.

An emotion as ageless as revenge entered Camilla's heart. She knew suddenly what could cause a lady to lose her balance and topple.

Falling in love.

STRAT: 1899

Twice that day, Strat felt the presence of Annie. Twice he reached into thin air, thinking to grasp her and haul her through to him. Twice he caught only the wind.

She is near, he thought, but a year or a century divides us.

He could have wept or screamed or even thrown himself off the Pyramid, but he managed to laugh and go on taking photographs of tourists and saving the money to send to Katie.

The third time he so intensely felt the presence of Annie, he lost his grip on the heavy wooden tripod that held his camera. It tipped to the side, falling heavily against a pile of stones. Oh, no! If his camera were broken . . .

Strat's heart sank.

But what was damaged was the stone.

Impossible. A stick of wood could not break stone. Strat kicked the stone with his boot—and it broke. He picked up a piece and rubbed it—and it turned to white dust in his palm.

It was plaster.

Who would apply plaster to a stone in the desert?

Strat opened his penknife and stabbed experimentally at the stones around him. He was surrounded by plaster. He, Strat, was standing on the entrance to a tomb. Some royal tomb had been camouflaged by that plaster for thousands of years, and *he*—not the brilliant archaeologists! not the scholars! not the historians!—*he,* Strat, had found it.

I'll be famous. I, Hiram Stratton, Jr.—

—but he did not want anyone else knowing he was Hiram Stratton, Jr. Already he felt vulnerable and anxious, because Archibald Lightner knew the truth. What if word spread?

Father, thought Strat ruefully, you have truly followed me to the grave. Luckily, it isn't *my* grave. And though I dare not take credit, for publicity would tell you where I am, at least I can take photographs.

He could not wait to tell Dr. Lightner. He ran across the sand and rubble to the dig and saw, several hundred yards away, Dr. Lightner talking with a tall slim girl in a long romantic skirt.

Annie had come.

The other night when he climbed to the top of the Pyramid, he *had* reached her. Time *had* let his prayer cross the century.

His body leaped forward and his heart followed. He soared toward her, as an eagle soars on rising heat. He plunged over the crevasse where some archaeologist was digging in the hope of finding a buried tomb ship. He raced over trenches where yet another hoped to find a queen's tomb. He could not slow his steps and he certainly could not slow his heart.

And when he arrived, plunging down a slope, leaping from rock crest to sand hill, he saw that the girl had blond hair.

Annie's was dark.

CAMILLA: 1899

"Let us descend," said Dr. Lightner at last. "There is work to do."

Down was easier than up. There were fewer occasions on which it was necessary to cling to each other. Camilla could not bring herself, an athlete, to pretend she needed help when she did not.

Halfway down Dr. Lightner said, "Tell me what sort of ball games you delight in."

She was touched that he had been paying attention to her from the first. "Basketball. Have you ever had the pleasure?"

"Oh, yes! We play basketball here for amusement. My young men all played for their colleges. How your team must relish you! You are so magnificently tall."

Camilla stared at Dr. Lightner's weathered face. Sun had burned it to bronze and split it in cracks.

They walked slowly toward the tents, finding much to say. How marvelous to be with a man who was not letting go of her hand. How marvelous, in fact, were hands.

A boy about Camilla's own age suddenly came bounding and yelling toward them.

Camilla was pretending to be thirty, which seemed like the right age for a seasoned reporter sent halfway across the world to write about scientific events, but in fact, she was seventeen. The boy too had the air of somebody pretending to be older, but in fact, still in his teens.

She had the oddest sense that he was racing toward *her.* That they knew each other. She even had the thought that she shocked him; that he was not prepared for the sight of her.

It was not until he pulled up next to them, breathless and excited, that Camilla saw he was astonishingly handsome and very unkempt. His jacket was in desperate need of button reattachment and his trousers needed mending.

"Dr. Lightner! Sir!" he cried. "I have found an undiscovered tomb."

Camilla laughed out loud at this pathetic claim. It was surely the daydream of every tourist: I'll stoop down, find pottery with hieroglyphs, kick away a rock and expose a tomb, which will be filled with gold.

"I knocked over my tripod whilst preparing my camera," said the boy. "The wooden legs are heavy and topped with brass casings. They hit against a desert stone and when I looked, it was not stone at all, but plaster camouflaged as a rock!"

Dr. Lightner quivered. "Perhaps I should take a look."

He and the boy walked with measured pace, though Camilla thought they wanted to fly through the air, dive into the sand and come flailing to the surface with their arms full of Egyptian gold.

In moments, the entire expedition was trooping along, whispering and wondering. What a gathering of fine young men! Camilla gathered that these were intellectuals from the great universities of the world, taking six months or a year to indulge a passion for archaeology. She wondered what it could be like to have the money to do such a thing.

"What is the significance of the plaster?" she asked one of them.

"In my studies at Yale," he told her, "I learned that in ancient times, the entry to a tomb was often disguised with plaster dyed to match the desert."

It did not seem to Camilla it had been necessary to wedge Yale into the response. She decided that she, in turn, would wedge an important women's college into the conversation, as if she too recalled tidbits from otherwise dull lectures.

"You are a lucky reporter, Miss Matthews," said one of the young men. "A real scoop. What an article you will write!"

Camilla was horrified. She didn't know a thing about reporting. She had planned to fake all that.

"What newspaper are you from?" asked the Yale man. "Boston?" he said. "New York?" It had to be one of these; no other city mattered.

"I'm from Kansas," she said, preparing to hand him

the fake card she had had printed up to support her fake credentials.

They burst into uproarious laughter at the idea that people in Kansas could read, or even printed newspapers.

Furious and embarrassed, Camilla took pad and pencil from her satchel and pushed her way to the front. Ladies did have a few advantages in this world. No man would think of pushing back.

A few taps of the chisel and it was established that behind the plaster were flat stones, easily dragged aside, and below them . . . a man-made rectangle. The entrance, perhaps, to the shaft of a tomb.

Dr. Lightner stood for the boy to photograph him above the unopened site. He contained his excitement poorly. He could not stay motionless for the lengthy time a photograph required.

Camilla found she had already written three paragraphs.

The removal of rubble from the shaft began.

The Egyptians were told to work faster, but that did not occur. They had a tempo. They did not rush. After all, thought Camilla, the rocks have been there five thousand years. It's Americans who rush.

Long before they had made much progress, the shadows were too thick for work to go on. People sighed, agreeing to leave the rest for the morrow, and went sadly and separately to their tents.

Camilla, however, approached the boy. She was amazed by his physical beauty. Burnished by the

Egyptian sun, the youth shone. He had retreated over the sand, and was facing the Sphinx, but his thoughts were clearly on a tiny envelope in his hand.

The envelope was not two inches long, the color of an American sky before an autumn storm: gray with tints of angry yellow. He held it to his lips. It was not a kiss, more a communion.

Communion.

She was Camilla Mateusz again, thinking of all the Sundays in this wicked year in which she had not gone to Mass and had not taken Communion and had not been a good person. Her eyes blurred with shame.

The boy put the envelope in his shirt pocket, so that it lay over his heart. Uncertainly, Camilla interrupted and was met by a sweet half-smile.

"Might we sit upon one of the Pyramid stones and talk to each other?" asked Camilla. "If you are willing, tell me the details of your discovery for my article."

They circled the Sphinx. The serpent charmers had packed up, the watermelon vendors were sold out and the tables of souvenirs had vanished. The boy took her arm as if they were off to a dance, and they walked over a vast pavement, tilted now by the ravages of Time, and arrived at Khufu's Pyramid.

The best spot was several stones up and they climbed together. "Girls can't usually swing up like that!" he said respectfully. "I've known only one."

"What was her name?" asked Camilla.

"Annie." His voice was so soft she could hardly hear. He traced the outline of the tiny envelope in his pocket.

"What is that in your pocket?" she asked. Working for Duffie had destroyed her inhibition against asking about people's private lives. She must remember that ladies did not pry. Of course, reporters always pried. Perhaps she could not be both.

He answered with courtesy. "Once, long ago, I loved a young lady. We left each other. There was no choice in the matter. All I have of her, and all I ever will, is a lock of her hair."

He carried that girl's token against his heart. Camilla's own heart was assaulted. Would any man ever feel that way toward her? She could not prevent a prayerful vision of herself and Dr. Lightner together, and had to blush at such foolishness. A great scholar? Interested in a half-educated girl, half his age, pretending to be a reporter?

Perhaps she really could be a reporter. Then there would be one true thing in her life. She would not entirely be a tissue of lies. "You and I were never introduced," she said. "I must have your name for my article so that you may receive credit for finding the shaft. I am Miss Camilla Matthews, newspaper reporter from Kansas."

"Really?" he said with interest. "Tell me about Kansas."

Camilla had never been west of New York City, so her answers lacked validity, but Strat repeated her words carefully. He would probably carry them around all his life.

"This has been a lovely night," he said then. "Allow

me to escort you to the tent that Dr. Lightner has arranged for you, Miss Matthews."

"I still do not know your name, sir."

"You need not use my name in your article, Miss Matthews."

She was astonished. "This discovery could be your future."

He shook his head, not interested in his future.

"What shall I call you then, since I am to stay at your camp for some time?" She extended her hand, firmly and in a masculine fashion, so he would not become confused and think she wanted to lean on him.

"People call me Strat," he said finally.

The son of the man who had murdered her father shook Camilla's hand.

III

Time to Fear

ANNIE

Reeds as thick as Annie's wrist, but unnaturally shaped in triangles—like no plant on earth she had ever heard of—towered around and above her. Lacy fronds and leaves closed out the sky. Fat roots fondled the mud in which they grew, and the mud caught her toes and sucked at her heels.

Birds shrieked. Water lapped. A cloud of purple dragonflies needled past and a frog vaulted out of the water, its wet skin brushing her ankle.

Annie had never known such heat. Sweat poured off her, soaking through her clothes. A white-winged heron rose languidly in front of her, as if half-asleep; as if all creatures, herself included, could not fully waken in this heat.

Gripping the heavy stems—trunks, almost—of the reeds, she tried to find her way out. Out of what? she thought, trying not to sink into terror as she was sinking into mud. Into what?

Leaves as hot as if they had been fried slapped her in the face. The air was so thick with moisture that no matter how deeply she breathed, she failed to find enough oxygen.

"Strat!" she screamed, for he must be here. The only reason Time had hurled her here—wherever she was—was to find Strat.

Nobody answered.

Huge rotting plants rimmed the edges of deep water. She could find no land, no solid earth. To break through these reeds would take a machete. The clothing bought in hope of an adventure was drenched and stinking and the wonderful shoes full of mud and probably leeches, even now sucking on the bottoms of her feet.

In front of her, the water turned gray, developed slick spots and heaved. Two bulging eyes stared at Annie. A pink mouth as large as a trash can opened up and the beast bellowed, its fat teeth as big as her palm.

When it sank back down, a wave lashed up and soaked Annie to the knees.

A hippopotamus. Not the sweet little blue pottery hippo sold in the museum shop. The real thing. The real hideous and dangerous thing.

Annie thrashed around, screaming for help.

Any help. Any people, from any time.

But only the hippo returned to stare at her.

Lockwood Stratton

The boy named Lockwood Stratton had never had a fainting spell, nor ever been dizzy, nor ever needed glasses.

Now he seemed to be struggling with all three.

His fingers shivered over the white tablecloth. He concentrated on figuring the tip and putting the bills down. What he had just seen—or not seen—was strange, but more strange was that he had come to the museum at all.

He had no interest in his family background. Any mention of ancestors and he fell asleep or left the room, moaning. And yet when he had read the article about the Egyptian exhibition (he, who never read anything, not even his assignments!), he thought: My ancestor was the photographer at that dig.

His mother would have been thrilled that her son was having a cultural moment.

His father would have been astonished that he even remembered from whom he was descended.

But he had not told them. He had come into the city

alone. Nobody did that. What fun was it to be alone in New York?

Well, I'm not alone now, he said to himself.

He and this Annie Lockwood would go back upstairs and finish seeing the special exhibition. How amazing that she and he shared a name and a history.

"Well, let's head on back," he said cheerfully, although he was not cheerful. He was still shaken by the way she had—but it was impossible. He had not seen that, because it hadn't happened.

"We still have half the exhibition to look at," he told her.

Nobody answered.

In fact, when he forced himself to raise his eyes from the tablecloth and look around, nobody was there. Not Annie, not the couple arguing at the next table, not even a waiter. The restaurant was empty and quiet. He walked uneasily toward the exit. He saw Annie Lockwood nowhere. She was distinctive, with that falling black hair.

She's got to be right here, he told himself. Waiting for me in the hall.

But she wasn't.

He saw the sign for the ladies' room, so he sat on a bench with some other men and waited patiently. But she didn't come out.

Great. I've lost her. Maybe she lost me, too, and she's gone back to the exhibition looking for me.

So he trooped back up the Grand Staircase, but she was not there.

He was embarrassed by how upset he was. Had she fallen into his life, full of delight and stories and lovely dark hair he yearned to touch, and he was so boring she just got up and left?

Although what he had seen was not exactly getting up and leaving.

He circled the special exhibition, pausing at the photograph under which he and this Annie Lockwood had met. The photograph seemed different. As if somebody had been added, or subtracted.

Impossible, he said to himself, shaking off a return of the dizziness that had struck in the restaurant.

He heard Annie scream for help, and he swerved, eyes wide open, to see where it had come from, but the room was empty, except for a guard who stared at him with a strange heavy-lidded antique look.

She went downstairs to the regular Egyptian collection, he told himself. I'll find her at the Temple of Dendur, sitting by the reflecting pool.

Renifer

Pankh poled the little skiff through the papyrus reeds while Renifer sang.

Fat pads of lotus swirled by, while brick-red swallows dipped and swerved in their quest for bugs. The hoopoe, a bird Renifer loved beyond all others, followed them, jumping from one papyrus frond to the next. Once she saw the snout of a crocodile, and, distantly, she heard the shrieks of baboons.

Renifer had had the servants put together a picnic basket and she fed Pankh dates and they drank sweet fig juice from the same bowl. She offered him cold duck and he nibbled the meat right down to her fingers. They dipped bread in salted oil and shared a block of cheese.

Twice he kissed her, and the reed boat trembled as they fought for balance, both physical and emotional. He was so handsome. When she looked at Pankh, she could think of nothing but marriage and the joy it would bring. Father, however, had lost his joy in the coming event. He was quiet. He was, in fact, fearful.

What could it mean?

Marriage must not be entered into lightly. She must

be sure of Pankh, and he of her. So Renifer said to him, "We must talk of important things."

He had to laugh at the idea that girls had important things in their lives. He poled into the swamp until the papyrus towered above them, six and eight and ten feet of strong triangular stalks, the wide flat heads darkening the sun.

"You are the most beautiful girl in Egypt," said Pankh. "I am all that is important to you. I will give you everything."

"But what I want, Pankh, is the truth. Tell me what is between you and Father."

"That is between men, Renifer. Men make choices in life. Your father has made his. He will live with them or he will die with them. It is not your place to consider truth or lack of truth. It is your place to obey. Yesterday you obeyed your father; from now on, you will obey me."

Renifer had stopped listening to him. She was watching the most amazing terrifying thing she had ever seen. A spirit was materializing before her. First there was mist. Then shape. Then color and movement.

It was a *ka*.

Renifer had known all her life, and worshiped the fact, that the *ka* returned one day to the body. That was why it was necessary to save the corpse. Without a body, no *ka* could find its way home. But she and Pankh were deep within a jungle of papyrus. There could be no body buried here. The *ka* was lost.

Renifer could think of nothing more dreadful. She

prayed that the *ka* would depart without touching them. Its shape was thickening now, and taking on human form, creating its own body, here in the papyrus! Renifer gazed in awe and terror.

Pankh, realizing he had lost his audience, turned to look where she looked.

"It's a lost *ka,*" whispered Renifer, so frightened she could not think what god to call upon.

But the *ka* saw them and cried out.

"Hetepheres," whispered Pankh. He fell to his knees and the reed boat, fortunately stable and hard to sink, shuddered under the weight of his collapse.

How could it be the *ka* of Hetepheres? wondered Renifer. Why would the name Hetepheres even enter Pankh's mind? She has been dead for a year. Besides, the queen was buried so well and so richly. If ever a *ka* had a good place to return to, it is the queen's tomb.

"Go home!" Pankh yelled at the *ka*. "Get away from us!"

But if it were a *ka,* it did not appear Egyptian. It came closer, and the tears it wept were real tears. It smelled bad, as foreigners did.

Renifer decided to treat it as she would a sacred animal—an ibis, or a cow dedicated to Hathor. The first thing was to feed it. She held out a date in the palm of her hand and in her other hand, a cup of fig juice, although it was doubtful that a creature so primitive would know how to drink from a cup, any more than a cow would.

But the creature seized the cup, drinking noisily, and

then bit down hard on the date. It seemed astonished that the date contained a pit and spat the whole thing out. Renifer gave the creature bread instead, and it consumed the bread like a wild dog. Then it stood panting and whimpering.

Pankh had calmed down. "I don't think it's a *ka,*" he said. "Maybe a slave girl in the dress of her native land? She has run away, perhaps, and is trying to hide in the papyrus swamp."

How frightening to be lost here! Papyrus was delicate with arching fronds, forming hieroglyphics of their own against the brown Nile and the blue sky. But millions of them . . . mile upon mile of them . . . and they interlaced like prison walls. Feet sank into mud and roots clung to ankles and crocodiles sprang out of dark water. No wonder the poor thing was frightened.

Its clothing was stranger than Renifer had seen even in the slave bazaar. Egyptians did not normally have slaves. Their servants were not sold in streets. Slaves were prisoners of war, and came from distant places that must be thrashed until they understood Egyptian superiority.

But Pankh was correct about the creature being female, and probably also that it was foreign, for its skin was as pale as bleached linen. It looked unhealthy to Renifer. Its hair was very long and must be very hot.

The creature tried to grab the pole with which Pankh pushed the little boat through the reeds but he jerked it out of her reach. "Pankh!" said Renifer severely. "We have to rescue her."

"No, we don't. It isn't a pet," said Pankh. "Don't touch it."

Renifer paid no attention to him. "It's all right," called Renifer, reaching toward the creature. "You may get in the boat with us. I'm going to take you home and bathe you. Don't be afraid. We won't leave you in the swamp."

Renifer held out her arms and the girl came, and Renifer felt its heartbeat, the heat of its skin and the wet of its tears.

Pankh kept the boat pole between himself and the pale creature. "Her skin is the color of a worm from under a rock," he said in distaste. "Perhaps that's the color of a returning spirit."

"Now, Pankh. You just said she was an escaping slave. She cannot be both." Renifer coaxed the girl to sit in the bottom of the boat. She picked out a sweet pastry and the creature ate it, but refused the beer, which looked fine to Renifer, although maybe it needed to be strained again. Nile beer was rather thick. "The gods have sent her to us, Pankh. They even made you cry out the name of Hetepheres. She is not a *ka,* but perhaps sent by the queen's *ka*! I cannot imagine the purpose. But soon the gods will reveal all. Our task will be made clear to us."

"It is clear to me," said Pankh, "that we should leave her here."

Renifer patted the girl's hand and said soothingly, "We're going to go home now. You're going to have a nice bath and put decent clothing on."

"She's the color of a rat's tail," said Pankh.

"She's the color of ivory," said Renifer. Even Pharaoh possessed little ivory, for it was so precious and rare. Father, of course, in his wealth, had acquired a number of pieces. Renifer lifted her voice to the gods and sang a song of thanksgiving for being honored with a girl of ivory.

Pankh swore at the same gods. He poled much more vigorously out of the papyrus than he had coming in.

The creature—or runaway slave—or foreigner—or *ka*—slid into the bottom of the boat and slept.

ANNIE

Humans!

Annie rushed forward. They were in a funny little boat with a swan's neck prow. But the people in the boat did not want her, and the man shoved her away with his oar.

"No, no," she said desperately. "There are crocodiles in there. Take me with you. Please? I'll do anything."

The man continued to push her away, but the girl behind him suddenly smiled at Annie, elbowed the man aside and drew Annie into the safety of the funny little boat. She was desperately relieved to have her feet out of the mud.

Her rescuer was younger than Annie. Very pretty, with rich warm golden-brown skin. Her black hair was extremely decorative, in many tiny tight braids, falling evenly to her shoulders, and heavily laced with beads. The man was bare except for a white kilt.

The boat was a sort of glorified raft. It was made, Annie realized, of hundreds of the very triangular reeds which had so terrified her. The woven reeds were dried out and stiff, and when she pressed her fingernail into them, they felt like Styrofoam, not wood.

"Papyrus," said the girl, smiling at Annie.

RENIFER

Once home in the women's quarters, Renifer could not get the girl to remove her dreadful clothing and Renifer could not figure out how to remove it herself. It was tied together in some bizarre foreign way.

The servants were laughing too hard and were also too afraid to be of any use.

Whatever tribe the girl came from, it was very primitive. Clearly, she had no acquaintance with gold or adornment. Her ears were pierced, so at some time in her life, she had worn something. But the only jewelry she possessed now was a plain leather wrist strap with a speckled circle.

Renifer decided on gold for a bribe.

Offering jewelry, one piece at a time, she coaxed the girl into a bracelet, and then a necklace and then another. Finally, Renifer got her to remove the strange clothing. The top piece gripped by means of little circles stuck through holes. It had sleeves, such as Renifer had seen on warriors from the Far East, when they had been captured by superior Egyptian forces.

What a relief to strip the girl naked and scrub away

her foreign smell and dress her in clothing through which the cleansing desert air could pass.

When at last she was clean and well oiled—a process she resisted rather vigorously—Renifer chose one of her finest gowns. They had a clash over how the dress hung, as the girl wanted it to cover her upper body. Renifer tried to demonstrate that breasts were a girl's best asset and the girl of ivory had a fine pair, and must display them. In fact, Renifer had makeup for them, but when she tried to apply it, the girl flung herself across the room and even handed back the gold.

Renifer could only laugh and put the girl in a dress that hung from the shoulders.

Renifer decked the girl in her very finest jewels, the ones Father had acquired during the last year, which she wore only at private dinners, because Father said they mustn't let neighbors realize how successful he had become. The necklace had a swollen solid gold collar from which hung gold lace and intense blue lapis lazuli. The finger rings were shaped like coiled serpents and sacred beetles. The earrings were paper-thin plates of hammered gold, six inches across.

When she was finally dressed, she no longer looked like a fish rotting on the shore. She was almost attractive. Once her face was properly made up, she might even be rather lovely. Renifer had never seen anything quite like her.

"A goddess sent you," said Renifer softly. "I'm sure of it. Tomorrow morning, or perhaps by the setting sun, the goddess will tell me your purpose."

Renifer's nurse sniffed. "She looks like a sacrifice. She is white like the best oxen and you have dressed her in white, like the best priestess. I think she is here to die."

They stared at her, while the pale girl herself stared at her new jewelry.

Renifer shivered, wondering to whom and for what the creature would be sacrificed.

ANNIE

All her life, Annie had loved those paintings of Egyptian women, their sloe eyes, dark lids and romantic mysterious glances. Renifer painted her just like that, the makeup going from the corners of her eyes all the way back into her hair. Annie sat and enjoyed it. She wasn't even trying to talk. The sounds Renifer made—if in fact her name was Renifer; it could just as easily be Zrnykr or Bjzhirhoo—did not sound like language.

Annie felt oddly as if she had not changed millennia; these were just girls gathered in a girl's bedroom, playing dress-up, putting on new makeup and sharing hairstyles.

Whereupon Renifer took off her hair.

Annie nearly screamed. Renifer was bald. She shaved her head!

Renifer laughed and pointed through a shuttered window at the huge yellow disk of the sun.

They shave their heads to keep cool, thought Annie, and wear wigs to keep off the sun, the way I'd wear a baseball cap. "Don't even think about shaving off my hair," said Annie. "Bad enough you put me in a see-through dress with nothing on underneath it."

Renifer and her maids burst into giggles at the duck-quacking sound of Annie's language. Then she tied Annie's hair into a knot on top of her head to get rid of it, while a servant brought out a magnificent wig.

It was a deeper black than Annie's real hair, with hundreds of the tight twisted braids like the ones in Renifer's wig. Into the wig, Renifer and the serving girl worked a series of gold ornaments, and then Annie was permitted to stand.

She knew by the delight on their faces that she was beautiful; that they were pleased.

Finally, Renifer decked Annie in gold necklaces. In Annie's world, a gold necklace was a slender thread, a mere suggestion of gold. Ancient Egyptians were not so restrained. The necklace Renifer fastened around Annie's throat was splendid. Its weight astonished her.

The wig and the eyepaint had the nice result of making her feel invisible, the way you felt behind sunglasses. You could see other people, but they couldn't see you. And this was a good thing, because Renifer took Annie's hand and led her into a garden and displayed her in the sheer dress.

The garden was enchanting. The dark plumes of palm trees bowed in the evening breeze. Against a tawny mud-brick wall stood an ancient sycamore, bark peeling into leopard spots. Acacia were powdered with yellow blooms. There were oleander, and limes, and roses blooming as if for a score of weddings.

Every tree and shrub stood inside its own little puddle of Nile water. Gardeners were walking about refilling the puddles. Outside each puddle, the dirt was as hard and dry as wooden planks.

Geese and ducks wandered. A cat sunned itself on a wall. Annie's gown was pleasantly cool against her skin. Renifer led her up a ladder to a roof garden. From here, Annie could see children playing tag, leaping from rooftop to rooftop. Men in the street below were coming home from work—fishermen with their catch; vendors with their wagons. They wore cotton nightgowns, like baggy T-shirts to the ankle.

On the desert horizon, Annie saw two pyramids. She caught her breath. Every picture she had ever seen showed three. It didn't precisely tell her the year, but it did tell her the time: She had arrived in Egypt before the third pyramid had been built. What had she just read on the plaques in the museum? Had not Khufu built his Pyramid around 2500 B.C.?

She tried to think how Strat fit into this and realized that she was going to find Strat, here in antiquity. How he must be rejoicing at his good fortune! What archaeologist has not dreamed of falling through Time to the very place he digs?

Annie turned away from the sights of Memphis to find Renifer's friend Pankh—the one-syllable name was easy to learn—staring at her with loathing. He stepped back when she approached, rubbing his arms, as if she literally made his skin crawl. Annie stuck close to Renifer. Pankh wore a pleated white cloth tied diaper-fashion between his legs. To Annie, he appeared comical, but Renifer certainly admired him.

A man who seemed to be Renifer's father greeted them, raising his eyebrows at the sight of Annie, but shrugging. When Pankh's back was turned, the father sent him looks. Just so had Annie and Tod looked at the woman with whom their father had had that affair. If looks were sharp knives, the woman would have died a quick death.

So, thought Annie, Renifer's father hates Renifer's boyfriend.

There was no time to dwell on this interesting problem, because a little sister and several brothers came pounding up the steps to the roof patio, and surrounded Annie, patting her as they did their pet goose and their pet monkey. The children were naked and dusty and beautiful and she found herself laughing and romping with them.

For dinner, there were roast pigeons with onion. There was baked perch with pomegranate sauce. The bread was delicious and also sandy, as if they had made the bread outside on a windy day. There were cakes drizzled with honey and many kinds of cheese.

Annie began nodding off, a giggly little brother on each side of her keeping her upright. Renifer led her away. She was so tired she could hardly make it down the roof ladder.

Renifer's bedroom was so full of beautiful objects. Every possession looked worthy of a king's tomb, but it was the bed Annie wanted to try out. It was wood framed and tilted toward the feet, with a footboard to keep Renifer from sliding off and one of those wonderful wooden pillows, like a torture rack.

But Annie did not get a bed or even a wooden pillow. Mats kept under Renifer's bed were unrolled and all Annie had for comfort was an inch of reed on a mud-brick floor.

She meant to stay awake for hours, memorizing all she had seen so she could tell Strat, but she fell asleep the moment her cheek touched the mat.

She did not know that when the servants unrolled their mats, tiptoeing around her, they carefully placed amulets on all four sides of her, to protect themselves.

CAMILLA

The following morning, the shaft which young Stratton had discovered was speedily emptied, but spirits sank as soon as the first person descended. The space below was small and unadorned. There were no gilt ceilings. No fine statues. No fabulous treasure. There were the remains of furniture, the wood having disintegrated, only the gold leaf which had wrapped each leg or arm still there. The only other object in the tomb was a huge unopened stone sarcophagus, sealed in antiquity.

"That means," the Yale man told Camilla, "that the tomb was robbed of anything easily carried, while the big pieces were abandoned."

"But surely, if the sarcophagus is sealed," Camilla protested, "there will be a coffin inside. A king's mummy and lots of gold."

"Nothing is for sure in ancient Egypt," said Dr. Lightner ruefully. He was lowered by rope down the sharply slanted shaft. Strat followed, carrying his camera equipment.

Camilla stared down the opening through which Hiram Stratton's son had just disappeared. If only he would rot down there. If only some tomb curse would close in upon him, smothering him with rocks. Then Hiram Stratton would find out what it was like to lose somebody he loved!

She sipped warm water from her canteen, wishing there were a way to keep drinks cold. To make ice, perhaps. She tried to imagine a method of creating ice in hot weather but gave up.

Dr. Lightner emerged from the shaft. He was excited and happy. "Look at this!" he cried.

He sounded like one of her little sisters or brothers bringing home some treasure found on the sidewalk. A bright penny or a lost pencil. Camilla was touched.

He held in his hand something that had been buried thousands of years ago. For the first time, it was struck by sun.

It was a sandal of gold.

Camilla had rarely seen gold. The gleam astonished her. No wonder the world had fallen in love with this metal; no wonder that conquistadors and pirates, presidents and archaeologists wanted it. She wanted that sandal. She was amazed by the ferocity of her desire. She asked permission, and received it, to touch the shoe. But when she did, a strange damp terror crept into her and she pulled her hand back as if from a hot iron.

"It was lying on the floor," said Dr. Lightner. "Just one sandal. Not the other. It's solid gold. Not intended for actual wear."

"Yet it was worn," said Camilla. "See? The sole of the sandal is scraped."

They stared in astonishment. She was right. The sandal had once slid onto the bare foot of an Egyptian girl, its intricately designed gold rope between her toes.

It was an Egyptian Cinderella's slipper, thought Camilla. She was leaving the ball, and her magic slipper fell off and was left behind. Somewhere in time, she still wears her other slipper.

Dr. Lightner held the gold sandal against his cheek, to feel its history. "Would the slipper fit you, Miss Matthews?" he asked.

"It was made for a small and slender foot," she told him. "My foot is far too large. You will have to find a princess."

"Miss Matthews, say no such thing. Among women, you are a queen."

Camilla blushed and then, being truthful, extended her right foot. Grinning, he stuck his out next to it. Dr. Lightner's feet made her own look delicate. They stood in each other's footprints, lost their balance, and gripped each other to keep from falling. Before it could become impropriety, of course, they stepped back and pretended to be doing other things.

"Might I descend the shaft?" said Camilla eagerly, merely being polite, not expecting to need permission.

But Dr. Lightner refused. She was a lady, he explained.

On the one hand, Camilla loved being a lady: too important to take risks or get dirty. On the other hand, she hated being a lady: too *un*important to participate in the fun.

The mystery of the tomb, however, was not so much the single sandal, but its owner. When torches were brought into the depths, and the hieroglyphs on the stone coffin read, it turned out to be the sarcophagus of Hetepheres, mother of Khufu, who built the Great Pyramid.

Impossible. This little hole—a queen's tomb?

Pharaoh forced his people to labor for decades to create *his* tomb—and stuck his mother into an undecorated closet?

"Surely, inside that sarcophagus lies the queen herself," said the young man from Yale.

"How fabulous her mummy will be!" said the boy from Princeton.

Dr. Lightner spread his hands in a shrug. "One does not know these things in advance. Egypt likes to hold her secrets."

"We must have a ceremony for the opening of her sarcophagus," said the youth from Harvard, having been raised to expect things to go his way, "and invite all the important archaeologists in Egypt. Within easy reach are scholars and dignitaries from Germany and Austria, France and Italy, America and England."

The site was chaotic as dusk fell. Egyptian workmen scurried and carried. Men from other digs in Giza came to discuss the find and the possibility of treasure. Camels spat and donkeys bellowed. The shadow of the Pyramid sketched a black line over the sand.

Camilla kept track of every member of the expedition.

The moment finally came in which nobody was looking in her direction. Camilla felt the nuns who had taught her calling *Stop it!* She ignored them.

She wrapped the gold sandal in her scarf and drifted away.

All the action was around Hetepheres' tomb. She walked swiftly to the long low tent where young Stratton and the college boys slept.

She was now a thief. She could never deny that in this life, and in the next life, she must face her Maker, and when asked which commandments she had broken, she would have to admit that she had stolen.

But Hiram Stratton, Sr., had stolen a life.

There were five cots in the tent, each with some gear stacked by. Which was Strat's? By the bed closest to the door, on a small scarred wooden trunk, lay one of Dr. Lightner's volumes with a folded letter half-tucked into it. Camilla withdrew the letter.

Dear Katie,

Your letters continue to make me feel worthless and self-indulgent. I participate in the opening of tombs—and you serve the most wretched humans on earth. That sickness terrifies me, Katie. One day, I fear, you will be what they are. And yet you chose that life. I will never understand. But I will always be proud.

I sold my best photograph of the Sphinx to a London newspaper! I had to keep a bit of money to resole my boots; sand is hard on footgear. But here is the rest. Katie, buy vegetables and milk, so you resist illness. Go ahead, laugh. You know I *despise vegetables and milk. But I worry. You might spend this on chocolate for your patients, instead of upon yourself.*

Today we descend into the tomb I found! Pray I will take a photograph good enough to sell. Then I will have lots of money to send you.

Your very dear friend,
Strat

Camilla stood for a moment. Then she opened the trunk.

Strat had few possessions. A spyglass, that he might see across the desert. Notebooks and pens. A few changes of clothing and linen. A Bible, with a red ribbon marking his place.

She lifted the Bible, intending to see what book and chapter he was reading, but out fell the tiny envelope. It was not sealed, but the flap gently tucked in. Camilla opened it, too. The lock of hair Strat had told her about was black and shimmery as silk. It was very straight and did not want to be in such a small space, but leaped toward the opening, straightening itself as if it still lived and grew.

Annie, thought Camilla, and the dank terror that had come through the gold sandal spread through her limbs once more.

She freed herself from the spell of the hair, put the gold sandal inside one of Strat's shirts and stumbled away.

* * *

"The wind has brought tears to your eyes," said Dr. Lightner, handing Camilla his handkerchief.

She blotted her tears.

From Spain Camilla had sent a cable to Duffie, telling him that Strat was with Dr. Lightner's dig in Giza. Shortly she would send another cable. It would contain the news of the son's ruin. A man who stole gold from an archaeology site was destined for the hellhole of an Egyptian prison.

Hiram Stratton would have no joyful reunion. Perhaps no reunion at all. Men do not live long in such prisons, what with cholera and typhus and murder.

"See how the desert has changed, sir," she whispered. "In the dark, it stretches on like death."

"That is the very horror Pharaoh tried to fend off," agreed Dr. Lightner. "All these stones he piled into a mountain, a ladder to his eternal life, because he so feared death. That I can understand. But what possible explanation can there be for the tomb Strat found? Why did Khufu not equally prepare his mother for *her* eternal life?"

She gave back the handkerchief. Her deeds had shadowed her soul, and she was worthy of nothing, not even a square of linen.

"Miss Matthews," said Dr. Lightner, "might I ask a most special favor of you?"

"Of course, sir," she said drearily.

"The French embassy is giving a dinner party. It seems that a major American art collector is arriving in Cairo. Over the years he has purchased many a French oil painting. We are privileged to meet him and of course invite him to our excavation."

Camilla kept forgetting she was here as a reporter. Dr. Lightner would want this event in the newspapers back in America and so would the art collector. She had never read a society column in her life. She had no idea what to write about such an event.

"Miss Matthews," said Dr. Lightner, "would you do me the honor of allowing me to escort you to this dinner?"

She was not to attend as a female reporter with work to do. She had been asked as a guest. A man—a *tall* man—had sought out her company. "You are so kind, sir," she said, her words stumbling on her tongue. "I regret, however, that when I packed my trunks, I did not plan for a ball at the French embassy."

He beamed. "I have already communicated with a friend whose wife has a plentiful wardrobe and will be delighted to assist you."

Men, Camilla thought. Whoever she is, her clothing won't fit *me*. It's too late to call a dressmaker. I have literally nothing to wear on such an evening.

But she was too touched by his eagerness to tell him how silly he was; that she, Camilla Mateusz, made even dressmakers laugh. And then she remembered that Camilla Mateusz did not exist. "Dr. Lightner, it will be my privilege."

And privilege it was.

Two dressmakers used up two gowns to create one

for Camilla. With anyone else, Camilla would have been weeping. Lady Clementine made it a party.

The maids cleverly stitched an entire ten inches to the length of one gown by using the ruffles off the other. "I feel like Cinderella," said Camilla, laughing.

"Indeed," said Lady Clementine, smiling. "And here are your borrowed slippers. Silver-toed. Are they not fashionable? Luckily, my feet are large for me and your feet are small for you."

Slippers . . .

Was the gold slipper even now being discovered in Strat's trunk? Would Dr. Lightner arrive at Lady Clementine's shocked and heartsick, having learned that his cameraman was a thief? Was Strat even now in some dark prison, without light or air or hope?

What price revenge? thought Camilla. My soul. Strat's future. But I do not care about either one. I want Hiram Stratton to suffer, and he will.

"Now stand tall, my dear," said Lady Clementine. "Do not slump. Dr. Lightner is halfway in love with you, and it is your splendid height that attracts him."

"Halfway in love? With me?"

"Of course. You are as tall and strong as a pillar of Karnak, I believe he said. He is quite smitten. Of course archaeologists are a difficult group, my dear. Think twice. They are apt to be demanding, pernickety and dusty."

Camilla laughed.

"Capitalize upon your height. Throw your shoulders back. Be tall."

Nobody had ever instructed Camilla to do that.

Lady Clementine became very serious. "I see you are well educated and more than capable of presenting fine arguments during table discussions. Remember that ladies in search of a husband do not demonstrate brains." Lady Clementine fixed around Camilla's throat a beautiful necklace of shimmering pearls.

In the looking glass, Camilla found, as many a girl before her, that the wearing of beautiful clothing and jewels made her lovelier and more worthy.

"Perfect!" cried Lady Clementine. "Just so must you blush and lower your eyes. It draws men's eyes toward your bosom, you know, and away from your mind. You must not display your mind."

"Thank you," said Camilla gratefully, and they pantomimed hugs, such as decoratively dressed and coiffed women give one another.

ANNIE

Since dawn, Annie had been pointing toward the Great Pyramid. By the time Pankh arrived in mid-morning, Annie's gestures had crossed the language barrier. Renifer coaxed Pankh to take them to see the Pyramid.

Pankh was unwilling.

It took considerable pouting and pleading to change his mind. Renifer was excellent at both. Flouncing around in her dress, a very thin gauze pressed in stiff pleats, Renifer made it clear that neither gold nor gifts would make her happy. Only an excursion to the Pyramid.

Finally Pankh shrugged and nodded.

Annie held Renifer's hand as they threaded through narrow streets shaded by canvas canopies, lined with stalls selling spices and cookpots and shoes. They passed walled houses and tenements, donkeys tied in stable yards, geese in the road and even a royal procession.

Everybody knelt to gaze lovingly at a young woman on a litter covered in beaten gold. A princess, perhaps, reclining on pillows under her fringed shade? Four bulky men in tiny white kilts carried the litter on their shoulders. They walked rhythmically, one counting, like rowers on a crew team.

At the waterfront, Pankh commandeered a boat. Two men rowed half-standing, toes braced against a shelf. They moved quickly on the river, a breeze bucketing inside a much-mended sail. Annie was mesmerized by the water traffic: little boats, tubby boats, oared boats and sailboats, barges loaded with stone or casks, logs or bales.

Along the banks of the Nile, hundreds of men labored, making bricks out of mud. Villages were perched on the heights, their little mud-brick dwellings like piles of little brown wren houses.

From the Nile, they entered a canal, straight-sided as a ruler, slicing through fields and orchards, palm trees and grazing sheep. They steered into a square lake, neatly sided by cut stone, and pulled up to a wharf. Soldiers paced up and down. Small sphinxes were being set in rows.

Pankh swept his two women before him and up to a vast temple.

So modern and harsh was its design Annie felt it could have been an electric power plant in Chicago or Detroit. They did not enter the temple, but walked through a vast portico and emerged on a paved pedestrian street with awnings stretched over pillars. Flowers had been laid on the whole length of the road, bouquet after bouquet, and their feet crunched on the sun-dried petals.

At the end of the shining road was Khufu's Pyramid.

In the museum photograph, the Pyramid had been tiers of great lumps, two million brown sugar cubes, each the size of a dining room table. But at its creation, the Pyramid was slick with polished white limestone. It was surrounded by a sea of baby pyramids, flat-topped pyramids, temples, graveyards, mausoleums, steles—and one vast Sphinx, being chipped out of bedrock as Annie watched.

She began laughing with excitement. Strat must be here! This was the very place where he had taken his photographs. She must keep her eyes open.

She examined every passing man, giggling at the thought of Victorian Strat wearing a white gauze kilt like Pankh.

Renifer

Renifer thanked the gods for letting her live now; a time which would last for all time, embodied in this very Pyramid.

The girl of ivory was gasping in awe. Wherever she was from, she had never seen anything like this. But then, nobody had.

I was right to insist that Pankh bring us today, thought Renifer. The girl herself made it clear that this is where she must be. The reason she was put in my hands will be presented to me now.

They passed a priest in a robe of panther skins. As he approached, the priest lifted a large ostrich feather fan and hid his face behind it. Renifer was mildly surprised, because priests of the City of the Dead were the proudest men in Egypt. They did not hide their status. When she looked after him, to see which temple he entered, the priest was half-running.

They approached the burial place of Queen Hetepheres. Her chapel was a delicate structure, sitting at the foot of the thirteen-acre Pyramid like a child's toy. Over the portico, the blue and white stripes of the awning fluttered in the wind and the reflection from the silver floor was blinding.

On two blessed occasions, Renifer had been privileged to help Princess Meresankh honor her grandmother. Renifer had done the actual carrying of food to the dead queen. A royal ornament, Meresankh had never once used her hands. Handmaidens were so called because their hands did all work.

Now Renifer knelt to honor Pharaoh's mother, motioning the girl of ivory to join her. Putting their weight on one knee, they leaned forward, extending the other leg back so as to achieve a position both graceful and helpless.

Here in the shade of the awnings, the silver had not gotten too hot to touch. Reverently, Renifer kissed the floor. Here had she prayed and knelt with the queen's granddaughter. Here had she scattered droplets of sacred water and the petals of flowers.

And puddling out of the doorway onto the silver floor was something wet and red, but not sacred.

Profane.

Blood.

IV

Time for Sacrifice

Renifer

The girl of ivory scrambled to her feet. Yanking Renifer up from her position of humility, she dragged her behind a screen of immense potted ferns just as two tomb police staggered out of the chapel. Both were bleeding heavily.

One was holding together a dreadful wound in his side, so deep it could never be sewn together; a gash from which he would die. "Pen-Meru!" he cried in a gurgling voice, and fell onto the silver pavement.

Pen-Meru? thought Renifer dizzily. But her father was not involved with the tomb police. He was a controller of the Nile, a measurer of floods and opener of canals.

The second soldier sank to his knees. Renifer thought he might live. She would tear up her dress and use it for bandages. She—

But the second soldier also whispered, "Pen-Meru."

There must be some other Pen-Meru of whom Renifer had not heard.

Pankh sprinted forward from where he had been

waiting in the shade of another temple while Renifer prayed. He pulled his dagger from its sheath.

Renifer's heart soared with pride. Pankh would be clothed in glory! For of course the tomb robbers who had done this terrible deed were inside the chapel. Brave Pankh was going to finish them off.

But Pankh did not enter the chapel. Lifting high the thin shining blade, he stabbed to death the still living tomb policeman who had sunk to his knees.

Renifer clutched the slender lotus pillar of the portico. What could this mean? How could Pankh do that? The man had been helpless! Already wounded for Pharaoh's sake.

Now Pankh was a blur, springing into the chapel itself. From within came a cry of terror. "No, Pankh! I promise—"

There was a groan and a thud.

There was silence.

The hot sickening smell of blood filled the air.

Renifer had to understand what was happening. She slipped inside the queen's chapel, careful not to block the sun, whose glint off the silver floor provided the only illumination to the interior. It took a moment to focus in the gloom. The walls were painted with scenes from the queen's life. From painted arbors hung thick purple grapes and heavy green leaves. On a ceiling of deep blue, gold stars were scattered.

Pankh stood panting in the center of the chapel. His knife stuck out of the chest of a third tomb policeman, now prostrate on the floor. In the shadows, pressed against the sacred illustrations, stood her father, Pen-Meru.

There were no other men inside the little chapel.

There was no other exit from which the killers might have fled.

No, thought Renifer. My father did not do this. Pankh did not do this. I am a slow thinker. In a moment I will understand.

She pasted herself against the wall, as if she too had been painted there.

"Good job, Pankh," said Renifer's father, grinning.

The two men slapped hands in victory and laughed. Then they frowned down upon the corpse at their feet.

"Now what?" said Pankh.

Renifer stepped forward, startling her father and her beloved, who whirled to see who was there. Father gripped a bloody dagger and Pankh tightened his fist around his own knife.

They had forgotten she existed at all, let alone that she was witness to this carnage. For one terrible moment, she thought herself in danger from the two men she loved most.

She saw now a rectangular opening in the chapel floor. Three paving stones had been lifted aside to reveal a great black shaft: the entrance to Hetepheres' tomb. It should be entirely filled with rubble—thirty feet down, all sand and rock. If the shaft was empty, then the queen's tomb had been emptied by robbers. No doubt the space below contained little of value now. The three dead policemen had walked in on the robbery.

And now her thoughts spun all too fast. Renifer felt as if she were drowning in the Nile. Mud-brown water silted up her heart. "You are tomb robbers," whispered Renifer. "It was *you* they caught."

Her father shrugged. "I have always been a tomb robber, my daughter. And your uncle with me. And Pankh."

"No! It cannot be! Father, I cannot believe it of you!"

Her father snorted. "You know perfectly well we live beyond the means of any controller of the Nile. *You* are the one yearning for gold. You and your mother insist on necklaces here and bracelets there. *You* are the ones for whom five servants are not enough; no, you must have fifteen," he snapped.

She thought of the chests of gold at home, all those jewels fit for a queen. The Sekhmet fit for a Pharaoh. Indeed. To a Pharaoh and a queen had they once belonged.

"I regret you are here, my love," said Pankh, "but since you are, you will participate."

In murder? thought Renifer. Never. She stared in loathing at their blood-flecked chests and arms.

"So far we are safe," said Pankh. "Easy lies will get us out of this. We say we are the ones who caught robbers in the act. Regrettably, they escaped, having first murdered three brave and true protectors of the queen's chapel."

Pankh and Pen-Meru laughed.

They had slain three loyal men of Pharaoh's and found it funny? Renifer felt as if she had been thrown into a sewage ditch. She could never be cleansed of the evil her father had done.

"I think, Pankh, we should say that you and I captured the actual robbers," said Pen-Meru. "They are being tortured even now, and dispatched to the Land in the West."

"What if He asks to see the prisoners?" said Pankh.

Pen-Meru shrugged. "We stake out a few peasants."

Renifer was appalled. "You would execute innocent men, pretending they robbed this tomb? But this is Egypt! Such things do not happen here."

"Would you rather that I and your future husband got staked out in the desert?" said Pen-Meru.

Renifer remembered how Pankh had stroked the goddess Sekhmet. It had not been worship, or lack of worship. It had been blackmail. *Your daughter marries me, Pen-Meru, or I bring Pharaoh into your gates to see what you have stolen from Him.*

I am the daughter of a tomb robber, thought Renifer. I will be made to marry a tomb robber. My father and husband will force my sons to be tomb robbers.

Renifer caught the distant scent of incense being burned. Somewhere a priest was obeying the sacred rites. Much good it did him, when people like her father were abroad in the land.

Here had Princess Meresankh prayed as Renifer sang, "Sky and stars make music for you. Sun and moon praise you. Gods exalt you and goddesses lift their voices." But Meresankh's grandmother was not exalted now. Renifer's family had brought her down.

Her father said to Pankh, "Even if Pharaoh believes our story, I think we will be executed. Pharaoh will find out that not only is His mother's tomb nearly empty, but her mummy is gone. He'll execute everyone in sight. He might execute the whole battalion of tomb police, even those not on duty this month."

"You stole the queen's mummy?" cried Renifer. Her family would be haunted forever. The powerful *ka* of the queen would waylay them by night and set traps for them by day. Renifer's children would be doomed to lives of terror.

Horror curdled in her stomach like goat's milk in the sun. She was not going to have children. She too would be staked out in the desert, three days dying, jackals waiting. Renifer's eternity would be spent in limbo, with neither rest nor joy. She hardly minded (although probably she would mind when they actually drove the stake through her). Such a fate was richly deserved by a family that profaned the tomb of a queen.

"We took the inner coffin, Renifer," said her father irritably, "because it contained the finest jewels. Of course it had her mummy in it."

"Where did you put the mummy?" said Renifer, trying not to sob. "We'll put it back. She must lie among her remaining tomb goods."

"I tossed the mummy in the desert after I peeled away the gold and silver," said Pen-Meru.

The verb he used—*toss*—was horrible in its simplicity. Children tossed balls. Her father had tossed aside the mummy of a queen as if it had no more meaning than a child's toy.

"Did you always know about this?" Renifer said in Pankh's direction. She could not face him.

"I've been helping since I was twelve." His voice was proud and even sassy, as if he had always wanted to swagger in front of her with this information, and now at last, his real self could stand before her: tomb robber.

Renifer was weeping. "Does Mother know?" she asked her father.

"She pretends not to. Like you."

"But I didn't know," she cried.

They lost interest in her silly vapors and returned to the problem at hand.

"More soldiers will be here soon," said Pen-Meru gloomily. "That means Pharaoh will be told soon. They'll go down the shaft and report to Pharaoh that not only was His mother's tomb robbed, her bones are gone. We are dead men."

"I've got it," said Pankh excitedly. "We tell Him that we, in our glory, prevented the robbery. The valor of Pen-Meru and his future son-in-law, Pankh, led to the deaths of some robbers—but the others fled. We tell Pharaoh that since the escaped evildoers now know where the opening of the queen's tomb is, we recommend an immediate solution to Pharaoh."

Pankh was almost jumping up and down in his delight. Renifer wondered how she had ever found this man attractive.

"You will recall, Pen-Meru," said her beloved, "that adjacent to that temple being constructed close to the Pyramid is an unused tomb. It was built for Princess Nitiqret of Blessed Memory, but she chose to be buried in her husband's tomb. How we will praise the vacant tomb! We will convince Pharaoh that it is fit for the *ka* of His mother. Even now, we will explain to Him, we are swiftly removing the tomb furniture from this defiled spot and have taken the blessed body of Hetepheres to its new and safe resting place." He folded his arms over his chest, swollen with pride at his brilliant idea.

"It's not much of a tomb," said Pen-Meru doubtfully. "It's hardly a closet. They sank it very deep, but since Nitiqret was buried elsewhere, they never began the wall paintings or finished up—"

"Who cares?" said Pankh impatiently. "Pharaoh is never going to descend the shaft to see. He will believe you. You in your radiance will have acted swiftly and with reverence to rescue a queen whose safe harbor has been invaded. I will treat you as a god before Him, marveling in the splendor of your quick thinking and willingness to die for the queen. He'll fall for it."

"Maybe," said Renifer's father. "But maybe not. Pharaoh isn't stupid."

"May I remind you what will happen if we allow Pharaoh's servants to climb down that shaft?"

And then the time for planning was over. The chapel filled with more tomb police. Shocked and saddened by the loss of their colleagues, they let Pen-Meru take charge. He motioned them into a huddle, giving instructions.

"We work quickly to transfer the remaining tomb furniture," said Pen-Meru. "Pharaoh will kill every one of us for failing to keep His mother's tomb safe. But if He thinks that in the end, we *did* keep her safe . . . Well, then. Not only do we survive, He will pay us each a great reward."

The tomb police, afraid of the wrath of Pharaoh, agreed.

Renifer felt there was a flaw in the plan. Everybody knew where tomb entrances were. The moment a chapel was raised, the world understood that the tomb lay beneath.

Does Pharaoh think nobody knows where He will lie? wondered Renifer. Having built the largest pyramid in the world above His shaft? Not that anybody could ever shift those stones. Still . . .

For the first time she realized that *Pharaoh would not bury Himself beneath His Pyramid.* He would have a real grave site, hidden and safe. The Pyramid was many things, and one was trickery.

Every tomb policeman went to work immediately. They delegated and planned, summoning laborers and torches, planks and ropes, carts and baskets.

Although Hetepheres' sarcophagus weighed many tons, removing it was not difficult, as the equipment was close at hand and used every day. Once lifted up, it was placed on rollers, hitched to ropes that were hitched to men, and moved to the mouth of the new tomb.

Nitiqret's shaft was far deeper. Affixing the strongest of papyrus ropes, the men lowered the sarcophagus easily, their only worry that the ropes would split under the weight and the coffin drop to the bottom and break into a thousand pieces. But that did not happen.

The remaining pieces of tomb furniture—only a bed canopy and a carrying chair had not been stolen—were taken down and piled against the wall. The gold hieroglyphs of the queen's name glittered against the black ebony of her bed.

"Now," said Pen-Meru, "we go to Pharaoh."

Renifer did not want to imagine the scene with Pharaoh, as her father and her future husband outdid themselves with lies to the Living God. If Pharaoh believed the untruths Pen-Meru put before Him, would it prove that He was man and not God? And if He were man, and not God, what then was Egypt? What were the sun and the Nile? Who controlled them and made them great?

Renifer felt bludgeoned by the heat and sun, the shock and shame.

"The more distinguished the ceremony of reburying Hetepheres," said Pankh, "the less Pharaoh will question the details. Girls are useful in ceremonies. They add a feeling of reverence and grace. You, Renifer, will sing. He loves your voice. And the girl of ivory we will dress as a handmaiden. She is just the kind of gift to please Pharaoh."

Renifer had forgotten the girl of ivory.

Was she indeed a *ka*? Could she be Queen Hetepheres' *ka*? Once Father had thrown Hetepheres' body to the jackals, had the *ka* lost its way in the papyrus swamp? Or could the girl of ivory be a messenger sent by Hetepheres?

Why had Pankh cried out the name of the queen when he first saw the girl of ivory? Because he knew what he had done to Hetepheres? Or because her *ka* put those syllables in his mouth?

Renifer found the girl still in the shade of the silver portico among the fronds of the green ferns. She seemed neither afraid nor confused, but lightly embraced Renifer, as if to say that she understood.

The great sun was sinking now in bloodred splendor. Pharaoh's barge was visible in the square lagoon far down the causeway.

"The timing is good," said Pankh. "Tomorrow Pharaoh has planned a great feast to welcome the return of the admiral from Lebanon. Not only did the admiral successfully acquire twelve ships of cedar logs, he brought dancing bears and trained dwarfs. Pharaoh will want to complete the reburial tonight, so that tomorrow He can concentrate on the celebrations."

Renifer was beginning to believe the outrageous plan might succeed.

Her father said, "You, Renifer, will utter the sacraments when we seal His mother in darkness. You will describe how the girl of ivory arrived; how she was sent by a *ka*. Pharaoh loves omens from the next world. Don't say she's just a foreigner who needed a bath. Then, deep in the night, we bring Him to the top of the new shaft. We let Pharaoh catch a glimpse of gold at the bottom, shining in the moonlight. He will assume that everything originally with the queen is still with the queen! And because we left behind her stone sarcophagus—after all, it has no resale value—He will think her silver and gold coffin is within."

"What do you bet," said Pankh, "that in His gratitude, He even invites us to the feast for the admiral?"

Pen-Meru laughed and bet the golden Sekhmet. Pankh bet six gold necklaces. They slapped hands to seal the bet.

Farmers were yanked from a field. They insisted they were not tomb robbers. But of course, that is what a robber would shout as he was carried to the desert edge. Once they understood their fate, they began screaming and fighting, but to no avail. The stakes were driven in slowly, to prolong the pain.

Renifer felt the stakes through her own heart; through all her hopes.

"What if the girl of ivory runs away or behaves badly?" asked Father.

"She loves gold," said Pankh. "Adorn her in much gold and she will be happy."

CAMILLA

Oh! the compliments of the men as they gathered for dinner at the French embassy in Cairo. The smiles with which the men greeted Camilla, upon being introduced. The admiring eyes. The tender remarks. Dizzy with excitement, Camilla flirted and laughed.

"If only we were not going to war!" cried the British officers. "We would surely beg the pleasure of your company at our dances, Miss Matthews."

How splendid the British were, chests crossed by sashes, hung with bejeweled military crosses, decked out in many-colored ribbons.

Dr. Lightner bowed to them, saying with great courtesy, "I hope you will join us for a dance I will give in her honor."

"But of course!" cried the guests. "Such a beautiful woman deserves everything in her honor."

"Ah," said the French, sounding so intimate that Camilla blushed, *"quelle perfection."*

Camilla could not stop smiling. Neither could Dr. Lightner. Camilla could have swirled around the room forever, height forgotten, as she and Dr. Lightner drifted from group to group.

"What a pleasure this is," said Dr. Lightner, as they waltzed in graceful circles. "Normally I am the outcast. The tedious scholar who writes books. Tonight, I have grace and appeal, Miss Matthews, because of your company."

Her very height prevented even Dr. Lightner from knowing how young she was; it was a disguise in inches. She was by far the youngest at the party, but she was holding her own. She wanted the introductions to go on forever, but of course, eventually the guest of honor arrived and they must all sit down for a formal dinner.

The guest of honor was very fat, strapped into his dinner jacket and cummerbund. His jowls layered down onto his chest and his arms were so thick he could hardly bend at the elbows.

"A very rich man indeed," said a British officer, admiring the amount of meat and brandy it took to achieve such girth.

"Excellent mustache," said another.

The guest had a strong American accent. The British flinched slightly at his vulgar words and the French raised their eyebrows. The Germans could not be bothered to cross the room. But Dr. Lightner was most eager to meet the gentleman. "An American art collector!" he whispered. "It's very new. All the best people are doing it now. It gives one hope for America. We will bring him to the excavation."

And then for the first time that evening, Dr. Lightner's face drooped into tired lines. "He will expect glory," said the archaeologist sadly, "and find only potsherds. He will expect gold. I did not want to sully this lovely evening, Miss Matthews, with the sad fact of what happened this afternoon. We cannot find the gold sandal."

Camilla was so flushed with excitement that another layer of pink in her cheeks was not noticeable. "It must have been mislaid," she said.

"Nobody mislays gold. They do, however, steal it."

"No!" cried Camilla. "Surely not. Who at your dig would stoop so low?" She wondered when they would search the gentlemen's tent. They might not, now that she thought of it. It would be too great an insult for young men so full of importance.

"Hush," murmured Dr. Lightner. "Let us not speak of regrettable events during this fine occasion. Come, it is our turn to be presented to the guest of honor."

Camilla was oddly afraid. This close, the body did not seem grand, but gross. The mustache not lush, but graying moss creeping over the lips and into the mouth. The swollen hand that gripped hers was girded in rings so tight that the flesh burst out around them. The man's breath stank of pipe tobacco and he had already had too much brandy.

The party felt infected.

"And this lovely lady?" he said. A smile crawled out from behind the moss of his mustache.

Camilla tried to smile, but did not achieve it.

"This," said Archibald Lightner proudly, "is my guest, sir. Miss Camilla Matthews."

A flicker of amusement went through the man's eyes, and Camilla felt owned, as a slave might be, or a factory hand.

"Ah, yes," said the guest of honor. "The famous Miss Matthews. The reporter from Kansas."

In all America, only Mr. Duffie knew there was a Camilla Matthews who claimed to be a reporter. Mr. Duffie and one other man. Camilla tried to step back, but the man did not release his grip, as a gentleman should. "Hiram Stratton, Sr., at your service, ma'am," said he.

Camilla tried to extricate her hands from his paws but he did not allow it. She would have to scrub her fingers as she had scrubbed herself from the dread of leprosy.

I would rather have leprosy than touch Hiram Stratton, she thought. Why did I not realize that he would come? It is my own telegraph that brought him. Of course he would not trust me to bring his beloved son home. After all, I had no intention of doing it. I intended his son to live out his days, or at least a few years, in an Egyptian prison.

But I have failed.

Whether or not the gold sandal is found among Strat's belongings, nothing will happen to the boy. Hiram Stratton's power is tangible even in this room that belongs to another government. His power will work anywhere. In Egypt, being paid off has been a tradition for thousands of years. There will still be a joyful reunion, and father and son will go home to burn down yet another factory.

"Mr. Stratton, sir!" cried Dr. Lightner. "What a privilege to encounter a man of your stature. It is my hope to be permitted to bring you to Giza, that I may myself escort you among the ancient Egyptian monuments, and have the great pleasure of showing you the excavation under my supervision. Just this week, we uncovered a hitherto unknown tomb. It is full of mystery."

"Fine, fine," said Hiram Stratton, already bored.

"In fact, my good sir," said Dr. Lightner, now somewhat uneasy, "among the young men spending a year with me in lieu of being broadened by travel in the more usual places, young men educated at Harvard and Yale, Princeton and Dartmouth . . ." Dr. Lightner paused, as if hoping he need not go on.

"Among those young men," said Hiram Stratton, "is my own son. Do not be uncomfortable with the admission. It is I who am ashamed. He went to Yale, but did not succeed. He has not, in fact, succeeded anywhere. He lacks capacity for anything except failure."

The French were horrified that a father would speak like that. The British were expressionless. The Germans, of course, had still not bothered to cross the room.

"I've come to bring him home," said Hiram Stratton. "He belongs in prison and I plan to put him there." The man's face split open in what must have been a smile. Camilla could not look at it.

"In prison?" repeated Dr. Lightner, appalled. "Surely not, Mr. Stratton. He seems a delightful fellow. Has taken fine pictures. In fact, he's the one who found the tomb about which I am so excited!"

"I was not blessed with a good son," said Hiram Stratton. "Throughout his life it has been necessary to curb him. I incarcerated him in an asylum for the good of the community."

You did not! thought Camilla. You locked him up because he defied you. It was easy to show the factory workers who was boss: burn their jobs. It was easy to show your son, too. Whip Strat until he cringed in the manner you like to see in dogs.

"He escaped," said Hiram Stratton. "Attacked the staff and vanished. Not only that, he kidnapped two innocent children."

He did not! They were not children. They went with him joyfully. He was saving them. Their own families do not want them back!

"I have come here," said Hiram Stratton, "to see Egypt, of course. To admire your excavation, of course. To consider a major donation. But alas, to administer a lasting punishment to my son." He did not mean that word alas. He gloated.

Camilla had thought that Duffie's lies were about the nature of St. Rafael's patients; Duffie feared she would not agree to get near leprosy. How terribly wrong she had been. His lies were about the reason for locating the son. Camilla had not been sent to arrange a joyful reunion. She had been sent so that the father could ruin his own boy.

Camilla had chosen not to believe Katie's version of Strat's character. But Katie, who knew so much of cruelty, had singled Strat out as a true and decent friend.

Why did I not believe Katie? thought Camilla.

Far from ruining Hiram Stratton, she had played into his hands. Not simply locating the boy, but putting the boy into an immensely worse situation. Whatever lies and fabrications Mr. Stratton brought from America, it would be no lie that the missing gold sandal was in Strat's possession; that Strat had dishonored the entire dig; that he was a thief.

"He was also," said the French attaché thoughtfully, "involved in some way in the death of those two young men who fell from the Pyramid."

"No, no," said Dr. Lightner, "we've been through that, he was in no way involved except that I instructed him to deliver the bodies to you."

"Since he is a kidnapper," said Hiram Stratton, "it would not surprise me if he were also a murderer. It is for trial that I bring him back to New York. I spawned a criminal and as a criminal he will be treated."

The man is happy, thought Camilla. He looks forward to throwing his own child to the jackals. He rejoices at the thought of his son suffering.

Why? Because the son is beautiful while he is gross? Because the son is kind while he believes in cruelty? Or because Hiram Stratton, Sr., is truly evil?

Hiram Stratton could not be allowed to continue. Such verbiage would simply ruin the festivities. Lady

Clementine and the ambassador's wife bustled about, tugging here and there to line the guests up for their entry into the dining room.

"My dear Miss Matthews," said the French ambassador.

I am not evil, thought Camilla, but I am in its neighborhood. Having placed young Stratton in jeopardy, I must now save him. The sandal, in fact, is minor. Kidnapping and assault are not. I cannot let his father have him.

She smiled at the French ambassador, who said, "Might I escort you to the dinner table, my dear, where if you will be so kind, I will seat you next to our guest of honor."

Camilla's bare arm rubbed against the sleeve of Hiram Stratton's dinner jacket. Her left hand brushed his when she picked up a fork and he a spoon.

She was unable to eat, but in a world where fainting delicate women were prized, failure to eat was much admired. She was unable to speak, but in a world where only the words of men had value, a quiet woman was a jewel.

"My dear Miss Matthews," said Hiram Stratton, "I detest a woman who babbles and you, dear girl, have a great capacity for silence. What a pleasure. I have never permitted one of my wives to chatter."

"*One* of your wives, sir?"

"I am in the midst of divorcing my fourth."

It was an admission so outrageous, Camilla could not believe he had said it in public. Even to use the word divorce at an elegant gathering like this was vulgar. She trembled at the suffering of those four women, sharing a life and a bed with this monster. "I assume your fourth wife babbled," she said.

"Precisely." Hiram Stratton laughed hugely and spilled red wine. "*And* demanded *and* whined *and* argued. A man cannot be expected to put up with that."

"Of course not," said Camilla.

"Miss Matthews," said Hiram Stratton very softly, "you are a fine detective. Nothing escapes you, does it? You should know, my dear, that nothing escapes me either."

Their eyes met. What could he mean? Had he already discerned that she was making plans for Strat's escape?

Hidden by the starched white damask tablecloth, the man had the gall to put his hand on her knee. He began to inch her skirt upward, in order to touch her bare skin.

Camilla's choices were few. To stab him with her fork would be a breach of manners. How would the French feel then about Dr. Lightner, bringing so uncouth a creature to their party? Lady Clementine would take back her dress and her pearls, knowing Camilla had not the grace to handle situations like a lady.

Yet she could not allow it to happen.

It dawned on her that this was what Hiram Stratton referred to. He had noticed Camilla and she belonged to him, having accepted his false letter of introduction and his money, and he would take her in other ways as well.

Camilla could not think clearly. Failure to think clearly had happened to at least four other women in the presence of Hiram Stratton, Sr. She looked desperately at Lady Clementine and found she had underestimated this fine person. Lady Clementine tapped her silver knife gently against a crystal glass, and a sweet note rang out through the room. The ladies stood, and quickly the men rose with them.

Hiram Stratton struggled to join them, his bulk and the difficult position into which he had maneuvered his hands slowing him down.

"Gentlemen," said the ambassador's wife graciously, "we leave you to your dessert and brandy, so your conversations may turn to war and politics, while we retire to the garden, and our conversations turn to fashion and weddings."

A servant pulled Camilla's chair out for her and the gentlemen bade the ladies *au revoir*. Hiram Stratton said into Camilla's ear, "Do not forget that you are my employee. You will do all that you are told." A smirk lay behind his moss mustache. *"All."*

ANNIE

Annie was very impressed by the clothing placed on her body.

A shift of fine linen hung straight from shoulder to ankle. Over that was placed an entire dress of linked beads, gold and blue and a rich dark red, laced into a thousand one-inch squares. When she moved, the beads rearranged themselves in a chorus of clicks.

Renifer's servant painted Annie's eyes far into her hairline, and into her hair worked a garland of shiny green leaves and bright flowers. On her feet were placed gold sandals, which glowed as if they contained the sun and eternity itself. Annie had never seen workmanship so beautiful, so impossible.

Of course, she might as well have been wearing lead slabs. She did not see how she was going to walk, but it turned out that walking didn't matter. She and Renifer were lifted like dolls into a double sedan chair, placed gently on soft pillows and carried on the shoulders of men whose muscles bulged as they strained.

The streets of Memphis were quiet. It was very late.

Most torches had been put out; most music had ended; most people slept.

All afternoon and all evening, Annie had thought about the three dead men, killed, it seemed, by Pankh and Pen-Meru.

There had been police, full of questions; their uniforms and weapons different from police in her time, but their demeanor and posture the same.

With so much coming and going among guards and so much confusion as they shifted things from one tomb to another, Annie could have vanished into the vast acreage of tombs and blocky mausoleums. But Time had surely given her into Renifer's hands for a purpose. It had to be Strat. And yet there had been no sign of him.

It was not fair. She had expected to find Strat. To love and be loved once more. Strat must be above her in time, pushing a trowel into the very sand on which she stood. Annie felt betrayed and angry. She wanted to yell at somebody, but nobody shared her language. She had tried to comfort Renifer when the girl wept over the farmers plucked from the fields like chicken for dinner.

But Renifer had sunk into a silent despair and nothing brought her out of it.

When they were dressed by the maids, Renifer refused every single piece of gold and jewelry.

Pankh and Pen-Meru were at the door constantly, demanding speed.

The maids were frightened. Annie tried to keep her own composure, but it was difficult, understanding so little of the events, and feeling so very sorry for Renifer, in love with a man who made a habit of stabbing policemen to death.

She and Renifer sat shoulder to shoulder in the litter, Annie's beads making dents in both of them. At last Renifer roused herself. She took Annie's first finger and pressed it against Annie's lips, shaking her head twice: *No.* Then she pressed her own finger against Annie's lips and raised her eyebrows.

She was requesting silence. Annie smiled and nodded agreement, rather proud to be communicating so clearly. With her thumbs, Renifer flattened the edges of Annie's smile away. Again she shook her head.

Whatever they were about to do, it was no laughing matter.

Oh, Strat! thought Annie. What is going to happen? Why aren't you here?

They were carried to the river and aboard the same barge that had been at the Pyramid lagoon that morning. Trimmed in gold, fluttering with flags and bright with paint, it was fit for a king. Along its deck, soldiers swung spears whose shafts were encircled with gold.

Not king, thought Annie. *Pharaoh.*

Khufu himself.

She was to be in the presence of the most powerful man on this earth? When she could not understand what anybody said? When she had seen how readily they murdered people here?

In front of his feet, as in front of the queen's chapel, the deck was silver. In the torchlight, it possessed a mysterious flickering gleam.

She and Renifer were lifted out of the sedan chair, while Pen-Meru and Pankh stepped ahead to kneel. They knelt in the awkward gymnast's perch that Renifer had used, one leg extended behind, other knee touching the floor, forehead pressed against the silver. In such a position, a man was helpless. If an order were given to have them killed, how simple it would be.

Fear was palpable. In their anxiety, people breathed so deeply it almost caused the sails to billow forth.

Annie suddenly realized the men were kneeling to Pharaoh. His throne was so immense, so high, and he so utterly still that she had not seen him. He did not seem to breathe at all. Wrapped against the evening chill in a magnificent cape of leopard skin, a towering crown upon his head, he did not appear to notice the humans at his feet. He did not even seem real.

Perhaps he's a mummy, thought Annie. Perhaps they worship a dead man.

But Pharaoh was very much alive, and very angry.

Whatever Renifer's father said infuriated the king. In one hand was a staff that he pounded against the deck of the ship, and in the other a short whip, which he flailed through the air, causing men to fling themselves flat on the deck.

Renifer was trembling badly. Annie tried to stave off her own fears. Much as she wanted Strat, she hoped he was not here. There was too much danger.

The barge left the wharf and moved slowly on the river, rowed by men sitting below the deck. Annie watched the rising and falling tips of the oars and heard the gentle slap as they entered the Nile.

Abruptly Pharaoh waved Pen-Meru to silence. Pen-Meru dashed his forehead on the deck and Pharaoh stood up. He barked short syllables, angry and quick. Renifer whimpered, and then guided Annie forward. It was almost impossible to move in the beaded dress and the inflexible gold sandals. Renifer positioned Annie in front of Pharaoh, running a hand up Annie's spine to keep her standing, while she herself knelt.

Pharaoh stared at Annie. He seemed made of wood. His eyes blinked slowly and thickly, as if fastened to hinges rarely used.

Courtiers reverently removed the great crown, placing it upon a pedestal designed to hold that amazing headgear. Pharaoh swung the great cape off his shoulders. He was bare-chested except for a medallion encrusted with jewels, and his muscular body was scarred from some danger he had survived. Claw scrapes, perhaps, from the very leopard whose skin he now wore.

This man, thought Annie, would skin anybody if he felt like it.

But it was Annie whose skin interested Pharaoh.

She tried to breathe as infrequently as he did. To show this man her fear would be a grave error. Not one man or woman on this barge had dared look Pharaoh in the eye. Annie stared right at him. For a moment, their gazes locked: a king and a blue-eyed trespasser from another time.

Her stomach churned. The slabs of gold on her feet seemed to drag her down.

Pharaoh seemed almost to smile, and the smile was one she had seen before. Where? On what face? Because she had certainly never seen his.

The barge arrived at the square lake and the harsh temple. Far down the torchlit causeway loomed his Pyramid, stunning and graceful by night.

Annie and Renifer were lifted once more into their sedan chair, while Pharaoh was placed on a similar, but immensely larger, chair. It took eight men to lift him.

A procession was formed.

Annie had thought Pharaoh would be attended by a cast of thousands. But only a dozen soldiers and a few priests accompanied the king.

They passed through the portals of the stern temple and under the banners of its pillars. They walked with measured pace along the causeway. They passed the chapel where the murders had happened. Renifer held tight to Annie. Her hand felt as thin and cold as bones.

Instead of lighting more torches for more light, the priests doused torches for *less* light.

What dark ceremony, what dark thoughts were soon to be expressed? What dark deeds?

They stopped at the shaft down which Pen-Meru and Pankh and their cohorts had lowered the sarcophagus. Annie and Renifer were lifted from their conveyance and brought to stand next to Pharaoh at the opening in the earth.

The priests chanted, and rocked on their heels, and

anointed surfaces with oil from holy vessels. Renifer sang. What a beautiful soprano she had! The notes soared among the tombs and the dead, echoing off a million stones.

Pharaoh closed his eyes in prayer.

Annie prayed to Time. *Take me to Strat.*

She could hear Time laughing, and turned quickly, but it was Pankh.

Renifer

Renifer stood with her head bowed and her eyes fixed on her painted toes. She knew now why her father smirked at power. Power was held by those who told the best lies.

For Pharaoh had believed Pen-Meru. He accepted Pankh's lies. Renifer stood in shame as deep as the mud in which peasants toiled.

If Pharaoh did not understand, and she did, was it Renifer's duty to speak the truth? Should she crush Him with the knowledge that His mother's bones were scattered and dishonored?

Pharaoh, God Himself, must bring order to the chaos of living. His power caused the Nile to rise, bringing the water that grew the grain that baked the bread that kept Egypt alive. To upset Pharaoh was to ruin the lives of all. Therefore silence was best.

Or was it?

One priest anointed the site with sacred oils while another burned incense. An acolyte set down a freshly killed duck and a basket of dates.

O Hetepheres! Your interment should include a train

of priestesses! Paid musicians and a choir. A parade and seventy days of feasting. Petals of roses strewn for hundreds of yards and fine perfumes distributed among thousands of mourners.

"It's a hundred feet down the shaft, Great King," said Pen-Meru, gleeful with success. "Infinitely more secure than the previous tomb. All was accomplished with speed but sacred dignity. Those laborers who moved her tomb goods have been sent West."

Renifer was sick. So every worker her father had commanded this afternoon had been executed. Oh, the foul deaths for which her father was responsible!

I cannot atone, thought Renifer. No matter what parts of this ritual I do, it will mean nothing.

She washed her face and hands with holy drops and sang to the Nile, because the river was Egypt and Egypt was the river.

When Pharaoh had added His blessing, He said, "The priestess of ivory does not sing?"

"She has no language, sire," said Renifer.

Seven times, she stepped forward and then backward to sanctify the shaft. Kissing each one, she placed before the new tomb four amulets: cat, scarab, cow and ibis. From a spun-glass goblet of holy water, Renifer sipped first, and then gave each person present a taste of the holy water. Even the girl of ivory.

The ritual was complete.

Pharaoh stepped up to the hole and gazed steadily down the open shaft.

Nobody dared speak. Perhaps the God was praying in

His heart. Or perhaps He had some plan of which He had not yet spoken.

"In very ancient times," said the Living God slowly, "a queen was buried with her living servants. I sometimes wonder if it is sufficiently reverent to allow dolls to represent those servants."

The hundreds of dolls which represented palace staff had of course been stolen early on. They were easy to sell. Well-to-do people needed them for their own burials and never asked when the dolls had been made or for whom.

Pharaoh flicked a wrist and two of His palace guards stepped forward. They carried between them a long open box, whose weight caused their muscles to bulge and quiver with effort. It contained gold. Necklaces were draped over tiaras, earrings tumbled through armpieces, bracelets tangled among pectorals.

Pankh and Pen-Meru gasped. Only Renifer knew that it was not with reverence. It was with greed.

"For the most part," said Pharaoh, "I agree with the new theory of symbolism. For the most part, I agree that when the queen my mother is given eternal life, her servants will arise to wait upon her. But the queen my mother has been wrenched from the resting place she herself prepared."

"It is so," spoke the listeners, because agreeing with a king was always correct. It was not permitted to look into Pharaoh's eyes, but that was easy, because their eyes were fastened on all that gold.

"The beautiful silent priestess, the color of ivory," said Pharaoh, "will be perfect."

Pen-Meru nodded.

Pankh nodded.

The soldiers, the priest and his acolyte nodded.

Renifer nodded. Ancient custom might erase some of what her family had done. Only the whitest bulls and cows were sacrificed, and was this not the whitest of females? Had not Renifer's own nurse seen from the first that the girl was intended for sacrifice?

The girl of ivory was not aware of their survey, nor had she any way of knowing what Pharaoh had just decreed: that she was to serve Hetepheres for eternity. She was staring at Pharaoh's Pyramid as if she could not believe that she stood beside it.

Soon, thought Renifer, you will stand below it.

It was imperative that the girl should neither scream nor fight. She must not understand what was happening. Normally she would have been given a special drink to prepare her body, but none was prepared for this event. Renifer wondered how to be sure that the girl participated graciously and fully.

An extraordinary thing occurred. Pharaoh Himself began to clothe her in the gold he had brought along. Around her neck He fastened a gold pectoral of spread wings, which not only covered her throat but fell almost to her waist. He Himself adjusted the weight behind her neck to keep the pectoral at the right height. One by one, He slid gleaming bracelets over her wrist and past the curve of her elbow, until her arms were solid with gold.

When He was done, the girl could scarcely have moved, so weighted was she now by gold. And such was the glory of gold that the girl was hypnotized by it. They needed no specially prepared drink to control her behavior. Wearing the gold was her drug.

It is good, thought Renifer. Her heart eased, knowing that the queen had this lovely servant for eternity.

Pharaoh studied the awesome triangle of His Pyramid. When at last He spoke, His voice seemed directed to the stars in the sky. "Such a perfect sacrifice," He said finally, "must have an escort into the tomb."

Pankh and Pen-Meru stiffened with panic. If Pharaoh designated a priest to go down the shaft, the priest would see there were hardly any tomb furnishings; that the seal on the sarcophagus was brand new and the tomb pitifully small for a queen. He would bellow the news, Pharaoh Himself might descend, and all would be executed after all.

"It worries me a little," said Pharaoh, "that the girl of ivory might cry out and defile the moment of her sacrifice."

There was sand and dust and the cold wind of night.

Renifer with her bare shoulders shivered.

Pharaoh looked into her eyes and she tried to keep her eyes on the ground where they belonged, but her eyes were caught on His and she could not even blink.

"Perhaps, my little singer of song," said Khufu, his smile broad and kingly, "you would lead the sacrifice into the tomb. With you by her side, she will be smiling."

Renifer listened to the faint lap of water from the lagoon, the distant voices of the crew on the barge. Khufu was asking her to travel down into the tomb. He was not suggesting that she would ever travel back out of it.

Her father said, "What an honor for my daughter, Great King."

Her once beloved said, "What an honor for my bride, Great King."

Wind whistled through stones stacked for future tombs.

"Will you, little singer of song, do me this honor?" asked Pharaoh.

As if Renifer had a choice. As if she were permitted to say, "No, thank you," and go home to her mother.

To the Lord of the Two Lands, Renifer said, "I will."

Annie

Annie did not see how they were all going to descend into Hetepheres' tomb. Especially her. With all this gold she probably weighed as much as the Statue of Liberty.

Renifer was lowered first, in a basket, like some scary ride at an amusement park. Annie was clearly next, then Pharaoh himself. Renifer held a torch in her hand but Annie was not given one. Renifer was lowered gently and without any bumping or lurching. Annie swallowed nervously and went down after her.

Pharaoh said something, his thin smile flickering like a flame or a snake's tongue.

That's who he reminds me of, she thought. A viper.

She was relieved when her basket fell below the level of the earth and beyond the power of his eyes. The shaft was very steep. She touched gouges in the stone, toeholds, perhaps for those without ropes or baskets.

At the bottom of the shaft, yet more gold glittered in the light of Renifer's torch.

Where do they get all this gold? she thought. Is Egypt

full of gold mines? Or do they send pirates abroad, to loot and pillage?

At the bottom, she was surprised and disappointed. It was just a small stone room. Nothing there except the few pieces shifted from the other tomb. The vast sarcophagus, the bed canopy, the sedan chair. The gold she had seen from higher up was just one tray, far less than she had on her own body.

Well, it sure isn't Tutankhamen's tomb, she thought. But probably this is just the outer room. Once we start exploring, we'll see the better rooms.

She wondered what ceremonies would take place underground.

She could hear Pharaoh being lowered, his basket not coming down quite so lightly as her own, for it seemed to smack the walls. She looked toward the shaft, but the feet of Pharaoh did not appear. A great slab was being lowered on ropes. Renifer's torchlight showed it to be no beautiful painted object. Just rock.

Annie could make no sense of it.

When the huge stone had settled onto the bottom, the person above let go of the ropes. They fell into a coil of their own. Were she and Renifer meant to do something with those ropes?

A second stone was lowered onto the ropes from the first stone. Together, the two stones sealed the shaft. There was no longer an opening. Nobody else could come down.

Nobody could go back up, either.

A terrible racket began. It took Annie several moments to realize that rocks were being dropped down the shaft. Rocks that hit and ricocheted and echoed. Filling the shaft. Filling it for eternity.

Annie and Renifer were being buried alive.

V

Time for Ghosts

Strat

Strat was sitting about ten courses up the Pyramid, feet dangling, head resting in the corner made by two huge stones. Across the Giza plateau, by carriage and sedan chair, by donkey and camel came the party guests, having spent the night in Cairo, and only now returning to the dig.

Miss Matthews and Dr. Lightner were astride donkeys so small their feet dragged in the dust. Strat hoped Miss Matthews had enjoyed herself. In his youth, he had been to many parties and enjoyed them. But he was nineteen now and felt no desire to attend more. The girl whose company had made him happy had been lost.

He was touched to see the stern Archibald Lightner so smitten. It was in part Miss Matthews' height: Dr. Lightner need not stoop to deal with her, as if she were a child. It was in part her independence. Elderly British ladies traveled alone all the time (although of course with a maid and a companion). But Miss Matthews had come truly alone, not even a maid. Strat tried to imagine a father or brother permitting her to be a reporter at all, let alone voyage by herself to a place quite primitive.

Laughing, Dr. Lightner and Miss Matthews dismounted easily, since they were taller than their rides, and walked the last quarter mile holding hands. Strat wanted to embrace them both in his joy for them.

He could hardly wait to tell the archaeologist about his latest discovery.

When the great man had left yesterday evening for Cairo, the entire camp had been distressed by the missing gold sandal. All spirits had sunk. Had the only true treasure in the tomb waited thousands of years—only to be stolen in 1899?

This morning, Dr. Lightner's college assistants had decided to search every tent and trunk, but Strat, unwilling to trespass upon the belongings of others, continued his own investigation. He had convinced himself that if *one* pile of rock turned out to be plaster hiding a tomb entrance, *another* pile of rock would surely turn out to be plaster, and hiding a tomb entrance.

Since dawn, he had been walking about with a small ball peen hammer, swinging it against rocks, hoping each time for a sifting of plaster. A hour ago, such an event had occurred.

Strat put up no flag to mark the location, but he knew exactly where it was. If he paced parallel to the causeway precisely forty-six steps, heel pressed against toe, from Hetepheres' shaft, he would see the tiny white smash mark of his hammer on a long flat thin stone.

A surprisingly large group was returning with Dr. Lightner. Clearly he intended to show off his excavation to many who had attended the French party. Strat hoped the gold sandal had been located by now, as it was sure to impress the visitors.

He recognized two German scholars from a dig in Saqqara; two Italians who wished to study Dr. Lightner's finds; a handful of British army officers; the hieroglyphic expert; and even the French military attaché.

Finally, in a small open carriage pulled by two straining donkeys, their keeper hitting them continually with sticks lest they give up and fall down, rode a very heavy man, all belly and jowls, with a dusty wrinkled hide like a rhinoceros.

No, thought Strat. It cannot be.

He closed his eyes for a moment, and tried again. The image did not change.

It was good that he wasn't at the top of the Pyramid, Strat thought, or he would have followed the example of the two young Frenchmen, and just rolled off. Arriving dead at the bottom would be better than encountering his father.

Father was a word that should be precious, redolent of respect and honor; of example and pride. This was not the case for Strat.

What mattered to his father were investments. All life was an investment: a servant, a wife, a factory, a dinner party. All investments must pay off or be discarded. At no time would a losing investment be kept . . . even if that investment were his only son.

Chained up in the asylum, Strat had promised God that if he ever got out, he would not follow his father's example. Rather, he would help others. Much harder, he would accept help, and not arrogantly insist that he could stand alone.

But it was Katie who had fulfilled those promises. She was help even to lepers beneath the feet of the Lord. And her greatest gift, the one that dazzled and shamed him, came when Katie chose to say good-bye, so Strat might have a life unencumbered by a deformed girl he could not forever pretend was his sister.

I have helped nobody, he thought now. I have leaped into adventure and thrown away my promise. And the Lord knows exactly how I have behaved.

Dizzily, Strat stared at Hiram Stratton clambering out of the carriage. Now Father stood inside Strat's new life; touched Strat's tent and cot; spoke to Strat's friends and colleagues.

How could Hiram Stratton, Sr., have located Strat? And why would he care enough to travel all the way to Egypt? His father loathed exercise and particularly loathed hot weather. What could he be doing here? Such a man might have anything in mind, but not anything good.

A commotion sprang up among the tents, of course. His father could not bear peace or calm. He must have action and argument. He must provoke and antagonize, because destroying the serenity of others demonstrated power. Nobody, not anywhere on this earth, not even in the desert, could hide from the personality of Hiram Stratton, Sr.

From this distance Strat was indistinguishable from the hordes of tourists, both European and Egyptian, climbing and picnicking on the rugged edges of Khufu's Pyramid. In a trice, Strat could mingle with the crowd below; buy from a vendor a robe of the sort worn by local men. He could wind around his head a turban and then hire a camel. He could vanish up the Nile, as British troops were vanishing into the misty unknown of darkest Africa.

This time he would be sufficiently intelligent to use another name.

Strat slipped down from his perch. What name to use? Perhaps Annie's. He could call himself Lockwood. Yes, that was it. He would be Strat Lockwood.

Yet if he fled, he would lose the respect of Dr. Lightner; lose his precious camera; lose Katie's letters; lose the chance to become a brilliant photographer; lose the glorious moment in which he showed Dr. Lightner the second tomb entrance he had found.

And lose, above all, the miniature envelope with the lock of Annie Lockwood's shining black hair.

Strat looked up at the peak of the Pyramid, five hundred feet above. The sky around those bronze stones was blue as a child's paint box. There had Strat knelt and asked Time to give Annie back to him.

In a few short weeks, a new century would arrive: the twentieth. Its first decade would belong to science and science alone. And here was Strat, abandoning rational thought, pretending Time was a power to move souls.

It might even be that Father was correct, and Strat *had* lost his sanity when he believed in the existence of a girl from another time.

At the dig, men were running back and forth and gesticulating. He could tell Dr. Lightner and Miss Matthews apart by their great height and he could tell his father by his great width.

Strat walked behind the Sphinx, briefly blinded by the shock of shadow. Usually when he stood by the Sphinx, the past overwhelmed him, but now he felt only the future. Future hovered around the great paws and blew sand on its back. Future gnawed its face and chewed its broken nose.

In Father's presence, he thought, my future is also broken, swallowed in the desert of his hatred. But I will not flinch from it. I will not run.

He squared his shoulders. He would not go slouching and timid into his father's presence.

The sand across which he trekked sucked at his boots and the wind tore at his face. The blue sky turned slightly yellow as the sand whirled across it.

The members of the dig saw Strat coming and they grew silent and still. Strat had the appalling thought that it was not his father of whom he must be afraid, but his companions. How could that be?

The visiting scholars, the French attaché, the Egyptians, the college boys . . . all in a row, staring at him. They looked like a firing line. Strat wanted to bolt, but kept his stride even and his face calm. He wondered what his father would say to him, after two years with no word between them.

But it was Archibald Lightner who spoke. "You lied to me, young Stratton. You claimed mere estrangement from your father. In fact, you are an escapee from an asylum, where you were incarcerated for the safety of your neighbors. You attacked and badly hurt an innocent physician who dedicated his life to helping his desperate patients. Most wretchedly, you kidnapped an innocent girl and defiled her to accomplish your escape."

That he could be accused of hurting Katie! Katie whom he loved as a sister! And that anybody could call Dr. Wilmott a dedicated innocent physician! The man was a monster who had delighted in torturing the helpless, smiling as they suffered.

Anyway, Strat had just hit him over the head with a lamp. Far from being badly hurt, Dr. Wilmott gave chase himself.

"And *now,*" cried Dr. Lightner, "you have defiled my excavation!"

Strat could not believe that statement. What of his contribution to the dig? His photographs, saving for all time the accomplishments of the entire group?

"You stole that gold sandal," accused Dr. Lightner. "You squirreled it away in your own bag. You who travel so lightly, burdened only with lies, no doubt planning to run away and continue your life against society."

The insult was too deep to be borne. That he would take a possession belonging to another man? Never!

The wind rose higher, engulfing them in dust, drying their throats and hurting their eyes, making them hotter and angrier.

At last the father spoke to the son he had not seen in

two years. "I had you found," said Hiram Stratton. "I hired a detective. I plan to bring you back to America to stand trial for kidnapping and attempted murder. I considered the possibility that you were attempting to become a better person and thus deserved mercy. But I arrive to find you are a common thief."

"Father, I stole nothing. I never have. Nor did I hurt Katie in any way."

"I stand here as future patron to this excavation," thundered his father, "and this is what I must deal with first. The low base treachery of my own son."

Patron? Impossible. His father had never shown generosity. Unless, of course, he got something in exchange. And what might that be? The Stratton name on a museum wing? Strat doubted that his father had ever entered a museum.

"You stole the gold," said his father. "Nor can you deny it. You hid it deep inside your own miserable pile of clothing." Gladly, he waved the gold sandal as proof.

Strat, aghast, looked at his former friends. They met his eyes steadily and with contempt. "I found it," said the boy from Princeton. "Hidden among your clothes."

How could it have gotten there? It could only be that he had some enemy; some person in this very company who wished to destroy him.

His eyes sought understanding, and found it immediately. Miss Matthews, head and shoulders above the gloating bulk of Hiram Stratton, was staring out into the desert, cheeks red, chin high and eyes wet.

She stole the sandal, thought Strat, and made it look as if I did. She must be the detective Father hired. Father paid her to make me a thief.

Poor Dr. Lightner, in love with one who betrayed people for a living. There was no point in accusing her. Father paid so well. Impossible for truth to override that much money.

He faced his father again, and saw in his father's hand, almost invisible in the grip of that fat thumb and forefinger, the tiny envelope in which Strat kept Annie's lock of hair. It was the only possession Strat could never replace. Father, too, was a thief, having taken it from Strat's Bible, where it lay pressed when he did not keep it against his heart.

He made the error of showing that it mattered. Father, quick to see the weakness of others, opened the envelope and shook out the contents. The wind, which swirled around knees and raced, dust-laden, through shirts, now whisked away the silken tresses of Annie's hair and flung them out across the sand.

Strat's heart opened as if a wrench had been applied, turning until his valves burst and his heart broke.

"It is my belief," said the French attaché, stepping forward, "that you are also a murderer, young Stratton. Tell us how the two young men fell from the Pyramid."

"I thought it was an accident!" cried Dr. Lightner's Yale aide.

"Surely it was just carelessness," said one of the Germans, who had little use for the standards of the French.

"It was the work of ghosts," said an Egyptian.

"You heard Mr. Stratton," argued the French attaché. "In America, the boy tried to kill. In Egypt, he succeeded."

Just so had false accusations landed Strat in the asylum. His father was an expert at arranging the lies of strangers. Strat thought of Annie, who had saved him once. The wind increased, so that the sand it flung was painful to bare skin. All of Strat was raw: heart and hope. There was no Annie to save him this time, and he would never have wanted her here. She was the very reason Father had had him locked up, and Father would recognize her. He trembled to think what Hiram Stratton, Sr., would do to her. Desperately, Strat revoked his plea to Time.

"We will lock him up," said the French attaché grandly, looking forward to having an American behind bars.

"No, *we* will lock him up," said a British army officer, appalled that the French might have any power in a British protectorate.

"No," said Dr. Lightner decisively. "This has occurred in my establishment and it is my choice to put the young man under house arrest. He will not be shackled nor placed under lock and key. He will not be handed over to Egyptian authorities nor British. I wish to give you the opportunity, young Stratton, to demonstrate that you are a man of honor. Should you run, it will be proof of guilt. An innocent man has nothing to run from."

This is like a witch hunt in Old Salem, thought Strat. If I am innocent, I will be taken home to be punished. If I am guilty, I will be taken home to be punished.

But the gentlemen of Egypt, France, Italy, England, Germany and America, to whom honor was everything, awaited his response.

"I give you my word," said Strat quietly. "I am under house arrest. Under house arrest I will stay."

Camilla

Camilla forced herself to look at the young man Katie had asked her to honor. Instead, Camilla had wronged him. The son was innocent of all charges, past and present. Far from avenging her own father, Camilla had sunk to the level of Strat's father.

She must find a way to save Strat. If nothing more, she owed Katie that.

But a curious thing was happening. The boy seemed to have forgotten his accusers and his witnesses. He had turned slightly, and was staring toward the Pyramid, looking at once both bewildered and excited. He took a quick shocked breath and held it, his shoulders high and motionless.

Camilla, too, looked toward the Pyramid. She caught a glimpse of shining gold, half-seen, as through gauze. There was a rasp of shoes on sand and a girl's laughter, half-heard, as through a door. It was Time, leaving its ghosts and passing on.

Camilla did not faint, but she lost strength and balance. People cried, "Are you all right?" and said to one another, "It's the heat. Put her in the shade. Put a wet cloth on her forehead."

Hiram Stratton, Sr., having lost his son's attention, grabbed Strat's arm. When Strat jerked free, all the men jumped forward to prevent a fight. Or perhaps to encourage one.

Miss Matthews was walked into her tent by Dr. Lightner, for only he was tall enough to take her arm. Dr. Lightner ducked beneath the tent flap and set her gently on the edge of her cot. Anxiously, he fanned her face with the brim of his canvas hat. Through the tent opening, she could see the broken nose of the Sphinx.

To every tourist the Sphinx was a mystery that must be plumbed. All paused before it to cry, Who are you? From whence do you spring?

Who am I? thought Camilla Matthews. I who rejected my gender, my family, my honor and my faith.

Egyptians had worshiped the Nile and the sun, their kings and their mummified cats. How strange and marvelous were all religions: the eternal need to find greater substance.

Camilla had shrugged over greater things. Immersing herself in low and ugly deeds, she had created a low and ugly situation. "Oh, Dr. Lightner," she said desperately. "I must confess that I have done a terrible thing."

"Nonsense," he said roundly. "Here. A damp cloth will cool your thoughts."

Pressing the comforting cotton against her burning eyes, Camilla made her confession. "I set young Mr.

Stratton up for this crime. I took that gold sandal. Yes, it was I. I placed it in the young man's trunk so you would blame him. He is innocent."

Relief washed over Camilla. At last, she had done a good thing. She might be flung out of camp or thrown onto the next ship. She even might be the one sent to prison. But at least Strat would not suffer at her hands. She risked a humiliated glance at Dr. Lightner.

But he was regarding her with great esteem. A soft smile crossed his face. "Nothing," said Dr. Lightner, "is so beautiful as a woman who sacrifices for a man. Miss Matthews, how kind and generous is your feminine heart. You wish to save the boy from punishment. How I respect you. But no one will believe that trumped-up story. Your truthfulness and honor are visible to all who have met you."

It had not occurred to Camilla that she would not be believed. "Truly, sir, it was my doing. I committed the act."

"Now, now. You have enough troubles merely enduring the great heat. Ladies should not be here at this time of year. As for the theft of the sandal, it is too much for your feminine sensibilities to accept that some men are evil and do evil things. I think it best for your sake to remove you to Lady Clementine's abode. She delighted in your company, as of course do I, but her villa is better for you than this hot and dusty encampment."

"But you must explain to everyone, Dr. Lightner, what really happened. Especially it must be made clear to the French, who have jumped to dreadful conclusions."

"Dear girl, we know what really happened. Young Stratton is his father all over again. I fear he does not deserve your assistance. One day he too will clench a cigar in his teeth, looking and smelling like the smokestack of his factory. He too will burn down that factory in order to get his way."

Camilla gave a little cry and hid once more behind his handkerchief.

"You know of that fire?" His arm had gone around her shoulder and she felt the comforting heat of his body. "That factory burned when I was in America raising money for this expedition," he told her. "Innocent people died in that fire. I'm told there was no investigation. Mr. Stratton simply paid off everyone involved."

Not everyone, thought Camilla. I wonder if Mama would have accepted his money, if he had offered it, to keep us in school. I accepted money from him. Passing it through Mr. Duffie's hands does not cleanse it. I am a sinner with my hands dipped in Stratton money.

Oh, there were too many moral problems here, and she without her church. "I do not think young Strat is like his father," she said. Tears filled her eyes, she who was supposed to be like a man and never weep. She could not help quoting Katie. "I think he is a good and decent and generous boy."

She was talking as if she really were a decade older than Strat, but in fact she was two years younger.

Remembering that she was only seventeen made her want to behave seventeen, and weep on Dr. Lightner's shoulder, and be taken care of. But that was not her lot in life, and she must not weaken.

Dr. Lightner burst out, "How touched I am by your tender heart! No matter what your height and frame say of boldness and strength, in fact you are gentle and full of love. Willing to sacrifice so that a young man might go free! Oh, Miss Matthews."

Camilla had completed the task of making him fall in love with her, weeks ahead of schedule. He was too good for her and she must walk away from him, but perhaps she could use the trap she had set for Dr. Lightner to undo the trap she had set for Strat.

"Honored sir," said Camilla shakily, "might we discuss a way to extricate the boy from his father's grasp? Such a wicked man does not tell the truth. I believe Hiram Stratton lies even about his son. I believe there were no such events as the kidnapping and the attack. Please. Let us conjure a way to set Strat free."

Dr. Lightner fiddled with some shards of pottery on which undeciphered hieroglyphs awaited his expertise. His thumb stroked letters incised thousands of years ago by a scribe. "If you have fallen in love with the young man, Miss Matthews," he said bravely, "I will do all within my power to assist you in saving him."

Camilla dropped the handkerchief and all pretense. How gallant he was! And how she agreed that nothing was more beautiful than one person sacrificing for another. "I have fallen in love with you, sir. But I am in a position to know that the father is truly evil and to extricate the son I do require your utmost assistance."

Dr. Lightner wrapped her hand tightly in his and kissed the top of it. "Do you mean that?" he whispered. "That you—that you—" The words were too intimate to be repeated.

Camilla nodded.

"Here is a way out then," he said. He patted her hair and cheeks, afraid to overstep his rights, but too emotional to keep a correct distance. "The British love war so very deeply. The wars in India have run out, and war in the Sudan may end within days, but luckily, war looms in South Africa. Those Dutchmen down there, Boers they call themselves, are trying to throw the British out. Everybody is happy. There's nothing like a good fight. I shall suggest young Stratton to my British friends as a cameraman. Off he goes to fight the Dutch. Thousands of miles once more between him and his father. This time we shall see that he uses a false name."

It was perfect! Strat would be saved. On her way back to America, Camilla would disembark in Spain to give Katie money and news. She would tell the truth about her own foul deeds and then she would find the priest of the convent at the hospital, and tell him the truth also. She would get her religion back if she got nothing else, and once home, she would no longer spy for Mr. Duffie. Somehow she would keep her brothers in school, but not that way.

Maybe I really could sell my first article as Strat sold his first picture, she thought, and from there go on to a splendid career. I shall be a spinster, but with fewer regrets, for I shall shine on my own.

Dr. Lightner stood. "I shall go then, and see how this may be managed."

Camilla looked into his face and immediately had more, not fewer, regrets. She did not want to be a spinster. She wanted Archibald Lightner. "And the French?" she said, jumping up. "What about their silly accusation?"

"Please, my dear. Sit back down and rest. The heat tired you."

"I'm over it," said Camilla crossly. "How will you handle the French?" She opened the tent flap for him instead of the other way around.

He laughed. "I don't know yet. First, let's make sure the young man himself will go along with our plan."

STRAT

The gold sandal had been set upon the dusty table where Dr. Lightner wrote up his notes in the evening. It seemed to Strat that the slipper actually sang: an ancient high quaver, a golden voice from the past. He touched the delicately incised gold rope under which a girl's toes had once slid.

Strat's heart actually stopped. It hit his ribs once, with a huge thrust of energy, and then it ceased to beat.

Annie had worn that sandal.

Around him, the figures and their speech glazed, as raw umber over oils on a painting. The angry men grew solid and still, fixing themselves as people on paper. There was light and shadow and heat. There was not sound.

A camel train appeared on the horizon, like liquid slowly poured over the sand, long black shadows spilled behind.

And Strat spilled out of the picture, falling and tumbling, like the French boys from the top of the Pyramid. His bones smashed against its rocky sides, and Strat could not understand this, because he was not on the

Pyramid, but on the sand. His skin was laid open by the scrape and assault of the stones. His mind broke apart, thoughts scattered like seed from a clumsy hand.

He spun into the vortex of the past. There were faces with him: hideous, unknown others being wrenched through Time.

And then he hit bottom, and it was stone.

CAMILLA

The members of Dr. Lightner's dig were turning in circles in the sand, like dogs deciding whether to lie down. The German scholars and the French attaché were puzzled and embarrassed. They could not produce Strat for Dr. Lightner and Miss Matthews.

"Where did you put your son?" Camilla demanded of Mr. Stratton. "Surely you have not already incarcerated him? It was agreed that he would stay upon his honor."

Mr. Stratton was bewildered and angry. "He was here a moment ago."

"He ran," opined the French attaché.

"He couldn't have," objected the Yale assistant. "He must be here. We'll help you look, Miss Matthews."

But nobody could find Strat. There was not a trace of him.

"He has fled," said Dr. Lightner sadly.

"Proof of guilt!" said Hiram Stratton gladly.

"Strat said he would put himself under house arrest,"

said Camilla through stiff lips. "He will be back by dark. He gave his word, and I accept that."

Oh, Strat, she thought, if you are not back . . .

No man here will forgive you for breaking your word. Even Dr. Lightner may refuse to help you after all.

STRAT

Above Strat spread a sky vast and dark, pierced by a thousand stars and a sliver of moon. Torches burned in tall posts, illuminating pyramid, pillar and stone.

He stood exactly where he had been standing in another time, fifty feet from the causeway. He had arrived at the beginning, when Khufu's Pyramid was perfect. It was a ghost, or he was.

Strat's breath came in shallow spurts, as if he were afraid of antique air. Slowly his lungs returned, his legs and strength, and he could feel again the sweet beating of his heart.

He was surrounded by temples and mastabas and monuments he could not identify because they did not exist in 1899. He could not see the Sphinx. The causeway, mostly destroyed or buried in his time, was lined with statues, covered by awnings and scented by flowers in massive pots.

He became aware of a steady, rhythmic tapping. He turned and looked toward the Nile. The sound of feet marching, he decided; guards, perhaps, walking back and forth during their night watch. Partially visible through the tall pillars of an open temple, motionless in the water of a lagoon that had vanished long before Strat's time, lay a large and well-lit boat. Although he judged the hour to be very late, there was a good deal of activity on its deck.

It seemed best not to attract attention. Strat stayed well away from the torchlight.

First he would examine the Pyramid. He had climbed it, photographed it, fallen in love with it—but only its core. Think of seeing it as Khufu's architects had planned! Strat was astonished to see a wall around the Pyramid, with the obvious intent of preventing visitors from scaling the monument. The year 1899 had its advantages after all; you need not just stand at the bottom and stare up.

Suddenly he saw the Sphinx. It existed, not half-broken, but half-carved.

O mystery of mysteries, thought Strat reverently. You are a creation of man, and that man must be Khufu!

He was startled by a sudden clatter and some sharply issued orders.

In ancient Egyptian! He was thrilled. He strained to hear, for nobody in 1899 knew how to pronounce the words so painstakingly translated from hieroglyphs.

A phalanx of soldiers was forming near the lagoon. They marched through the temple, pivoted sharply and turned onto the causeway. Their boots and the shafts of their spears slammed against the pavement. Strat drew deeper in the shadows. There were not many soldiers, and yet the sound they made was the sound of many: the relentless echo of men who would show no mercy and give no quarter . . . men not unlike his own father.

The procession was both beautiful and threatening. In the midst of the soldiers was carried a huge litter. Strat could not see the occupant, but he recognized the tall crown from tomb paintings: the headgear of the Lord of the Two Lands.

Pharaoh.

The man was so motionless in his litter that Strat decided this was a representation of the Lord of the Two Lands, and not the king himself.

All too aware of his khaki-colored trousers and shirt, Strat dropped down into the sand, that he might cast no shadow. The sand was cold, having no capacity to hold heat. The desert that had failed to roast a man by day tried to freeze him by night. Strat shivered. Farther out in the sand, a high vicious yapping began.

A pack of wild dogs? No, he thought, this is Egypt. *Jackals.*

The jackals were much too close and far too interested. Also not unlike his father.

Next in the procession came men who seemed neither soldier nor priest, another litter and more soldiers.

Fearful of discovery, Strat inched backward over the sand, although moving into range of the jackals did not seem wise either. But the parade stopped well away from him. They did not pause in front of one of the temples or mastabas or baby pyramids. They gathered, it seemed to Strat, around a shadowy circle in the causeway itself.

He squinted to see better, and writhed in the sand for a better angle. It looked like a manhole, like a—

Strat was embarrassed. This was ancient Egypt. There was no room for confusion under these circumstances. It must be a tomb entrance.

Pharaoh's litter was set down. Soldiers assisted Pharaoh out of it. They removed his crown and he himself swung off his cape. So he was real. His chest was as hung with medals and ribbons and sashes as any British officer bound for war. He was spectacular.

There were prayers, with hands held up to the sky; there was anointing with oil; there was sharing of the cup.

From the second litter, two girls in white gowns were brought forward. One knelt, kissed the ground, and sang from a kneeling position. The cool high notes of her psalm rang between the vast stones, echoing in the night air. Was she a priestess? A daughter or wife of Khufu?

Strat knew the name of Khufu's mother, Hetepheres; he was sure he could hear those syllables in the girl's song. Now he recognized the notes. It was the song of the gold sandal, when he had held it in his hands.

As the ceremony went on, ropes were rigged. Two rock slabs were hauled across the sand, each perhaps four feet across and six or eight inches thick. Heavy, but nothing compared to the two-ton stones that made up the Pyramid. Many baskets, also containing something very heavy, were carried up.

The second girl sang nothing and did nothing, but stood motionless. She wore so much gold that she herself was scarcely visible.

Now Khufu himself spoke, and even the jackals were silent as Pharaoh expanded his voice, and his orders filled the City of the Dead.

The singer was lifted into a sort of basket on ropes and lowered gently into the tomb. The girl wrapped in gold was put into the next basket and also lowered. Torches dipped forward, in fascination or reverence. There was a great spill of light and the second girl was no longer shadow under jewels. Strat could see her features and her eyes.

It was Annie.

He had hardly begun rejoicing at the marvelous ways of Time—the miraculous conjunction of souls—the perfect meeting soon to occur in the perfect place—when the next lowering into the shaft occurred.

It was not a priest or a soldier who went down. It was the first rock-hewn slab.

Promptly, the second slab was lowered over the first, and the men began a great and dreadful warbling. They hooted like robed birds gone mad, bowing and nodding to the earth. Then, one by one, man by man, they emptied the baskets down the shaft. Sand and rock and pebble.

Filling it.

Annie

Annie and Renifer were in a small room with a large bed. The pile of soft pillows awaited. So did death.

It was a parody of a slumber party. But they had not dressed Annie for a party. They had dressed her for eternity.

She did not speak to Renifer and Renifer did not speak to her, because they shared no language and because there was nothing to say.

Annie took off the magnificent necklace, the crown, the thick bracelets, the anklets and amulets. She laid them in a row at the foot of the bed. Gold was beautiful, but you could not, in fact, take it with you. When she slithered out of the netted gown, its bright beads tumbled onto the floor, tangled beyond hope. She slid out of the gold sandals but when her bare feet touched the stone floor, she couldn't stand it. There might be spiders or beetles or rats down here. So she kept the sandals on and fingered the pleats in her stiff white undergown.

Time, you vicious spirit. How could you do this to me? Renifer's torch will burn out. We will sit in the dark while we suffocate.

Annie had contemplated death, of course. All thinking people contemplate death. Her own age was particularly fascinated with it. Whenever they had a poetry assignment, half the kids wrote about death. But none of them ever expected to sit inside their own tomb with lots of time to consider the future of their own dead body.

I am going to become a mummy, she thought.

Annie had read that the Egyptians had not really needed to mummify their dead; the desert would do it for them. Egypt was so dry that bodies behaved like autumn leaves, turning color and turning crispy.

The torch had burned down too low for Renifer to hold it anymore. She set the bit of flaming wood against the stone sarcophagus, where it burned brightly, casting shadows along the incised hieroglyphs. The ceiling was quite high. Annie watched the smoke rise. Perhaps she should breathe deeply and get it over with.

It was uncommon for an American to feel helpless. Annie's generation and country did not believe in that kind of thing. If you had character and intelligence, you did not permit yourself to be helpless. You solved everything.

Annie would not solve this.

She would not solve thirst, hunger, fear or rage. She would not teach Renifer to speak English, so they could mourn together. She would not dismantle the tomb from the inside, nor tug away granite slabs as large as picnic tables and then empty the shaft so she could climb up.

Instead, she would listen to her heartbeat and wonder what it would be like when that stopped. And then it would stop.

The torch flickered. Annie did not think she could bear being in total dark. "Renifer," she whispered.

Renifer took Annie into her arms and sang gently, as in a lullabye.

Rock me to sleep, thought Annie. Let me not remember in my sleep that I have been buried alive. Let me not wake, but just drift away and not have to feel what is happening to me.

And as she fell asleep, she understood what Time had done.

In 1899, Strat was going to dig up bones that had been interred for thousands of years.

And they would be Annie's.

VI

Time to Die

RENIFER

Renifer hoped she would be the first to die. It was bad enough to lie next to an empty sarcophagus in the dark. She didn't want to lie next to the corpse of the girl of ivory. Renifer's mouth was dry. Thirst was not yet torture, but that would come. She and the girl of ivory would not die easily.

She could neither pray nor summon happy memories. The image of her mother shopping, her little brothers playing ball, her sister stealing her eye makeup, her girlfriends casting eyes at Pankh—none of these could she remember.

She pictured instead the hand of her father dropping a rock as his contribution to the sealing of his living daughter's tomb. The smile of Pankh as he took his turn. How Pharaoh would honor them. How their careers would soar.

I do not mind dying for thee, O queen, thought Renifer. *But to die while Father and Pankh laugh at Pharaoh! To die neither embalmed nor prayed over, while Father and Pankh are given tombs in the best part of the City of the Dead. I mind that.*

Pankh had not spoken to Renifer as she was led to her fate. He had touched his forehead to the ground at Pharaoh's feet, but he had not touched the cheek or hand of his beloved. Nor had he touched the girl of ivory. His eyes had done that for him: caressing the gold she wore. In Pankh's eyes had been heat and excitement such as Renifer herself had never generated.

It was lust for gold.

Pankh will rob this tomb, thought Renifer.

He would wait until the girls were dead. He would wait a month or year. Until Pharaoh was busy with other affairs. Until new guards had been given new bribes. Until the gold he already possessed was not enough and he must have more.

He would empty the shaft. It would take several nights. He would remove rubble, cart it away, temporarily plaster over the cavity, open it up again the next night. Lifting the two slabs at the bottom would be easy, since the ropes still lay tied around them. He would step over the bodies, pleased that the girl of ivory had stripped off her gold and stacked it so neatly.

His wife would wear it. For Pankh would marry soon. His station required it. Possibly he would marry Renifer's little sister, thus keeping the secrets in the family.

In the darkness, Renifer inched away from the sleeping pale girl and went to her knees and prayed.

Sekhmet! Destroy Pankh who destroys queens. Destroy him who loves gold more than love. I beg thee, in honor of my willing sacrifice, with thy power, make him suffer.

Renifer sat back on her heels, hugging her knees to

her chest. Never had she been so sure that a prayer had been heard.

She sat in terrible darkness, where not even gold had value, and dreamed of what Sekhmet would do to Pankh. And then began the terror. Not for Pankh, who deserved it! For Renifer herself.

Queen Hetepheres began to open her sarcophagus from the inside.

There was a creaking of bones as joints moved, and the sound of old dead laughter.

Renifer imagined the fingernails of a dead queen raking her face.

But Father had destroyed the mummy! There was no queen within that coffin.

The girl of ivory awoke and they gripped each other in the dreadful dark.

No longer did the sound seem to come from the sarcophagus. It was on all sides: above and below, left and right.

Was it the sound of a *ka* rejoining its mummy? But there was no mummy to find!

What rage would the *ka* exhibit when it learned the evil truth? It seemed to be trapped in the walls, fighting in the shaft, scrabbling on the surface. What would it do to Renifer and the girl of ivory when it got into the room with them?

Renifer prayed aloud, desperate to reach the ears of the coming *ka*. "No," she prayed. "O queen, I gave myself for you. I die for you. Do not attack me in the dark. O grandmother of Meresankh, whom I served, pity me!"

There were grunts and scrabbles. Scrapes and moans. A trickle, as of many pebbles; and a cry, as of pain.

I would rather have been impaled in the desert in the sun, thought Renifer. At least I could see and understand my death.

Beloved gods! Do not allow the fingers of the dead to feel the skin of my face.

Pankh

Pankh was permitted the honor of escorting Pharaoh back to the royal barge. The royal hand lay upon Pankh's forehead; the royal blessing bestowed upon Pen-Meru. But already Pharaoh's mind was elsewhere. His mother was safe and now He must get a good night's sleep.

Pankh did not consider Pharaoh a fool. The Lord of the Two Lands was as strong a king as Egypt had known. But He believed too much in His own people. He believed in loyalty.

It was Pankh's experience that men were more loyal to gold than to kings. A hundred men had gasped at the sight of that gold. Chains of gold, circles of gold, hanks of gold, crowns of gold—draped upon the girl of ivory, who neither bent nor sagged, but stood white and flawless, a statue of marble, carrying it into eternity.

Or . . . as long as it took for tomb robbers to relieve her of the burden.

Pharaoh went to His chamber. The procession

dispersed. Torches were doused. Priests went to their beds. Soldiers changed watch. Pen-Meru was rowed to Memphis, his arms full of treasure to replace his daughter.

Pankh, however, drifted toward the docks and piers. He knew the waterfront well. The dark was his friend. Half a mile upstream, he eased out into the desert. Silently and carefully, he circled the City of the Dead, keeping to the shadows, more uneasy about jackals than tomb police. He would approach the girls' tomb from the vacant western desert instead of the busy Nile.

Pankh would not be the only one who wanted that gold, but he was definitely the only one bold enough to take it the very same night Pharaoh dedicated it. In Pharaoh's own procession had been at least one tomb guard and one priest known to assist robbers. But did these men know there was a second shaft? That it had not been filled? Did they know the exact location? Or would it take them years of poking to locate the spot?

Pankh had purchased the architect's plans for the tomb of Princess Nitiqret of Blessed Memory. But that did not mean the plans had been sold only once.

He must retrieve the gold before dawn. At the sun's first rays, the next police shift would arrive. Priests would be performing morning ablutions, tourists gawking, families picnicking. Acolytes would be anxiously reporting for their first day and vendors setting up their tables to sell cheap straw hats. The girl of ivory had worn so much gold! But if she could wear that much, he could carry or hide that much.

Pankh slipped among the minor pyramids to find the second shaft.

He regretted that the girls would not yet be dead.

In a way, he reasoned, it would be an act of generosity to speed them on their way. Less suffering. Yes, he was being kind.

ANNIE

Annie and Renifer were holding each other so tightly she could not tell whose heart was pounding so loudly: her own, Renifer's, or the intruder's.

It was the dark that was so very terrible. Although she had looked around carefully when there was still torchlight, and knew how small was the room in which they were trapped, higher than it was wide, now that it was utterly dark, she did not know. She could not bring herself to reach forth in the pitch black and touch a wall or a floor and the ceiling was far too high to be touched.

And then, through her fear, she became aware of something most odd. She felt a strong draft. There should not be fresh air in a sealed tomb, let alone a breeze.

Somehow, somewhere, an airway had been opened. Only the hand of man could move rocks and let in a draft. So . . . the scrapes—could those be rocks as they were dragged away? The grunts—from a living man's chest? The rasping—soles of shoes sliding down stone?

Could this be *rescue*?

But who would rescue them?

She understood now that Pharaoh had ordered their deaths. His soldiers would not march back to retrieve the sacrifice. The priests had been proud to participate. In the faces of all assembled, Annie had seen reverence.

That left Pankh and Pen-Meru. Had Annie misjudged them? Were they good people after all? Helpless to act when surrounded by Pharaoh's finest soldiers? Had they returned, at hideous risk to themselves, to save Renifer?

If it is them, thought Annie, they'll save Renifer, but they won't save me. I'm the sacrifice. They'll leave me here.

The draft lifted her hair. Whoever was coming had opened a considerable airway.

And I'm climbing up it, she told herself. Pankh buried me alive; I have the right to smash him in the head.

She still wore the gold sandals. She slid one off and gripped it firmly in her hand. It was a good solid weapon. She'd knock him out in the dark and shinny out of her tomb.

There was a long scraping drag as stone was pulled over stone.

Trembling, the girls waited. Annie had lost any sense of direction in the little room and did not know where to look to find the shaft down which they had been lowered. But light, when she saw it at last, did not appear in the wall where the shaft had been. It was in the ceiling. A stone was being dragged away and slowly a slit was appearing. Fingers gripped the edge of the stone and shifted it more. Grunts and gasps followed. The fingers vanished, and returned gripping a torch.

Behind the murky smoke that swirled up to fresh air and life was a dark and half-seen face.

If Pankh can get down, I can get up, she said to herself. She had not a moment to waste. Lifting the magnificent sedan chair on which Queen Hetepheres had once rested, she hauled it onto the high bed and propped it against the headboard.

Above her, the torch was set on the edge of the hole. Pankh could not both hold the torch and lower himself. He sat on the edge of the hole above her and came down feet first. Annie tightened her grip on the sandal and climbed up onto the sedan chair. She was high enough to break Pankh's kneecaps, but not high enough to smash in his skull. Perhaps she should just break his fingers off.

Annie had never had impressive upper arm strength. She prayed adrenaline would give her enough kick so she could haul herself up into the hole.

The soiled shoelaces of Pankh's scratchy old leather boots had come undone.

I could grab him by the feet and yank him down, she thought. If I'm lucky, he'll break his spine on the floor.

She drew her arm back, preparing to whack him with all her might.

An inch of bright red sock showed at the top of the boots. The legs were encased in khaki trousers with frayed hems. She had not seen Pankh in anything but bare legs and a little white kilt.

The body lowered.

Annie held her sandal at the ready.

A waist appeared, and its belt. A shirt appeared, and its buttons. Elbows unfolded. Hanging from his fingers was Strat.

"Don't hit me," he said.

She could not speak. She could neither laugh nor cry. She could not even touch him, because with one hand she held her weapon and with the other was steadying herself against the wall.

"You're beautiful," he said to her.

She nodded. "Fit for a king," she told him.

"I was there. I saw. It was Khufu, wasn't it?"

"Who cares about him? Oh, Strat! How did you get here? Where did you come from! I was scared of death and pain and darkness and then there was all that noise and I thought you were a mummy coming out of the sarcophagus."

"In 1899 when we open that sarcophagus," said Strat, "there is no mummy. It's something of a mystery. I can't hang here much longer, Annie. It's either let go or haul back up."

"If you let go, you're going to spike yourself on the bedstead. I'll hop down from the sedan chair and move the furniture."

It didn't work that easily. She broke the arm of the chair by stepping wrong and fell backward onto the mattress. Strat kicked the sedan chair off the bed and fell onto the mattress with her.

She felt his face, every inch of it, to be sure this was

her Strat, the one she remembered so vividly, the one she had wanted so very very much. He caught her long hair in his knotted fist and kissed her. "Oh, Annie. Of all the terrible things that happened, the worst was losing your lock of hair. All this time, I have cherished it. And this afternoon, my father threw it into the wind and it vanished in the desert."

They clung to each other.

"You got away, then?" Annie said to him. "You escaped Dr. Wilmott and all the dangers that pursued you? I never knew. I could only guess and hope."

"Oh, Annie, it was just so for me. Did you suffer after we parted? Did I behave wrongly? I have agonized over it," he said. "It was a terrible decision, and so little time in which to make it. But I had to save Katie. You were strong and could survive. Katie was fragile and could not." He kissed her cheeks and lips, her throat and hair.

Even now he cannot overstep the bounds of propriety, thought Annie.

How she loved him!

"I begged Time to let me see you again, Annie," he said, feasting his eyes on her. The torch, still lying on the edge of the hole in the upper room, gave a faint shadowy glow to the room. "I climbed to the top of Khufu's Pyramid to ask it, because the natives say that the ghosts of Time are present in the night." He tightened his embrace.

In his time, a lady was not merely covered with undergarments of lace, silk and satin, but also strapped into corsets, so that the actual form and feel of the lady was unavailable to anybody, including the lady. Surely what his hands told him now of Annie Lockwood was beyond the bounds of propriety. He comforted himself that this was ancient Egypt, however, and for that, she was properly dressed.

"Not only did Time bring us together," said Strat, "but amid such excitement."

"If you call being buried alive excitement," said Annie. "The two of us are supposed to suffocate to death down here. I think there's a famous opera where that actually happens."

"Aida," said Strat. "In days gone by I often attended such musical torture."

They held each other, their tears dampening their close cheeks.

"How did you know how to get down to us?" asked Annie. "I can't stand feeling so confused."

"I found a second shaft in real life," he told her. "Well, 1899 life. Just this morning. Except forty-five hundred years from now, if I remember Khufu's dates correctly. I paced it off exactly, and of course the same markers are here, because this came first. So Time flung me down on the sand, and I regained consciousness, and had the astounding privilege of seeing Pharaoh in a royal procession, and the shocking reality of seeing two human sacrifices, and just as the second sacrifice was lowered in her basket, I recognized her."

Annie buried her face in his throat.

He said, "I'm not sure if you were sent to save me or if I was sent to save you. Had I stayed in my time, I would have been in terrible difficulties."

"Had you stayed in your time," said Annie, "I would have been dead. Was it you the other day in the museum? Did you buy me lunch?"

He was puzzled. "Lunch?" he said confusedly. "What museum?"

"I forgot. It hasn't happened yet. But I'm sure it's you."

She had the oddest sense of wanting to get back and check on him in the museum. First, we'd better get out of our tomb, she thought, sitting up abruptly.

"Tell me how it worked for you," he said, sitting up with her. He slid his hand under the mass of her silky hair and rubbed her spine.

"Your photographs," said Annie. "You had told me you were going to Egypt to be an archaeologist, do you remember? I never found out a single thing about what happened to you. You vanished. But I happened to pick up the Sunday *New York Times,* which my parents don't often buy and I almost never touch. And I felt you through the print. You were in a museum article. So I went to the museum to find you. I have only four days, which is the first problem. You see, my parents just got married, Strat. It was a lovely ceremony, and they're having a very short honeymoon so I thought we could have a very short reunion or ask Time to stretch it or bring you back with me or stay here with you."

Strat decided not to ask why her parents had just gotten married. It seemed late, what with their daughter in her teens. But who was he, whose father was on wife number four, to quibble about the marriages of parents? "The ceremony I just watched was also lovely," he teased. "You made a beautiful sacrifice."

"Thank you," said Annie. "I threw Pharaoh's gold on the floor over there. I think, but I'm not sure, that Renifer's actual father and her actual boyfriend handed her over to Pharaoh to be sacrificed. Those two men enjoyed every minute of shoving Renifer underground."

"I cannot accept such a statement," said Strat. "Her own father? Her own beloved? I expect they were so fearful of Pharaoh that they could not move to save their darling girl."

"Since when have you thought highly of fathers?" Annie demanded. "Your own father did the same thing to you. Or have you already forgotten being thrown down the shaft, so to speak, into the asylum?"

Strat did not like to think that the world—now, then or ever—had fathers who behaved that way. He liked to think of his own father as an unpleasant exception. He liked to think that when he became a father, he would be an excellent one. Under the circumstances, both 1899 and now, however, he did not actually expect to reach adulthood and have the privilege of being a father.

"Tell me everything," said Annie. "Tell me about your life, and Devonny, and Harriett and Katie and what happened and where everybody is and all that."

"First let's get out of here," said Strat. He got up off Queen Hetepheres' bed and paced the tiny room. He smiled at Renifer, who was backed against the wall, holding her hand up to keep him away. "Don't be afraid," he said to her. "I came to save you both."

Renifer just held both hands up like traffic signals.

"I don't know how much time we have, Annie," said Strat, suddenly worried. "Dawn will come soon. We have to get up out of here, but once we are out on the sand, we'll be very visible. The soldiers won't take kindly to finding Pharaoh's sacrifices running around laughing."

"How hard will it be to get out?" asked Annie, staring up at the hole.

"Easy. I had to remove some stones, which took me a while, but once the shaft was revealed, there's a ladder. We just go up and we're fifty feet or so from Hetepheres' chapel. I'll go first, and then reach down and help each of you up."

Standing tiptoe on the bed frame, Strat was able to get his fingers around the stone rim of the ceiling hole. With the wonderful upper arm strength of boys, he hauled himself upward.

"I couldn't do that in a thousand years," said Annie.

"You don't need to," said Strat. "Hand Renifer up first."

But Renifer would not go.

RENIFER

Renifer's heart was still beating, which she thought amazing, considering what she had been through.

The thing was male, she could tell from the voice and shape of it.

It was foreign, she could tell from the smell and clothing of it.

It was not a *ka,* because a ghost could pass through stone but this creature had needed an opening, as humans did.

Renifer had pretended that it would be Pankh, coming to prove his love. For a space of time so brief the words had hardly formed in her mind, she even asked Sekhmet to dismiss her prayer for revenge. But she had been right the first time. Pankh's love was gold, and he would come for that.

The rescuer, on the other hand, had not glanced at the treasure on the floor. It meant nothing to him. He cared about the girl. And the girl, whom Renifer had thought chained by the gold, had forgotten it also, swept away by the presence of the boy. Even now, begging, they were not thinking of gold, but of her.

They wanted to save her.

I cannot go, she said, without words, because neither of them could understand Egyptian, and because she did not think they could understand in any language. The Living God had decreed that she stay here and die. Yes, this was terror. She had felt great terror when she had stood above, and grasped what Pharaoh wanted of her. She felt greater terror in the hours of knowledge below the earth.

But now, Renifer could make the choice herself. Live or die?

Her family had betrayed Pharaoh in all ways. She, Renifer, could atone. She could die for Hetepheres.

She climbed on top of the sarcophagus, and lay down on her back, carefully adjusting her gown and folding her arms over her chest as neatly as if she had been laid out by the priests. She stared silently upward at the unpainted ceiling.

The girl of ivory begged and plucked at her and the boy called from his hole in the ceiling. Arguments in a foreign language were presented. Tears were shed. For a while, it even seemed that the boy might come back down and they would try to force Renifer into the fresh air.

How many human sacrifices had to fight for the privilege of staying dead?

"Go," said Renifer irritably. "Go!" She flicked her fingers at the girl as one might snap at a bug and hoped the girl would understand. Of course she did not, being a foreigner, and instead stamped her foot like Renifer's little sister having a tantrum.

Renifer returned her gaze to the ceiling. She was faintly amused by what was happening. Hetepheres' reburial had been arranged so speedily that none of the priests and courtiers on the barge and none of the soldiers at the shaft had paused to remember that an unused tomb probably had more than one open shaft. In a week or a year, some dedicated priest of Pharaoh would remember.

But would he do anything?

Renifer doubted it. Innocent men had already died because of Hetepheres' tomb. Why be numbered among them?

A dedicated priest might even decide to check that second shaft and fill it in himself, to be sure the queen's tomb could not be robbed yet again. But Renifer had recognized Pharaoh's priest last night. It was the man who had held his ostrich fan in front of his face, fleeing the unfortunate event of Pen-Meru caught in the act of robbing Hetepheres' tomb. No doubt that priest was very dedicated. To gold.

Which meant there had been at least three tomb robbers present at the reburial of Hetepheres: the priest, her father, her beloved. Poor Pharaoh, she thought. You do not know with whom You consort.

"Renifer!" said the girl of ivory fiercely, trying to drag her right off the sarcophagus.

Renifer made a universal sign: finger slicing her throat. Quit!

Muttering, the girl expended considerable effort replacing the queen's sedan chair on top of the mattress.

At first Renifer thought the girl was going to do a little tomb robbing after all, but then she understood the girl wanted to be sure that Renifer could change her mind. If Renifer stood on top of that sedan chair, she might be close enough to the ceiling to pull herself through.

Coming back to the sarcophagus, the girl kissed her own fingertips and placed those fingertips on Renifer's forehead, drawing on her skin a sign Renifer did not recognize. A blessing, perhaps, or a salute. Renifer would never know. She did not let herself meet the girl's eyes. In a moment of weakness, she might surrender, cry out and go with them.

Pankh was weak. She, Renifer, would be strong.

She held her breath and all her muscle and bone against weakness and while she lay rigid and unyielding, the boy lifted his girl into the upper chamber. A treasure room empty, Renifer supposed, of anything except air.

Although, in its way, air was a treasure.

The boy did not slide the stone over the ceiling opening. She would lie here knowing she could leave, and that was difficult knowledge to possess. The flow of fresh air meant that she could not die easily in gathering sleep, and would die in the dreadful pain of thirst. But they were foreigners, and did not understand these things, and she had no means to explain.

She could tell by the sounds of their feet that a ladder remained in place inside the shaft; that he went first and she second up the shaft and from thence to freedom and life.

And then they were gone.

Renifer's tears puddled on the cold stone at her back. Then she prayed, composing a song for her own soul. How glorious and magnified was her voice in the stone chamber. She imagined her soprano rising like smoke, ascending to heaven, and knew that Pharaoh would be pleased.

She decided to die wearing Pharaoh's gold, so that when she passed into the next world, she could present that gold to Hetepheres and be acquitted of the evil deeds of her family.

She dressed slowly, finishing just as the torch the boy had left by the ceiling hole went out.

The weight of the gold was great. She feared falling over, getting disoriented in the dark or hurting herself. She wanted to die in dignity. So, keeping a grip on the edge of the sarcophagus to steady herself, Renifer knelt to pray once more.

She asked for one thing only.

That Hetepheres' tomb should not be robbed twice.

PANKH

Pankh pressed his back against a small obelisk, faced directly west and counted paces. He need only kick aside a few rocks, breaking the plaster that held them together, and shift a few large flat stones. According to the plans, these were not slabs requiring a team of men or ropes.

The torches on the causeway had been doused by the priests themselves to provide secrecy for the reburial of Hetepheres. Pankh felt his way through the gloom and shadows toward the entrance to the second shaft. He had almost finished the pace count when he saw on the ground a darker dark. A hole.

Somebody else had gotten to the second shaft before him. His hand flew to the hilt of his dagger. *That gold is mine,* he thought. *I will kill them!*

He was already making plans: better, perhaps, to shove the stones back over the hole, entrapping the robbers, and wait a few weeks, when both tomb robbers *and* girls would have died! Or perhaps he should just join the ongoing robbery. At least he would get some of the gold.

Although Pankh did not share well, and still meant to have it all.

But a hand stopped him.

Pankh whirled, ready to slash, and found himself facing two puzzled tomb police. If they were part of the robbery, they would have knifed him from behind. So they were simply doing their jobs, wondering who was wandering around in the dark, and why.

Luckily, he was wearing his best clothing and his finest jewelry. His uniform would give him some control. "Good evening," he said, smiling, and guiding them away from the half-visible hole. "What good luck that you have appeared," he told them. "Perhaps you would spend a moment or two to help me."

He managed to draw them around the corner of an old mastaba, with flat roof and sloping sides. To face him, the police would have their backs to the shaft opening. "I dropped an amulet of Sekhmet during Pharaoh's night ceremony, the one finished only an hour or two ago, in which I was honored to participate. I hoped to see my amulet still lying here."

Pankh sneered at amulets and religious symbols. When men or women hung such things about their necks, or built little shrines in their gardens, or more comical still, erected temples, Pankh laughed. Tomb robbers were atheists and knew what the common run of people did not. Nothing mattered except possessions.

"Why don't we wait for the sun to rise," said one policeman, "so we can see better?"

In the east, the sand had brightened. In a moment,

dawn would explode over the desert. Surely Pankh was not too late to get the gold! "Let's go over to the causeway," he suggested, herding them. "I'm sure my precious amulet is lying on the stones."

"Then why were you coming from the desert?" asked one policeman pleasantly.

"The Lord of the Two Lands required a sacrifice to the jackals and to Anubis, jackal god of the dead, because of the urgency of Pharaoh's prayers and the need for celestial guidance."

The guards were unconvinced. He did manage to jostle them onto the causeway, however.

"Here it is!" exclaimed the other policeman, astonished. "Such a tiny ornament on such a vast surface! You are very lucky, sir." He stooped to retrieve an amulet which he first drew over his lips to obtain its blessing and then handed to Pankh.

It was a miniature Sekhmet, so perfectly carved it seemed the handwork of a god, not of man. Pankh had never owned such a thing, much less dropped it. Its slender chain was woven of tiny gold plackets, but the Sekhmet herself was made of a material he did not at first recognize.

He rubbed the tiny goddess between his thumb and forefinger. It was ivory.

From his palm, the little Sekhmet snarled at him. Under his heavy wig, Pankh's shaved scalp quivered.

Then he remembered he had no patience with religious superstition, and he put the necklace on. "I owe you," he said to the policeman. "I will see that you are well paid for your prompt assistance."

The necklace was surprisingly chilly against his skin. Nor did the heat of his body warm the slender chain. Although the chain was long and did not press up against his throat, he felt strangled by it, and he rubbed his windpipe, straining for air.

"Look there," said the first guard softly. "What are those two doing?"

In the growing light, Pankh made out two people a hundred yards away, admiring the Pyramid. The man, dressed in the ludicrous trousers of northerners, vaulted onto the stone wall that enclosed the Pyramid, built to keep just such people from touching its sacred sides. Little boys had proved particularly annoying in this regard, scrambling over the wall and then with their bare toes trying to find cracks between the Pyramid slabs, so they could crawl upward. They fell and broke bones and their mothers sobbed.

"Tourists even at this hour," said the second guard, shaking his head. "Amazing. And behaving badly, of course, since they're foreigners."

The foreigner stretched out his hand, that he might help his woman up onto the wall with him, and as she was drawing onto her toes, Pankh saw her white gown and long black hair, and recognized the girl of ivory.

Impossible.

But true. This foreigner had opened the second shaft. How could a foreigner have known the location? Who could the man be? Some crafty slave, perhaps, or escaped criminal. And what of Renifer? Where was she?

And who had the gold?

For had the girl of ivory still been clothed in gold, he would easily see it from here.

Giving their names to Pankh, so they could be rewarded, the policemen ambled off to deal with the tourists. Pankh had no more time to waste. Slipping around the mastaba, he strode up to the hole. Even in the few minutes that had gone by, there was enough light to see quite well. He descended the long ladder in two steps, crossed the empty treasure room and knelt beside the open trapdoor.

"I will have my gold!" he whispered. "I care for nothing but the gold!"

Pankh stroked the little Sekhmet as if beseeching her.

He forgot that there was one other thing he cared about.

Life.

STRAT AND ANNIE

The first rays of dawn glinted off Annie's dark hair. Her long white pleated gown lifted gently in the breeze. She seemed ancient and silvery. She could have been a goddess.

"I am starving to death," said Annie dramatically.

He looked at her with great affection. He had saved her from starving to death. Whatever else he had done wrong in his life—and Strat felt assaulted by all he had done wrong in his life—at least he had rescued Annie.

He said, "No one will ever excavate it, because archaeologists care only for kings, but I know where the workmen's village is from here. It takes hundreds of men to do all the stonework, the painting, the road building, the engineering, the cooking. Would a gold sandal be a fair exchange for a jug of water, a loaf of bread and a seat in the shade?"

Annie giggled. "Let's hold out for two jugs of water. Although I would really like an ice cream sundae with chocolate sauce."

He loved her instant recovery. She was not having the vapors, or in need of a rest cure, or weeping on his shoulder, the way girls would in his day. She was bouncing and eager for whatever came next.

He felt a ripping in his soul, as of tendons wrenched from bones because of a fall in a ball game.

What *would* come next?

He sat above her on the wall, Annie standing between his knees staring up at him, thinking his the most beautiful face she had ever seen. Of my precious four days, she thought, more than two are gone. Time is so stingy. "How I missed you," she said, "all these months. But you did the right thing when you saved Katie, Strat, and I have held your noble act in my heart as an example of how to live."

Annie imagined saying those words in 1999 to a boy in her high school. The situation would not come up, though, because boys in her class liked to be examples of how *not* to live. Noble conduct was not a goal in her century.

"Here comes trouble," said Strat softly.

Guards were walking toward them, motioning at Strat to get down. But there was nothing scary about them. They were not armed and dangerous like her tomb escorts. They were just nice guys keeping people off tourist attractions. Annie smiled and waved.

Strat hopped down onto the pavement. "I don't think they know you," he murmured. "They probably weren't part of the sacrifice ritual. They've lost interest now that I'm off their wall. Let's find the workmen's village and buy some food."

Already the cool breezes were gone and the air parched. Huge numbers of people had arrived to take advantage of the short time before the blistering heat began.

Crews were getting to work on funerary chapels and memorial temples. Teams were erecting statues and walling in family cemeteries. Flowers were being delivered, and fine spices and incense being burned. Daughters were visiting their dead mothers and sons paying respect to their ancestors.

Where they had been alone only minutes ago, Annie and Strat were among hundreds now.

"I can hear a choir rehearsing somewhere," she said. "This is so much more fun with you here. I really feel part of ancient Egypt. Of course, I almost *was* part of ancient Egypt. The dead part."

"We are in the center of the City of the Dead," he agreed.

"Thank you," she said, "for keeping me in the city of the living instead," and she began to cry. "Oh, Strat," she whispered, "what should we do about Renifer? She didn't choose the city of the living. Should Renifer have to obey our choice, and not be allowed her choice? Is she still a sacrifice or has she become a suicide?"

Strat looked around him. In the west, where the sands deepened into hills, just before the hills soared into cliffs hundreds of feet high, somewhere tucked among those hills was the workers' village.

"I know," said Annie. "At some point in the day when

nobody's around, we'll go back down and offer her a second chance. I know I'd take it. I'd be sick of dying by then."

Strat took a deep breath. "I think it would be better if we went right now and closed the shaft."

"Strat! You can't mean it!" How had she ever thought that Strat was noble of heart and generous in deed? "That's horrible. Absolutely not! Leaving her there was bad enough. We're not going to be the ones who seal her in!"

"People are going to walk by and find that open hole. They'll explore. They'll find Renifer. She won't be dead because it takes days to starve. Then what? They drag her out? They hand her back to Pharaoh? Will she suffer an even more terrible fate because she circumvented Pharaoh's plan?"

"What could be more terrible than being buried alive?" Annie demanded.

Strat pointed toward the edge of the desert. A hundred yards away, the mutilated corpses of dead men stuck up into the air on tall sharp spikes. Annie had seen that happen; she just hadn't been willing to remember. There was, after all, something worse than running out of air.

"If we close up the shaft, we'll actually be keeping Renifer safe," said Strat. "When it's dark tonight, and everyone else is gone, we pull away the stone and offer her a second chance."

Annie's heartbeat returned to normal. He was a gentleman after all; he had saved Katie; he would save Renifer. It was good.

"Too late," said Strat sadly. "Look. The shaft is already surrounded."

"I can't see," whispered Annie, starting to cry. "What's happening?"

"I don't dare get closer," said Strat. "Quick, up that hill. We can see from there."

They staggered across the sand, which was first hard and flat and then sinking and ankle-breaking, scrabbled up a ragged hillside of sand and climbed rocks that collapsed under their weight. Some places were so steep they were forced to crawl.

"Be careful at the edges," said Strat. "The wind chews on the undersides of these hills, leaving crags supported by nothing."

The crest of the hill was wild and wonderful. Fingers of rock poked out into thin air. The peak of the Pyramid was half a mile away, but eye level. The necropolis stretched on and on. Thousands of distant tomb structures glittered like sugar cubes in the sun.

And where Renifer's open shaft might be, Annie had no idea.

"Let your eye travel down the causeway," said Strat, "and look for a dozen workers with baskets."

"Baskets?" said Annie blankly.

"Rock and sand," said Strat quietly. "That's how they filled in your shaft. Basket after basket. Rock after rock."

And there it was, a team lifting one basket after another from a series of donkey-drawn carts. Somebody somewhere had known about the second shaft.

Strat and Annie clung to each other. They could not, mercifully, hear the sound of the rocks as they dropped down.

But Renifer would.

Annie prayed to her own God that Renifer would not be scared. That she remained proud of her choice. That the end would come quickly for her.

Strat held her until she had stopped weeping.

The sun scorched the desert floor on four sides. He knew that the workmen's village was not far below, but the twists and turns of the jagged hill hid it entirely. Alone, they perched on a rock ledge.

"You're wearing only one sandal," said Strat.

"The other one fell off in the tomb," said Annie. "It's there with Renifer, I guess. I don't know how I managed to keep this one."

Strat took it in his hand. I also held this sandal in another life. Or stole it, depending on who tells the story. He remembered what he had to go back to.

When he set the sandal down, Annie's white dress blew over it, hiding it.

Beyond them, spread out like a painting in five stripes, lay Egypt. Two outside stripes of yellow desert. Narrow green stripes of farmland inside those. The placid brown ribbon of the Nile in the middle. "The river is a sort of vertical oasis, isn't it?" said Annie.

"You are my oasis," said Strat.

He was not sure just how much time he spent telling her that and showing her that. Long enough to know he wanted it to last forever, but long enough to know that time was passing. The heat of noon would be too much on this exposed spot. They must get out of the sun or die under it.

He pulled her even closer, to tell her what he thought they should do next, and Annie screamed.

PANKH

Pankh was amused.

The foreigners were in each other's arms, oblivious to the world, cooing. He had completely surprised them.

He knew how impressive he looked. Of course, foreigners were always deeply impressed by Egyptians. His white kilt was starched and finely pleated, unlike their sweat-stained garb. His wig was heavy and flawlessly braided, unlike the messy sandy locks of the foreigners. But most important, his dagger was heavy and strong in his hand.

The girl, pleasingly, had screamed.

She would scream more before he was done.

Hetepheres' tomb had been empty. He had spat down the trapdoor, trying to spit on the queen's sarcophagus, but missed.

These were the possibilities: The foreign male had carried the gold in some basket or bundle that Pankh had not seen; or the man had buried it to retrieve later; or somebody else had the gold.

Pen-Meru? Could he have moved so swiftly?

But it was unlikely that Pen-Meru would trust a foreign male. And although Pankh could possibly imagine Pen-Meru saving Renifer, why would anybody save the girl of ivory?

Pankh had climbed out of the tomb, retreated behind the mastaba, dusted himself off and straightened his wig. He was preparing a lie should he encounter the same tomb police when Pharaoh's crew arrived to fill in the shaft.

So Pharaoh had known of the second shaft; known its precise location and that it was empty. But his men had certainly not known that the stone would be moved away and the shaft gaping open, down to where the living sacrifice probably still lived. Pankh laughed grimly to himself as they swore oaths not to tell Pharaoh. His retreat was covered by the racket of rocks they threw down as quickly as they could, to keep the spirit of the sacrifice from reaching out toward their bare feet and cursing their lives.

And there, beyond, were the two foreigners, on the edge of the desert, climbing the cliff. Nobody went toward the desert, where there was no water, no shelter and no hope. People went toward the Nile. Had there been time already to bury the gold up on that cliff? Were they carrying it with them? Or did they expect to meet others with the gold at that spot?

Pankh would get the gold before he threw them off the cliff. No need to worry about bodies. Tomb police didn't bother with this piece of sand. Jackals did.

But now, standing before them, Pankh felt the rage of

frustration working through his chest. They had no gold with them. But they certainly knew where it was; the girl had removed it and placed it somewhere. "Gold," said Pankh clearly. He drew bracelets around his arms and a necklace around his throat and raised his eyebrows.

The foreign boy and girl were puzzled.

"Gold!" he shouted, hating them for not understanding a civilized language. "Where is the gold?"

Their eyes flew open and their jaws dropped. They stared as if seeing somebody rise from the dead.

"The gold," he spat. "Where is the gold?"

"I have the gold," said Renifer, behind him.

Pankh whirled.

Renifer stood on the very edge of the cliff. She was so weighted down with that beautiful gold he did not know how she could possibly have scrambled up here. Behind her was nothing but air.

Pankh recovered quickly. "How beautiful you are, my beloved," he whispered. "How wonderful that you survived Pharaoh's evil trick. How glad I am to see you in the land of the living."

Renifer said nothing. He could not see her breathe or blink. She did not look as if she belonged to the land of the living. Her face was as expressionless as if she had died.

Pankh had his back to the foreign man. He was vulnerable. And yet, he felt in some way that the danger came from Renifer herself. "Come, my beloved. You will hide in my house, lest Pharaoh learn that you survived. But what pleasure we will have in being together, you and I."

Renifer said nothing.

Pankh took a few steps away, hoping Renifer would step toward him. The rims of this kind of cliff frequently caved in, and her weight was putting her in danger. Although of course he could simply retrieve the gold from her corpse. "Renifer, it wasn't my fault. I didn't intend for Pharaoh to sacrifice you. Who could have dreamed that such an idea would enter the mind of a civilized Egyptian? Come to me, my beloved."

Renifer said nothing.

She had not an inch between herself and falling. He extended his hand. But she seemed not to see it. "Your father and I were forced to agree with Pharaoh. My beloved, let us leave these strangers to their own devices. Let us go home and rejoice that you live."

She was still and unearthly in her gold. How *had* she gotten up the steep and difficult slope? Had she been lifted? By what power?

The thin chain of the amulet of Sekhmet seemed to cut his neck.

By now some laborer or priest or guard would have noticed this strange scene playing out on the distant hill. Somebody would investigate. Pankh could not permit Renifer to delay any longer. They would be out of time. "Renifer, come let your beloved Pankh embrace you."

Renifer removed one arm piece. Its gold was over an inch thick. He could not take his eyes off it. Underhanded, she threw the bracelet. The heavy circle sailed in a great arc out beyond the cliff and then vanished in a long curving silent fall.

The sand below was soft. The heavy gold would dig its own hole, the sand would close over it and Pankh would never find it. "No, no, my beloved!" protested Pankh. "You and I will need that gold in our marriage. Think what it will cost to protect you for all time from the wrath of Pharaoh."

Renifer threw a second bracelet into the air.

"Beloved," he said coaxingly, inching toward her.

She almost smiled. She almost softened. She was almost his. When she held out her arms, Pankh acted swiftly, grabbing for those gold-laden wrists, but Renifer leaned back over the cliff edge, planning to fall, still willing to die for Pharaoh.

Pankh's velocity was great. He could not stop himself. Together they would hurtle over the cliff and hundreds of feet down to their deaths. He tried to brace himself against her; let her fall while he saved himself.

But the arm of the foreign male, in its loathsome jacket of heavy cloth, pulled Renifer to safety while Pankh spun out into the air and was lost.

The amulet flew up in Pankh's face, and the last thing he saw before death was the image of Sekhmet, goddess of revenge.

Renifer

Renifer stood within the embrace of the foreign male.

She did not need to follow their language to know what they were asking. Fascinated, amazed, they were crying—how did you get here? how did you know? are you all right? we're so glad to see you!

Had the gods sent these strangers to save Renifer—or had she been sent to save them? "I was kneeling beside the sarcophagus while I prayed," she explained, as if they had been given Egyptian along with life. "Pankh looked into the tomb. He did not see me. He had eyes only for gold and thought the tomb empty. He swore, yet again defiling Hetepheres. He damned her for not making her gold available to him. He spat, promising to kill you, O girl of ivory."

The girl had been entrusted to Renifer's care. Handed to Renifer, as it were, in the midst of Pharaoh's papyrus swamp. Renifer could not let Pankh kill the girl of ivory. She had almost literally been on Pankh's heels as he ascended the ladder out of Hetepheres' tomb, too busy muttering to himself and uttering threats to look back. When Pankh hid behind a mastaba, she walked behind a chapel, and then Pharaoh's crew arrived.

For a few moments, she stared at them, as they filled in forever the shaft out of which she had just escaped. She heard their oaths to say nothing to Pharaoh and understood their terror.

Heavy lay the gold on her body. She followed Pankh as he chased the girl of ivory and the foreign male. There was a perfectly fine path up the cliff, but the foreigners and Pankh hadn't seen it, so they struggled up the worst and most crumbling side. Renifer walked slowly along the path. The workers in the village saw her—a goddess, as it were, clothed in gold, going back to her home in the cliffs, and they fell on their faces in the sand and let her pass.

Beyond the Pyramids, the Nile sparkled under the sun. Renifer could see the city of Memphis, her beloved and beautiful home. She could see, from here, the entire world.

And many of its inhabitants, running in her direction.

Pankh had not cried out, but witnesses had. Tourists and guides, vendors of carved wooden hippos or hot spicy sausages—all had shouted to the tomb police that somebody had fallen. A crowd was gathering at the foot of the cliff, exclaiming over Pankh's body. He was an officer of Pharaoh, wearing his uniform. There was no hope of explaining these extraordinary events.

Foreigners would be held responsible.

Nobody would believe any version of Pankh's death except the worst: that he had been pushed to his death by the foreign male. Renifer could see all too clearly what was going to happen now. The boy, who had come to save the girl of ivory and who had just now saved Renifer herself, would be accused of murder, and pay the ultimate price.

The crowd began pointing and shouting, and Renifer knew what they were shouting for. The foreign male.

The girl of ivory turned even more pale, if that were possible, and she and the boy exchanged frightened looks. They had reason to be frightened.

"Go into the desert," said Renifer, pointing at the massive hills in the west. The Nile was truly cupped in a valley, and the sides of the cup were high and brutal. No civilized person went west of the Nile.

"Sekhmet saved me," she said quietly, "and you who protected me will be given protection. Be not afraid. I will prevent the mob from reaching you."

Even now, the boy worried more about Renifer than himself. He wanted her to come too.

She shook her head. "Go, and go swiftly," she said, giving him a gentle push in the right direction.

Coming out of the west, borne on a high wind, was a cloud of sand. It stood up vertically, like an approaching god. The boy and girl walked toward it, while the girl of ivory called farewell, waving, and repeating her accented version of Renifer's name.

How powerful were the gods. Sekhmet had answered every one of Renifer's prayers: Hetepheres' tomb would not be robbed twice, the queen was avenged and Pankh had suffered.

The terror and joy of dying for Pharaoh disappeared. Renifer was astonished and glad to be alive.

She followed the path back down, arriving at the bottom exactly when the soldiers did. They froze at the sight of her.

Renifer extended her long slender arms and stood under the blazing sun, all gold and white, all shimmer and ghost. She sang the chants of the dead, her soprano rising and shivering, curling around the tops of temples as she walked. She flung her head back and addressed the sky and the hidden stars. She called upon Hetepheres to be with her, and Sekhmet to avenge her. She called upon jackals and queens, upon crocodiles and princesses.

Long before she finished her song, the tourists had scurried back to the temples and the guards had fled to the safety of their headquarters. Tomb robbers they would fight. Ghosts and *ka*s would be left to their own devices.

Renifer lowered her arms. They trembled from the weight of the gold.

The tall thin windstorm spread and deepened, until it sailed like a ship over the desert. It flung sand over the half-carved Sphinx, hiding an entire paw. It flung sand over tourists too foolish to shelter in a mausoleum. It smothered the pots of flowers and put out the fires of incense.

Renifer ignored the sand. It would wrap her forever or let her go. She walked on, accepting the will of her gods.

Strat

Strat had known they would not die in the tomb of Hetepheres, because when it was uncovered in 1899, it contained no bones. But out here, in the vicious true desert, the one that reached all the way to the Atlantic Ocean, here they could die. No one would know, either. Not in Khufu's time, not in Strat's and not in Annie's.

The footing was terrible.

From a great distance, he had been able to make out tiny paths twisting up those towering cliffs, probably followed by wild goats and greedy robbers. Up close, there were a hundred possible ledges or routes, and no way to tell which actually went somewhere. But in his heart, Strat knew that nothing out here went somewhere. They were headed toward nothing. No town, no oasis, no road, no water.

The sandstorm was no longer a single column. It now covered an entire width of desert. Like a blustery sheet of sand or a hurricane all in a row, its hope was to fill lungs, blind eyes, deafen ears, bury bones.

They came to a bluff, and had to scramble up it, but

their feet sank. They circled it, tripping and stumbling on rocks and rubble. They plunged once more into sand; sand; sand. The wind hurled sand into Annie's eyes, and she cried out, and clung to Strat, wiping at her eyes with her free hand. "It will kill us," she shouted. "We have to go back!"

But they had nothing to go back to. When Strat turned, even the Pyramid of Pharaoh had been obliterated. "Tuck your face beneath my shirt, Annie," he ordered her, "and we will grip each other tightly and hope not to be torn apart by the strength of the wind."

They would be buried where they stood. For a moment he bowed his head over Annie's grit-filled black hair and accepted his defeat. But only for a moment. "No!" he shouted. "I will not be beaten again!"

Strat recognized this shred of his father in him: the refusal to admit defeat. Well, then he had one good thing from Hiram Stratton, Sr., and he would take it.

"Annie," he commanded, "step through Time."

The pain in his heart was so fierce he could not tell whether it was dying of sorrow or of sand. "You go first, Annie. I cannot live a second time in fear that I abandoned you or that you suffered without me. Go. Quickly."

But just as Renifer had refused to leave her tomb, so Annie refused to leave hers. "No, Strat. I love you. Now when Time has finally brought us together, you think I'm leaving? Forget it! Whatever happens, it will happen to both of us."

"Annie, all that can happen to us is death. We have no water, we have no transportation, you don't even have shoes. We cannot live here, only die here. We must cross through Time again."

"But Time won't let us go together and I want to be together. When this storm ends, we'll steal a camel," said Annie. "We'll be our own little wagon train to Morocco. Then we'll build a boat and row across the Atlantic to New York. Although there won't be much around in Manhattan, forty-five hundred years ago." She giggled.

"Stop playing games," said Strat, although this was why he adored her. She could always laugh. Perhaps it was her century; a time when girls seemed to have so much more than the girls in his time. "Anyway, there are no camels in ancient Egypt. If you want to steal a camel, you have to come to 1899 with me."

He expected to hear one of her peculiar words, from the vocabulary of her amazing decade: Okay or Deal.

But Annie's hair swirled across his face in a black cloud, her eyes opened wide, and screaming, she filtered away from him. It was as quick as the death of Pankh. She was in his arms and then his arms were empty.

Strat tried to follow her, stumbling through the sand, falling over rocks, tumbling off the cliff they had so desperately climbed. He felt himself surrounded by all the troops of Pharaoh, reaching and grasping, and then in the sand, he was alone again, retching and gasping. He eluded them, neither dying nor living, just staggering on, calling her name.

Annie.

And eventually, he was defeated. Sand filled his shirt and hair, his shoes and the hem of his trousers. His determination not to be beaten had been beaten.

Many things were stronger than one man's heart.

VII

The Sands of Time

Renifer

She walked along the edge of the straight-sided canal, wakened a sleeping sailor and ordered him to take her to Memphis. The sandstorm tore his sails and he had to row. Memphis was closed up tight, every shutter and door sealed against the storm. She walked alone through her city.

Sand piled up against the mud-brick walls that enclosed every garden and home. Sand ripped the leaves from the sycamores and tore down the nests of birds. When she reached her own door, she knocked for a long time before the doorkeeper let her in.

Her father, Pen-Meru, was standing in the garden, mournfully surveying the damage from the sandstorm.

Up on the roof, no sand had fallen. On its pedestal still stood the gold statue of Sekhmet. "Greetings, Father, from the *ka* of Hetepheres," said Renifer.

He whirled.

He saw her, goddess and *ka,* cloaked in gold. He who had buried her fell to his knees.

She found it quite pleasing to stand above him. "The

queen sent me home. The queen requires you, Father, to treat me as *her* daughter, instead of your own."

Pen-Meru beat his forehead against the dirt and she let this go on for some time. "Enough. The queen requires you to cease stealing. She has, after all, an empty tomb in which to store your living body, should you disobey."

"I obey," whispered Pen-Meru.

Renifer walked into the women's rooms. She would worry about Pharaoh another day. Today she would see her mother, take a hot bath, throw the dreadful gold into a pile by the bed. And maybe she would spend it one day, and maybe she would not. And maybe she would marry one day, and maybe not.

She would not worry. The gods held her in the palm of their hands.

STRAT

He was buried only up to his ankles, and he shook that sand away, and was aware of raw skin, burning eyes and the terrific heat that rose up to slap him now that the wind had passed. Beyond him stood three Pyramids. One Sphinx. A dozen tents.

Eternity, however desirable, was not here.

Strat was a prisoner of Time. His own.

There was no sign of Annie Lockwood. Instead, he was facing the same group he had left, thousands of years, or only an hour, ago. There stood the girl reporter, his father's hireling, Miss Matthews. How tall she was, her straight spine so unusual. Most females had terrible posture, being desperate to stand lower than their men. The only other girl he knew who was proud of her backbone was Annie herself.

I will never wed, thought Strat. I will never say vows of perpetual love. I will never look for a girl to equal Annie. For there is none.

Dr. Lightner said in an odd voice, "Strat. How can you be holding that gold sandal?"

Strat brushed sand from his eyebrows and hair and

tried to focus on the world in which he was about to be beaten once more. I've just convicted myself, he thought ruefully, staring down at the gold in his hand. I would rather have her lock of hair. This gold sandal is not Annie. And if I learned one thing in the sands of Time, it is that gold has no value. Only decency toward others is to be valued.

"I myself opened the tomb," said Dr. Lightner. "There was but one sandal, Strat, and I hold that in my hand. Where did you find that other one?"

Strat was aware of his father's bulk on his left. The shifting confused figures of the other members of the dig on his right. The flapping of tents and the whisk of brooms, the smack of shovels. There had been a sandstorm. The crew was digging them out.

How could I have let go of Annie, he thought, sunk in misery, and kept my grip on a worthless piece of metal? "It was lying in the rubble," said Strat finally, "up in the hills."

Water was brought, and Strat drank gratefully. Sweet cool water. Now that was treasure.

People spoke of the damage from the sandstorm and of its wondrous works, flinging up from its hidden depths the very partner of the sandal Dr. Lightner had found in a tomb. Strat could not quite hear. The winds of Time spun through his ears and thoughts and made him deaf.

He became aware that his father was speaking, almost courteously. His father seemed to be apologizing. Strat stared at his parent.

"I have judged you wrongly," said Hiram Stratton, Sr. "You are not a thief."

Around them, in this necropolis, more generations of fathers and sons were on display than anywhere on earth. Here had a thousand generations loved and hated. And what was Strat's destiny? To love or to hate?

"I wish you to come home with me," said Hiram Stratton, Sr., "and be my son."

"You said that once before, Father," said Strat softly. "When you snatched me from school and put me in an insane asylum."

"I was wrong," said his father.

Neither Strat nor any other person had ever heard those words from the mouth of Hiram Stratton, Sr. Strat was touched beyond measure that his father would make such an effort, such an admission. Could it be? he thought. Could my father and I be at peace? Could that be the gift of Time?

Not Annie, but my father? My family? Those I want so badly to love and cannot?

CAMILLA

Camilla Matthews was looking at Hiram Stratton, Sr. She was looking at evil.

Good people, because they are good, want to believe in good. She saw Strat wanting to believe that his father was good. Leaning into the hope that his father cared for him after all. Would welcome him home. Would love him.

How the world was driven by love. This was a desperate love; a son's love.

Hiram Stratton was gloating, revenge within his reach. Camilla understood because she, too, was a friend of revenge. This was a man who excelled at cheating and pretending and convincing all around him to believe his untruths.

Camilla said softly, "Strat, there is a place for you in the British war. Go south. Vanish again. Use a different name. Carry on in a different life." She took his hand and turned him and gave him a slight shove toward the south.

Far away, as if somebody at that very moment were painting her on a gold background, Camilla could almost make out a shadowy girl in a white gown. "Go, Strat," said Camilla softly and insistently. "Go, and I will give you time."

Strat stared into Camilla's eyes. *"You were sent by Time?"*

"Go," she said, and he went.

Hiram Stratton, Sr., opened his huge maw to bellow after his son.

Camilla caught the sleeve of the man's jacket. He weighed far more than she, but she was taller and her touch startled him, and he paused.

"It is not your son, at this moment, who matters, Mr. Stratton."

The great man looked at her with annoyance and shook himself loose.

"I am the daughter of Michael Mateusz, whose death you gladly caused when you burned your factory. I stand here, Hiram Stratton, to accuse you of murder."

STRAT

Strat ran after Annie. "We'll go to the Sudan!" he shouted over the sand. "The British are having a wonderful war! I'll get another camera. We'll sell your gold sandal and have enough to live on for a while. We'll sail up the Nile and catch the army and I'll be a famous photographer! Annie! Wait!"

He struggled on and on in the sand. He could not seem to reach her. He told himself he would catch up. "We'll get married," he said. "It would be unseemly to travel together otherwise. I know that I am but nineteen, Annie, and I have no means of properly supporting you. But I have faith in my wits and my abilities!"

He was exhausted. His voice did not carry the way he wanted it to. He was not getting closer to her. "Be my wife, Annie! We shall find a missionary on the banks of the Nile! Or in South Africa! Or on board some fine ship!"

He and Annie would repeat their vows in the presence of God and this company, whoever the company might be. Strat was not picky. He had known the worst of companies. Annie was always eager for adventure. She was no shrinking violet, like the girls in his time.

But like a violet, Annie shrank. He could see her and he could not.

His voice—or perhaps it was hers—cried out, "It isn't fair!"

He lunged forward, sure he could take her hand. But Annie whirled like some dervish of ancient Egypt, spinning and diminishing and vanishing. No! thought Strat. We're going to honeymoon in a far land and make a home as homes are meant to be: children and hope and joy and love.

He could see the Nile in the distance, a dark and shining ribbon, like the ribbons of Annie's hair, and he ran on and on, sure he could reach them both.

ANNIE

"No!" screamed Annie Lockwood. "It isn't fair! I came all the way through Time for you, Strat, and you—"

Her voice had no sound and her lungs no air. She wanted to beat her fists upon the chest of Time. This isn't fair! You brought me all this way! I deserve Strat!

How many times had Annie or her classmates shouted that? It isn't fair! In nursery school, when other kids got pushed on the swings and your turn never came. In third grade, when other kids got to sit next to their best friend, but you had to sit with a creep. In sixth, when other kids got to go to Disneyland for vacation, but you just grilled hotdogs in the backyard. In ninth grade, when you paid some attention to the world, and found that some citizens were treated a lot better than other citizens.

It isn't fair!

But by then, enough things had not been fair that you could shrug. Life isn't fair, you said to one another. But this is me, thought Annie. I should be an exception.

Time, like all the great powers, like gravity or velocity, continued on. It did not acknowledge what happened inside or outside its span. Annie fell, hair in her face, all sweat and tangles, desperate for a drink of water. The thirst of the desert had taken all moisture out of her. She could not open her eyes in the tremendous glare.

Slowly the rushing shriek of wind and Time left her ears. She tried to listen to the sounds around her, to separate speech from noise, but she was too battered by Time and loss. She tried to see where she was, but the immensity of sun blinded her, and she could make out only stones and mirages of water and palm. She wavered in her heart, as if she were nothing but heat on sand, a figment, impossible to catch up to, impossible to be.

It didn't really matter where or when Annie was, because she was not quite where or when. She was among but had not arrived.

She knew that Egypt did not care. Egypt had seen too much. From Alexander the Great consulting the oracle out in the western sands to the invasion by Napoleon. From Antony romancing Cleopatra on the deck of a Roman ship to the canal at Suez. From the ancient scribe who chiseled a decree of Ptolemy V on a slab of black basalt to Champollion who translated the Rosetta Stone, two thousand years later.

I don't care one little twitch about history! thought Annie. I want Strat. It isn't fair.

She had never felt quite so American or quite so spoiled brat, but she did not want to set an example. At last she stood up and stumbled over stones and steps toward a drinking fountain. The water was cold and refreshing and she drank as if she had not had a sip of water in a thousand years. She felt as if she had not showered in a thousand years either. She tottered back to the seat she had left.

I love you. I want to marry you. We'll have children and joy and hope and love.

Had she said that? Or had Strat? Or were the words a dream?

I love you. I want to marry you. We'll have children and joy and hope and love. Couldn't have been me saying that, thought Annie dully. In my time, the most a girl ever says is, "You wanna go to a movie?" and the most a boy ever says is, "Yeah, okay, if I got nothin' else to do."

"The museum is closing," said a bored voice.

Annie looked up, jarred. For a moment, she almost recognized the man; his ancient dark features; somebody's father, somebody's murderer—he was—no. He was only a guard, sweeping through the museum at closing. And she, Annie, was only a tourist, not even a New Yorker.

She was just a silly girl in silly clothing, wearing silly hopes.

"Oh, Strat," she said, heart bursting with grief.

And across the room—not a room, really, but a vast, glass-ceilinged case; a case large enough to hold an entire ancient temple and an entire reflecting pool and three entire classes of middle school children on a field trip—across that room, somebody heard.

"Annie?" said Strat.

CAMILLA

The unfounded accusations of a girl had no effect.

Hiram Stratton, Sr., merely explained who and what she was, a paid lackey of his own, a piece of chicanery whose ticket he had paid for.

The silly and very rude words of Miss Matthews embarrassed the company. The French were appalled, as always, by the manners of American females. The Germans were amused by so dramatic a woman, built to sing opera, to stand by the Rhine and bellow songs across the water.

Hiram Stratton, Sr., shoved the girl aside and demanded of all of them—servant and scholar, expert and passerby, "Find my son. Now."

The Americans returned to the dig and the tourists got bored. The Egyptians melted away and the British remembered that they were en route to war.

Camilla went to her tent to pack. What would become of her now? Her dream of becoming a great reporter had been silly to start with, but now she had proved herself a liar and a fake, and nobody needed a reporter with those vices. Her tears soaked into the clothing she was folding.

She had not avenged her father.

She had not done anything, really.

She no longer knew what she had been thinking of—telling Strat to run off into the desert. It was true that great heat caused a lady to hallucinate.

Well, she could do one thing: sail to Spain and talk to Katie, who knew right from wrong, action from apathy and hope from sorrow.

"Miss Matthews?" called Dr. Lightner through the flimsy tent walls. "Might we speak?"

She wiped away her tears. Men were undone by ladies' weeping and that was not fair. Oh, the scorn Dr. Lightner would face, having been tricked by a mere girl. "Of course, sir. Please come in. I am packing. I shall not abuse your hospitality another hour."

He entered, stooping of course, because neither he nor she could stand upright in the tents. He pulled up a stool and sat beside her. "You should have told me. I would not have exchanged a syllable with the man had I known that he truly is a beast and a murderer."

"You believe me?"

"Of course I believe you. You have not forgotten the life and death of your father, nor should you. How proud your father would be, Miss Matthews. Such courage! To become a famous reporter and cross half the world!"

She faced him squarely. "But you know that isn't true. I am not Camilla Matthews, age thirty and a seasoned reporter. I am Camilla Mateusz and I am seventeen." She lifted her chin and told him every detail, those he had heard already in front of witnesses and those she had lacked the courage to state.

When she finished the true narrative of her life, he was staring aghast. She awaited his contempt. But no, he was shouting with laughter. Kissing her!

"Forgive me," he said. "I was forward. I deeply apologize. But oh, Miss Matthews! I thought you a queen all along. In my thoughts, I compared you to the queens of ancient Egypt. Partly, that was your fine height and straight spine, your carriage and manner. Although of course," he corrected himself, "the real queens of ancient Egypt, whose mummies I myself have examined, were short and bent. Yet I was correct. You are as royalty. What zest! What courage! Camilla, how proud I am that you trust me with the truth."

She had to laugh. "I have no royal blood, sir. I am the daughter of Polish immigrants. And I have no idea what is to become of me except that I must leave."

"Leave? Do not think of such a thing! Might I have the honor of asking you to become Camilla Lightner?" he said. His words tumbled over one another in his excitement. "We will live in Cairo. I will support your family. I promise, no matter how badly I need donations, to accept none from Hiram Stratton. If necessary, I will become a professor of history in some obscure American college attended by dull and unworthy students. I will do anything to support you properly and not compromise your high standards."

He was a good man.

Was it possible that she could be a good woman?

She thought of Katie, and thought she could hear Katie laughing, saying, of course you can. Goodness is a decision. Make it now.

"Yes," said Camilla.

"What children we will have!" cried Archibald Lightner, kissing her once more. "How brave and strong they will be!"

"And tall," said Camilla.

ANNIE

The person coming toward her . . . was he the boy from lunch? Or could it possibly be Strat from another century? He looked like Strat and he didn't. He wore cargo pants and a navy sweater. Strat in Egypt had worn khaki trousers with frayed hems, red socks inside scratched old boots.

The boy worked his way through a crowd of departing kids, dodging their swinging backpacks. "Here you are!" he said, laughing. "I've been looking and looking for you. I don't know how we got separated. Did you finish the special exhibition without me?"

"Hurry it up, kids," said the guard. "Take a left out that door, please."

They took a left out that door and walked like strangers away from the Egyptian Room. So, Time, what are you up to? Annie wanted to know. Flinging me from century to century? Giving me an hour here and a minute there? And who is this? And why isn't his identity clear?

"I'm taking a train home," she said to the boy. "I'm walking to the station. It's a long way on foot, but a beautiful part of the city." She framed her next sentence the way Strat would have. "Might I have the pleasure of your company?"

"I love how you said that. Now I feel like an usher at a wedding." He put out his arm for her to take. They walked down an aisle strewn with sculpture instead of wedding guests. "This has been the weirdest day," he confided. "I was trying to find you, since I didn't want to lose my new Lockwood on the very day we met, and I guess I dozed off in the Egyptian Room. I dreamed I was on the Nile, sailing upstream with a bunch of British soldiers. We didn't have enough to eat and the tribes were attacking from both banks and what I did have was a camera. On a tripod, isn't that a kick? I lost it in a swamp. There was a crocodile."

Annie was trembling. She swallowed hard and asked the important thing. "Was there a girl with you? Did she catch up? Did you have company?"

But he was frowning at his watch, lifting his wrist and tapping on the watch face. "It isn't working," he said, completely distracted by not knowing the time.

I don't know Time very well, either, thought Annie. "Don't worry about the watch," she told him. "All it is is Time. We're going to have enough."

He smiled at her. "I love how you said that, too. I love people who are sure of things." He took the watch off and squinted at it to see what was wrong.

Then they were outdoors, the wide magnificent museum steps stretching down to the street. "Two at a time," he told her, and in the lamplit night, they vaulted down the wide steps two at a time until they reached the sidewalk below.

It was a beautiful evening. The air was crisp but not cold. New York glittered with early Christmas lights and hundreds of people moved swiftly to their unknown destinations. The whole world seemed eager to get home in time.

The boy balled up his watch and aimed for a trash barrel.

"Don't throw your watch out," cried Annie.

"It's a really cheap one. I shouldn't have expected it to last. You can't get this kind of watch fixed, you can only get another."

"May I keep it for a souvenir?" said Annie quickly, and blushed at his stare. "After all, I don't meet extra Lockwoods all the time."

He laughed and gave her the watch. "I've noticed," he said as they walked, "that just about every sentence we've said has the word time in it." He said, "Are you warm enough without gloves?" He took her hand in his. "Listen," he said, "speaking of time, what are you doing next Saturday?"

Who cares about other times and other worlds when you can dream about next weekend? thought Annie. The best time is always now. "I'm free," said Annie Lockwood to Lockwood Stratton.

She put the broken watch on her own wrist because she had seen right away why the watch didn't work.

It was full of sand.

FACTS

The Metropolitan Museum of Art did have an exhibition in November 1999 presenting the tomb artifacts of Hetepheres, mother of Khufu, who built the Great Pyramid. It was a mysterious tomb. Her sarcophagus, although sealed in antiquity, contained no mummy. The tomb, small as a closet, contained much less than a queen should have. George Reisner, who excavated that tomb in real life in 1925, guessed that it was a hurried reburial, possibly after a botched robbery.

The tomb entrance was found during the Reisner dig when the cameraman's tripod broke some plaster.

That did not happen, however, in 1899, and the cameraman was not Strat.

No Hiram Stratton, Sr., or Hiram Stratton, Jr., existed or made donations to the museum.

BE SURE TO READ ALL FOUR BOOKS IN THE TIME TRAVEL QUARTET!

Imagine moving to a different century and making things worse, not better, on both sides of time.

Meet 15-year-old Annie Lockwood, a romantic living in the wrong century. When she travels back 100 years and lands in 1895—a time when privileged young ladies wear magnificent gowns, attend elegant parties, and are courted by handsome gentlemen—Annie at last finds romance.

But Annie is a trespasser in time. Will she choose to stay in the past? And if she does, will she be *allowed* to stay?

Be Sure to Read All Four Books in the Time Travel Quartet!

Annie Lockwood exists; everyone admits it. Everyone has seen her. But only Strat insists that Miss Lockwood traveled 100 years back in time to be with them in 1895. Now Strat is paying an enormous price; his father has declared him insane and had him locked away in an asylum.

When Time calls Annie back to save Strat, she does not hesitate, even though her family is falling apart and desperately needs her.

Can Annie save the boy she loves, or are she and Strat and her family back home out of time?

Tod Lockwood has never wanted to be anyone's knight in shining armor. In fact, he wants to avoid having anything to do with girls, at least for the present. But that's before Devonny Stratton steps into his life out of the nineteenth century.

As for sixteen-year-old Devonny, she has no plans for marriage until her father arranges to wed her to the contemptuous but well-connected Lord Winden. Devonny has only one hope: Someone must rescue her. Can Tod Lockwood be Time's answer to her prayers? Life never seems simple to Devonny, but do the solutions to her problems await her in the future? Or will she only become a prisoner of a different time?

From #1 *New York Times* bestselling author David Baldacci comes a moving family drama about learning to love again after heartbreak and loss.

ONE SUMMER

It's almost Christmas, but there is no joy in the house of terminally ill Jack and his family. With only a short time left to live, he spends his last days preparing to say good-bye to his devoted wife, Lizzie, and their three children. Then, unthinkably, tragedy strikes again: Lizzie is killed in a car accident. With no one able to care for them, the children are separated from one another and sent to live with family members around the country.

Just when all seems lost, Jack begins to recover in a miraculous turn of events. He rises from what should have been his deathbed, determined to bring his fractured family back together. Struggling to rebuild their lives after Lizzie's death, he reunites everyone at Lizzie's childhood home on the oceanfront in South Carolina. And there, over one unforgettable summer, Jack begins to learn to love again, and he and his children learn how to become a family once more.

ACCLAIM FOR

ONE SUMMER

"If you know David Baldacci only as a thriller writer, you need to read more of David Baldacci. In ONE SUMMER, he writes as beautifully and insightfully about the pathways of the human heart as he does about the corridors of power. The twists and turns in this hugely emotional and unforgettable novel come from the resilience of one father's spirit and the revelation of the love that binds a family, in this world and even beyond."

—Lisa Scottoline, *New York Times* bestselling author of *Save Me* and *Think Twice*

"The last few pages are packed with enough action to rival Baldacci's thrillers... [Fans] will find in these pages a good message and a big heart."

—*Washington Post*

"Readers better have their hankies ready."

—*RT Book Reviews*

"A beautifully told story of the fate of a family devastated by loss and healed by love. ONE SUMMER has it all, humor, grace, and redemption, delivered with humanity and wisdom in the capable and sure hands of America's great storyteller."

—Adriana Trigiani, *New York Times* bestselling author of *Very Valentine* and *Lucia, Lucia*

Also by David Baldacci

Absolute Power
Total Control
The Winner
The Simple Truth
Saving Faith
Wish You Well
Last Man Standing
The Christmas Train
Split Second
Hour Game
The Camel Club
The Collectors
Simple Genius
Stone Cold
The Whole Truth
Divine Justice
First Family
True Blue
Deliver Us from Evil
Hell's Corner
The Sixth Man
One Summer
Zero Day
The Innocent
The Forgotten
The Hit

DAVID BALDACCI

One Summer

VISION

NEW YORK BOSTON

To Spencer, my little girl all grown up.
And I couldn't be prouder of the
person you've become.

Vision
Hachette Book Group
237 Park Avenue
New York, NY 10017
www.HachetteBookGroup.com

Vision is an imprint of Grand Central Publishing.
The Vision name and logo is a trademark of Hachette Book Group, Inc.

Printed in the United States of America

Originally published in hardcover by Hachette Book Group
First international mass market edition: May 2012
First U.S. mass market edition: May 2013

10 9 8 7 6 5 4 3 2 1
OPM

1

Jack Armstrong sat up in the secondhand hospital bed that had been wedged into a corner of the den in his home in Cleveland. A father at nineteen, he and his wife, Lizzie, had conceived their second child when he'd been home on leave from the army. Jack had been in the military for five years when the war in the Middle East started. He'd survived his first tour in Afghanistan and earned a Purple Heart for taking one in the arm. After that he'd weathered several tours of duty in Iraq, one of which included the destruction of his Humvee while he was still inside. That injury had won him his second Purple. And he had a Bronze Star on top of that for rescuing three ambushed grunts from his unit and nearly getting killed in the process. After all that, here he was, dying fast in his cheaply paneled den in Ohio's Rust Belt.

His goal was simple: just hang on until Christmas. He sucked greedily on the oxygen coming from the line in his nose. The converter that stayed in the corner of the small room was on maximum production, and Jack knew that one day soon it would be turned off because he'd be dead. Before Thanksgiving he was certain he could last another month. Now Jack was not sure he could make another day.

But he would.

I have to.

In high school the six-foot-two, good-looking Jack had varsity lettered in three sports, quarterbacked the football team, and had his pick of the ladies. But from the first time he'd seen Elizabeth "Lizzie" O'Toole, it was all over for him in the falling-in-love department. His heart had been won perhaps even before he quite realized it. His mouth curled into a smile at the memory of seeing her for the first time. Her family had come from South Carolina. Jack had often wondered why the O'Tooles had moved to Cleveland, where there was no ocean, a lot less sun, a lot more snow and ice, and not a palm tree in sight. Later, he'd learned it was because of a job change for Lizzie's father.

She'd come into class that first day, tall, with long auburn hair and vibrant green eyes, her face already mature and lovely. They had started going together in high school and had never been separated since, except long enough for Jack to fight in two wars.

"Jack; Jack honey?"

Lizzie was crouched down in front of him. In her hand was a syringe. She was still beautiful, though her looks had taken on a fragile edge. There were dark circles under her eyes and recently stamped worry lines on her face. The glow had gone from her skin, and her body was harder, less supple than it had been. Jack was the one dying, but in a way she was too.

"It's time for your pain meds."

He nodded, and she shot the drugs directly into an access line cut right below his collarbone. That way the medicine flowed directly into his bloodstream and started working faster. Fast was good when the pain felt like every nerve in his body was being incinerated.

After she finished, Lizzie sat and hugged him. The doctors had a long name for what was wrong with him, one that Jack still could not pronounce or even spell. It was rare, they had said; one in a million. When he'd asked about his odds of survival, the docs had looked at each other before one finally answered.

"There's really nothing we can do. I'm sorry."

"Do the things you've always wanted to do," another had advised him, "but never had the chance."

"I have three kids and a mortgage," Jack had shot back, still reeling from this sudden death sentence. "I don't have the luxury of filling out some end-of-life bucket list."

"How long?" he'd finally asked, though part of him didn't really want to know.

"You're young and strong," said one. "And the disease is in its early stages."

Jack had survived the Taliban and Al-Qaeda. He could maybe hold on and see his oldest child graduate from college. "So how long?" he'd asked again.

The doctor said, "Six months. Maybe eight if you're lucky."

Jack did not feel very lucky.

He vividly remembered the morning he started feeling not quite right. It was an ache in his forearm and a stab of pain in his right leg. He was a building contractor by trade, so aches and pains were to be expected. But things soon carried to a new level. His limbs would grow tired from three hours of physical labor as opposed to ten. The stabs of pain became more frequent, and his balance began to deteriorate. His back finally couldn't make it up the ladder with the stacks of shingles. Then it hurt to carry his youngest son around after ten minutes. Then the fire in his nerves started, and his legs felt like an old man's. And one morning he woke up and his lungs were like balloons filled with water. Everything had accelerated after that, as though his body had simply given way to whatever was invading it.

His youngest child, Jack Jr., whom everyone called Jackie, toddled in and climbed on his dad's lap, resting his head against his father's sunken chest. Jackie's hair was long and inky black, curled up at the ends. His eyes were the color of toast; his thick eyebrows nearly met in the middle, like a burly woolen thread. Jackie had been their little surprise. Their other kids were much older.

Jack slowly slid his arm around his two-year-old son. Chubby fingers gripped his forearm, and warm breath touched his skin. It felt like the pierce of needles, but Jack simply gritted his teeth and didn't move his arm because there wouldn't be many more of these embraces. He slowly turned his head and looked out the window, where the snow was steadily falling. South Carolina and palm trees had nothing on Cleveland when it came to the holidays. It was truly beautiful.

He took his wife's hand.

"Christmas," Jack said in a wheezy voice. "I'll be there."

"Promise?" said Lizzie, her voice beginning to crack.

"Promise."

2

Jack awoke, looked around, and didn't know where he was. He could feel nothing, wasn't even sure if he was still breathing.

Am I dead? Was this it?

"Pop-pop," said Jackie as he slid next to his father on the bed. Jack turned and saw the chubby cheeks and light brown eyes.

Jack stroked his son's hair. Good, thick strands, like he used to have before the disease had stolen that too. Curious, Jackie tried to pull out the oxygen line from his father's nose, but he redirected his son's hand and cupped it with his own.

Lizzie walked in with his meds and shot them into the access line. An IV drip took care of Jack's nutrition and hydration needs. Solid foods were beyond him now.

"I just dropped the kids off at school," she told him.

"Mikki?" said Jack.

Lizzie made a face. Their daughter, Michelle, would be turning sixteen next summer, and her rebellious streak had been going strong since she'd become a teenager. She was into playing her guitar and working on her music, wearing junky clothes, sneaking out at night, and ignoring the books. "At least she showed up for the math test. I suppose actually passing it would've been asking too much. On the bright side, she received an A in music theory."

Jackie got down and ran into the other room, probably for a toy. Jack watched him go with an unwieldy mixture of pride and sorrow. He would never see his son as a man. He would never even see him start kindergarten. That cut against the natural order of things. But it was what it was.

Jack had experienced an exceptionally long phase of denial after being told he had little time left. That was partially because he had always been a survivor. A rocky childhood and two wars had not done him in, so he had initially felt confident that despite the doctors' fatal verdict, his disease was beatable. As time went by, however, and his body continued to fail, it had become clear that this battle was not winnable. It had reached a point where making the most of his time left was more important to him than trying to beat his head against an impenetrable wall. Most significantly, he wanted his kids' memories of his final days to be as positive as possible. Jack had concluded that if he had to die prematurely, that was about as good a way to do so as there was. It beat being depressed and making everyone else around him miserable, waiting for him to die.

Before he'd gotten sick, Jack had talked to his daughter many times about making good life choices, about the importance of school, but nothing seemed to make a difference to the young woman. There was a clear disconnect now between father and daughter. When she'd been a little girl, Mikki had unconditionally loved her dad, wanted to be around him all the time. Now he rarely saw her. To her, it seemed to Jack, he might as well have been already dead.

"Mikki seems lost around me," he said slowly.

Lizzie sat next to him, held his hand. "She's scared and confused, honey. Some of it has to do with her age. Most of it has to do with..."

"Me." Jack couldn't look at her when he made this admission.

"She and I have talked about it. Well, I talked and she didn't say much. She's a smart kid, but she really doesn't understand why this is happening, Jack. And her defense mechanism is to just detach herself from it. It's not the healthiest way to cope with things, though."

"I can understand," said Jack.

She looked at him. "Because of your dad?"

He nodded and rubbed her hand with his fingers, his eyes moistening as he remembered his father's painful death. He took several long pulls on the oxygen. "If I could change things, I would, Lizzie."

She rested her body next to his, wrapped her arms around his shoulders, and kissed him. When she spoke, her voice was husky and seemed right on the edge of failing. "Jack, this is hard on everyone. But it's hardest on you. You have been so brave; no one could have handled—" She couldn't continue. Lizzie laid her head next to his and wept softly. Jack held her with what little strength he had left.

"I love you, Lizzie. No matter what happens, nothing will ever change that."

He'd been sleeping in the hospital bed because he couldn't make it up the stairs to their bedroom even with assistance. He'd fought against that the hardest because as his life dwindled away he had desperately wanted to feel Lizzie's warm body against his. It was another piece of his life taken from him, like he was being dismantled, brick by brick.

And I am, brick by brick.

After a few minutes, she composed herself and wiped her eyes. "Cory is playing the Grinch in the class play at the school on Christmas Eve, remember?"

Jack nodded. "I remember."

"I'll film it for you."

Cory was the middle child, twelve years old and the ham in the family.

Jack smiled and said, "Grinch!"

Lizzie smiled back, then said, "I've got a conference call in an hour, and then I'll be in the kitchen working after I give Jackie his breakfast."

She'd become a telecommuter when Jack had gotten ill. When she had to go out, a neighbor would come over or Lizzie's parents would stop by to help.

After Lizzie left, Jack sat up, slowly reached under the pillow, and pulled out the calendar and pen. He looked at the dates in December, all of which had been crossed out up to December twentieth. Over three decades of life, marriage, fatherhood, defending his country, and working hard, it had come down to him marking off the few days left. He looked out the window and to the street beyond. The snow had stopped, but he'd heard on the news that another wintry blast was expected, with more ice than snow.

There was a knock at the door, and a few moments later Sammy Duvall appeared. He was in his early sixties, with longish salt-and-pepper hair and a trim beard. Sammy was as tall as Jack, but leaner, though his arms and shoulders bulged with muscles from all the manual labor he'd done. He was far stronger than most men half his age and tougher than anyone Jack had ever met. He'd spent twenty years in the military and fought in Vietnam and done some things after that around the world that he never talked about. A first-rate, self-taught carpenter and all-around handyman, Sammy was the reason Jack had joined the service. After Jack left the army, he and Sammy had started the contracting business. Lacking a family of his own, Sammy had adopted the Armstrongs.

The military vets shared a glance, and then Sammy looked over all the equipment helping to keep his friend alive. He shook his head slightly and his mouth twitched. This was as close as stoic Sammy ever came to showing emotion.

"How's work?" Jack asked, and then he took a long pull of oxygen.

"No worries. Stuff's getting done and the money's coming in."

Jack knew that Sammy had been completing all the jobs pretty much on his own and then bringing all the payments to Lizzie. "At least half of that money is yours, Sammy. You're doing all the work."

"I got my Uncle Sam pension, and it's more than I need. That changes, I'll let you know."

Sammy lived in a converted one-car garage with his enormous Bernese mountain dog, Sam Jr. His needs were simple, his wants apparently nonexistent.

Sammy combed Jack's hair and even gave him a shave. Then the friends talked for a while. At least Sammy said a few words and Jack listened. The rest of the time they sat in silence. Jack didn't mind; just being with Sammy made him feel better.

After Sammy left, Jack lifted the pen and crossed out December twenty-first. That was being optimistic, Jack knew, since the day had really just begun. He put the calendar and pen away.

And then it happened.

He couldn't breathe. He sat up, convulsing, but that just made it worse. He could feel his heart racing, his lungs squeezing, his face first growing red and then pale as the oxygen left his body and nothing replenished it.

December twenty-first, he thought, *my last day.*

"Pop-pop?"

Jack looked up to see his son holding the end of the oxygen line that attached to the converter. He held it up higher, as though he were giving it back to his dad.

"Jackie!"

A horrified Lizzie appeared in the doorway, snatched the line from her son's hand, and rushed to reattach the oxygen line to the converter. A few moments later, the oxygen started to flow into the line and Jack fell back on the bed, breathing hard, trying to fill his lungs.

Lizzie raced past her youngest son and was by Jack's side in an instant. "Oh my God, Jack, oh my God." Her whole body was trembling.

He held up his hand to show he was okay.

Lizzie whirled around and snapped, "That was bad, Jackie, bad."

Jackie's face crumbled, and he started to bawl.

She snatched up Jackie and carried him out. The little boy was struggling to free himself, staring at Jack over her shoulder, reaching his arms out to his father. His son's look was pleading.

"Pop-pop," wailed Jackie.

The tears trickled down Jack's face as his son's cries faded away. But then Jack heard Lizzie sobbing and pictured her crying her heart out and wondering what the hell she'd done to deserve all this.

Sometimes, Jack thought, living was far harder than dying.

3

Jack awoke from a nap late the next day in time to see his daughter opening the front door, guitar case in hand. He motioned to her to come see him. She closed the door and dutifully trudged to his room.

Mikki had auburn hair like her mother's. However, she had dyed it several different colors, and Jack had no idea what it would be called now. She was shooting up in height, her legs long and slender and her hips and bosom filling out. Though she acted like she was totally grown up now, her face was caught in that time thread that was firmly past the little-girl stage but not yet a woman. She would be a junior in high school next year. Where had the time gone?

"Yeah, Dad?" she said, not looking at him.

He thought about what to say. In truth, they didn't have much to talk about. Even when he'd been healthy, their lives lately had taken separate paths. *That was my fault,* he thought. *Not hers.*

"Your A." He took a long breath, tried to smile.

She smirked. "Right. Music theory. My only one. I'm sure Mom told you that too. Right?"

"Still an A."

"Thanks for mentioning it." She looked at the floor, an awkward expression on her features. "Look, Dad, I gotta go. People are waiting. We're rehearsing."

She was in a band, Jack knew, though he couldn't recall the name of it just now.

"Okay, be careful."

She turned to leave, and then hesitated. Her fingers fiddled with the guitar case handle. She glanced back but still didn't meet his gaze. "Just so you know, when you were asleep I duct taped your oxygen line onto the converter so it can't be pulled off again. Jackie didn't know what he was doing. Mom didn't have to give him such a hard time."

Jack gathered more oxygen and said, "Thanks."

A part of him wanted her to look at him, and another part of him didn't. He didn't want to see pity in her eyes. Her big, strong father reduced to this. He wondered whom she would marry. Where would they live? Would it be far from Cleveland?

Will she visit my grave?

"Mikki?"

"Dad, I really got to go. I'm already late."

"I hope you have a great... day, sweetie."

He thought he saw her lips quiver for a moment, but then she turned and left. A few moments later, the front door closed behind her. He peered out the window. She hopped across the snow and climbed into a car that one of her guy friends was driving. Jack had never felt more disconnected from life.

After dinner that night, Cory, in full costume, performed his Grinch role for his father. Cory was a chunky twelve-year-old, though his long feet and lanky limbs promised height later. His hair was a mop of brown cowlicks, the same look Jack had had at that age. Lizzie's parents had come over for dinner and to watch the show and had brought Lizzie's grandmother. Cecilia was a stylish lady in her eighties who used a walker and had her own portable oxygen tank. She'd grown up and lived most of her life in South Carolina. She'd come to live with her daughter in Cleveland after her husband died and her health started failing. Her laugh was infectious and her speech was mellifluous, like water trickling over smooth rocks.

Cecilia joked that Jack and she should start their own oxygen business since they had so much of the stuff. She was dying too, only not quite as fast as Jack. This probably would also be her last Christmas, but she had lived a good long life and had apparently made peace with her fate. She was uniformly upbeat, talking about her life in the South, the tea parties and the debutante balls, sneaking smokes and drinking hooch behind the local Baptist church at night. Yet every once in a while Jack would catch her staring at him, and he could sense the sadness the old lady held in her heart for his plight.

After Cory finished his performance, Cecilia leaned down and whispered into Jack's ear. "It's Christmas. The time of miracles." This was not the first time she'd said this. Yet for some reason Jack's spirits sparked for a moment.

But then the doctor's pronouncement sobered this feeling.

Six months, eight if you're lucky.

Science, it seemed, always trumped hope.

At eleven o'clock he heard the front door open, and Mikki slipped in. Jack thought he saw her glance his way, but she didn't come into the den. When Jack was healthy they had kept a strict watch over her comings and goings. And for months after he'd become ill, Lizzie had kept up that vigil. Now she barely had time to shower or snatch a meal, and Mikki had taken advantage of this lack of oversight to do as she pleased.

When everyone was asleep, Jack reached under his pillow and took out his pen. This time he wasn't crossing off dates on a calendar. He took out the piece of paper and carefully unfolded it. He spread it out on a book he kept next to the bed. Pen poised over the paper, he began to write. It took him a long time, at least an hour to write less than one page. His handwriting was poor because he was so weak, but his thoughts were clear. Eventually there would be seven of these letters. One for each day of the last week of his life, the date neatly printed at the top of the page—or as neatly as Jack's trembling hand could manage. Each letter began with "Dear Lizzie," and ended with "Love, Jack." In the body of the letter he did his best to convey to his wife all that he felt for her. That though he would no longer be alive, he would always be there for her.

These letters, he'd come to realize, were the most important thing he would ever do in his life. And he labored to make sure every word was the right one. Finished, he put the letter in an envelope, marked it with a number, and slipped it in the nightstand next to his bed.

He would write the seventh and last letter on Christmas Eve, after everyone had gone to bed.

Jack turned his head and looked out the window. Even in the darkness he could see the snow coming down hard.

He now knew how a condemned man felt though he had committed no crime. The time left to him was precious. But there was only so much he could do with it.

4

Jack marked off December twenty-fourth on his calendar. He had one letter left to write. It would go into the drawer with the number seven written on the envelope. After he was gone, Lizzie would read them, and Jack hoped they would provide some comfort to her. Actually, writing them had provided some comfort for Jack. It made him focus on what was really important in life.

Jack's mother-in-law, Bonnie, had stayed with him while the rest of the family went to see Cory in the school play. Lizzie had put her foot down and made Mikki go as well. Bonnie had made a cup of tea and had settled herself down with a book, while Jack was perched in a chair by the window waiting for the van to pull up with Lizzie and the others.

Sammy came by, stomping snow off his boots and tugging off his knit cap to let his long, shaggy hair fall out. He sat next to Jack and handed him a gift. When Jack opened it he looked up in surprise.

It was five passes to Disney World, good for the upcoming year.

Sammy gripped Jack by the shoulder. "I expect you and the family to get there."

Jack glanced over to see Bonnie shaking her head in mild reproach. Bonnie O'Toole was not a woman who believed in miracles. Yet Jack knew the man well enough to realize that Sammy fully believed he would use those tickets. He patted Sammy on the arm, smiled, and nodded.

After Sammy left, Jack glanced at the tickets. He appreciated his friend's confidence, but Jack was the only one who knew how close he was to the end. He had fought as hard as he could. He didn't want to die and leave his family, but he couldn't live like this either. His mind focused totally on the last letter he would ever compose. He knew when his pen had finished writing the words and the paper was safely in the envelope, he could go peacefully. It was a small yet obviously important benchmark. But he would wait until Christmas was over, when presents were opened and a new day had dawned. It was some comfort to know that he had a little control left over his fate, even if it was simply the specific timing of his passing.

He saw the headlights of the oncoming van flick across the window. Bonnie went to open the front door, and Jack watched anxiously from the window as the kids piled out of the vehicle. Lizzie's dad led them up the driveway, carrying Jackie because it was so slick out. The snow was still coming down, although the latest weather report had said that with the temperatures staying where they were, it was more ice than snow at this point, making driving treacherous.

His gaze held on Lizzie as she closed up the van, and then turned, not toward the house, but away from it. Jack hadn't noticed the person approach her because his attention had been on his wife. The man came into focus; it was Bill Miller. They'd all gone to school together. Bill had blocked on the line for Jack the quarterback. He'd attended Jack and Lizzie's wedding. Bill was single, in the plumbing business, and doing well.

Jack pressed his face to the glass when he saw Bill draw close to his wife. Lizzie slipped her purse over her shoulder and swiped the hair out of her eyes. They were so close to one another, Jack couldn't find even a sliver of darkness between them. His breath was fogging the glass, he was so near it. He watched Bill lean in toward Lizzie. He saw his wife rise up on tiptoe. And then Bill staggered back as Lizzie slapped him across the face. Though he was weak, Jack reared up in his chair as though he wanted to go and defend his wife's honor. Yet there was no need. Bill Miller stumbled off into the darkness as Lizzie turned away and marched toward the house.

A minute later he heard Lizzie come in, knocking snow off her boots.

Lizzie strode into the den, first pulling off her scarf and then rubbing her hands together because of the cold. Her face was flushed, and she didn't look at him like she normally did. "Time for the presents; then Mom and Dad are going to take off. They'll be back tomorrow, okay, sweetie? It'll be a great day."

"How's your hand?"

She glanced at him. "What?"

He pointed to the window. "I think Bill's lucky he's still conscious."

"He was also drunk, or I don't think he would've tried that. Idiot."

Jack started to say something, but then stopped and looked away. Lizzie quickly picked up on this and sat next to him.

"Jack, you don't think that Bill and I—"

He gripped her hand. "Of course not. Don't be crazy." He kissed her cheek.

"So what then? Something's bothering you."

"You're young, and you have three kids."

"That I get." She attempted a smile that flickered out when she saw the earnest look on his face.

"You need somebody in your life."

"I don't want to talk about this." She tried to rise, but he held her back.

"Lizzie, look at me. Look at me."

She turned to face him, her eyes glimmering with tears.

"You will find someone else."

"No."

"You will."

"I've got a full life. I've got no room for—"

"Yes, you do."

"Do we have to talk about this now? It's Christmas Eve."

"I can't be picky about timing, Lizzie," he said, a little out of breath.

Her face flushed. "I didn't mean that. I . . . you look better tonight. Maybe . . . the doctors—"

"No, Lizzie. No," he said firmly. "That can't happen. We're past that stage, honey." He sucked on his air, his gaze resolutely on her.

She put a hand to her eyes. "If I think about things like that, then it means, I don't want to . . . You might . . ."

He held her. "Things will work out all right. Just take it slow. And be happy." He made her look at him, and he brushed the tears from her eyes. He took a long pull on his oxygen and managed a grin. "And for God's sake, don't pick Bill."

She laughed. And then it turned into a sob as he held her.

When they pulled away a few moments later, Lizzie wiped her nose with a tissue and said, "I was actually thinking about next summer. And I wanted to talk to you about it."

Jack's heart was buoyed by the fact that she still sought out his opinion. "What about it?"

"You'll probably think it's silly."

"Tell me."

"I was thinking I would take the kids to the Palace."

"The Palace? You haven't been back there since—"

"I know. I know. I just think it's time. It's in bad shape from what I heard. I know it needs a lot of work. But just for one summer it should be fine."

"I know how hard that was for you."

She reached in her pocket and pulled out a photo. She showed it to Jack. "Haven't looked at that in years. Do you remember me showing it to you?"

It was a photo of the O'Tooles when the kids were all little.

"That's Tillie next to you. Your twin sister."

"Mom said she never could tell us apart."

Jack had to sit back against his pillow and drew several long breaths on his line while Lizzie patiently waited.

Finally he said, "She was five when she died?"

"Almost six. Meningitis. Nothing the doctors could

do." She glanced briefly at Jack, and then looked away. Her unspoken thought could have been, *Just like you.*

"I remember my parents telling me that Tillie had gone to Heaven." She smiled at the same time a couple of tears slid down her cheeks. "There's an old lighthouse on the property down there. It was so beautiful."

"I remember you telling me about it. Your grandmother... still owns the Palace, right?"

"Yes. I was going to ask her if it would be all right if we went down there this summer."

"The O'Tooles exchanging the sunny ocean for cold Cleveland?" He coughed several times, and Lizzie went to adjust his air level. When she did so he started breathing easier.

She said, "Well, I think leaving the Palace was because of me."

"What do you mean?"

"I never really told you about this before, and maybe I'd forgotten it myself. But I've been thinking about Tillie lately." She faltered.

"Lizzie, please tell me."

She turned to face him. "When my parents told me my sister had gone to Heaven, I... I wanted to find her. I didn't really understand that she was dead. I knew that Heaven was in the sky. So I started looking for, well, looking for Heaven to find Tillie."

"You were just a little kid."

"I would go up in the lighthouse. Back then it still worked. And I'd look for Heaven, for Tillie really, with the help of the light." She paused and let out a little sob. "Never found either one."

Jack held her. "It's okay, Lizzie; it's okay," he said softly.

She wiped her eyes on his shirt and said, "It became a sort of obsession, I guess. I don't know why. But every day that went by and I couldn't find her, it just hurt so bad. And when I got older, my parents told me that Tillie was dead. Well, it didn't help much." She paused. "I can't believe I never told you all this before. But I guess I was a little ashamed."

His wife's distress was taking a toll on Jack. He breathed deeply for several seconds before saying, "You lost your twin. You were just a little kid."

"By the time we moved to Ohio, I knew I would never find her by looking at the sky. I knew she was gone. And the lighthouse wasn't working anymore anyway. But I think my parents, my mom especially, wanted to get me away from the place. She didn't think it was good for me. But it was just . . . silly."

"It was what you were feeling, Lizzie." He touched his chest. "Here."

"I know. So I thought I'd go back there. See the place. Let the kids experience how I grew up." She looked at him.

"Great idea," Jack gasped.

She rubbed his shoulder. "You might enjoy it too. You could really fix the place up. Even make the lighthouse work again." It was so evident she desperately wanted to believe this could actually happen.

He attempted a smile. "Yeah."

The looks on both their faces were clear despite the hopeful words.

Jack would never see the Palace.

5

Later that night his father-in-law helped Jack into a wheelchair and rolled him into the living room, where their little tree stood. It was silver tinsel with blue and red ornaments. Jack usually got a real tree for Christmas, but not this year of course.

The kids had hot chocolate and some snacks. Mikki even played a few carols on her guitar, though she looked totally embarrassed doing so. Cory told his dad about the play, and Lizzie bustled around making sure everyone had everything they needed. Then she played the DVD for Jack so he could see the performance for himself. Finally his in-laws prepared to leave. The ice was getting worse and they wanted to get home, they said. Lizzie's father helped Jack into bed.

At the front door Lizzie gave them each a hug. Jack heard Bonnie tell her daughter to just hang in there. It was always darkest before the dawn.

"The kids are the most important thing," said her dad. "Afterward, we'll be right here for you."

Next, Jack heard Lizzie say, "I was thinking about talking to Cee," referring to her grandmother Cecilia.

"About what?" Bonnie said quickly, in a wary tone.

"Next summer I was thinking of taking the kids to the Palace, maybe for the entire summer break. I wanted to make sure Cee would be okay with that."

There were a few moments of silence; then Bonnie said, "The Palace! Lizzie, you know—"

"Mom, don't."

"This is not something you need, certainly not right now. It's too painful."

"That was a long time ago," Lizzie said quietly. "It's different now. It's okay. I'm okay. I have been for a long time, actually, if you'd ever taken the time to notice."

"It's never long enough," her mother shot back.

"Let's not discuss it tonight. Not tonight," said Lizzie.

After her parents left, Jack listened as his wife's footsteps came his way. Lizzie appeared in the doorway. "That was a nice Christmas Eve."

He nodded his head dumbly, his gaze never leaving her face. The tick of the clock next to his bed pounded fiercely in Jack's head.

"Don't let her talk you out of going to the Palace, Lizzie. Stick to your guns."

"My mother can be a little..."

"I know. But promise me you'll go?"

She nodded, smiled. "Okay, I promise. Do you need anything else?" she asked.

Jack looked at the clock and motioned to the access

line below his collarbone, where his pain meds were administered.

"Oh my gosh. Your meds. Okay." She started to the small cabinet in the corner where she kept his medications. But then Lizzie stopped, looking slightly panicked.

"I forgot to pick up your prescription today. The play and...I forgot to get them." She checked her watch. "They're still open. I'll go get them now."

"Don't go. I'm okay without the meds."

"It'll just take a few minutes. I'll be back in no time. And then it'll just be you and me. I want to talk to you some more about next summer."

"Lizzie, you don't have to—"

But she was already gone.

The front door slammed. The van started up and raced down the street.

Later Jack woke, confused. He turned slowly to find Mikki dozing in the chair next to his bed. She must have come downstairs while he was asleep. He looked out the window. There were streams of light whizzing past his house. For a moment he had the absurd notion that Santa Claus had just arrived. Then he tried to sit up because he heard it. Sounds on the roof.

Reindeer? What the hell was going on?

The sounds came again. Only now he realized they weren't on the roof. Someone was pounding on the front door.

"Mom? Dad?" It was Cory. His voice grew closer. His head poked in the den. He was dressed in boxer shorts and a T-shirt and looked nervous. "There's someone at the door."

By now Mikki had woken. She stretched and saw Cory standing there.

"Someone's at the front door," her brother said again.

Mikki looked at her dad. He was staring out at the swirl of lights. It was like a spaceship was landing on their front lawn. *In Cleveland?* Jack thought he was hallucinating. Yet when he looked at Mikki, it was clear that she saw the lights too. Jack raised a hand and pointed at the front door. He nodded to his daughter.

Looking scared, she hurried to the door and opened it. The man was big, dressed in a uniform, and had a gun on his belt. He looked cold, tired, and uncomfortable. Mostly uncomfortable.

"Is your dad home?" he asked Mikki. She backed away and pointed toward the den. The police officer stamped off his boots and stepped in. The squeak of his gun belt sounded like a scream in miniature. He walked where Mikki was pointing, saw Jack in the bed with the lines hooked to him, and muttered something under his breath. He looked at Mikki and Cory. "Can he understand? I mean, is he real sick?"

Mikki said, "He's sick, but he can understand."

The cop drew next to the bed. Jack lifted himself up on his elbows. He was gasping. In his anxiety, his withered lungs were demanding so much air the converter couldn't keep up.

The officer swallowed hard. "Mr. Armstrong?" He paused as Jack stared up at him. "I'm afraid there's been an accident involving your wife."

6

Jack sat strapped into a wheelchair staring up at his wife's coffin. Mikki and Cory sat next to him. Jackie had been deemed too young to attend his mother's funeral; he was being taken care of by a neighbor. The priest came down and gave Jack and his children holy communion. Jack nearly choked on the host but finally managed to swallow it. Ironically, it was the first solid food he'd had in months.

At my wife's funeral.

The weather was cold, the sky puffy with clouds. The wind cleaved the thickest coats. The roads were still iced and treacherous. They'd been driven to the cemetery in the funeral home sedan designated for family members. His father-in-law, Fred, rode up front, next to the driver, while he and the kids were squeezed in the back with Bonnie. She had barely uttered a word since learning her youngest daughter had been instantly killed when her van ran a red light and was broadsided by an oncoming snowplow.

The graveside service was mercifully brief; the priest seemed to understand that if he didn't hustle things along, some of the older people might not survive the event.

Jack looked over at Mikki. She'd pinned her hair back and put on a black dress that hung below her knees; she sat staring vacantly at the coffin. Cory had not looked at the casket even once. As a final act, Jack was wheeled up to the coffin. He put his hand on top of it, mumbled a few words, and sat back, feeling totally disoriented. He had played this scene out in his head a hundred times. Only he was in the box and it was Lizzie out here saying good-bye. Nothing about this was right. He felt like he was staring at the world upside down.

"I'll be with you soon, Lizzie," he said in a halting voice. The words seemed hollow, forced, but he could think of nothing else to say.

As he started to collapse, a strong hand gripped him.

"It's okay, Jack. We'll get you back to the car now." He looked up into the face of Sammy Duvall.

Sammy proceeded to maneuver him to the sedan in record time. Before closing the door, he put a reassuring hand on Jack's shoulder. "I'll always be there for you, buddy."

They were driven home, the absence of Lizzie in their midst a festering wound that had no possible healing ointment. Jackie was brought home, and people stopped by with plates of food. An impromptu wake was held; devastated folks chatted in low tones. More than once Jack caught people gazing at him, no doubt thinking, *My God, what now?*

Jack was thinking the same thing. *What now?*

Two hours later the house was empty except for Jack, the

kids, and his in-laws. The children instantly disappeared. Minutes later Jack could hear guitar strumming coming from Mikki's bedroom, the tunes melancholy and abbreviated. Cory and Jackie shared a bedroom, but no sound was coming from them. Jack could imagine Cory quietly sobbing, while a confused Jackie attempted to comfort him.

Bonnie and Fred O'Toole looked as disoriented as Jack felt. They had signed on to help their healthy daughter transition with her kids to being a widow and then getting on with her life. Without the buffer that Lizzie had been, Jack could focus now on the fact that his relationship with his in-laws had been largely superficial.

Fred was a big man with a waistline large enough to portend a host of health problems down the road. He tended to defer to his wife in all things other than sports and selling cars, which was the line of work that had brought him to Cleveland. He was a man who would prefer to look at the floor rather than in your eye, unless he was trying to sell you the latest Ford F-150. Then he could be animated enough, at least until you signed on the dotted line and the financing cleared.

Bonnie was shorter than her daughter. The mother of four grown children, she was now well into her sixties, and her figure had lost its shape. Her waist and hips had turned into a solid wall of flesh. Her hair was white, cut short and rather brutally, and her eyeglasses filled most of her square face. Fred kept sighing, rubbing his big hands over his pressed suit pants, as though attempting to rub some dirt off his fingers. Bonnie, who had kept on her black outfit, was sitting very still on the couch, her gaze aimed at a corner of the ceiling but apparently not actually registering on it.

Fred sighed again, and this seemed to rouse Bonnie.

"Well," she said. "Well," she said again. Fred eyed her, as did Jack.

She looked over and gave Jack a quick glance that was undecipherable.

Then came more silence.

Finally, a few minutes later Fred helped Jack get into bed, and then he and Bonnie went up to Jack and Lizzie's room. They would be staying here full-time until other arrangements were made.

Jack lay in the dark staring at the ceiling. The days after Lizzie had died had been far worse than when he'd received his own death sentence. His life ending he'd accepted. Hers he had not. Could not. Mikki and Cory had barely spoken since the police officer had come with the awful news. Jackie had wandered the house looking for his mother and crying when he couldn't find her.

Jack slid open the drawer of the nightstand and took out the six letters. He obviously had not written one on Christmas Eve. In these pages he had poured out his heart to the person he cherished above all others. As he looked down at the pages, wasted pages now, his spirits sank even lower.

Jack rarely cried. He'd seen fellow soldiers die horribly in the Middle East, watched his father perish from lung cancer, and attended the funeral of his wife. He had shed a few tears at each of these events, but not for long and always in a controlled way. Now, staring at the ceiling, thinking a thousand anguished thoughts, he did weep quietly as it finally struck him that Lizzie was really gone.

7

The next morning Bonnie took charge. She came to see Jack with Fred in tow. "This won't be easy, Jack," she cautioned, "but we really don't have much time." She squared her shoulders and seemed to attempt a sympathetic look. "The children of course come first. I've talked to Becky and also to Frances several times."

Frances and Becky were Lizzie's older sisters, who lived on the West Coast. The only brother, Fred Jr., was on active military duty, stationed in Korea. He had not been able to make it to the funeral.

"Becky can take Jack Jr., and Frances has agreed to take Cory. That just leaves Michelle." Bonnie had never called her Mikki.

"*Just* Michelle?" said Jack.

Bonnie looked momentarily taken aback. When she spoke, her tone was less authoritative and more conciliatory. "This is hard on all of us. You know Fred and I had planned to move to Tempe next year after things were more settled with Lizzie and the kids. We were going this year, but then you got sick. And we stayed on, because that's what families do in those situations. We tried to do our best, for all of you."

"We couldn't have gotten on without you."

This remark seemed to please her, and she smiled and gripped his hand. "Thank you. That means a lot."

She continued, "We'll take Michelle with us. And because Jack Jr. will be in Portland with Becky and Cory in LA with Frances, they will all at least be on or near the West Coast. I'm sure they'll see each other fairly often. It's really the only workable solution that I can see."

"When?" Jack asked.

"The Christmas break is almost over, and we think we can get all the kids transitioned in the next month. We decided it was no good waiting until the fall, for a number of reasons. It'll be better all around for them."

"For you too," said Jack. As soon as he said it, he wished he hadn't.

Bonnie's conciliatory look faded. "Yes, us too. Jack, we're taking care of all the children. They'll all have homes with people they love and who love them. You can't have an issue with that."

Jack touched his chest. "And me?"

"Yes, well... I was getting to that, of course." She stood but didn't look at him. Instead, she stared at a spot right over his head. "Hospice. I'll arrange all the details." Now she looked at him, and Jack had to admit, she didn't look happy about this. "If we could take care of you, Jack, in the time that you have left, we would. But we're not young anymore, and taking in Michelle and all..."

Fred added, "And Lizzie dying."

Jack and Bonnie stared at him for an instant. Each seemed surprised the man was still there, much less that he had spoken. Bonnie said, "Yes, and Lizzie not... well, yes."

Jack drew a long breath and mustered his strength. He said, "*My* kids, *my* decision."

Fred looked at Jack and then over at his wife. Bonnie, though, had eyes only for Jack.

She said, "You can't care for the kids. You can't even take care of yourself. Lizzie did everything. And now she's gone." Her eyes glittered; her tone was harsh once more.

"Still my decision," he said defiantly. He had no idea where he was going with this, but the words had tumbled from his mouth.

"Who else will take three kids? If we do nothing, the matter is out of our hands and they'll go into foster care. They'll probably never see each other again. Is that what you want?" She sat down next to him, her face inches from his. "Is that really what you want?"

He sucked in some more air, his resolve weakening along with his energy. "Why can't I stay here?" he said. Another long inhalation. "Until the kids leave?"

"Hospice is much cheaper. I'm sorry if that sounds callous, but money is tight. Tough decisions have to be made."

"So I die alone?"

Bonnie looked at her husband. Clearly, from his expression, Fred sided with Jack on this point.

Fred said, "Doesn't seem right, Bonnie. Taking the family away like that. After all that's happened."

Jack shot his father-in-law an appreciative look.

Bonnie fidgeted. "I've been thinking about that, actually." She sighed. "Jack, I'm not trying to be heartless. I care about you. I don't want to do any of this." She paused. "But they just lost their mother." Bonnie paused but didn't continue.

It slowly dawned on Jack, what she was getting at.

"And to see me die too?"

Bonnie spread her hands. "But you're right. You are their father. So I'll leave it up to you. You tell me what to do, Jack, and I'll do it. We can keep the kids here until... until you pass. They can attend your funeral, and then we can make the move. They can be with you until the end." She looked at Fred, but he apparently had nothing to add.

Jack was surprised, then, when Fred said, "Anything you want, Jack, we'll take care of it. Okay?"

Jack was silent for so long that Bonnie finally rose, clutched her sweater more tightly around her shoulders and said, "Fine, we can have an in-home nursing service come. Lizzie had some life insurance. We can use those funds to—"

"Take the kids."

Fred and Bonnie looked at him. Jack said again, "Take the kids."

"Are you sure?" asked Bonnie. She seemed to be sincere, but Jack knew this way would take a lot of the pressure off her.

He struggled to say, "As soon as you can." *It won't be long,* Jack thought. *Not now. Not with Lizzie gone.*

When she turned to leave, Bonnie froze. Mikki and Cory were standing there.

Bonnie said nervously, "I thought you were upstairs."

"You don't think this concerns us?" Mikki said bluntly.

"I think the adults need to make the decisions for what's best for the children."

"I'm not a child!" Mikki snapped.

Bonnie said, "Michelle, this is hard on all of us. We're just trying to do the best we can under the circumstances." She paused and added, "You lost your mother and I lost my daughter." Bonnie's voice cracked as she added, "None of this is easy, honey."

Mikki gazed over at her father. He could feel the anger emanating from his oldest child. "You're all losers!" yelled Mikki. She turned and rushed from the house, slamming the door behind her.

Bonnie shook her head and rubbed at her eyes before looking back at Jack. "This is a big sacrifice, for all of us." She left the room, with Fred obediently trailing her. Cory just stood there staring at his dad.

"Cor," he began. But his son turned and ran back upstairs.

A minute went by as Jack lay there, feeling like a turtle toppled on its back.

"Jack?"

When he looked over, Bonnie was standing a few feet from his bed holding something in her hand.

"The police dropped this off yesterday." She held it up. It was the bag with Jack's prescription meds. "They found it in the van. It was very unfortunate that Lizzie had to go back out that night. If she hadn't, she'd obviously be alive today."

"I told her not to go."

"But she did. For you," she replied.

The tears started to slide down her cheeks as she hurried from the room.

8

The room was small but clean. That wasn't the problem. Jack had slept for months inside a shack with ten other infantrymen in the middle of a desert, where it was either too frigid or too hot. What Jack didn't like here were the sounds. Folks during their last days of life did not make pleasant noises. Coughs, gagging, painful cries—but mostly it was the moaning. It never ceased. Then there was the squeak of the gurney wheels as the body of someone who had passed was taken away, the room freshened up for the next terminal case on the waiting list.

Most patients here were elderly. Yet Jack wasn't the youngest person. There was a boy with final-stage leukemia two doors down. When Jack was being wheeled to his room he'd seen the little body in the bed: hairless head, vacant eyes, tubes all over him, barely breathing, just waiting for it to be over. His family would come every day; his mother was often here all the time. They would put on happy expressions when they were with him and then start bawling as soon as they left his side. Jack had witnessed this as they passed his doorway. All hunched over, weeping into their cupped hands. They were just waiting, too, for it to be over. And at the same time dreading when it would be.

Jack reached under his pillow and pulled out the calendar. January eleventh. He crossed it off. He had been here for five days. The average length of stay here, he'd heard, was three weeks. Without Lizzie, it would be three weeks too long.

He again reached under his pillow and pulled out the six now-crumpled envelopes with his letters to Lizzie inside them. He'd had Sammy bring them here from the house before it was listed for sale. He held them in his hands. The paper was splotched with his tears because he pulled them out and wept over them several times a day. What else did he have to do with his time? These letters now constituted a weight around his heart for a simple reason: Lizzie would never read them, never know what he was feeling in his last days of life. At the same time, it was the only thing allowing him to die with peace, with a measure of dignity. He put the letters away and just lay there, listening for the squeaks of the final gurney ride for another patient. They came with alarming regularity. Soon, he knew it would be his body on that stretcher.

He turned his head when the kids came in, followed by Fred. He was surprised to see Cecilia stroll in with her walker and portable oxygen tank resting in a burgundy sling. It was hard for her to go outside in the cold weather, yet she had done so for Jack. Jackie immediately climbed up on his dad's lap, while Cory sat on the bed. Arms folded defiantly over her chest, Mikki stood by the door, as far away from everyone as she could be. She had on faded jeans with the knees torn out, heavy boots, a sleeveless unzipped parka, and a black long-sleeve T-shirt that said, REMEMBER DARFUR. Her hair was now orange. The color contrasted sharply with the dark circles under her eyes.

Cory had been saying something that only now Jack focused on. His son said, "But, Dad, you'll be here and we'll be way out there."

"That's the way *Dad* apparently wants it," said Mikki sharply.

Jack turned to look at her. Father's and daughter's gazes locked until she finally looked away, with an eye roll tacked on.

Cory moved closer to him. "Look, I think the best thing we can do, Dad, is stay here with you. It just makes sense."

Jackie, who was struggling with potty training, slid to the side of the bed and got down holding his privates.

"Gramps," said Mikki, "Jackie has to go. And I'm not taking him this time."

Fred saw what Jackie was doing and scuttled him off to the bathroom down the hall.

As soon as he was gone, Jack said, "You have to go, Cor." He didn't look at Mikki when he added, "You all do."

"But we won't be together, Dad," said Cory. "We'll never see each other."

Cecilia, who'd been listening to all this, quietly spoke up. "I give you my word, Cory, that you will see your brother and sister early and often."

Mikki came forward. Her sullen look was gone, replaced with a defiant one. "Okay, but what about Dad? He just stays here alone? That's not fair."

Jack said, "I'll be with you. And your mom will too, in spirit," he added a little lamely.

"Mom is dead. She can't be with anyone," snapped Mikki.

"Mikki," said Cecilia reproachfully. "That's not necessary."

"Well, it's true. We don't need to be lied to. It's bad enough that I have to go and live with *them* in Arizona."

Tears filled Cory's eyes, and he started to sob quietly. Jack pulled him closer.

Jackie and Fred came back in, and the visit lasted another half hour. Cecilia was the last to leave. She looked back at Jack. "You'll never be alone, Jack. We all carry each other in our hearts."

Those words were nice, and heartfelt, he knew, but Jack Armstrong had never felt so alone as he did right now. He had a question, though.

"Cecilia?"

She turned back, perhaps surprised by the sudden urgency in his voice. "Yes, Jack?"

Jack gathered his breath and said, "Lizzie told me she wanted to take the kids to the Palace next summer."

Cecilia moved closer to him. "She told you that?" she asked. "The Palace? My God. After all this time."

"I know. But maybe... maybe the kids could go there sometime?"

Cecilia gripped his hand. "I'll see to it, Jack. I promise."

9

They all came in to visit Jack for the last time. They would be flying out later that day to their new homes. Bonnie was there, as was Fred. Cory and Jackie crowded around their father, hugging, kissing, and talking all at once to him.

Jack was lying in bed, dressed in a fresh gown. His face and body were gaunt; the machines keeping him comfortable until he passed were going full blast. He looked at each of his kids for what he knew would be the final time. He'd already instructed Bonnie to have him cremated. "No funeral," he'd told her. "I'm not putting the kids through that again."

"I'll call you as soon as I get there, Dad," said Cory, who wouldn't look away from his father.

"Me too!" chimed in Jackie.

Jack took several deep breaths as he prepared to do what had to be done. His kids would be gone forever in a few minutes, and he was determined to make these last moments as memorable and happy as possible.

"Got something for you," said Jack. He'd had Sammy bring the three boxes to him. He slowly took them from the cabinet next to his bed and handed one to Cory and one to Jackie. He held the last one and gazed at Mikki. "For you."

"What is it?" she asked, trying to seem disinterested, though he could tell her curiosity was piqued.

"Come see."

She sighed, strolled over, and took the box from her father.

"Open them," said Jack.

Cory and Jackie opened the boxes and looked down at the piece of metal with the purple ribbon attached.

Mikki's was different.

Fred said to her, "That's a Bronze Star. That's for heroism in combat. Your dad was a real hero. The other ones are Purple Hearts for being . . . well, hurt in battle," he finished, looking awkwardly at Cory and Jackie.

Jack said, "Open the box and think of me. Always be with you that way."

Even Bonnie seemed genuinely moved by this gesture, and she dabbed at her eyes with a tissue. But Jack wasn't looking at her. He was watching his daughter. She touched the medal carefully, and her mouth started to tremble. When she looked up and saw her dad watching her, she closed the box and quickly stuck it in her bag.

Cecilia was the last to leave. She sat next to him and patted his hand with her wrinkled one.

"How do you feel, Jack, really?"

"About dying or saying good-bye to my kids for the last time?" he said weakly.

"I mean, do you feel like you want to let go?"

Jack turned to face her. The confusion, and even anger, seeping into his features was met by a radiant calm in hers.

"I'm in hospice, Cee. I'm dead."

"Not yet you're not."

Jack looked away, sucked down a tortured breath. "Matter of time. Hours."

"Do you want to let go?" she asked again.

"Yes. I do."

"Okay, honey, okay."

After Cecilia left, Jack lay there in the bed. His last ties to his family had been severed. It was over. He didn't need to pull out the calendar. There would be no more dates to cross off. His hand moved to the call button. It was time now. He had prearranged this with the doctor. The machines keeping him alive would be turned off. He was done. It was time to go. All he wanted now was to see Lizzie. He conjured her face up in his mind's eye. "It's time, Lizzie," he said. "It's time." The sense of relief was palpable.

However, his hand moved away from the button when Mikki came back into the room and held up the medal. "I just wanted to say that . . . that this was pretty cool."

Father and daughter gazed awkwardly at each other, as though they were two long-lost friends reunited by chance. There was something in her eyes that Jack had not seen there for a long time.

"Mikki?" he said, his voice cracking.

She ran across the room and hugged him. Her breath burned against his cold neck, warming him, sending packets of energy, of strength, to all corners of his body.

He squeezed back, as hard as his depleted energy would allow.

She said, "I love you so much. So much."

Her body shook with the pain, the trauma of a child soon to be orphaned.

When she stood, Mikki kept her gaze away from him. When she spoke, her voice was husky. "Good-bye, Daddy."

She turned and rushed from the room.

"Good-bye, Michelle," Jack mumbled to the empty room.

10

Jack lay there for hours, until day evaporated to night. The clock ticked, and he didn't move. His breathing was steady, buoyed by the machine that replenished his lungs, keeping him alive. Something was burning in his chest that he could not exactly identify or even precisely locate. His thoughts were focused on his last embrace with his daughter, her unspoken plea for him not to leave her. With the end of his life, with his last breath, the Armstrong children would be without parents. His finger had hovered over the nurse's call button all day, ready to summon the doctor, to let it be over. But he never pushed it.

As the clock ticked, the burn in Jack's chest continued to grow. It wasn't painful; indeed, it warmed his throat, his arms, his legs, his feet, his hands. His eyes became teary and then dried; became teary and then dried again. Sobs came and went. And still his mind focused only on his daughter. That last embrace. That last silent plea.

The nurses came and went. He was fed with liquid, shot like a bullet into his body. The clock ticked, the air continued to pour into him. At precisely midnight Jack started feeling odd. His lungs were straining, as they had been when Jackie had pulled the line out of the converter at home.

This might be it, Jack thought, button or no button; not even the machines could keep him alive any longer. He had wondered what the moment would actually feel like. Wedged in a mass of burning metal in Iraq after being blown up in his Humvee, he had wondered that too: whether his last moments on earth would be thousands of miles away from Lizzie and his kids. What it would feel like. What would be waiting for him.

Who would not be scared? Terrified even? The last journey. The one everyone took alone. Without the comfort of a companion. And, unless one had faith, without the reassurance that something awaited him at the end.

He took another deep breath, and then another. His lungs were definitely weakening. He could not drive enough oxygen into them to sustain life. He reached up and fiddled with the line in his nose. That's when he realized what the problem was. There was no airflow. He clicked on the bed light and turned to the wall. There was the problem; the line had come loose from the wall juncture. The pressure cuff had not come off, however, or he would've heard the air escaping into the room. He was about to press the call button but decided to see if he could push the line back in himself.

That's when it struck him.

How long have I been breathing on my own?

He glanced at the vitals monitor. The alarm hadn't

gone off, though it should have. But as he gazed at the oxygen levels, he realized why the buzzer hadn't sounded. His oxygen levels hadn't dropped.

How was that possible?

He managed to push the line back in and took several deep breaths. Then he pulled the line out of his nose and breathed on his own for as long as he could. Ten minutes later, his lungs started to labor. Then he put the line back in.

What the hell is going on?

Over the next two hours, he kept pulling the line out and breathing on his own until he was up to fifteen minutes. His lungs normally felt like sacks of wet cement. Now they felt halfway normal.

At three a.m. he sat up in bed and then did the unthinkable. He released the side rail and swung around so his feet dangled over the sides of the bed. He inched forward until his toes touched the cold tile floor. Every part of him straining with the effort, little by little, Jack pushed himself up until most of his weight was supported by his legs. He could hold himself up for only a few seconds before collapsing back onto the sheets. Panting with the exertion, pain searing his weakened lungs, he repeated the movement twice more. Every muscle in his body was spasming from the strain.

Yet as the sweat cooled on his forehead, Jack smiled—for good reason.

He had just stood on his own power for the first time in months.

The next morning, after the hospice nurse had come through on her rounds, he edged to the side of the bed again, and his toes touched the floor. But then his hands slipped on the bedcovers and he crumpled to the floor.

At first he panicked, his hand clawing for the call button, which was well out of reach. Then he calmed. The same methodical, practical nature that had carried him safely through Iraq and Afghanistan came back to him.

He grabbed the edge of the bed, tightened his grip, and pulled. His emaciated body slipped, slithered, and jerked until he was fully back on the bed. He lay there in quiet triumph, hard-earned sweat staining his hospice gown.

That night he half walked and half crawled to the bathroom and looked at himself in the mirror for the first time in months. It was not a pretty sight. He looked eighty-four instead of thirty-four. A sense of hopelessness settled over him. He was fooling himself. But as he continued to gaze in the mirror, a familiar voice sounded in his head.

You can do this, Jack.

He looked around frantically, but he was all alone.

You can do this, honey.

It was Lizzie. It couldn't be, of course, but it was.

He closed his eyes. "Can I?" he asked.

Yes, she said. *You have to, Jack. For the children.*

Jack crawled back to his bed and lay there. Had Lizzie really spoken to him? He didn't know. Part of him knew it was impossible. But what was happening to him seemed impossible too. He closed his eyes, conjured her image in his mind, and smiled.

The next night he heard the squeak of the gurney. The patient next door to him would suffer no longer. The person was in a better place. Jack had seen the minister walk down the hallway, Bible in hand. A better place. But Jack was no longer thinking about dying. For the first time since his death sentence had been pronounced, Jack was focused on living.

The next night as the clock hit midnight, Jack lifted himself off the bed and slowly walked around the room, supporting himself by putting one hand against the wall. He felt stronger, his lungs operating somewhat normally. It was as though his body was healing itself minute by minute. He heard a rumbling in his belly and realized that he was hungry. And he didn't want liquid pouring into a line. He wanted real food. Food that required teeth to consume.

Every so often he would smack his arm to make sure he wasn't dreaming. At last he convinced himself it was real. No, it wasn't just real.

This is a miracle.

11

Two weeks passed, and Jack celebrated the week of his thirty-fifth birthday by gaining four pounds and doing away with the oxygen altogether. Miracle or not, he still had a long way to go because his body had withered over the months. He had to rebuild his strength and put on weight. He sat up in his chair for several hours at a time. Using a walker, he regularly made his way to the bathroom all on his own. Another week passed, and four more pounds had appeared on his frame.

Things that Jack, along with most people, had always taken for granted represented small but significant victories in his improbable recovery. Holding a fork and using it to put solid food into his mouth. Washing his face and using a toilet instead of a bed pan. Touching his toes; breathing on his own.

The hospice staff had been remarkably supportive of Jack after it was clear that he was getting better. Perhaps it was because they were weary of people leaving this place solely on the gurney with a sheet thrown over their bodies.

Jack talked to his kids every chance he got, using his old cell phone. Jackie was bubbly and mostly incoherent. But Jack could sense that the older kids were wondering what was going on.

Cory said, "Dad, can't you come live with us?"

"We'll see, buddy. Let's just take it slow."

With the help of the folks at the hospice, Jack was able to use Skype to see his kids on a laptop computer one of the medical techs brought in. Cory and Jackie were thrilled to see their dad looking better.

Mikki was more subdued and cautious than her brothers, but Jack could tell she was curious. And hopeful.

"You look stronger, Dad."

"I'm feeling better."

"Does this mean?" She stopped. "I mean, will you . . . ?"

Jack's real fear, even though he did believe he was experiencing a true miracle, was that his recovery might be temporary. He did not want to put his kids through this nightmare again. But that didn't mean he couldn't talk to them. Or see them.

"I don't know, honey. I'm trying to figure that out. I'm doing my best."

"Well, keep doing what you're doing," she replied. And then she smiled at him. That one look seemed to make every muscle in Jack's body firm even more.

One time Bonnie had appeared on the computer screen after Mikki had left the room. Her approach was far more direct, as she stared at Jack sitting up in bed. "What is going on?"

"I'm still here."

"Your hospice doctor won't talk to me. Privacy laws, he said."

"I know," Jack said. "But I can fill you in. I'm feeling better. Getting stronger. How're things working out with Mikki?"

"Fine. She's settled in, but we need to address *your* situation."

"I *am* addressing it. Every day."

And so it had gone, day after day, week after week. Using Skype and the phone, and answering all the kids' questions. Jack could see that more and more even Mikki was coming to grips with what was happening. Every time he saw her smile or heard her laugh at some funny remark he made, it seemed to strengthen him even more.

It was on a cold, blustery Monday morning in February that Jack walked down the hall under his own power. He'd gained five more pounds, his face had filled out, and his hair was growing back. His appetite had returned with a vengeance. They had also stopped giving him pain meds because there was no more pain.

The hospice doctor sat down with him at the end of the week. "I'm not sure what's going on here, Jack, but I'm ordering up some new blood work and other tests to see what we have. I don't want you to get your hopes up, though."

Jack simply stared at him, a spoonful of soup poised near his lips.

The doctor went on. "Look, if this continues, that's terrific. No one will be happier than me—well, of course, except for you. All of my patients die, Jack, to put it bluntly. And we just try to help them pass with dignity."

"But," said Jack.

"But your disease is a complicated one. And always a fatal one. This might just be a false remission."

"Might be."

"Well, without dashing your hopes, it probably is."

"Have others in my condition had a remission?"

The doctor looked taken aback. "No, not to my knowledge."

"That's all I needed to know."

The doctor looked confused. "Needed to know about what?"

"I know I was dying, but now I'm not."

"How can you be so sure?"

"Sometimes you just know."

"Jack, I have to tell you that what's happening to you is medically impossible."

"Medicine is not everything."

The doctor looked him over and saw the new muscle, the fuller face, and the eyes that burned with a rigid intensity.

"Why do you think this is happening to you, Jack?" he finally asked.

"You're a doctor; you wouldn't understand."

"I'm also a human being, and I'd very much like to know."

Jack reached in his drawer and pulled out a photo. He passed it to the doctor.

It was a photo of Lizzie and the kids.

"Because of them," said Jack.

"But I thought your wife passed away."

Jack shook his head. "Doesn't matter."

"What?"

"When you love someone, you love them forever."

12

Two days later, Jack was in his room eating a full meal. He'd put on three more pounds. The doctor walked in and perched on the edge of the bed.

"Okay, I officially believe in miracles. Your blood work came back negative. No trace of the disease. It's like something came along and chased it away. Never seen anything like it. There's no way to explain it medically."

Jack swallowed a mouthful of mashed potatoes and smiled. "I'm glad you finally came around."

He saw his kids that night on the computer. He believed he actually made Jackie understand that he was getting better. At least his son's last words had been, "Daddy's boo-boo's gone."

Cory had blurted out, "When are you coming to see me?"

"I hope soon, big guy. I'll let you know. I've still got a ways to go. But I'm getting there."

Mikki's reaction surprised him, and not in a good way.

"Is this some kind of trick?" she asked.

Jack slowly sat up in his chair as he stared at her. "Trick?"

"When we left you, Dad, you were dying. That's what hospice is for. You said good-bye to all of us. You made me go live with Gramps and *her*!"

"Honey, it's no trick. I'm getting better."

She suddenly dissolved into tears. "Well then, will you be coming to take us home? Because I hate it here."

"I'm doing my best, sweetie. With a little more time I think—"

But Mikki hit a key and the computer screen went black.

Jack slowly sat back. He never heard the squeak of the gurney as the woman across the hall made her final journey from this place.

Day turned to night, and Jack hadn't moved. No food, no liquids, no words spoken to anyone who came to see him.

Finally, at around two a.m., he stirred. He rose from his bed and walked up and down the hall before persuading a nurse to scavenge in the kitchen for some food. He ate and watched his reflection in the window.

I'm coming, Mikki. Dad's coming for you.

A week later he weighed over one-sixty and was walking the halls for an hour at a time. Like an infant, he was relearning how to use his arms and legs. He would flex his fingers and toes, curl and uncurl his arms, bend his legs. The nursing staff watched him carefully, unaccustomed to this sort of thing. Families of other hospice patients observed him curiously. At first Jack was afraid they would be devastated by his progress when their loved ones still lay dying. At least he thought that, until one woman approached him. She was in her sixties and was here every day. Jack knew that her husband had terminal cancer. He'd passed by the man's door and seen the shriveled body under the sheets. He was waiting to die, like everyone else here.

Everyone except me.

She slipped her arm through his and said, "God bless you."

He looked at her questioningly.

"You give us all hope."

Jack felt slightly panicked. "I don't know why this is happening to me," he said frankly. "But it's an awfully long shot."

"That's not what I meant. I know my husband is going to die. But you still give us all hope, honey."

Jack went back to his room and stared at himself in the mirror. He looked more like himself now. The jawline was firming, the hair fuller. He walked slowly to the window and looked outside at a landscape that was still more in the grips of winter than spring, though that season was not too far off. He'd spent several winters apart from his family while he carried a rifle for his country. Lying in his quarters outside of Baghdad or Kabul he had closed his eyes and visualized Christmas with his family. The laughter of Mikki and Cory as they opened presents on Christmas morning.

And then there was the memory of Lizzie's smile as she looked at the small gifts that Jack had bought her before he was deployed for the first time. It had been the summer, so he had gotten her sunblock, a bikini, and a book on grilling. She'd later sent him a photo by e-mail of her wearing the bikini while cooking hot dogs on the Hibachi with mounds of snow behind her. That image had carried him through one hellish battle after another. His wife. Her smile. Wanting so badly to come back to her. That all seemed so long ago, and in some important ways it was.

He went to his nightstand and pulled out the bundle of letters. Each had a number on the envelope. He selected the envelope with the number one on it and slid the paper out. The letter was dated December eighteenth and represented the first one he'd written to Lizzie. He gazed down at the handwriting that was his but that also wasn't because the disease had made him so weak. Sometimes while writing he'd had to put down the pen because he just couldn't hold it any longer. But still it was readable. It said what he had wanted to say. It was the accomplishment of a man who was doing this as his final act in life.

Dear Lizzie,

There are things I want to say to you that I just don't have the breath for anymore. That's why I've decided to write you these letters. I want you to have them after I'm gone. They're not meant to be sad, just my chance to talk to you one more time. When I was healthy you made me happier than any person has a right to be. When I was half a world away, I knew that I was looking at the same sky you were, thinking of the same things you were, wanting to be with you and looking forward to when I could be. You gave me three beautiful children, which is a greater gift than I deserved. I tell you this, though you already know it, because sometimes people don't talk about these things enough. I want you to know that if I could've stayed with you I would have. I fought as hard as I could. I will never understand why I had to be taken from you so soon, but I have accepted it. Yet I want you to know that there is nothing more important to me than you. I loved you from the moment I saw you. And the happiest day of my life was when you agreed to share your life with mine. I promised that I would always be there for you. And my love for you is so strong that even though I won't be there physically, I will be there in every other way. I will watch over you. I will be there if you need to talk. I will never stop loving you. Not even death is powerful enough to overcome my feelings for you. My love for you, Lizzie, is stronger than anything.

Love,
Jack

He put the letter back in the envelope and replaced the packet in the drawer. He slipped the photo from the pocket of his robe and looked at it. From the depths of the color print, his family smiled back at him. He thought of all the others in this place who would never leave it alive. He had been spared.

Why me?

Jack had no ready answer. But he did know one thing. He was not going to waste a second chance at living.

13

A few days later, Jack Armstrong was discharged from hospice and sent to a rehab facility. He rode over in a shuttle van. The driver was an older guy with a soft felt cap and a trim white beard. Jack was his only passenger.

As they drove along, Jack stared out in childlike wonder at things he never thought he would experience again. Seeing a bird in flight. A mailman delivering letters and packages. A kid running for the school bus. He promised himself he would never again take anything for granted.

As they pulled up in front of the rehab building, the man said, "Never brought anybody from that place to this place."

"I guess not," said Jack. He held his small duffel. Inside were a few clothes, a pair of tennis shoes, and the letters he'd written to Lizzie. When he got to his room, he looked around at the simple furnishings and single window that had a view of the interior outdoor courtyard, which was covered in snow. Jack sat on the bed after putting his few belongings away.

He looked up when a familiar person walked into the room.

"Sammy? What are you doing here?"

Sammy Duvall was dressed in gray sweats and had on a checkered bandanna. "Why the hell do you think I'm here? To get your sorry butt in shape. Look at you; you've obviously been dogging it. And they told me you were getting better. You look like crap."

"I don't understand. You didn't come by the hospice. And I left you phone messages."

The mirth left Sammy's eyes, and he sat down next to Jack on the bed. "I let you down."

"What are you talking about? You've done everything for me."

"No, I haven't. I told you at the cemetery that I'd always be there for you, but I wasn't." He paused. Jack had never seen Sammy nervous before. That emotion just never squared with a man like him. Nothing rattled Sammy Duvall.

Sammy's voice trembled as he said, "I should've come to visit you. But... seeing you in that place, just waiting to..."

Jack put a hand on the older man's shoulder. "It's okay, Sammy. I understand."

Sammy wiped his eyes and said, "Anyway, I'm here now. And you're probably gonna wish I wasn't."

"Why?"

"I'm your drill instructor."

"What?"

"Worked a deal with the folks here."

"How'd you do that?"

"Told 'em you were a special case. And you need special treatment. And if you're okay with it, so are they."

"I'm definitely okay with it. That was one reason I called you. To have you help me get back in shape."

"Famous last words, boy, because I'm gonna kick your butt."

The weeks went by swiftly. And with pain. Much pain.

The sweat streaming off him during one particularly arduous workout, Jack told Sammy, "I can't do one more damn push-up. I can't!"

"Can't or won't? 'Cause that's all the difference in the world, son."

Jack did one more push-up and then another and then a third, until he could no longer feel his arms. Jack had gone on to pump thousands of pounds of weights, run on the treadmill until he couldn't stand the stink of his own sweat, perform more push-ups until his arms nearly fell off, jump rope until his knees failed.

He cursed at Sammy, who laughed at him and goaded him into doing more, and more.

"You call yourself an army ranger? Sam Jr. can work harder than you, and he's a big, fat baby."

And Sammy didn't just instruct. He got down on the floor and did the exercises with Jack. "If an old man like me can do this, you sure as hell can," was his usual taunt.

On and on it went. Sammy screaming in his face and Jack gnashing his teeth, furrowing his brow, and doing one more pull-up, one more push-up, one more mile on the treadmill, one more set of curls, a hundred more pounds on the squat bar. But the thing was, Jack was growing stronger with every rep.

He talked to his kids every day. They knew he was in rehab. They knew he was getting stronger.

On one joint Skype session, Jack showed Cory and Jackie his muscles.

"You're ripped, Dad," said Cory.

"Whipped," crowed Jackie.

Later that night he saw Mikki. She hadn't agreed to do a Skype session with him in a while, but repeated phone calls from him and finally Sammy had convinced her.

"You look great, Dad," she said slowly. "You really do."

"You look thin," he replied.

"Yeah, well, Grandma is watching her weight, which means we all eat like birds."

"Cheeseburger's on me."

"When?" she said quickly.

"Sooner than you think, sweetie. I know I probably should have come out to see you before now. And I miss you more than anything. But... but I want to do this right. When I was in the army and we'd go on patrol, I always analyzed everything that might come up. Some of the other guys liked to wing it. Just turn on the fly. And sometimes in combat you have to do that. But being prepared for everything because you've done your homework is the best way to survive, Mikki. I hope you understand. I want to do this right. For all of you."

"I get it, Dad." She added playfully, "And Skype will get you ready for when I go to college and you really miss me."

Finally, the day came on a surprisingly warm spring morning. Jack's bag was packed and he was sitting on his bed when Sammy came into the room. "It's time."

"I know it is," said Sammy.

"I couldn't have done this without you."

"Sure you could, but it wouldn't have been nearly as much fun."

While his discharge papers were being finalized, Jack sat in a chair outside the rehab office. The months had been a blur. He drew a long, measured breath, trying to collect his thoughts. He looked out the window, where winter had passed and spring had arrived. Crocuses were pushing through the earth and trees were starting to bud out. *The world is waking up from a long winter's nap, and so am I.* He opened his duffel and pulled out an envelope with the number two on it. He slid out the letter.

Dear Lizzie,

Christmas will be here in five days, and I promise that I will make it. I've never broken a promise to you, and I never will. It's hard to say good-bye, but sometimes you have to do things you don't want to. Jackie came to see me a little while ago, and we talked. Well, he talked in Jackie language and I listened. I like to listen to him because I know one day very soon I won't be able to. He's growing up so fast, and I know he probably won't remember his dad, but I know I will live on in your memories. Tell him his dad loved him and wanted the best for him. And I wish I could have thrown the football to him and watched him play baseball. I know he will have a great life.

Cory is a special little boy. He has your sensitivity, your compassion. I know what's happening to me is probably affecting him the most of all the kids. He came and got into bed with me last night. He asked me if it hurt very much. I told him it didn't. He told me to say hello to God when I saw him. And I promised that I would.

And Mikki.

At this point Jack's hand trembled a bit. He remembered stopping at this point too as he was writing the letter. There was an old teardrop that had made the ink blotch. He started to read again.

Mikki is the most complicated of all. Not a little girl anymore but not yet an adult either. She is a good kid, though I know you've had your moments with her. She is smart and caring and she loves her brothers. She loves you, though she sometimes doesn't like to show it. My greatest regret with my daughter is letting her grow away from me. It was my fault, not hers. I see that clearly now. I only wish I had seen it that clearly while I still had a chance to do something about it. After I'm gone, please tell her the first time I ever saw her, when I got back from Afghanistan and was still in uniform, there was no prouder father who ever lived. Looking down at her tiny face, I felt the purest joy a human could possibly feel. And I wanted to protect her and never let anything bad ever happen to her. Life doesn't work that way, of course. But tell her that her dad was her biggest fan. And that whatever she does in life, I will always be her biggest fan.

Love,
Jack

14

After being discharged, Jack rode with Sammy to his house. Along the way, he asked his friend to pass by his old home. Jack was surprised to see his pickup truck in the carport.

Sammy explained, "Went with the house sale, so I heard."

"Bonnie and the Realtor handled all that. Is that my tool bin in the back?"

"Yep. Guess that went too. All happened pretty fast." He eyed Jack. "Knew you'd beat that damn thing. Still got the tickets to Disney World?"

"Yeah," said Jack, staring glumly out the window.

Five of them.

Later, Jack drove to his bank. They had kept the account open to pay for expenses. It had a few thousand dollars left in it. That was a starting point. He had his wallet, and his credit cards were still valid. Driver's license was still good. Contractor's license intact. He drove to his old house and offered the owner eight hundred bucks on the spot for the truck and tools. After some negotiation back and forth, he got them for eight-fifty, the owner apparently glad to get the heap out of his driveway. Jack raced to the bank and got a cashier's check; the title was signed over, and he drove off in his old ride the same day.

He called the kids and told them he was out of rehab and getting a place for them all to live in. He next talked to Bonnie and explained things to her.

"That's wonderful, Jack," she'd said. But her words rang hollow. She asked him what his next step would be.

"Like I said, getting my family back. I'll be coming out there really soon."

"Do you think that's wise?"

"Bonnie, I'm their father. They belong with me."

That night he treated Sammy to dinner. While Sammy had a medium-rare burger, fries, and black coffee, Jack made three trips to the salad bar before settling down to devour his heaping plate of surf and turf.

"So what's the plan, chief?"

"Get my kids back pronto. But I need a place for us to stay."

"You're welcome to stay at my place, long as you want."

Sammy's place had one bedroom and a bathroom attached to the back with only an outside entrance; Sammy's massive Harley was parked in what he referred to as "the parlor." Besides that, his "puppy," Sam Jr., had the bulk of a Honda.

"That's fine for me, but with three kids, I'll need something a little bigger."

* * *

Late that night he slowly pulled his truck down the narrow roads of the cemetery. He'd been here only once, on a bitterly cold day, the ground flash-wrapped in ice and snow. And yet even though he'd been sick, he'd memorized every detail of the place. He could never forget where his wife was buried any more than he could ever fail to recall his own name.

He walked between the plots until he reached hers, represented by a simple bronze plate in the grass. He knelt down, brushed a couple of dead leaves off it. There was a skinny metal vase bolted to the plate where one could put flowers. There were roses in there, but they were brown. Jack cleaned them all out and placed in the vase a bunch of fresh flowers he'd brought with him. He sat down on his haunches and read the writing on the plate.

"Elizabeth 'Lizzie' Armstrong, loving wife, mother, and daughter. You will always be missed. You will always be loved."

He traced the letters with his fingers, even as his eyes filled with tears.

"I'm going to get the kids, Lizzie. I'm going to bring them home, and we're going to be a family again." He choked back a sob and tried to ignore the dull pain in his chest. "I wish you could be here with me, Lizzie. More than anything I wish that. But you were there for me in the hospital when I needed you. And I promise I will take good care of the children. I will make them proud. And I will raise them right. Just like you did."

The words finally failed him, and he lay down in the soft grass and wept. He finally became so exhausted, he fell asleep. When he woke he didn't know where he was for a few seconds, before he looked over and saw the grave. The dawn was breaking, the air chilly. As he looked overhead, he could see flocks of birds arriving for the start of spring.

Jack's clothes were damp from the dew. He coughed to clear his throat. His eyes and face were raw. In the distance he could hear the sounds of early-morning traffic on the roads that fronted the cemetery. He walked silently back to his truck and drove off without the one person he needed more than anyone else.

15

One day later, Jack found it, a house owned by an elderly couple who had moved to an assisted-living facility. They couldn't sell their home because it needed a lot of repairs. And with dozens of homes in default on their street, it was difficult to sell anyway. Jack called the Realtor and offered his labor for free to fix up the place in exchange for staying there at no cost. Since the couple wasn't making any money off the house anyway, they quickly agreed. It wasn't perfect, but he didn't need perfect. He just needed his kids under the same roof as him. Jack moved his few possessions in the next day, after signing a one-page agreement. He made some quick cosmetic changes and bought some secondhand furniture.

Now it was time.

Using his credit card, he booked his plane tickets, packed his bag, and left for the airport. He went to collect Mikki first, because he knew if he went to the sisters' homes first, they would be on the phone to their mother before he'd even left their driveways.

He landed in Phoenix, rented a car, and drove to Tempe. He reached Fred and Bonnie's house but then drove past it. He parked a little down from the house and waited. An hour later a car pulled into the driveway, and Fred and Mikki got out. She was carrying her schoolbag. His heart ached when he saw her. She'd grown even taller, Jack noted, and her face had changed too. She was wearing a school uniform, white polo shirt and checked skirt. Her hair was in a ponytail and had nary a strand of pink or purple in it. She looked utterly miserable.

They went into the house. Jack parked in their driveway, took a deep breath, climbed out of the car, and walked up to the door.

"Dad?"

Mikki stared at him openmouthed. When he held out his arms for a hug, she tentatively reached out to him. He stroked her hair and kissed the top of her head.

"Dad, is it really you?"

"It's me, sweetie. It's really me."

Bonnie and Fred came around the corner, saw him, and stopped.

"Jack?" said Fred. "My God."

Bonnie just stood there, disbelief on her features.

Jack moved into the house with Mikki. He held out his hand, and Fred shook it. He looked at Bonnie. She still seemed in a daze.

"My God," she said, echoing her husband's words. "It's true. It's really true. Even with all the phone calls and seeing you on that computer. It's not the same."

"What is all the commotion?" Cecilia came into the

room, skimming along on her walker, her oxygen line trailing behind her. When she saw Jack, she didn't freeze like Fred and Bonnie had done.

She cackled. "I knew it." She came forward as fast as she could and gave him a prolonged squeeze. "I knew it, Jack, honey," she said again, staring up at him and blinking back tears of joy.

They all sat at the kitchen table sipping glasses of iced tea. Jack eyed Bonnie. "Docs gave me a clean bill of health."

Bonnie just kept shaking her head, but Fred clapped him on the shoulder. "Jack, we're so happy for you, son."

Later, when they were alone, Bonnie asked, "How long will you be staying?"

"From here I'm heading to LA and then on to Portland."

"To see the kids?"

"No, to take them back with me, Bonnie. I've already told Mikki to start packing her things."

"But the school year will be done in less than two months."

"She can go to school in Cleveland as easily as she can here."

"But the house was sold."

"I'm renting another one."

"How will you support them?"

"I've started my business back up."

"Okay, but who will watch them when you're working?"

"Mikki and Cory are in school the whole day. And they're old enough now to come home and be okay by themselves for a few hours. Jackie will be in extended day care. And if unexpected things come up, we'll deal with them. Just like every other family does."

Bonnie pursed her lips. "Michelle has settled into her new life here."

Jack said nothing about how miserable the girl had been here. He simply said, "I don't think she'll mind."

"You could have called before you came."

"Yeah, I could have. And maybe I should have. But I don't see what harm it did."

"What harm? You just expect us to give her back to you, with no notice, no preparation? After all we've done."

"I've been in constant contact over the last few months. I kept you updated on my progress. Hell, you've *seen* me on the computer getting better. And I told you I would be coming to take the kids back. Soon. So this shouldn't come as a shock to you. And it's not like you're never going to see them again." He paused, and his tone changed. "Even though you did leave me by myself."

"You said it was all right. You told us to do it. And we thought you were dying."

"Come on, Bonnie, what else could I tell you under the circumstances? But for the record, dying alone is a real bitch."

As soon as Jack finished speaking, he regretted it. Bonnie stood, her face red with anger. "Don't you dare talk to me about dying alone. My Lizzie is lying dead and buried. There was no one with her at the end. No one! Certainly not you."

Jack eyed her. "Why don't you just say it, Bonnie, because I know you want to."

"*You* should be dead, not her." Bonnie seemed stunned by her own words. "I'm sorry, I didn't mean that." Her face flushed. "I'm very sorry."

"I *would* give my life to have Lizzie back. But I can't.

I've got three kids who need me. Nothing takes priority over that. I hope you can understand."

"What I understand is that you're taking your children from a safe, healthy environment into something totally unknown."

"I'm their father," said Jack heatedly.

"You're a single parent. Lizzie isn't here to take care of the kids."

"I can take care of them."

"Can you? Because I don't think you have any idea what's in store for you."

Jack started to say something but stopped.

Could she be right?

16

"Mr. Armstrong?"

Jack stared down from the ladder he was standing on while repairing some siding on a job site. The sun was high overhead, the air warm, and the sweat on his skin thick. He had on a white tank top, dirty dark blue cargo shorts, white crew socks, and worn steel-toed work boots. The woman down below was pretty, with light brown curly hair cut short, and she wore a pair of black slacks and a white blouse; her heels were sunk in the wet grass.

"What can I do for you, ma'am?"

"I'm Janice Kaplan. I'm a newspaper reporter. I'd like to talk to you."

Jack clambered down the ladder and rubbed his hands off on the back of his shorts. "Talk to me about what?"

"Being the miracle man."

Jack squinted at her. "Come again?"

"You are the Jack Armstrong who was diagnosed with a terminal illness?"

"Well, yeah, I was."

"You don't look terminal anymore."

"I'm not. I got better."

"So a miracle. At least that's what the doctor I talked to said."

Jack looked annoyed. "You talked to my doctor? I thought that was private."

"Actually, he's a friend of mine. He mentioned your case in passing. It was all very positive. I became interested, did a little digging, and here I am."

"Here for what?" Jack said, puzzled.

"To do a story on you. People with death sentences rarely get a second chance. I'd like to talk to you about the experience. And I know my readers would want to know."

Jack and the kids had been back for nearly four weeks now. With parenting and financial support resting solely on his shoulders, Jack barely had time to eat or sleep. Bonnie had been right in her prediction. He didn't have any idea what was in store for him. Mikki had really stepped up and had taken the laboring oar with the cooking and cleaning, the shopping, and looking after the boys. He had never had greater appreciation for Lizzie. She'd done it all, from school to meals to laundry to shopping to keeping the house clean. Jack had worked hard, but he realized now that he hadn't come close to working as hard as his wife had, because she did all that and worked full-time too. At midnight he lay in his bed, numb and exhausted—and humbled by the knowledge that Lizzie would have still been going strong.

"A story?" Jack shook his head as he dug a hole in the

mulch bed with the toe of his boot. "Look, it's really not that special."

"Don't be modest. And I also understand that you turned your life around, built your business back, got a house, and went to retrieve your children, who'd been placed with family after your wife tragically died." She added, "I was very sorry to hear about that. On Christmas Eve too, of all days."

Jack's annoyance turned to anger. "You didn't learn all that from my doctor. That really is an invasion of privacy."

"Please don't be upset, Mr. Armstrong. I'm a reporter; it's my job to find out these things. And I'm probably not explaining myself very well." She drew a deep breath while Jack stared at her, his hands clenching into fists with his anxiety. "It's strictly a feel-good piece. One man's triumph against the odds, a family reunited. These are hard times for folks, especially around here. All we hear is bad news. War, crime, people losing their jobs and their homes. I write about that stuff all the time, and while it is news, it's also very, very depressing. But this is different. This is a great story that will make people smile. That's all I'm shooting for. To make people feel good, for once."

His anger quickly disappearing, Jack looked around while he considered her request. He saw Sammy up on another ladder watching him intently. He waved to show him things were okay. Jack turned back to the woman.

"So what exactly do I have to do?"

"Just sit down with me and tell your story. I'll take notes, do a draft, get back to you, polish it, and then it'll be published in the paper and on our Web site."

"And that's it?"

"That's all. I really believe it will be positive for lots of people. There are many folks out there with what seem like insurmountable obstacles in front of them. Reading about how you overcame yours could do a lot of good. It really could."

"I think I just got lucky."

"Maybe, but maybe not. From the research I've done on your condition, the odds were zero that you would recover. No one else ever has."

"Well, I'm just happy I was the first. How about tomorrow after dinner?"

"Great. About eight?"

Jack gave her his address. She glanced at his exposed upper right arm and then his scarred calves. "I understand you were in the military. Is that where you got those?" She indicated the ragged bullet wound on his arm and the network of scars on his legs.

"Arm in Afghanistan and legs in Iraq."

"Two Purples then?"

"Yeah. Were you in the military?"

"My son just got back from the Middle East in one piece, thank God."

"I guess we both have a lot to be thankful for."

"I'll see you tomorrow."

The story ran, and a few days later Janice Kaplan called.

"The AP picked up my article, Jack."

Jack had just finished cleaning up after dinner.

"What does that mean?" he asked.

"AP. Associated Press. That means my story about

you and your family is running in newspapers across the country. My editor still can't believe it."

"Congratulations, Janice."

"No, thank *you*. It wasn't the writing; it was the story. And it was a great picture of you and the kids. And I think lots of families will be inspired by your struggle and triumph. I just thought I'd give you a heads-up. You're famous now. So be prepared."

17

Janice Kaplan's words proved prophetic. Letters came pouring in, including offers to appear on TV and to tell his story to major magazines; one publisher even wanted Jack to write a book. Overwhelmed by the blitzkrieg and wanting a normal life with his kids, he declined them all. He figured with the passage of time other stories would emerge and take the focus away from him. His fifteen minutes of fame couldn't be over soon enough for him. He was no miracle man, he knew, but simply a guy who got lucky.

A week after Kaplan's call, Jack was lying in bed when he heard voices downstairs. He slipped on his pants and crept down to the main level.

"Stop it, Chris!"

Jack took the last three steps in one bound. Mikki was at the door, and a teenage boy had his hands all over her as she struggled against him. It took only two seconds for Jack to lift the young man off his feet and slam him against the wall. Jack said, "What part of *no* don't you get, jerk?" He looked over at Mikki. "What the hell is going on?"

"We... he just came over to work on some... Dad, just let him down."

Jack snapped, "Get upstairs."

"Dad!"

"Now."

"I can handle this. I'm not a child."

"Yeah, I can see that. Upstairs."

She stalked up to her room. Jack turned back to the young man.

"I ever catch you with one finger on her again, they won't be able to find all the pieces to put you back together, got it?"

The terrified teen merely nodded.

Jack threw him outside and slammed the door. He stood there, letting his anger cool. Then he marched up the stairs and knocked on his daughter's door.

"Leave me alone."

Instead he threw open the door and went in. Mikki was sitting on the floor, her guitar across her lap.

"We need to get a few rules straight around here," Jack said.

She stared up at him icily. "Which rules? The ones where you're ruining my life?"

"What was I supposed to do, let that little creep paw you?"

"I told you I could handle it."

"You can't handle everything. That's why there are people called parents."

"Oh, is that what you're pretending to be?"

Jack looked stunned. "Pretend? I brought all of you back home so we could be together. Do you think I did that just for the hell of it?"

"I don't have a clue why you did it. And you didn't even ask me if I wanted to come back. You just told me to pack, like I was a child."

"I thought you hated it out there. You told me that a dozen times."

"Well, I hate it here too."

"What do you want from me? I'm doing the best I can."

"You were gone a long time."

"I explained that. Remember? I told you that story about being in the army? About taking your time and being prepared for every eventuality."

"That's crap!"

"What?"

"In case you hadn't figured it out, this isn't the army, Dad. This is about family."

"I did all that to make sure we *could* be a family," he shot back.

"A family? You don't have a clue what to do with us. Admit it. You're not Mom."

"I know I'm not, believe me. But you two were always arguing."

"That doesn't mean I didn't appreciate what she did for us. Now I do most of the cooking and cleaning and the laundry, and looking after Jackie. And your grocery-shopping skills are a joke."

Jack felt his anger continue to rise. "Look, I know I'm not in your mom's league, but I'm trying to make this work. I love you guys."

"Really? Well, Cory's being bullied at school. Did you know that? His grades are going down even though he's a really smart kid. The teachers have sent home tons of notes in his bag, but you never check that, do you? And Jackie's birthday is in two weeks. Have you planned anything? Bought him a present? Planned a party for his friends or even thought about a cake?"

Jack's face grew pale. "Two weeks?"

"Two weeks, *Dad*. So you might want to try harder."

"Mik, I—"

"Can you please just leave me alone?"

When he left her room, Cory was standing in the hall in his underwear.

Jack looked embarrassed. "Cor, *are* you being bullied at school?"

Cory closed the door, leaving his dad alone in the hall.

18

Jack and Sammy were unloading Jack's truck in his driveway after a long day at work. Jack nearly dropped a sledgehammer on his foot. Sammy looked over at him.

"You okay? Haven't been yourself the last couple of days."

Jack slowly picked up the tool and threw it back in the truck bed. "What do you think Jackie would like for his birthday? It's just around the corner, and I wanted to get him something nice."

Sammy shrugged. "Uh, toy gun?"

Jack looked doubtful. "I don't think Lizzie liked to encourage that. And where can I get a cake and some birthday things? You know like hats and... stuff?"

"The grocery store up the street has a bakery."

"How do you know that?"

"It's right across from the beer aisle."

Jack drove to the store and got some items for Jackie's

birthday. He was standing at the checkout aisle when he saw it. He had never been more stunned in his life. He was looking at *his* photo on the cover of one of the tabloid magazines that were kept as impulse buys at the checkout. He slowly reached out his hand and picked up a copy.

The headline ran, "Miracle Man Muddied."

What the hell?

Jack turned to the next page and read the story. With each word he read, his anger increased. Now he could understand the headline. The writer had twisted everything. He'd made it seem that Jack had forced Lizzie to go out on an icy, treacherous night to get his pain meds. And then, even worse, the writer had suggested that Jack thought his wife was having an affair with a neighbor. An obviously distraught Lizzie had run a red light and been killed. None of it was true, but now probably millions of people thought he was some kind of monster.

He left his items on the conveyor belt and rushed home.

On the drive there, it didn't take him long to figure out what had happened.

Bonnie had been the writer's source. But how could she have known? Then it struck him. Lizzie must've called her on the drive over to the pharmacy and told her what she was doing. Maybe she mentioned something about Bill Miller, and Bonnie had misconstrued what Jack's reaction had been, although it would have been pretty difficult to do that. More likely, Bonnie might've just altered what Lizzie had told her to suit her own purposes.

Jack could imagine Bonnie seething. Here he was getting all this notoriety, adulation, and sympathy, and Lizzie was in a grave because of him. At least Bonnie probably believed that. A part of Jack couldn't blame her for feeling that way. But now she had opened a Pandora's box that Jack would find difficult to close. And what worried him the most was what would happen when his kids found out. He wanted to be the first to talk to them about it, especially Mikki. He gunned the truck.

Unfortunately, he was too late.

19

Mikki was waiting for him on the front porch with a copy of another gossip paper with a similar headline. She was trembling and attacked him as soon as he got out of the truck. "This is all over school. How could you make Mom go out that night? And how could you even think that she would cheat on you?"

Jack exploded. "That story is full of lies. I never accused your mom of anything. I saw her slap Bill Miller. She and I had a laugh about it because he was drunk. And I didn't insist she go out that night. In fact, I told her not to."

"I don't believe you."

"Mikki, it's the truth. I swear. Tabloids make stuff up all the time. You know that."

"This never would have happened if you hadn't agreed to do that stupid Miracle Man story in the first place. That *was* your fault."

"Okay, you're right about that. I wish I hadn't but—"

"So now everybody thinks Mom was a slut and you're a jerk. And I'll spend the rest of the school year having people talking behind my back."

"Will you just listen to me for a sec—"

Before he could finish, she'd fled inside, slamming the door behind her. When he started to go in the house after her, he heard the lock click. Staring through the side window at him was Cory. He gave his father a furious scowl and ran off.

Jack ended up taking Cory and Jackie to Chuck E. Cheese's for Jackie's third birthday. Jack wore a ball cap and glasses so people wouldn't recognize him during his fifteen minutes of "infamy." On the table in front of him were a half-eaten cheese pizza and a mass-produced birthday cake. While Jackie jumped into mounds of balls along with a zillion other kids, Cory sat slumped in a corner looking like he would rather be attacked by sharks than be here. Jack didn't even know where Mikki was. The only moment in his life worse than this was when the cop told him Lizzie was dead.

Later, after they returned home, Jackie played with the monster truck that Jack had rushed out to buy him the night before. Cory had escaped into the backyard.

"You like the truck?" Jack asked quietly.

Jackie made guttural truck noises and rolled it across his dad's shoulder.

At least I've still got one kid who doesn't hate me.

Carrying his youngest son, Jack walked up the stairs and peered inside Mikki's bedroom. It was small, lighted by a single overhead fixture that gave out meager illumination, and her clothes were all over the floor. A half-empty jar of Nutella sat on a storage box. Her guitar and keyboard were in one corner. A device to mix musical tracks was on the floor. Sheet music was stacked everywhere. There was an old beat-up microphone on a metal fold-up table that she used as a desk.

Jack put his son down and then walked over and picked up some of the music. It was actually blank sheets with pencil notes written in, obviously by his daughter. Jack couldn't read music and didn't know what the markings represented, but they looked complicated. She could create this but couldn't even manage a B in math or science? Then again, he hadn't been a great student either, except in the subjects that interested him.

He took Jackie's hand and walked into the bedroom the boys shared. It was far more cluttered than Mikki's because it was smaller and housed two people instead of one. The beds were nearly touching. There was a small built-in shelf crammed with toys, books, and junk that boys tended to collect. Cory had stacked his clothes neatly in the small bureau Jack had gotten thirdhand. Jackie's clothes were on top of the bureau.

Jack noticed a box crammed with papers on the floor next to Cory's bed. He looked inside. When he saw the top page, he started going through the rest. It was printed information about his disease. He saw, in Cory's handwriting, notes on the pages.

"He thought maybe he could find a cure."

Jack spun around to see Mikki standing there.

She came forward. "He wanted to save you. Dumb, huh? He's only a kid. But he meant well."

Jack slowly rose. "I didn't know."

"Well, to be fair, you were pretty out of it at the time." She sat down on one of the beds, while Jackie rushed toward her and held out his truck for her to see. "That's really cool, Jackie." She hugged her brother and said, "Happy birthday, big guy."

"Big guy," repeated Jackie with a huge smile.

She glanced at her dad. "It's a nice gift."

"Thanks." He stared back at her. "So where does that leave us?"

"This is not where we say stupid stuff and hug and then bawl our eyes out and everything is okay, cue the dumb music. It's one day at a time. That's life. Some days will be good and some days will suck. Some days I'll look at you and feel mad; some days I'll feel crappy about being mad at you. Some days I'll feel nothing. But you're still my dad."

"The thing is, I was supposed to be gone, not your mom. I'd accepted that. But then your mother was gone. And somehow I got better. It just wasn't supposed to happen that way."

"But it did happen exactly that way. You *are* here. Mom isn't."

"So where do we all go from here?"

"You're really asking me?"

"You obviously know a lot more about this family than I do."

His cell phone rang. He looked at the caller ID. It was Bonnie's number. Now what? Hadn't she done enough damage?

"Hello?" he said, bracing for a fight.

It was Fred. He sounded tired, and there was something else in his voice that made Jack stiffen.

He said, "Fred, is everything okay?"

"Not really, Jack, no."

"What is it? Not Bonnie?"

"No." He paused. "It's Cecilia. She died about two hours ago."

20

Though she'd lived the last ten years in Ohio with her daughter and son-in-law, except for her short stint in Arizona, Cecilia Pinckney was a Southerner through and through. She'd requested to be buried in Charleston, South Carolina, in the family crypt. So Jack bundled the kids into a pale blue 1964 VW van with white top that Sammy had lovingly restored, and headed south. A large crowd gathered under a very hot sun and high humidity for the funeral. Bonnie looked older by ten years, shrunken and bowed. Seeing this, Jack couldn't bring himself to offer anything other than brief condolences. As she looked up at him, Jack thought he could see some affection for him underneath all the sorrow.

"Thank you for coming," she said.

"Cecilia was a great lady."

"Yes, she was."

"When some time has passed, we need to talk."

She slowly nodded. "All right. We probably should."

After the service was over, Jack and the kids drove back to the hotel, where they were crammed into one room. Jack had just taken off his tie and jacket when the hotel phone rang. He answered, thinking it might be Fred, but it was a strange voice.

"Mr. Armstrong, I'm Royce Baxter."

"Okay, what can I do for you?"

"I had the pleasure of being Mrs. Cecilia Pinckney's attorney for the past twenty years."

"Her attorney?"

"That's right. I was wondering if I could meet with you for a little bit. My office is only a block over from your hotel. Fred O'Toole told me where you were staying. I assumed you'd be heading back to Ohio soon, and I thought I would catch you before you left. I know the timing is bad, but it is important and it won't take long."

Jack looked around at the kids. Jackie was passed out in a chair, and Cory and Mikki were watching TV.

"Give me the address."

Five minutes later he was sitting across from the very prim and proper Royce Baxter, who was dressed in a dark suit. He was in his sixties, about five-ten, with a bit of a paunch and a good-natured face.

"Let me get down to business." Baxter drew a document out of a file. "This is Ms. Cecilia's last will and testament."

"Look, if she left me anything, I really don't feel that I should accept it."

Baxter peered at him over the document. "And why is that?"

"It's sort of complicated."

"Well, she made this change to her will very recently. She told me that even if you never used it, it would always be there for you."

"Well, what is it exactly?" Jack said curiously.

"The old Pinckney house on the South Carolina coast in a town called Channing."

"The Palace, you mean?"

"That's right. So you know about it?"

"Lizzie told me about it. But I've never been there. Once she moved to Ohio she never went back."

"Now, let me warn you that while it's right on the beach, it's not in good condition. It's a big, old, rambling place that has never been truly modernized. But it's in a lovely location. The coastal low country is uniquely beautiful. And I say that with all the bias of a proud South Carolinian. Ms. Cecilia told me that you're very good with your hands. I believe she thought you were the perfect person to take care of it."

"Beachfront? I couldn't afford the real estate taxes."

"There are none. Years ago Ms. Cecilia placed the property into a conservancy so it could never be sold and developed. She and her descendants can use the property but can never sell it. In return the taxes were basically waived."

"But we've got a home in Cleveland. The kids are in school."

"Ms. Cecilia thought that you might have some trepidation. But since most of the summer is still ahead of us, the issue of school does not come into play."

Jack sat back. "Okay. I see that. But I still don't think—"

Baxter interrupted. "And Cecilia said that you told

her that Lizzie was thinking of taking the kids there this summer."

"That's right, Lizzie was. She told me that. I thought it was a good idea but..." Jack's voice trailed off. He'd made Lizzie promise him that she would take the kids to the Palace. Now she couldn't.

Baxter fingered the will and studied him. "Would you like to see it before you make up your mind?"

"Yes, I would," Jack said quickly.

21

Less than two hours after leaving Royce Baxter's office, Jack and the kids pulled down a sandy drive between overgrown bushes after following the directions the lawyer had given him. He surveyed the landscape. There were marshes nearby, and the smell of the salt water was strong, intoxicating.

"Wow!" said Cory as the old house finally came into view.

Jack pulled the VW to a stop, and they all climbed out. Jack took Jackie's hand as they walked up to the front of the house, which was shaded by two large palmetto trees. It was an elongated rambling wood-sided structure, with a broad, covered front porch that ran down three-quarters of the home's face. A double door of solid wood invited visitors to the entrance. The wood siding was faded and weathered but looked strong and reliable to Jack's expert eye. The hurricane shutters were painted black, but most of the paint was gone, leaving the underlying wood exposed to the elements. Five partially rotted steps carried them up to the front entrance.

The furniture on the porch was covered. When Jack and the kids looked underneath, they found quite the mess, along with animal nests. One squirrel jumped out and raced up a support post and onto the roof, which had many missing shingles, Jack had already noted. A snake slid out from under a pile of wood, causing the older kids to scream and run. Jackie approached the serpent and attempted to pick it up before Jack snatched him away. He looked at the other kids, who were cowering by the VW.

"It's a black snake. Not poisonous, but it will bite, so stay clear of it." He watched as the snake slowly made its way down the steps and into the underbrush around the house.

"They don't have giant snakes in Cleveland," said a breathless Cory.

"It was only a three-footer, son. And there *are* snakes in Ohio."

That information did not seem to make Cory feel any better.

"Come on," said Jack. "Let's at least check it out while we're here."

Using the key Baxter had given him, he opened the front door and went inside with Jackie. He turned to check on the other two kids. They hadn't budged from next to the VW. "Remember, guys, that snake is out there with *you*, not in here with us."

A moment later, the two kids flew up the front steps and past their dad into the house, with Cory screaming and looking behind him for the "giant freaking snake."

Jackie and his father exchanged a glance.

Jackie pointed at his brother and said, "Corwee funny."

"Yeah, he's a riot," said Jack, shaking his head.

Inside, the spaces were open and large, with high, sloped ceilings where old fans hung motionless. The kitchen was spacious but poorly lighted by tiny windows, and the bathrooms were few in number and small. There was an enormous stone fireplace that reached to the ceiling in the main living area, a big table for dining that showed a lot of wear and tear, and several other rooms that served various purposes, including a laundry room and a small library. On the lower level were an old billiards table, its green felt surface worn smooth with use, and a Ping-Pong table with a tattered net. Water toys, flippers, flattened beach balls, and the like were stacked in a storage room.

The furniture was old but mostly in good shape. The floors were random-width plank, the walls solid plaster. Jack knocked on one section and came away impressed with the craftsmanship. Yet when he stepped toward the back of the house, he drew in a breath. The rear of the house was mostly windows and glass doors; there was also a second-floor screened-in porch with stairs leading down to the ground. The view out was of the wide breadth of the Atlantic, maybe two hundred feet away, the sandy beach less than half that distance.

Jack breathed in the sea air and pointed out to the ocean. "There's really not a drop of land between here and Europe or Africa," he said. "Just water."

As the kids stared out at the views, Jack looked down at the backyard. It was sandy, with dunes covered in vegetation. He stepped back inside and smelled the burned wood of fires from long ago.

They clumped upstairs and looked through the shotgun line of bedrooms there, none of them remarkable, but all functional. Where others might have seen limitations, builder Jack saw potential. All the bedrooms had views of the ocean, and the largest one had a small outdoor balcony as well.

"What do you think is up there?" This came from Mikki, who was pointing to a set of stairs at the end of the hall going up another half flight.

"Attic, I suppose," he said.

Jack eased open the door and fumbled for a light switch. Nothing happened when he flicked it, and it occurred to him that the power had been turned off when the place became uninhabited. The room was under the eaves of the house, and the ceiling slanted upward to a peak. It was large, with two windows that threw in good morning light, though now the sun had passed over the house and was going down. There was a bed, an old wrought-iron four-poster, a large wooden desk, a shelf filled with books, and an old trunk set in one corner. A door led to a closet that was empty. Jack stepped cautiously over the floor planks to test their safety.

"Okay," he said after his inspection was complete. "Explore."

Cory made a beeline for the trunk, while Jack led his youngest over to the desk and helped him open drawers. He glanced back at Mikki, who hadn't budged from the doorway.

"You going to look around?"

"Why? You're not thinking about moving here, are you?"

"Maybe."

Her face flushed with anger. "I already had to move to Arizona. And all my friends are in Cleveland. My band, everything."

"I'm just looking around, okay?" But in his mind, Jack was already drawing up plans for repairs and improvements.

In his mind's eye, there was Lizzie seated next to him on the bed, on what would turn out to be her last day of life.

You never know, Jack, you might enjoy it too. You could really fix the place up. Even make the lighthouse work again.

"So Grand left you this place?" asked Mikki.

Jack broke free from his thoughts. "Yeah, she did."

"Well, why don't you sell it, then? We could certainly use the money."

"I can't. It's a legal thing. And I wouldn't have felt right selling it even if I could."

Mikki shrugged and leaned against the doorway, adopting a clearly bored look.

Jack glanced over at Cory, who'd nearly tumbled into the large trunk he'd opened in his eagerness. He came up wearing on old-fashioned top hat, black cloak, and a half mask covering the upper part of his face.

"Moo-ha-ha-ha," he said in a dramatically deep voice.

"That Corwee?" said Jackie, uncertainly, hugging his father tighter.

"That's Cory acting funny," said Jack encouragingly as he gently pried his youngest son's frantic fingers from around a patch of his hair.

Jack picked up a book and opened it, and his jaw dropped.

"What is it?" asked Cory, who had seen his reaction.

Jack held up the book. There was a bookplate on the inside cover.

"Property of Lizzie O'Toole," read Jack. "This was your mother's book," he said. "Maybe they all were." He looked excitedly around. "I bet this was your mom's room growing up."

Now Mikki stepped into the room and joined them. "Mom's room?"

Jack nodded and pointed eagerly to the desktop. "Look at that."

Carved into the wood were the initials *EPO*. Mikki looked at her dad questioningly.

He said animatedly, "Elizabeth Pinckney O'Toole. That was your mom's full name. Pinckney was Grand's maiden name. She kept her last name even after she married."

"Why did Mom leave her books behind?" she asked.

"Maybe she thought she would come back," replied Jack uncertainly.

"I remember her telling me about a beach house she grew up in, but she never really said anything else about it. Did you know much about it?"

"She told me about it. But I'd never been here before."

"Why'd she never bring us here?" Mikki asked.

"I know that she wanted to. In fact, she was planning to bring all of you here this summer after I... Anyway, that was her plan."

"Is that why we're here, then? Fulfilling Mom's wishes?"

"Maybe that's part of it."

Jackie tugged on his dad's ear.

"Corwee?" asked Jackie.

Jackie was pointing at his brother, who was now wearing a pink boa, long white gloves, and a tiara.

"Still Cory," said Jack, smiling broadly. "And obviously completely secure in his masculinity."

He glanced at Mikki, who was running her fingers over her mom's initials.

Jack looked out the window. "Hey, guys. Check this out."

The kids hurried to the window and stared up in awe at the lighthouse that rose into the air out on a rocky point next to the house.

"It's really close to the house," said Mikki.

Cory added, "Do you think it belongs to us too?"

Jack said, "I know it does. Your mom told me about it. It was one of her favorite places to go."

They rushed outside and over to the rocky point. The lighthouse was painted with black and white stripes and was about forty feet tall. He tried the door. It was locked, but he peered through the glass in the upper part of the door. He saw a spiral wooden staircase. There were boxes stacked against one wall, and everything was covered in dust.

"What a mess," said Mikki, who was looking through another pane of glass.

On the exterior wall of the lighthouse was an old, weathered sign. He scraped off some of the gunk and read, "Lizzie's Lighthouse." Jack stepped back and stared up at the tall structure with reverence.

Cory looked at the hand-painted sign. "How could this be Mom's lighthouse?"

"Well, it was one of her favorite places, like I said,"

answered his father, who was now circling the structure to see if there was another way to get in. "Isn't it cool?"

"It's just an old lighthouse, Dad," Mikki said.

He turned to look at her. "No, it was your *mom's* lighthouse. She loved it."

Jackie pulled on his dad's pants leg again. He pointed at the lighthouse.

"What dat?"

Cory said, "It's a lighthouse, Jackie. Big light."

"Big wight," repeated Jackie.

Jack gazed around at the property. "I'm sold."

"What?" exclaimed Mikki.

"This will be a great place to spend the summer."

"But, Dad," protested Mikki. "It's a dump. And my friends—"

"It's *not* a dump. This is where your mother grew up," he snapped. "And we're moving here." He paused and added in a calmer tone, "At least for one summer."

22

Back in Cleveland, they moved out of the rental and parked their few pieces of furniture at Sammy's place, because he'd decided to come with them to South Carolina.

"What am I gonna do by myself all summer?" he'd said when told of the family's plans. "And Sam Jr. expects the kids to be around now. Whines all the time when they're not here. I mean, I can get by without you folks, but it's the damn dog that troubles me."

They closed up Sammy's garage house and pushed Sam Jr.'s big butt into the VW, and off they went. Sammy drove the VW, and Jack followed in his pickup truck with Sammy's Harley tied down in the cargo bed. They made one stop, though, to Lizzie's grave. Jack knew it would be hard on everyone, but he also didn't want the kids to leave without going there to visit their mom.

They put fresh flowers in the vase, and each of the kids

said something to their mother, though Mikki's remarks were inaudible. Jack stood behind them, trying to hold the tears back. When Jackie wanted to know where his mom was, Mikki told him that she was sleeping. Jackie lay down next to his mom's grave and started whispering things as though he didn't want to wake her. At that point Jack disappeared behind some bushes and cried into his hands.

They split the trip up into two days, spending the night in adjoining rooms at a motel outside of Winston-Salem, North Carolina. They left Sam Jr. in the van with the windows down and a big pan of water; he was too big to climb through the opening. But around midnight he started howling so mournfully that Jack and Sammy had to run out and bundle him into their room before anyone could see them. That night, Sam Jr. slept curled up around Jackie on a blanket on the floor.

Jack woke up early in the morning and went outside to get some fresh air. He found Mikki already fully dressed and leaning against the VW.

"What's up?" he asked, stretching out his back.

"Why are we doing this?" she said in a surly tone.

"Doing what?"

"You know what!"

He walked over to her. "What is your problem?"

"I don't have a problem. Do you?"

"What's that supposed to mean?"

"We just settled back in Cleveland, Dad. And now you're moving us down to South Carolina."

"Yeah, to the home where your mom grew up."

"Okay, Dad, but in case you didn't realize it, Mom's not there."

She turned and walked back to her room.

Jack stared after her, shook his head, and headed off to get ready for the rest of the trip.

They got an early start and arrived in Channing, South Carolina, before lunch. Jack had had the electricity and water turned back on at the beach house before they got there. He'd also found a cable TV provider, so when they hooked up the TV they'd brought it actually worked. Huge TV watchers Jackie and Cory were immensely relieved by this development.

It didn't take them long to unload. They put the Harley under a side deck. As they were carrying things in, Jack found an envelope on the knotty pine kitchen table. It was addressed to him with a Post-it note on the outside from the lawyer, Royce Baxter. It read,

> *This is a letter that Ms. Cecilia left for you, with instructions to deliver it to you when you moved into the beach house.*

"Man," said Sammy, dumping his old army duffel bag on the floor and looking around. "This place is something else."

"This 'something else' needs a lot of work," said Jack. "But it's got great bones. I made a list when I was down here before. We'll need materials and a lot of sweat. There's a hardware store the lawyer recommended that's not too far from here."

Sammy looked at him curiously. "Fixing it up? You said you couldn't sell it."

"That's right, I can't."

"So why are you planning to fix it up?"

"Because Lizzie—I mean, because we might be staying down here."

"Staying down here? For how long?"

Jack didn't answer but pointed out the window.

Sammy exclaimed, "Is that a lighthouse?"

"Yep."

"Does it work?"

"No. But it used to. That's Lizzie's Lighthouse."

"Lizzie's Lighthouse?"

"Yeah. It was kind of her place."

Sammy eyed the letter that Jack was holding. "What's that?"

"Just something from Cecilia's lawyer." Jack stuffed the letter into his pocket, and they all spent the next several hours putting things away, cleaning up, and exploring. After that they changed into bathing suits. The kids sprinted toward the water, with Mikki in the lead, Cory second, and Jackie bringing up the rear. Sam Jr. stayed back with him, keeping pace with the chubby-legged three-year-old, who ran on his tiptoes. Sammy and Jack carried towels, a cooler, beach chairs, and an umbrella to stick into the sand. They'd found the chairs and umbrella in the lower level of the Palace.

After playing in the water for a while, Cory went up to the house and returned with a tattered old football.

"Hey, Dad," he called out. "Can you throw with me?"

Jack didn't look thrilled by the request; he was tired. However, right before he was about to decline, a memory struck him.

It had been a basketball, not a football. In his driveway. His father had driven up after work, and six-year-old Jack was bouncing his new ball. He'd asked his dad to play with him. He wasn't sure if his dad had even answered. All he'd remembered was the side door closing with a thud. And if that memory had stuck with him all these years?

He got up from his chair. "You're on, Cor."

Sammy said, "Okay, big guy, show your old man some moves."

They threw for more than an hour. Jack hadn't lost his touch from high school. And Cory, after a few dropped balls, started catching everything that came his way. Jack could see the athleticism showing through his son's chubby, prepubescent frame. Jackie, and even Mikki, finally joined them, and Jack ran them through some old high school football plays he remembered.

After everyone was sufficiently exhausted, Cory said, "Thanks, Dad, that was great."

Jack rubbed his son's head. "Nice soft pair of hands you got. Wish I had you on my football team in high school."

Cory beamed and Jackie squealed, "Me too?"

Jack snatched Jackie up, held him upside down, and ran to the water. "You too."

Hours later, the sun started to set while the kids were still running around in knee-deep water, building castles, chasing wide-butted Sam Jr., and throwing a Frisbee that they'd also found in the house. Sammy and Jack sat back in the tattered beach chairs, Jack with a Coke and Sammy with a Corona.

Sammy finally tipped his baseball cap over his eyes and leaned back, settling himself so deeply in the chair that his butt touched the sand. Jack drew the letter out of his pocket and opened it. In spidery handwriting, Cecilia sent her love and hope that Jack and the kids would find as much fun and contentment from the house as she and Lizzie had. As Jack read the letter it was as though Cecilia was talking to him in her richly soothing, Southern cadence.

She wrote:

My life on earth is over of course, or else you wouldn't be reading this letter. But I had a fine, old run, did everything I wanted to do, and, hell, the things that might've got left out I didn't need anyway.

I'd never seen a little girl who loved the ocean and sand more than Lizzie. And she loved this old house, even though, as you know, it carries some bad memories. And Lizzie's Lighthouse, as she called it. That child was always up there. I think Mikki, Cory, and dear Jackie will love this place too; at least that's my hope. And I feel sure that you, Jack, will find some comfort and peace in the place where Lizzie grew up.

I know it has been a most difficult and heartbreaking time for you. I know that you loved Lizzie more than anyone could. And she loved you just as much back. Fate dealt you a terrible hand by separating you two long before you should have been. But remember that every day you wake up to those three darling children, you are waking up to the most precious things that you and Lizzie ever made together. Because of that, you will never be apart from the woman you love. That may not seem like nearly enough right now, when you want to be with her so badly. But as time goes by, you will realize that it will actually make all the difference in the world. It's not so much that time heals all wounds, honey, as it is that the passage of the years lets us make peace with our grief in our way.

I know they called you the miracle man after you got better. But just so you know, I considered you a miracle from the moment you came into Lizzie's life. And I know she felt the same way. You got a second chance of sorts, son, so you live your life good and well. And Lizzie will be waiting for you when your time has run too. And I'll probably come by for a cup of coffee myself. Until then, keep hugging those precious children and take care of yourself.

Love,
Cecilia

Jack slid the letter back in his pocket, drew a long breath, and wiped his eyes. Even though he had never been to this place before, he felt like he'd just come home. He rose, took off his shoes, and jogged out toward the water to be with his kids. When they were tired out and headed inside for a late dinner, Jack stayed behind, walking along the beach as the sun dropped into the horizon, burning the sky down to fat mounds of pinks and reds. The warm waters of the Atlantic washed over his feet. He stared out to sea, one of his hands absently feeling for the letter in his pocket. It had been a good first day.

"Hey, Dad!"

He turned to see Cory frantically waving to him from the rear screen porch.

He waved back. "Yeah, bud?"

"Jackie turned the hose on."

"Uhhh... okay?"

"After he dragged the other end in the house."

Jack started to walk fast to the Palace. "In the house? Where's Sammy?"

"In the bathroom with a magazine."

Jack started to jog. "Where's Mikki?"

Cory shook his head helplessly. "Dunno."

Jack started to run faster as he yelled, "Well, can't you turn the hose off or pull it out of the house?"

"I would, but the little knobby thing came off in my hand and Jackie won't let go of the end of the hose. He's a lot stronger than he looks." Cory's eyes grew a little wider. "Is it bad that stuff's starting to float, Dad?"

Oh, crap.

Jack started to sprint, rooster tails of sand thrown up behind him. "Jackie!"

My three precious children. This one's for you, Cecilia.

23

The next day, while Sammy stayed with the other kids, Jack and Mikki drove in the pickup truck to the hardware store in downtown Channing, about three miles from the beach house. Along the way, they reached a stretch of oceanfront that was lined with magnificent homes, estates really, thought Jack. There was serious money down here. If he could catch some work from some of these wealthy folks, it might really be good.

Mikki said, “Are those like condo buildings?”

“They’re mansions. This is prime beachfront property here. Those places are worth millions each.”

“What a waste. I mean, who needs that much room?” she said derisively.

He glanced at her. “Are you feeling better about things?”

“No.”

As they passed one house that was even larger than

the others, a teenage girl came out into the cobblestone driveway dressed in a bikini top and tiny shorts with the words HUG 'EM printed on the backside. She was blond and tanned and had the elegant bone structure of a model. She climbed into a Mercedes convertible about the same time a tall, lean, tousled-haired young man came hustling up the drive. He had on wakeboard shorts and a tank top. He hopped in the passenger seat, and the car roared off, pulling in front of their old truck and causing Jack to nearly run off the road.

Mikki rolled down the window and yelled, "Jerks!"

The girl made an obscene gesture.

"Catch up to them, Dad; I want to kick her butt."

"Since when did you develop such anger issues, my little miss sunshine?"

"What are—" She stopped when she saw him smiling.

She muttered, "Shut up."

They reached Channing and climbed out of the truck. Jack had on jeans and a white T-shirt and sneakers. Mikki was dressed in knee-length cotton shorts and a black T-shirt. Her skin was pale, and her hair was now partially green and purple. His daughter's supply of hair colors seemed endless.

Mikki looked around as Jack checked his list of supplies.

"Looks like something right out of Nick at Nite," she said. "Pretty old-fashioned place."

Jack looked around and had to admit, it was a little like stepping back in time. The streets were wide and clean and the storefronts well maintained. The shops were mostly mom-and-pops. No big-box retailers here, it seemed. A bank, grocery, large hardware store, barber's shop with a striped pole, restaurants, an ice cream parlor, and a sheriff's station with one police cruiser parked in front were all in his line of sight. They also saw a public library with a sign out front that advertised free Wi-Fi service inside.

Mikki said, "Well, at least we can get online here."

People walked by in shorts and sandals; some of the older ladies had scarves around their heads. One elderly gent had on seersucker shorts, white socks, and white sandals. Others rode bikes with wicker baskets attached to the fronts. A few people had dogs on leashes, and some kids ran up and down the street. Everyone was very tanned. There was also a sense of prosperity here. Most of the cars parked along the street were late-model luxury sedans or high-dollar convertibles. Some had out-of-state license plates, but most were from South Carolina. But then Jack noted dented and dirty pickup trucks and old Fords and Dodges rolling down the street. The people in those vehicles looked more like he did, Jack thought. Working stiffs.

They passed a shabby-looking building with a marquee out front that read, CHANNING PLAY HOUSE. An old man was sweeping the pavement in front of the double-door entrance. Next to the entrance was a glass ticket window. The man stopped sweeping and greeted them.

"What's the Channing Play House?" Jack asked.

"Back in its day it was one of the finest regional theater houses in the low country," said the man, who introduced himself as Ned Parker.

"Regional theater?" said Jack.

Parker nodded. "We had shows come all the way down from New York City to perform. Singers, dancers, actors; we had it all."

"And now?" Jack said.

"Well, we still have the occasional performance, but it's nowhere near what it used to be. Too many video games and big-budget movies." He pointed at Mikki. "From your generation, missy."

Mikki pointed to the marquee, which read, CHANNING TALENT COMPETITION. "What's that?"

"Hold it every year in August. Folks compete. Any age and any act. Baton, dancing, fiddling, singing. Lot of fun. It's a hundred-dollar prize and your picture in the *Channing Gazette*."

They continued on, and Jack and Mikki went to the local, well-stocked hardware store and purchased what they needed. A young man who worked at the store helped Jack load the items. Jack noticed that the boy was giving Mikki far more attention than he was Jack. He stepped between the young man and his daughter. "Some of this stuff won't fit in my truck bed," Jack pointed out.

Before the helper could answer, a stocky man in his seventies with snow-white hair strolled out. He was dressed in pleated khaki pants and a dark blue polo shirt with the hardware store's name and logo on it.

He said, "That's no problem; we deliver. Can have it out there today. You're in the Pinckney place, right?"

Jack studied him. "That's right; how'd you know?"

He put out his hand and smiled. "You beat me to it. I was coming out to see you later today and formally introduce myself. I'm Charles Pinckney, Cecilia's 'little' brother." He turned to Mikki and extended his hand. "And this must be the celebrated Mikki. Cee wrote me often about you. Let me see, she said you could play a guitar better than anyone she'd ever heard and were as pretty as your mother. I haven't heard you play, but Cee was spot-on with her assessment of your beauty."

In spite of herself, Mikki blushed. "Thanks," she mumbled.

Pinckney looked at the young helper. "Billy, take the rest of these materials and set it up for delivery."

"Yes, sir, Mr. Pinckney." He hurried off.

Jack said, "Now I remember. You were at the funeral, but we didn't get a chance to talk."

Pinckney nodded slowly. "I'm the only one left now. Thought for sure Cee would outlive me, even though she was a lot older."

"There were ten kids? At least that's what Lizzie told me."

"That's right. Mother and Dad certainly did their duty. I was the closest with Cee. We talked just about every day. Feel like I lost my best friend."

"She was a fine lady. Really helped me out."

"She was one of a kind," agreed Pinckney. "She was duly proud of her heritage. Not many ladies of her generation kept their maiden name, but it wasn't a question for her. In fact, she told her husband he could change his surname to Pinckney if he wanted, but she wasn't switching." He chuckled at the memory.

"Sounds like Cecilia."

"She thought a lot of you. I suppose that's why she left you the Palace. She loved that place. Wouldn't have left it to just anyone."

"I appreciate that. But it came as a total shock. I knew about the place and all, but I'd never been here."

"Cee actually talked to me about it. I know she wanted you to have it, and I was all for it. Especially after Lizzie died. She loved the place too, maybe more even than Cee."

Mikki, who'd been listening closely, added, "If she loved the place so much, why did they move to Cleveland?"

Pinckney said, "I think it had to do with Fred's work."

"People don't buy cars down here?"

"Mikki, knock it off," said her father.

"So why do you call it the Palace?" asked Mikki.

Pinckney grinned. "It was our mother's doing. Her mother and father, my grandparents, were quite the Bible thumpers, but she wasn't. Naming it the Palace made it seem like it was a casino or a saloon or something. It worked. Her parents never visited there, far as I know," he added with a smile.

"Sounds like my kind of woman," Mikki said tartly.

Pinckney looked at the materials in Jack's truck. "So, fixing the place up?"

"Yeah."

"Cee said you were great with your hands."

"If you hear of anyone who needs work done, let me know. I'm not in a position where I can just take the summer off. I've got a lot of mouths to feed."

"I'll put the word out. Good luck with the Palace. Love to see the old place like it used to be."

"Thanks," Jack said. "It has great bones, just needs some TLC."

"Don't we all," said Pinckney. "Don't we all."

24

"Friendly people," remarked Mikki grudgingly as they continued down the street.

"Southern hospitality, they call it. Hey, how about some lunch before we head back?"

"Dad, you don't have to—"

"It's just lunch, Mik. Work with me here, will you?"

"Fine," she said dully.

As they rounded the corner, the Mercedes sports car that had almost caused them to wreck earlier flew around the same corner. The girl's head was swaying to the music blasting from the car's radio. The same young man was in the front seat next to her.

Mikki yelled, "Hey!"

"Mik," said her dad warningly.

But she was already in the street flagging the car down. The girl hit her brakes and snapped, "What the hell do you think you're doing?"

"First, turn off that crap you think is music," said Mikki. The girl made an ugly face, but the guy hit the button and the sounds died.

"*You* cut us off earlier and almost made my dad roll his truck."

The girl laughed. "Is your hair naturally that color, or did someone throw up on it?"

The guy grimaced. "Tiff, knock it off."

The girl gave Mikki a condescending look and then laughed derisively. "Okay, whatever. Hey, sweetie-pie, now, why don't you go on off and play somewhere." She hit the gas, and they sped off.

"Creeps," Mikki screamed after them. She glared over at her dad. "Wow. So much for Southern hospitality."

When she saw the sign a few moments later, her face brightened. "Okay, *that* is the place for lunch."

Jack looked where she was pointing.

"Little Bit of Love Bar and Grill?" Jack read. "Why is that the place?"

"Come on, Dad, I have to see if this is what I think it is."

She hurried inside, and Jack followed. There were twenty retro tables with red vinyl covers on them and chairs with yellow vinyl covers. The floor was a crazy pattern of black-and-white square tiles. The walls were covered with posters of famous rock-and-roll bands. Behind the bar, which took up one entire wall, were acoustic, bass, and electric guitars along with various costumes actually worn by band members, all behind Plexiglas. Stenciled on another wall were lyrics from famous rock songs.

Mikki looked like she'd just discovered gold in a tiny coastal town in South Carolina. "I knew it. So cool."

Most of the tables were occupied, and the bar was doing a brisk business. Waiters and waitresses dressed in jeans and T-shirts were moving trays of food and drink from the kitchen to the patrons. Along another wall were old-fashioned pinball machines, all with a musical theme.

A woman about Jack's age headed toward them.

"Two for lunch?" the woman said.

Jack caught himself staring at her. She was tall and slim and had dark hair that curved around her long neck. Her eyes were a light blue, and when she smiled Jack felt his own mouth tug upward in response.

"Um, yeah," said Jack quickly. "Thanks."

They followed her to a table, and she handed them menus.

"I can take your drink order."

They told her what they wanted. She wrote it down and said, "Haven't seen you before."

Jack introduced himself and Mikki.

"I'm Jenna Fontaine," she said. "I own this pile of bricks."

"As soon as I saw the name, I just knew," said Mikki.

Jack looked at her. "What do you mean?"

Jenna and Mikki exchanged smiles. Mikki said, "Def Leppard, am I right?"

"You know your rock-and-roll lyrics." When Jack still looked puzzled, Jenna said, " 'Little Bit of Love' is a Def Leppard song."

"So you're into music?" said Jack.

"Yes, but not nearly as much as that guy."

She pointed to a tall, lanky teenager with long black hair who was setting plates full of food down at the next table.

"That's Liam, my son. Now, he's the musical madman in the family. When I decided to chuck the life of a big-city lawyer and move here and open a restaurant, the theme and décor were his idea."

Mikki eyed Liam and then turned back to her. "Does he play?"

"Just about any instrument there is. But drums are his specialty."

Mikki's eyes glittered with excitement for the first time since stepping foot in South Carolina.

"I take it you're into music too," said Jenna.

"You could say that," said Mikki modestly.

"So where y'all staying?"

"My great-grandma left us a house."

"Wow. That's pretty impressive. Well, enjoy your lunch."

She walked off, and Jack looked down at the menu but wasn't really seeing it.

Mikki finally touched his hand, and he jumped.

"Dad?"

"Yeah?"

"She's really pretty."

"Is she? I didn't notice."

"Dad, it's—"

"Mik, let's just get something to eat and get back, okay? I've got a lot of work to do."

After Mikki took refuge behind her menu, Jack snatched a glance at Jenna as she seated another party. Then he looked away.

25

It took several days of backbreaking work to thoroughly clean the house, and all the kids pitched in, although Mikki did so grudgingly and with a good deal of complaining. "Is this how the summer's going to go?" she said to her dad as she scrubbed down the kitchen sinks. "Me being a slave laborer?"

"If you think this is tough, join the army. There you clean the floor with a toothbrush, and it only takes about twelve hours, until they tell you to do it again," Jack told her. She glared at him darkly as he walked off with a load of trash.

They next attacked the outside, cleaning out flower beds, pruning bushes, clearing away dead plants, and power washing the decks and the outdoor furniture. The rest of the acreage was beyond their capability—and Jack's wallet.

With much tugging and cursing, Jack and Sammy were finally able to get the door to the lighthouse open. As

Jack stepped into the small foyer, dust and disturbed spiderwebs floated through the air. He coughed and looked around.

The rickety steps looked in jeopardy of falling down. He looked through some of the boxes stacked against the wall. There was mostly junk in them, though he did find a pair of tiny pink sneakers that had the name "Lizzie" written on the sides in faded Magic Marker. He held them reverently and imagined his wife as a little girl prancing around in them on the beach. He looked through some other boxes and found a few things of interest. He carried them up to his bedroom.

They all trooped down to the beach that afternoon and ate lunch, letting the sun and wind wash over them. After the meal was over, Jack looked at Mikki, grinned, and said, "Let me show you something."

"What?"

"Stand up."

She did so.

"Okay, grab me."

"What?"

"Just come at me and grab me."

Mikki looked around, embarrassed, at the others. "Dad, what are you doing?"

"Just grab me."

"Fine." She rushed forward and grabbed him, or tried to. The next instant she was facedown on the sand.

She lay there for a second, stunned, then rolled over and scowled up at him. "Gee, Dad, thanks. That was really a great closer after a picnic on the beach."

He helped her up. "Let's do it again, and I'll show you exactly what I did."

"Why?" she asked. "Is this like National Kick Your Daughter's Butt Day and nobody told me?"

Sammy interjected. "He's showing you some basic self-defense maneuvers, Mik."

Mikki looked up at her dad. He said, "So you can handle yourself in certain situations. Without me helping," he added.

"Oh," she said, a look of understanding appearing on her face.

They went through the moves a dozen more times, until Mikki had first her dad, then Sammy, and even Cory lying facedown in the sand. Jackie begged until she did it to him too, and then started crying because he got sand in his eyes.

"Hello!"

They all turned to see Jenna Fontaine walking down the beach. She had on shorts and a tank top and a broad-brimmed sun hat. She was waving and holding up a picnic basket. "I brought you some things from the café."

Jack came forward. "There was no need to do that."

"No trouble. I know how it is coming to a new place." She showed him what was in the basket, and then Jack introduced her to Cory, Sammy, and Jackie. His youngest son hid behind his dad. She smiled and squatted down. "Well, hello, little man. You look just like your daddy."

"Daddy," said Jackie shyly, hiding his face.

Mikki asked, "So where do you live, Jenna?"

Jenna pointed to the south. "About a half mile that way. We have a rocky point too. So when you hit the rocks, our house is the pile of blue shingles with the vibrating roof."

"Vibrating roof?" said Mikki curiously.

Jenna looked at Jack. "It's another reason I stopped by.

Charles Pinckney said you were a whiz at building things. He was the one who told me you were staying here. What I really need—to stop myself from either killing my son or committing myself to a mental institution—is a soundproof room for his music studio."

"He has a music studio?" exclaimed Mikki.

"Well, he calls it that. Most of the equipment is secondhand, but he's got a lot of stuff. I don't understand most of what it does, but what I do know is it's killing my ears." She looked at Jack again. "Want to come by and give me an estimate?"

Jack looked uncertain for a moment but then said, "Sure, I'd be glad to."

"You want to stop by tomorrow evening? Liam will be there, and he can sort of tell you what he needs."

"It might be a little expensive," said Jack. "But we've done soundproofing before. You'll notice a big difference."

"I think saving my hearing and my sanity is worth any price. Say about eight?"

"That'll be fine," said Jack.

Jenna told them her address, waved, and headed off.

Jack watched her go. When he turned back, he saw Mikki and Sammy staring at him. Jack said nervously, "Uh, I've got some stuff to do."

He handed the picnic basket to Mikki and trudged back to the Palace.

Sammy looked at Mikki. "Is he okay?"

Mikki glanced in Jenna's direction, then up to her dad, who was just entering the house. "I don't know," she said.

Jack fell asleep that night with the tiny pair of pink sneakers on his chest.

26

Mikki had insisted on coming along with Jack to the Fontaines' house, so Sammy stayed behind to watch the boys. They drove there in Jack's pickup truck.

Jenna met them at the door and ushered them in. The house was old but well maintained, and the interior was surprising. Instead of a typical beach look, it was decorated in a Southwestern style, with solid, dark, and what looked to be handcrafted furniture. There were textured walls faux painted in salmon and burnt orange, oil paintings depicting both snowcapped mountains and smooth deserts, and brightly colored woven rugs with geometric patterns.

Jenna sat across from him. Jack ran his gaze over her and then looked away. She was wearing white capri pants and a pale blue pullover, and her feet were bare.

"Nice place," said Jack.

"Thanks. We tried to make it feel like home."

"Where's that?" asked Mikki as she looked around. "Arizona? I was just there recently."

Jenna laughed. "I've never been to Arizona or the Southwest in general. That's why I decorated the house this way. Probably as close as I'll ever get, and I love the look and feel of it. We originally came from Virginia. I went to college and law school up there. Ended up in D.C., though."

"You look pretty young to have a teenager," said Mikki.

"Mik!" her father began crossly, but Jenna laughed.

"I'll take that as a huge compliment. Truth is, I had Liam while I was in high school." She pursed her lips but then smiled. "The best thing that came out of that marriage was Liam."

"So how did you end up down here?" asked Jack.

"Got tired of the rat race in D.C. I'd made really good money and invested it well. We came down to Charleston one summer, took a drive, happened on Channing, and fell in love with it." She glanced keenly at Jack. "When I talked to Charles Pinckney, he told me about his sister leaving you the Palace. It's a great old place. Never been inside, but I've always loved that lighthouse."

"Yeah, it's pretty cool," said Mikki, looking at her dad.

"My wife grew up in that house," said Jack.

"Charles told me about that too." She paused and added solemnly, "And I'm very sorry for your loss."

"Thanks," said Jack quietly.

Jenna stood and reassumed a cheery air. "Well, do you want to see the mad musician's space?"

Mikki jumped up. "Absolutely."

Mikki could see at a glance that it was set up as a recording studio, albeit on a tight budget. To her expert eye, the soundboard, mixing devices, mikes, and the like were old and looked jury-rigged. She knew because she and her band had done the very same thing. New equipment was far too expensive. A piano keyboard was against one wall; a bass guitar sat in a stand in a corner. A banjo and a fiddle hung on hooks on the wall.

And yet there were no sheets of music. No songbooks.

"Where's Liam?" Mikki asked. "I thought you said he'd be here."

"He's on his way. He was taking some inventory at the restaurant. What will you be next year, a junior?"

"Yeah."

"Liam too. He goes to Channing High. Only high school in town."

"He's a big kid," said Jack. "Does he play ball?"

Jenna smiled and shook her head. "He's a good athlete, but this"—she pointed at the room—"this is where his heart is."

Mikki slid over to the bass guitar. "Do you think he'd mind?"

"Go for it."

Mikki strapped the guitar on, placed her fingers, and started to play.

"Wow," said Jenna. "That's really good."

She started to take off the guitar, but a voice said, "Play those last two chords again."

They all turned to see Liam standing in the doorway. He had on wire-rimmed glasses and a T-shirt that said, SAVE THE PLANET, CUZ I STILL LIVE HERE.

"Liam, I didn't hear you come in," said his mother. "Everything okay at the Little Bit?"

"A place for everything, and everything in its place."

He looked at Mikki again. "So knock those last two chords out."

Surprised, but pleased at his request, she did so. The sound rocked the room again.

He walked over to her and placed her index finger on the guitar neck in a slightly different spot. "Try that; it'll give the sound more depth," he said.

Her grin disappeared, and she flushed angrily. "I know how to place my fingers. I've been playing since I was eight."

He seemed unfazed by her hostility. "So let me hear it now."

"Fine, whatever." She checked the new position of her index finger and played the chord. Her eyes displayed her amazement. The sound was far richer. She looked at him with new respect. "How did you figure that one out?"

He held up his hand. His fingers were amazingly long and the tips heavily calloused. "Anatomical."

"What?"

"The fingertip has different strength points on the surface. Once you understand where they are and place your fingers accordingly, the tightness on the strings is increased. Gives a fuller sound because there's less vibration coming off the neck."

"You worked that out on your own?"

"Nope. I'm not that smart. Read about it in an article in *Rolling Stone*," he said. "So what's your name?"

"Mikki Armstrong. That's my dad."

Jack and Liam shook hands.

"Mr. Armstrong is here to see if he can save my hearing," said Jenna.

Jack said, "Just call me Jack."

Liam grinned. "Think you can help Mom out? I don't

want her going deaf on me. But then again, that might have its advantages."

Jenna smacked him lightly on the arm. "Don't make me put you over my knee at your age."

Jack surveyed the room and then went around the space knocking on the walls. "Drywall on two-by-four studs set at standard width." He reached up and tapped the low ceiling at regular intervals. "Same here. Yeah, I can handle it if the hardware store has what I need."

Jenna looked impressed. "When can you start?"

"Soon as I get materials. I'll work up an estimate so you know how big a hit your pocketbook will take."

Mikki blurted out, "My dad is great at this stuff. He can build anything."

Jenna smiled. "I believe it."

Mikki eyed the room. "Liam, where's your music?"

He tapped his head. "All up here."

"But what about new pieces? You need sheet music to learn them."

"I can't read music. I play by ear."

"Are you kidding?"

He grinned. "Want to test me?"

She looked down at the bass guitar she was still holding. When she saw what it was, she exclaimed, "This is a Gibson EB-3 from the late sixties. Jack Bruce from Cream played one. It's vintage. How'd you score it?"

"EBay. Saved up two summers for it. Got a great deal. Its box is so smooth, and the sound is so pure. I think it's the best four-string ever made."

Jenna looked at Jack. "I don't know about you, but I don't speak this language. You want some coffee while our kids talk shop?"

Jack hesitated, but after a pleading look from Mikki he said, "Sure."

After they left, Mikki said, "Okay, Mr. Play-by-Ear, here's your test." She played a minute-long piece of a song she'd recently composed. She handed him the Gibson.

"Okay, go for it."

He strapped on the bass, set his fingers, and played back her song, note for perfect note.

Mikki exclaimed, "You're like Mozart only on percussion and bass. Ever been in a band?"

He scoffed. "There are no bands in Channing."

"Who're your faves?"

"Hendrix, AC/DC, Zeppelin, Plant, Aerosmith, to name a few."

"Omigod, they're like my top five of all time."

Liam picked up his drumsticks. "Want to score a few sets?"

She strapped the bass back on. "I'm dying to try out my new fingertip strength points."

27

Jenna and Jack were sitting out on her rear deck with their mugs of coffee when the music started up. The deck flooring really did appear to vibrate.

"Now do you see why I need the soundproofing?" she asked, covering her ears.

Jack nodded and laughed. "Yeah. I get it. We finally had to get Mikki to start practicing at another kid's house back in Cleveland. Even with that I'm not sure I can hear out of my right ear."

"The long-suffering parents of musical prodigies. Want to carry our coffee down to the beach? My head is already hurting."

They strolled along the sand together. It was well after eight but still light outside. A jogger passed them heading in the opposite direction, and an elderly couple were throwing tennis balls to a chubby black Lab. As the dog ran after a ball, the man and woman held hands and walked along.

Jenna eyed them and said, "That's how it's supposed to turn out."

Jack glanced at her. "What?"

She pointed at the couple. "Life. Marriage. Growing old together. Someone to hold hands with." She smiled. "A fat dog to throw balls to."

Jack watched the old couple. "You're right, it is supposed to turn out that way."

"So your wife grew up here?"

"Yeah."

"Is that why you came down here? Memories?"

"I guess so," Jack said slowly. He stopped and turned to her. "And my wife planned to bring the kids down here this summer. So I thought I'd do it for her. And I wanted to see the place too."

"You'd never been here before?"

Jack shook his head. "My wife had a twin sister who died of meningitis. They lived here for a while longer. But then I guess it just wasn't that . . . um . . . good," he finished, a bit awkwardly.

"I'm so sorry."

They started walking again. She said, "So how're the kids dealing with the move and all?"

"With three kids, they all sort of handle things differently."

"Makes my job seem simple. I've only got one."

"Well, Mikki is pretty independent. Just like her mom."

"She seems fantastic. Liam is not easily impressed when it comes to music."

"She and I butt heads a lot. Teenage girls. They need . . . stuff that dads just aren't good at."

"I feel that deficiency with Liam too, just on the flip side."

"He looks like he's doing fine."

"Maybe in spite of me."

"So you're divorced now?"

"Long time. Right after Liam was born. My ex moved to Seattle and has nothing to do with him. I just have to put it down to my poor choice in men."

"How'd you manage college and law school with a kid?"

"My parents were a huge help. But sometimes I'd take Liam to class with me. You do what you have to do."

Jack stopped, picked up a pebble off the beach, and threw it into the oncoming breakers. "Yeah, you do."

Jenna sipped her coffee and watched him. "So are y'all just down here for the summer?"

"That's the plan. Look, I'll write up that estimate and get it to you tomorrow."

"I tell you what. Why don't I just give you a check tonight to help cover the materials and you can get started."

"You don't want an estimate?" he said in surprise.

"No."

"Why not?"

"I trust you."

"But you don't know me."

"I know enough."

"Okay, thanks for the coffee." He smiled. "And the trust."

"Stop by the Little Bit again. Have to try the killer onion rings."

As they walked back, she said, "I really am sorry about your wife."

"Me too." Jack glanced back at the old couple still walking slowly hand in hand. "Me too."

28

Mikki awoke the next morning in her attic bedroom. She stretched, yawned, and sat back, bunching her pillows around her. Then she rose, picked up her guitar, and started playing a new song she'd been working on, using the new technique Liam had taught her. The long fingers of her left hand worked the neck of the instrument, while her right hand did the strumming. She put down the guitar, went to her desk, picked up some blank music sheets, and started making notations and jotting down some lyrics. Then she started singing while she played the guitar.

A minute later, someone knocked on her door.

Startled, she stopped singing and said, "Yeah?"

"Are you decent?" Jack called through the door.

"Yes."

He opened the door and came in. He had a breakfast tray in hand. Bacon, eggs, an English muffin smeared with Nutella, and a glass of milk. He set it down in front of her. Mikki put the guitar aside.

"How'd you know I like Nutella?"

"Did some good old-fashioned reconnaissance." He pulled a rickety ladder-back chair up next to the bed.

"What?"

"Okay, I looked in your room back in Cleveland. Dig in before it gets cold."

Mikki began to eat. "Where's everybody else?" she asked.

"Still sleeping. It's early yet. Did you have fun last night with Liam?"

Mikki swallowed a piece of bacon and exclaimed, "Omigod, Dad, he is, like, so awesome. That thing he showed me with the fingers, the pressure points? It works. We played some sets together, and he likes the bands I like, and he's funny, and—"

"So is that a yes?"

"What?"

"You did have a good time last night?"

She grinned sheepishly. "Yeah, I did. How did things go with Jenna?"

"I agreed to do the job. She gave me a check to start. Sammy and I will get the materials and go from there."

"She seems really cool. Don't you think?"

"She's very nice." Jack slipped something from his pocket and handed it to her. "I found this in a box in the lighthouse this morning."

"The lighthouse? Pretty early to have already been out there."

"Look at the picture."

Mikki held it tightly by the edges, her brow furrowing. "Is this Mom?"

"Yep. There's a date on back. Your mom was right about your age in that photo. It was taken down here at the beach. It must've been the summer before she moved to Cleveland. The lighthouse is in the background." He paused. "You see, don't you?"

"See what?"

"That you look just like her."

Mikki squinted at the image of her mom. "I do?"

"Absolutely you do. Well, except for the weird hair color and goth clothes. Your mom was more into ponytails and pastels."

"Ha-ha, real funny. And my clothes are not goth, which is, like, so last century anyway."

"Sorry. Why don't you finish your breakfast and we can go for a walk on the beach before things get going."

"Is this part of you being a dad thing?" she asked bluntly.

"Partly, yeah."

"And the other part?"

"I had a long time to be alone after you guys left, and I hated it. I never want to be alone again."

As they hit the sand, the sun was slowly coming up and the sky was a sheet of pink and rose with the darkened mass of the ocean just below it. There was a wind that had dispelled most of the night's heat. Gulls swooped and soared over the water before diving, hitting the surface and sometimes coming away with breakfast in the form of a wriggling fish.

"It's really different down here," said Mikki, finally breaking the silence.

"Ocean, sand, hotter."

"Not just that."

"I guess no matter where we'd be right now, it would be different," he replied.

"I wake up sometimes and think she's still here."

Jack stopped walking and looked out to the ocean. "I wake up every morning expecting to see her. It's only when she's not there that I realize..." He started to walk again. "But down here, it's different. I feel... I feel closer to her somehow."

Mikki gazed worriedly at her dad but said nothing.

They threw pebbles into the water and let the fingers of the tides chase them up and down the sand. Mikki found a shell that she pocketed to later show her brothers.

"You've got a great voice," he said. "I was listening outside the door this morning."

"It's okay," she said modestly, although it was clear his praise had pleased her.

"Do you want to study music in college?"

"I'm not sure I want to go to college. You didn't."

"That's true."

"I'm not sure the sort of stuff I want to play would be popular in college curriculums or in the mainstream music industry."

"What kind is it?"

"Are you asking just to be polite, or do you really want to know?"

"Look, do you have to make everything so complicated? I just want to know."

"Okay, okay. It's very alternative, edgy beats, nontraditional mix of instrumentals. No blow-you-out-of-the-house cheap synthesizer tricks. And no lollipop lyrics. Words that actually mean something."

Jack was impressed. "Sounds like you've given this a lot of thought."

"It's a big part of my life, Dad; of course I've thought about it."

"It's nice to have something you're so passionate about."

"Were you ever passionate about anything?"

"Not until I met your mother; then she sort of took up all the passion I had."

Mikki made a face. "That is, like, so gross to tell your own daughter."

"I didn't mean it like that. Before your mom came along, I was just drifting. I had my sports and all that. But not much else. And my dad was dying of cancer."

"But you still had your mom."

"Yeah, but we had our issues."

"Didn't get along? Like you and me?" she added, poking him in the side.

"Let's just say I spent a lot more time at the O'Tooles' instead of my house."

"What was the issue?"

His expression turned serious. "I've never really talked about this with anyone, except your mother. There were no secrets between us."

"Fine, I was just curious. You don't have to tell me."

Jack stopped walking, and she pulled up too.

"Okay, full confessional. It got to the point where I really wondered if my mom actually loved me."

Mikki looked shocked. "She had to love you. She was your mother."

"You'd think so, wouldn't you?"

"Why did you think she didn't?"

"Probably because she left when I was seventeen. Right after my dad died."

"What? Nobody ever told me that."

"Well, it's not the sort of thing you announce to the world."

"What happened?"

"She met some guy and moved to Florida. She kept the house in Cleveland, and I lived there until I married your mom and enlisted. She died in a boating accident when you were still a baby and I was still in the army."

Mikki looked at him in amazement. "You lived there, what, by yourself?"

"Didn't have any other relatives, so yeah."

"But you weren't even out of high school yet."

"But I was over sixteen. It wasn't like foster care was an option. I got part-time jobs to pay for expenses."

"My God, Dad. I mean, you were all by yourself."

"*You* like to spend time alone."

"Yeah, but I could come downstairs and everybody would be there."

"Well, I had your mom. She was my best friend. She helped me through some really tough times."

When they got back to the Palace, Mikki said, "Thanks for the walk and talk."

"Hope it's one of many this summer."

As she ran up the deck steps ahead of her father, Sammy appeared from around the side of the house. "You got an early start." He glanced at Mikki as she went into the house. "Little father-daughter time?"

"She's a pretty amazing kid, Sammy. Half her life I was carrying a gun for my country. The other half I was driving nails. I've got a lot to learn about her."

"Probably why I never got married," said Sammy. "Too complicated."

"You ever regret it? No kids, no wife?"

"I didn't, until I started hanging out with you Armstrongs."

29

Later that week, before her dad left for work and she had to watch the kids, Mikki pulled on some shorts, tennis shoes, and a tank top, stretched her legs, and headed to the beach to run. She was naturally athletic, taking after her dad, but she'd never gone out for any school sports teams. The jocks at her school were obnoxious, she thought. And she disliked the competitiveness of sports. She simply liked to run, not try to beat someone running next to her.

She headed down the beach, listening to tunes on her iTouch. She'd put on lots of sunblock because her skin was still pale from the bleak Ohio winter and cold spring. The sun felt great; the views were breathtaking. Her arms pumped, and her long legs ate up ground at a rapid pace. People were fishing from the shore; kids were playing in the sand; teenagers were body surfing in the rough breakers. Though it was still early, a few people were already lying out on beach blankets, reading and talking.

"What the—" she gasped.

The guy had run right up beside her.

"Hey," he said, grinning.

Mikki saw that it was the boy from the Mercedes convertible. He had on board shorts, no shirt. He was lean and muscled. Up close he looked like a Ralph Lauren model, which meant she instantly despised him.

She took out her earbuds, though she kept running.

"The beach is pretty wide," she said back, trying to look indifferent, "so pick another spot."

"I'm Blake Saunders." As they ran, he put out his hand to shake.

She ignored it. "Good for you."

"Can we stop running for a sec?"

"Why?"

"It's important."

She stopped, and he did too.

"Okay, what?" she demanded.

"I wanted to apologize for what happened the other day. Tiff can be a real piece of work."

"Tiff?"

"Tiffany, Tiffany Murdoch."

Mikki snorted. "She looks like a Tiffany."

"Yeah, she's pretty spoiled. Her dad was some big-shot investment guy in New York before they moved down here and built the biggest house on the beach."

"So why do you hang out with her?"

"She can be fun."

Mikki gave him a scathing look. "Oh yeah, I'm sure she can be fun." She slapped her behind. *"Hug 'em?"*

"No, I didn't mean it that way."

Mikki said, "I'm going to finish my run."

"Mind if I jog along with you? I'm the quarterback on the high school football team and I'm trying to keep in shape."

"Suit yourself, QB."

"And your name?"

She hesitated but then said, "Mikki. Mikki Armstrong."

They ran on.

"So what grade are you in?"

"Junior next year."

"I'll be a senior. So you guys just moved down here?" said Blake.

"Yeah, from Cleveland."

"Wow, Cleveland."

She looked to see if he was making fun of her. "Yeah, Cleveland. Got a problem with that?"

"No, I meant that was cool. You have a pro football team. Although no more LeBron James."

"Yeah, but we have the Rock and Roll Hall of Fame."

"That's cool. You play music?"

"Some, yeah. Mostly guitar. And bass."

"I'd like to hear it sometime."

"Why?"

"You're hard to get to know."

"Yes, I am."

"Maybe we can hang out sometime."

"Again, why? If Tiffany is your type, it would be a waste of time. Because I'm not a *Tiffany* by any stretch of the imagination."

"Because it's nice to meet some people who aren't from around here. Small towns can be pretty boring."

"Well, I plan to run on the beach about this time every day."

"Great. Maybe next time I won't get the evil eye as much."

He playfully punched her in the arm, and Mikki let slip a tiny smile.

"Finally, a crack in the armor," he kidded.

"Do you know Liam Fontaine?" she asked.

"Yeah, he's cool but a little odd."

"Odd? Why?"

"No sports, though I know he's a good athlete."

"Well, he works at the restaurant and he has his music. Not much time for anything else."

"Sounds like you already know him."

"I met him. He's an amazing musician."

Blake grinned. "Maybe you should ask him out."

"Please. I don't really know him."

"That's all I'm asking for. A chance to get to know you."

Later, they finished their run. Blake said, "See you tomorrow?"

"Okay."

"You're a good runner."

"So are you," she conceded.

"Have a good one."

He took off at a full sprint, and she caught herself admiring his tanned, muscled back and legs. Then she headed on to the Palace.

30

At the Channing hardware store, Jack and Sammy loaded up the truck with the materials for the work at Jenna Fontaine's house. Charles Pinckney came outside to see them, and Jack introduced him to Sammy.

"Appreciate the referral, Charles," said Jack, as he hoisted another box into the truck bed. "And thanks for putting a rush on these materials for me. I know it's not stuff you'd normally keep in stock."

"Glad to do it. And Jenna is a fine person. She runs the most popular restaurant in town, so she can be a great lead for other work."

"And gorgeous to boot," said Sammy.

Both men were wearing cargo shorts, tank tops, and work boots. It was still morning, but the temperature was already in the eighties.

"Charles, I had a question," said Jack. "I was wondering about the lighthouse. Its history."

"My father built it along with the house. It was originally listed on the official navigational charts. But one day it just stopped working."

"Anybody ever try to get it running again?"

Pinckney looked surprised. "Why, no. What would be the point? By the time it broke, they didn't use it for a navigational aid anymore."

"Just asking," said Jack.

He and Sammy left Pinckney and drove on to Jenna's house. She'd already left for the restaurant, but she'd pinned a note to the front door telling them that the entrance on the lower level was unlocked. They hauled the materials in, and after covering all of Liam's musical instruments and the furniture with drop cloths, they began to tear out the existing drywall. The plan was to backfill the wall and ceiling spaces with soundproofing materials and then replace the original drywall with specialized denser material that would also act as a sound block.

Around one o'clock they heard someone upstairs.

"Hello?" It was Jenna's voice.

"Down here," called out Jack.

She came down the steps carrying a large white bag.

She held up the bag. "Well, I hope you boys haven't eaten yet."

"You didn't have to do that," said Jack.

"Well, I'm glad you did. I'm hungry," exclaimed Sammy.

Jenna smiled and unpacked two large turkey and cheese sandwiches, chips, pickles, cookies, and sodas on a table against a wall. While she did this, she gazed around the room. "Boy, you two have been busy."

Jack nodded. "It's going better than I thought it would. That means it'll be less expensive for you."

Sammy put down his tools, wiped off his hands on a clean rag, walked over, and examined the food she'd brought. He bowed formally and said, "You are a goddess sent from above for two weary travelers."

Jenna laughed. "It's so nice to meet a real gentleman."

Jack rinsed off his hands using a bottle of water and a rag and sat down across from Sammy. He looked at Jenna. "You didn't bring yourself anything?"

"I always eat early before the lunch crowd gets in. Place is packed. Always is during the summer."

"Looks like you have a gold mine there," Jack noted.

She sat on a small hassock, crossed her legs, and said, "We do fine. But the profit margins are small and the hours are long."

"Buddy of mine ran a restaurant," said Sammy after he swallowed a bite of his sandwich. "Said it was the hardest work he'd ever done."

Jack munched on a chip and said, "So why do you do it, then, Jenna?"

Jenna had on a black skirt and a white blouse. She'd slipped her heels off and was rubbing her feet. Jack's gaze dipped to her long legs before quickly retreating. If she noticed, she didn't react.

"I'm my own boss. I'm a people person. I admit I get a kick out of walking into the Little Bit and knowing it's mine. And it's something I can leave for Liam, if he wants it, that is. He'll probably be off touring with a band. But it'll be there for him."

"Nice legacy for your kid," said Sammy.

"I know about Jack, but do you have any children, Sammy?"

"No, ma'am. Uncle Sam was my family. That was enough."

"Uncle Sam? You mean?"

Jack answered. "Sammy was in the army. 'Nam. After that, Delta Force."

Jenna looked at Sammy in awe. "That's pretty impressive."

Sammy wiped his mouth with a napkin. "Well, Jack won't tell you about himself because he's too damn modest. So I'll do the honors."

"Sammy," Jack said in a warning tone. "Don't."

"Two Purple Hearts and a Bronze Star," Sammy said, giving Jack a defiant look. He pointed to Jack's bullet wound on his arm. "Purple for that." He pointed to Jack's scarred calves. "And a Purple for that. And the Bronze for saving a bunch of his buddies from an ambush that almost cost him his life."

Jenna gazed at Jack, her lips slightly parted, her eyes wide. "That's amazing."

"What it was, was a long time ago." Jack finished his meal and balled up the paper, putting it in the white bag she'd brought. "Really appreciate the lunch, Jenna." He rose. "We need to get back to work, Sammy."

Jack started cutting out more of the walls.

Jenna eyed Sammy.

In a low voice, he said, "He's a complicated guy."

As Jenna watched Jack attack the walls, she said, "I'm beginning to see that."

31

Later that night, after the kids were asleep, Jack grabbed a flashlight and headed out to the lighthouse. He opened the door and shone his light around. He'd already gone through the boxes lining the walls, but now he walked up the rickety stairs carefully, testing each step before continuing on.

He heard scurrying feet and flashed his light in time to see a mouse rush past his foot. He kept going as the old wooden stairs creaked under his weight. He finally reached the top platform, directly under the access door that led into the space where the light mechanism was located.

As Jack moved his light around, it picked out things in the darkness; the images flew by like a reel of black-and-white film on an old projector. He stopped at one point and drew closer. It was an old mattress. He knelt down and touched it. Sitting on the mattress with its back against the wall of the lighthouse was an old doll. Jack reached down and picked it up. The doll's hair was grimy and moldy, its face stained with dirt and water. Still, he looked at it as though it were a bar of gold. He *knew* this had been Lizzie's. He'd seen her holding it in an old photo of her as a child.

He stood and moved the light around some more. His beam froze on a picture that had been drawn with what looked to be black Magic Marker on the wall. It was a little girl with pigtails and a huge smile. Under the figure was the name "Lizzie." Next to the picture of the girl was a drawing of the lighthouse with the beam on. Above that was written the word "Heaven." Jack noted that the lighthouse beam had been extended out to encompass the word.

He was about to move on when his light caught on something else. He knelt down and held the flashlight close to the wall. The image had been partially rubbed out, but Jack could still tell what it was. It was another drawing of a little girl, with pigtails. At first Jack thought it was merely a second drawing of Lizzie. But as he eyed the faded image more closely, he saw there was a major difference. In the drawing the little girl wasn't smiling. Her mouth pointed downward.

"Not a happy girl," whispered Jack. His gaze shot lower. He edged closer to read what was written there on the wall. Three letters: "T-i-l."

It had to refer to Tillie, Lizzie's twin sister, who'd died of meningitis. He sat back on his haunches and viewed the drawing in its entirety. The remaining letters had faded too badly to be read.

The drawing of the beam of light from the lighthouse extended outward but fell short of encompassing the image of Tillie. She remained firmly in the dark.

"You never found Heaven, Lizzie. And you never found Tillie."

Jack felt tears creep to his eyes, and his lungs suddenly couldn't get enough air.

Holding the doll under one arm, he pushed open the door that led to the catwalk encircling the top exterior of the lighthouse. Jack stared up at the dark sky. Heaven *was* up there somewhere. And, of course, so was Tillie.

And now Lizzie too.

He held up his hand and waved to her. And then, feeling slightly foolish, he let his hand drop but continued to stare up. Right this minute his wife seemed so close to him. He shut his eyes and conjured her face. It couldn't possibly be more than six months since he'd heard her voice and her laugh, felt her skin or watched her smile.

It can't possibly be that long, Lizzie.

He reached up. His finger covered a star that was probably a trillion light-years away and the size of the sun. But his finger covered it all. How close Lizzie must be to him, if he could cover up an entire star with his finger.

Heaven must be right up there.

He carefully set the doll down and slipped the envelope from his pocket. It had the number three written on the outside. The letter was dated December twentieth. He already knew what it said. He'd memorized every word of every letter. But if Lizzie could not read them, he would do it for her.

Dear Lizzie,

Christmas is five days away and it's a good time to reflect on life. Your life. This will be hard. Hard for me to write and hard for you to read, but it needs to be said. You're young and you have many years ahead of you. Cory and Jackie will be with you for many more years. And even Mikki will benefit. I'm talking about you finding someone else, Lizzie.

I know you won't want to at first. You'll even feel guilty about thinking about another man in your life, but, Lizzie, it has to be that way. I cannot allow you to go through the rest of your life alone. It's not fair to you, and it has nothing to do with the love we have for each other. It will not change that at all. It can't. Our love is too strong. It will last forever. But there are many kinds of love, and people have the capacity to love many different people. You are a wonderful person, Lizzie, and you can make someone else's life wonderful. Love is to be shared, not hidden, not hoarded.

Jack paused for a moment as a solitary tear plunked down on the paper.

And you have much love to share. It doesn't mean you love me any less. And I certainly could never love you more than I already do. But in your heart you will find more love for someone else. And you will make him happy. And he will make you happy. And Jackie especially will have a father to help him grow into a good man. Our son deserves that. Believe me, Lizzie, if it could be any other way, I would make it so. But you have to deal with life as it comes. And I'm trying my best to do just that. I love you too much to accept anything less than your complete and total happiness.

Love,
Jack

Jack slipped the letter into the envelope and put it back in his pocket. He picked up the doll and stared out over the ocean for a long time. He finally walked back down the stairs and out into the humid night air. He stared up at the lighthouse.

Lizzie's Lighthouse.

He walked back to the house, his heart full of thoughts of what should have been.

32

Mikki rolled over in her bed. Outside she could hear the breakers. The physics of waves crashing on sand had been completely foreign to her a short while ago. Now she'd grown so accustomed to their presence that she wasn't sure she ever wanted to be without the sound.

She yawned, sat up, and did a prolonged cat stretch. Glancing at her clock, she saw it was six thirty a.m. She liked to take her run around now so she could get back before her dad and Sammy left for work.

She slipped off the long-sleeve T-shirt she normally slept in and pulled on running shorts, a tank shirt, ankle socks, and sneakers. She made a pit stop at the bathroom and tied her hair back in a ponytail. On the way out she looked in on both her brothers, who shared a room at the end of the hall next to her dad's bedroom. They were both still asleep. Cory was sprawled on his stomach, while Jackie was on his back, but with both legs bent so his covers made a tent.

She smiled as she listened to her brothers' gentle snores.

As Mikki passed her dad's room, she could hear him stirring.

She rapped on the door. "Dad, I'm going running. I'll put the coffee on. Be back in about an hour."

"Okay. Thanks," came his sleepy response.

She put on the coffee and laid out two mugs for her dad and Sammy. The men got their own breakfast, but Mikki had been making her brothers' meals. Sometimes it was just cereal. But other times she'd pull out the black skillet and whip up eggs, bacon, and something called grits, apparently a Southern thing, which her brothers had instantly loved but she couldn't stand.

She bounced down the steps and passed through the dunes to the flat beach. She did a more thorough stretch and started her run. She kept to the hard, compacted sand, and her long strides carried her down the beach at a rapid clip. About a half mile into her run, Blake joined her. They talked as they ran. All normal subjects that teens gabbed about. She found herself liking him more, in spite of his association with someone like Tiffany Murdoch. He made her laugh.

He said his good-byes a few miles later and jogged back up to the street.

Mikki made her turn to head back toward the Palace when she saw someone out in the surf.

"Liam?"

She jogged down closer to the edge of the water as he stood up and waved.

"Early-morning swim?" she asked.

He high-stepped through the surf to stand next to her.

"Musicians and short-order cooks come here to keep in shape. And I'm not into running."

She smiled and looked out at the water.

"My mom taught me to swim in a wading pool in our backyard," she said.

"Always a good skill to have." He brushed sand out of his hair. "You look like you're working out. Don't let me interrupt you."

"Just a few more miles to go."

"Miles! I'd be puking."

"Come on! You look like you're in awesome shape."

"If I keep eating at the Little Bit, they'll have to start wheeling me out of the kitchen."

"My dad says the soundproofing is coming along."

"Then we can really jam. And my mom won't kill me."

"Looking forward to it."

Back at the Palace, Mikki showered and changed her clothes. Her dad had surprised her by making breakfast for everyone. Pancakes and ham.

"I help," announced Jackie. He proceeded to pour about a gallon of syrup on his dad's pancakes.

Before her dad and Sammy left, Mikki ran back up to her closet to get some things to take down to the beach later with the boys. Her bag spilled over, though, and when she started crawling around the floor picking things up, she noticed a loose floorboard near the rear of the closet. When she pressed the board up, she saw the edge of the photo. She pulled it out and studied the images. She went downstairs and showed her dad, who was finishing up his breakfast.

Jack looked at the picture of Lizzie as a young girl. She was surrounded by her family. A much younger Fred and Bonnie. And her siblings.

"See, Dad," said Mikki. She pointed to one of the people in the photo.

"Yeah, honey, I see."

"That was Mom's twin, right? The one who died?"

"Yes. Her name was Tillie."

"Is that why they left here? Not because of Gramps' job? But because it was so sad with her dying and all?"

"Yeah," admitted Jack. "I guess that was part of it."

"I don't know what I'd do if something happened to Cory or Jackie. And to lose a twin. It's like you lost a part of yourself in a way."

"I think you're right."

He held out his hand for the photo, but Mikki drew it back.

"Do you mind if I keep this?"

"No, sweetie, I don't mind at all."

33

"Bonnie?"

When Jack had opened the door in answer to the knock, his mother-in-law was the last person he expected to see.

She was dressed casually in slacks and a turquoise blouse, with sandals on her feet. She slid off her sunglasses and said, "Can I come in?"

"Of course." He moved aside and looked behind her.

"Fred didn't come with me," she said.

"When did you get in?"

"A couple of days ago. We're renting a house on the marsh."

"Here?"

"Yes. This *is* my hometown."

"Of course. I was just surprised."

They sat on the couch in the front room.

"I have to say, I was surprised that Mother left the place to you," she began.

"No more than I was."

"Yes," she said absently. "I suppose not."

Jack hesitated and then just decided to say it. "I heard Lizzie tell you she wanted to bring the kids here after I died."

Bonnie shot him a glance but said nothing.

"That stunned you, didn't it? Her wanting to come back here?"

"Where are the kids?" she asked, ignoring his question.

"On the beach. I can call them up."

"No, let's talk first." She looked around. "I noticed the new boards on the porch and steps, and the yard looks good."

"Sammy and I have been doing a little work to it. Electrical, plumbing, roofing, some landscaping."

"Probably more than a little." She stared at him. "I suppose that's why she left you the place. You could fix it up."

"Like I said, it came as a total shock."

"She left me a letter that explained things."

"She left me one too."

"Mother always did think of everything," Bonnie noted dryly.

"I've been thinking about fixing up the lighthouse too. Lizzie's Lighthouse."

"Please don't do that. Do you know she became obsessed with that damn thing?"

"She told me about it," said Jack. "But she was a little kid."

"No, it lasted for years. She would go up in that lighthouse every night. She would make us turn on the light and shine it over the sky looking for Tillie."

"Heaven," said Jack.

"What?"

"Lizzie said she was looking for Tillie in Heaven."

"Yes, well, it was very stressful for all of us. And then the light stopped working and she became very depressed. When Fred got the job offer in Cleveland, we jumped at it to get away from here. And to answer your question, I *was* stunned when she told me she was thinking of coming back here."

"But she was a grown woman with three kids. She wasn't going to be searching the sky for Heaven and her dead sister."

"Can you be sure of that?"

"Yeah, I can."

"How?"

"Because I know Lizzie."

Bonnie looked away but did not appear to be convinced.

Jack decided to change the subject. "You and Fred are welcome to use the place anytime you want. It's certainly more your home than mine."

"That's very nice of you, but I really couldn't. It took everything I had just to come here today." She stood and went over to one doorjamb that had horizontal cuts in the wood. "I measured the kids' heights here. Lizzie grew faster than her older sisters. Drove them crazy."

"We saw that," said Jack. "I was going to start doing that for Cory and Jackie."

Bonnie went over to the window and gazed up at the lighthouse, and then shuddered again. "I can't believe the damn thing is still standing."

She sat back down. "I'd like to see the kids while Fred and I are here."

"Of course. Anytime you want."

Jack started to say something else but then caught himself. They were having such an unusually pleasant time together that he didn't want to shatter it. However, Bonnie seemed to sense his conflict.

"What is it?"

"The tabloid story about the Miracle Man?" he said.

"Disgusting. If I could have found that reporter I would have strangled him."

Jack looked confused. "If you could have found him?"

She stared at him, and then what he was thinking apparently dawned on her. Her face flushed angrily. "Do you really think I would have spoken to a trashy gossip paper about my own daughter?"

"But the things in the story. Who else would have known about them?"

"I don't know. But I can assure you it wasn't me. They made Lizzie out to be... well, someone she very clearly wasn't."

"But you never called about it."

"Why would I? I knew none of it was true. Lizzie cheating on you? As preposterous as you cheating on her. I knew you never would have suspected that about her."

"And her going back out that night for the meds? You brought me the bag of pills. You seemed really angry about it."

Bonnie looked embarrassed. "I *was* angry about it. But I knew it wasn't your doing. I called Lizzie thinking she was home. She was at the pharmacy. She told me you hadn't wanted her to go out, that you could do without them. I only acted that way toward you because... well, I'd just buried my daughter, and I was hardly thinking clearly. I'm sorry."

"Okay, I completely understand that."

"I care about the children. I want the best for them."

"I know; so do I."

She drew an elongated breath. "Jack, this is hard, but hear me out."

Okay, here it comes, thought Jack. *The real reason she's here.*

"I've spoken with numerous doctors since your recovery."

"Why would you do that?" he said sharply.

"Because they are only one parent from becoming orphans; that's why."

"I'm alive, Bonnie, in case you hadn't noticed."

"Every doctor I talked to said it's not possible. The disease you have is fatal, without exception. I'm sorry, but that's just what they said."

"Had. I *had* the disease. I don't have it any longer. I was given a clean bill of health."

"Which these same doctors—and one of them was from the Mayo Clinic—said was also impossible. It does not go away. It may go dormant, but it always comes back. And when it does, the consensus is that you won't have more than a few weeks."

"Bonnie, why are we having this discussion? Look at me. I'm not sick anymore."

"Those three children have been through so much. You on your deathbed. Lizzie dying. Having to be uprooted and moved around the country."

"That was your doing, not mine."

"And what choice did I have exactly? Tell me that."

Jack looked away. "Okay, maybe you didn't have a choice. But I don't see your point now."

"What if you get sick again? What if it comes back? And you die? Do you have any idea what it will do to them? A person can only take so much misery, so much sorrow. They're only children; it will destroy them."

"What do you want me to do? Give them back to you? Go crawl off in a corner and wait and see if I get sick again?"

"No, but you could come and live with us in Arizona. You and the kids. That way they can get into a stable routine. And if something does happen to you, we'll be there to help you, and the kids will be used to living with us."

Jack looked askance at her. "Are you telling me that you're willing to take me and all three kids?"

"Yes. Even though Mother left you the Palace, she also left me quite a bit of money. We're in a position to purchase a larger house and have the resources to support all of you."

"I appreciate that, but I can support my own family," he said firmly.

"I didn't mean it that way."

"Okay."

"I'm just looking to help you."

"I appreciate that."

"So you won't consider my offer?"

"No, I'm afraid not."

Bonnie stood. "Well, I guess that's that. Can I go and see the children now?"

"Absolutely. I can take you down there. And I want you involved in the kids' lives."

"I want that too."

34

On Sunday, while Sammy took his motorcycle for a spin, Jack piled all the kids into the VW and drove into Channing. He'd been working hard at Jenna's house and a few other jobs, and the kids needed a break from the Palace. Jack had gotten hold of Ned Parker, and he'd agreed to give the family a behind-the-scenes tour of the playhouse.

Parker met them outside the theater, and over the next hour he took them through the darkened spaces. He showed Cory how to manipulate the house lights, lift and lower scenery, move equipment on stage dollies, and work the trapdoor in the middle of the stage that would allow people to seem to vanish. Jackie in particular thought that was very cool.

They left the theater and walked along, looking at various restaurants. Someone called out to Jack from across the street. He looked over and saw Charles Pinckney hurrying over to them. He was dressed casually in khaki shorts and a short-sleeve button-down oxford shirt with a T-shirt underneath it; leather sandals were on his feet.

"Taking the Sabbath off to enjoy some sunshine and the pleasures of Channing?"

Jack nodded. "Get away from the house for a bit. See the town."

"You hungry?"

Jack said, "We're deciding where to go."

Charles's eyes twinkled. "Then there's only one real option."

"A Little Bit of Love," said Mikki immediately.

Jack said, "We've already been there. How about another place? There're three right here on this block."

"But Jackie and Cory haven't seen it." She turned to her brothers. "It's full of musical stuff; it's so cool."

"Cool," chimed in Jackie.

She smiled. "You want a bit of love, Jackie, huh?"

He jumped up and down. "Bitalove. Bitalove." He grabbed his dad's leg. "Bitalove. Bitalove."

Cory said, "That was, like, such a cheap trick, Mikki."

"Jenna does the best Sunday brunch in town, actually," advised Charles. "I was just heading there myself."

"Okay," Jack said in a resigned tone.

Jenna smiled when she saw them come in. The place was crowded, but she said, "I've got a nice window table. Catch some of the breeze from outside. Follow me."

She seated them at the table, handed out menus, and took their drink orders.

"Is Liam around today?" asked Mikki.

"In the kitchen, grilling. He's turned into quite the short-order cook."

"We'd arranged that I could come by tonight to do a few sets."

Jack looked at her. "You did?"

She stared back at him and said sharply, "Yeah, I did. Sitting home all day watching Cory and Jackie isn't exactly how I planned to spend my summer."

"You don't need to watch me," said Cory.

"Yeah," said Jackie. "Not me."

Jenna looked at Jack and, sensing his distress, said, "Well, your dad is working really hard on the soundproofing, but it's not done yet. And while you guys sound great together, I do like a little peace and quiet in the evening. But I tell you what: Come by around eight. Liam will be home by then, and that's when I take my walk on the beach. I'll be gone about an hour or so. Does that work?"

"That's cool, Jenna, thanks."

Jenna looked at Jack. "And is that cool with Dad?"

"Yeah," Jack said slowly.

"So where's your Delta buddy?" she asked.

"Out riding his Harley," answered Cory.

"Ah. Well, he better watch himself. I know a few single ladies of a certain age in this town who will snap him up."

"Snap!" cried out Jackie.

After Jenna left, Jack leaned over and whispered to his daughter, "This is strictly music between you and Liam, right?"

"Dad, please."

"Just asking." He turned to Charles. "Bonnie came by to see me."

"She told me she was."

"Did she tell you what about?"

"Yes. I saw her afterward too. She told me what you

two talked about. She told me what you said. And I told her I agreed with you. I don't think that's what she wanted to hear, but so be it."

Mikki, who'd been listening, said, "What didn't she want to hear?"

"Another time, Mik; not now," said her father, shooting a glance at the boys. Then he added, "Did you have a good visit with her, Mik?"

"She was more laid-back than in Arizona," Mikki replied. "There she was like a control freak. Drove me nuts."

Jack turned to Charles. "I checked out the lighthouse the other night."

"Did you? And how is it looking?"

"Not great, actually."

"It really was something in its day."

"I bet it was," said Jack. "I bet it was."

35

After lunch they were walking back to the van when Charles pointed across the street and said, "Speak of the devil."

Jack saw where he was pointing. Bonnie and Fred were just entering a gift shop. Mikki walked up beside him and said in a low voice, "Okay, Dad, what is going on with Grandma? Why is she really here?"

"She just came by to make an offer." Mikki waited expectantly. "For us all to go and live with her in Arizona."

"No way. You're not thinking of doing that, are you?"

"No, I'm not."

Mikki was about to say something else when she saw Blake Saunders coming down the street with two beefy young men. They were all wearing mesh football jerseys with CHANNING HIGH printed on the front.

"Hi," said Mikki. Jack looked at her questioningly. "Blake and I met on the beach when I was going for a run," she explained. "And we've run a few more times together since then."

"Thanks for telling me." He eyed Blake. "You look familiar."

Blake looked embarrassed. "I was in the car that almost ran you off the road that day."

"The girl's name is Tiffany," said Mikki. "And she's superrich. What a shock."

Blake said, "I told her to slow down, but she doesn't listen to anyone."

"Yeah, I bet," said Mikki.

Blake turned to her. "Hey, we're having a little party on the beach next Saturday. I was wondering if you'd like to come out and hang with us. There's food, a bonfire, and we play some tunes."

"And no alcohol, of course," interjected Jack.

"No, sir," said Blake right away, though his friends gave goofy grins.

"*Right.* She'll have to get back to you on that, sport," said Jack, while Mikki scowled at her father.

"Nine o'clock. About the midpoint of our run, near where the big yellow house is," he added.

"Right."

"Okay, hope to see you there."

The young men walked off.

"What was that all about?" demanded Jack.

"Do you have a boyfriend?" a grinning Cory wanted to know. "I thought you liked this Liam guy."

Mikki's face reddened. "Will you two just knock it off?"

"That guy doesn't even have an earring, and his hair is perfectly normal," said Jack. "He's not your type. He's a football player, for God's sake. You hate football players."

"Who told you that?"

"Your mom. She made a big joke out of it because she *married* a football player."

"I think I can decide for myself what my type is," Mikki said hotly.

"Well, I'm still your dad and I don't like the idea of—"

"Hey, Miracle Man!"

Jack jerked around to see where the voice had come from.

"Over here, Miracle."

Jack turned to see two large men sitting in the cab of a pickup truck staring at him. One man stuck his head out of the truck. "I need me a miracle. You want'a come over here and sprinkle some water on my head?" He waved a five-dollar bill. "I ain't expecting miracles for free. I'll pay good money for it." Both men burst out laughing. They got out of the truck and leaned against it, their big arms folded over their thick chests. They were dressed in jeans and dirty T-shirts, with greasy ball caps on their heads. Their bare arms were covered in tattoos.

Cory said fearfully, "Dad?"

"It's okay, son. We'll just keep on walking."

They passed by the men.

One of them said, "Hey, Miracle, you too good to stop for us poor folk?"

Mikki whirled around and said, "Grow up, you creeps!"

"Mikki," Jack snapped. "Just keep walking."

"Yeah, Mikki," mimicked one of the men. "Just keep walking, sugah."

Jack stiffened at this remark. He almost turned around, but his kids were with him, and he knew nothing good would come out of a confrontation. Jack said to the kids, "We'll go on down to the beach when we get back, and—"

"Hey, Miracle, was it true your slutty wife was cheating on you with your best bud?"

Jack moved so quickly, Cory's hand was still up in the air where it had been clutching his dad's. When Jack rushed at them, the first man threw a punch. Jack ducked it, grabbed the man's hand, ripped it back and then over his shoulder, swung him around, and slammed him headfirst into the truck. When the bloodied man turned back around and charged at Jack, he sidestepped the attack and leveled the guy with a crushing blow to the jaw. The second man slammed into Jack's back, propelling him forward and face-first into a lamppost. In the next instant he'd spun out of the man's grasp, laid a fist into his diaphragm, doubling him over, and then kicked his legs out from under him. Jack's elbow strike to the back of the man's neck sent him down to the pavement, where he stayed, groaning loudly.

Jack was bent over, his breaths coming in gasps and blood pouring down his face from where he'd hit the post. As he straightened up and looked around, it seemed like the entire town of Channing was staring back at him. No one moved; no one seemed even to be breathing. As he glanced across the street, he saw Jenna and Liam staring at him from the door to the Little Bit. When he looked to his left, he saw Bonnie and Fred gawping at him in shock from the entrance to the gift shop. Bonnie looked at Jack, then to the unconscious men, and then back at her bleeding son-in-law.

"Daddy!"

Jack looked over his shoulder. Jackie was standing

on the sidewalk bawling. Cory stood there looking in amazement at his dad, while Mikki glowered contemptuously at the two men lying on the pavement. "Idiots," she said.

Jack quickly piled his kids into the VW and drove off.

36

Jack sat at the kitchen table with ice wrapped in a paper towel and held over his left cheek. Dried blood was stuck to his forehead from the impact with the street lamp. When someone knocked on the door, Jack half expected it to be the police.

"Old man and wady," squealed Jackie after he managed to open the door.

Jenna and Charles strode in. She was carrying a small bag and sat down next to Jack. She started pulling things out: sterilized wipes, Band-Aids, an ice pack, and antibiotic cream.

"What are you two doing here?" asked Jack.

Jenna moved Jack's hand away from his battered face and cleaned up the cuts, applied the ointment, and covered it all with a large Band-Aid.

Charles said, "We thought you might need a little assistance."

"Those two idiots," said Jenna. "Going off half-cocked like that. Probably drunk."

"You know them?" asked Jack.

"They come into the bar every once in a while. But I can't really say I know them."

"They're from Sweat Town," added Charles.

Jenna frowned. "I despise that term."

"Well, it's not very nice, but I think the residents actually coined it," said Charles.

"What exactly is Sweat Town?" asked Mikki.

"Other side of the tracks," replied Charles. "Poor side of town. Every coastal area has them. Most of the people who do the actual work around here live there."

Jenna said, "Here's an ice pack. It'll work faster on that swelling."

"Thanks."

She closed up her bag, sat back, and studied Jack's face. "Okay, you should be good to go."

"You're pretty slick at that," said Mikki.

"Just your mom-standard-procedure stuff."

Jackie jumped up and down trying to get to her bag of medical supplies. Jenna finally placed a Band-Aid on his finger and kissed it. "Now your boo-boo is all gone too." She straightened back up and gazed steadily at Jack. "Looks like you didn't forget your army training. Those weren't small guys, and you put 'em down pretty fast."

Jack grimaced. "It was stupid. Never should've happened."

The door opened, and Sammy walked in carrying his motorcycle helmet. "Had a nice little ride—" When he saw Jack, he exclaimed, "What the hell happened? You fall off a ladder?"

Jackie yelled, "Daddy pighting." The little boy did a kick and then swung his fist so hard he fell over.

"Fighting? Who with?" demanded Sammy.

Mikki and Cory both started telling Sammy what had happened. The older man's features turned dark as he listened to them. When they got to the slur that the one man had called Lizzie, Sammy went over to his toolbox and pulled out a crowbar. "You tell me what they look like and where I can find these maggots."

"No, Sammy," said Jack.

"I'm not letting them get away with this crap," barked Sammy.

"I'll handle it."

"What, you think I'm too old to take care of myself?"

"That's not the point. You beat them up, your butt will land right in jail."

Charles said, "He's right, Sammy. That's not the way to go about it."

"Uh-oh," said Jackie. He was peering out the window into the front yard.

"What is it, Jackie?" asked his sister.

Jackie pointed to the door, his eyes so big they appeared to touch. *"Cop dude,"* he said in a very un-Jackie-like whisper. Then he sped into the next room to hide.

Jack looked sternly at his older kids. "Cop dude? Where did he learn that?"

Mikki looked uncomfortably at the floor. Cory studied the ceiling, his teeth clenched over his bottom lip.

"Great," said Jack stiffly as he rose to answer the door.

The sheriff identified himself as Nathan Tammie. He was a big man with a bluff, serious face and dark curly hair. He took Jack's statement and scratched his chin.

"That pretty much matches up with what other people said happened. But you *did* go after them."

"He was provoked. They were saying nasty things about our mom," exclaimed Mikki. "What did you expect him to do?"

Jenna said, "Sheriff, Charles and I saw the whole thing. It's exactly as Mikki said. He was provoked. Anybody would've done what Jack did."

"I'm not saying I wouldn't have done the same thing, Jenna, but I also can't let things like this happen in town without consequences. I've already told those two boys to back off. And I expect you to hold on to your temper, Mr. Armstrong. If something happens again, you come tell me, and I'll handle it. Do we understand each other? 'Cause if there's a next time, people are gonna end up in jail."

"I understand."

After the sheriff left, Charles said, "He's a good man, but he also means what he says." He looked at Jenna. "I can drive you back to town."

"Can you give me a minute, Charles?"

A sulking Sammy had gone into another room, and the kids had disappeared.

Jenna said to Jack, "Miracle Man?"

Jack stared at her, the ice pack held to his face. "It's a long story."

"I'm a good listener."

"I appreciate that, Jenna. It's just that..."

"I can tell you're the sort of man who doesn't open up easily. Keeps it all inside."

"Maybe we can talk about it. Just not right now."

"Well, you need anything else, just let me know." She rose to go.

"Jenna?"

She turned back to see him watching her. "Yes?"

He touched the Band-Aid on his face. "Thanks for coming over. Means a lot."

She smiled. "Only next time I hope I don't have to bring my first-aid kit."

37

The sound woke all of them. Lights burst on. Jack and Sammy made sure the kids were okay before checking the rest of the house.

"Sounded like a bomb going off," said Sammy. "Or a building collapsed."

Jack looked at him quizzically and then said, "Oh, damn!"

He ran toward the rear of the house.

"Jack! What is it?"

Sammy raced after him.

Jack sprinted across the backyard and over to the rocks. He ripped open the door of the lighthouse and stopped. The stairs had collapsed. He shone his light upward. Forty vertical feet of wood had tumbled down.

Sammy ran up next to him and saw what he was looking at. "Hell. Weren't you just up there?"

Jack nodded, his gaze still on the fallen structure. Now he couldn't get to the top.

"Close call, boy."

Jack turned to him. "I need to rebuild the stairs."

"What?"

"We can go get the materials tomorrow."

"But we still have to finish some other jobs. And Charles has got some more referrals for us. Lady named Anne Bethune has a big house on the beach. She wants a screen porch enclosed and some other stuff done. Good money."

"I'll do this on my own time."

"Yeah, all your spare time."

"I *have* to do it, Sammy."

Sammy looked at the jumble of splintered wood. "Gonna be expensive."

"Take it out of my share. And I don't expect you to help."

Sammy frowned. "Since when do we have shares and don't help each other?"

"But this is different, Sammy. I can't expect you to do this too."

Sammy looked at the hand-painted sign next to the door and said quietly, "We'll take some measurements in the morning. Get the materials. We'll do the paying stuff during the day and this after hours. Okay?"

"Okay," said Jack. As Sammy turned to go back in the house, he added, "Thanks, Sammy."

He turned around. "Never been married, Jack. But I understand losing somebody. Especially someone like Lizzie."

He continued on into the house, and Jack turned to look back at the lighthouse he was now going to rebuild.

* * *

"What's all this for?" Charles asked as Jack and Sammy finished loading the truck to capacity. He eyed the items in the truck bed. "Scaffolding, and you've ordered enough wood to build another Noah's ark?"

"Had a little accident at the Palace," said Sammy when it appeared Jack was not going to answer the man's question.

Charles looked alarmed. "Accident? Was anyone hurt?"

"Stairs in the lighthouse fell down," said Jack. "No one was hurt."

"So you're going to rebuild the stairs?" he asked, looking perplexed.

"Yes," said Jack tersely.

Sammy eyed Charles and shrugged.

"But the light doesn't even work."

"He plans on fixing that too," replied Sammy.

"But why? It's not registered as a navigational aid anymore."

Jack finished strapping everything down before he looked at Charles and pulled out a sheet of paper and handed it to him. "I found a schematic on the lighting system. I'd appreciate it if you could see if these pieces of equipment could be ordered."

Charles glanced down at the list. "Might take some time. And it won't be cheap."

Jack started to climb into the truck. "Thanks."

Sammy gave Charles a helpless look and got in the truck.

As they were driving out of town, Sammy said, "Isn't that Bonnie?"

Jack looked where he was pointing. It was indeed Bonnie. And she was sitting in a car with a younger man dressed in a suit.

"Who's the guy?" asked Sammy.

"Never seen him before."

"She's a strange bird."

"Yeah." Jack glanced back at the woman and then drove on.

They unloaded the materials at the Palace. Then Sammy took the VW and drove off to meet with Anne Bethune about what she needed done, while Jack continued on to Jenna's house in the truck.

Jenna met him at the door. She was still dressed in a robe and slippers.

"Sorry about my appearance. The restaurant business isn't nine to five; it's more like ten a.m. to midnight. You want some coffee?"

Jack hesitated.

"No extra charge," she said, smiling.

"Okay, thanks."

She poured out a cup and brought it down to him in the music room. She watched him work hanging new drywall.

"You really know what you're doing," she said.

"It's just drywall. Once you know what to do, it's pretty easy."

"Right. I can't even hang a picture."

"I doubt being a lawyer in D.C. was easy."

"Just a bunch of words, legal gobbledygook."

"If you say so."

Jenna sipped her coffee and continued to watch. "Our kids have really hit it off playing music together."

"Yeah, Mikki told me."

"First time I've seen Liam really take an interest in anyone down here."

"He seems like a fine young man. And Mikki's mood is a lot better. That's worth its weight in gold."

He put down his tool and took a sip of coffee. "Mind if I ask you a personal question?"

She eyed him with mock caution. "Should I be scared?"

"No."

"Then shoot."

"Ever think about getting married again?"

"I've thought about it, sure."

"I mean, from what you've said, you've been divorced a while. You're young, well-off, smart, and educated. And . . . really pretty."

"Can I hire you as my publicist?"

"I'm serious, Jenna."

She put her cup down, sat, and covered her bare knees with her robe. "There have been some men interested in a permanent relationship with me. Some right here in Channing."

"But?"

"But they weren't the right ones. And I'm a woman who's willing to wait for the real Mr. Right. Especially considering how *wrong* I got it the first time."

Jack picked up his tool again. "Lizzie and I met in high school. We would've celebrated our seventeenth wedding anniversary this year."

"Sounds like you found Mrs. Right on your first try."

"I did," he said frankly.

"I suppose that makes the loss that much harder."

"It does. But I've got our kids to raise. And I have to do it right. For Lizzie."

"And you, Jack. You're part of the equation too."

"And me," he said. "I hope you find Mr. Right."

"Me too," said Jenna wistfully, as she stared at him.

38

Sammy turned to Jack and said, "I think it's time to knock off. It's almost midnight."

"You go on. I'm just going to finish up a few things."

They were in the lighthouse. After working most of the last three days at Anne Bethune's house, Sammy and Jack had eaten a hasty dinner and worked another four hours on the lighthouse. They had cleared out all the wood from the collapsed stairs and assembled the scaffolding up to the top platform, which also needed repair. Fresh lumber delivered from Charles Pinckney's hardware store was neatly stacked outside in preparation for the rebuilding process.

"Jack, you've put in sixteen hours today. You need to get some rest."

"I will, Sammy. Just another thirty minutes."

Sammy shook his head, dropped his tool belt on the lower level of the scaffolding, stretched out his aching back, and walked slowly to the Palace.

Jack tightened down some of the scaffolding supports and then climbed up to the top and stepped out onto the catwalk. What he was trying to imagine was how Lizzie the little girl would have thought of the view from up here.

"Were you scared at first, Lizzie? Did you think you might fall? Or did you love it the first time you saw it?" He stared out at the dark ocean and let the breeze wash over his face. He eyed the sky, looking for the exact spot where little Lizzie had imagined Heaven to be perched. And also where her twin sister had gone.

And now where you are, Lizzie.

Farther out to sea he could see ship lights as they slowly made their way across the water. He closed his eyes, and his thoughts carried back to that frozen cemetery four days after Christmas, when they'd laid Lizzie into the ground. She was there right now, alone, in the dark.

"Don't, Jack," he said. "Don't. Nothing good will come from dwelling on that. Remember Lizzie in life. Not like that."

He looked to his right and was surprised to see someone walking along the beach. As the person drew closer, Jack could see that it was Jenna. She was holding her sandals in one hand, slowly swinging them as she walked close to the waterline. He looked at his watch. It was nearly one in the morning. What was she doing out here?

She suddenly looked up and under the arc of moonlight saw him. She waved and started toward the rocks.

She called up to him. "Working late?"

He said, "Just finishing up a few things. Surprised to see you out."

"I sometimes take a walk on the beach after closing

down the Little Bit. Helps to relax me." She gazed at the lighthouse. "Heard you were fixing it up."

"Trying." He added, "Guess it seems pretty crazy."

"I think it's a good idea," she said, surprising him.

"Why?"

"I just think it's a good idea. That's all." He didn't say anything. "By the way, you did a great job on the soundproofing. Can't hear a thing. It's raised the quality of my life a thousand percent. And I won't have to kill my only child."

"I'm glad I could help."

"Well, I guess I better head back."

Jack looked down the dark beach from where she had come. "Do you want me to walk back with you? It's pretty dark out there."

"No, I'll be fine. It's a safe place. And you look like you have some thinking to do still."

Before he could say anything, she'd turned and walked off. He slowly climbed back down the scaffolding. When he touched bottom, he passed through the doorway and then turned and looked at the hand-painted sign.

"I'm going to get it working," he said. "Lizzie, I promise that this light will work again. And then you can look down from Heaven and see it."

And maybe see me.

39

"Oh, great," said Mikki. It was Saturday night and she was at the beach party Blake Saunders had invited her to. There were lots of people already there, and one of them was Tiffany Murdoch, holding court by the large bonfire that spewed streams of embers skyward. There were quite a few large young men in football jerseys and teenage girls in short shorts, tight skirts, and tighter tops. A catering truck was parked on the road near the beach. Mikki, who'd brought a blanket and a bag of marshmallows, looked on in shock as men and women in white jackets carried trays of food and drinks around to the teens partying on the sand.

Blake spotted her and strolled over, a bottle in his hand.

"Hey, glad you could make it."

"Never been to a beach party that was catered before," she said in a disapproving tone.

"I know. But Tiffany's dad is a big football booster, and he pays for the party every year."

"So I guess that's why Tiff's here?"

"Oh, yeah. The center of attention as always. A real queen bee."

"Bees sting," Mikki shot back.

"What's in the bag?" he said.

"Nothing," she said quickly, hiding the bag of marshmallows behind her.

He held up the bottle. "Want a taste?"

"Thanks, but I'll pass."

"It's not alcohol."

"I'll take your word for it."

A little put off, he said, "Well, there's plenty of food and drink. Help yourself and then come join us."

He left, and Mikki went to the tables manned by other adults in white jackets. She asked for a Coke. The woman, weathered looking with stringy gray hair, poured it out for her.

"Thank you," said Mikki.

The woman looked surprised.

"What?" asked Mikki. She looked down at her jeans and T-shirt. "Something wrong?"

"You're not with that group, are you?" said the woman quietly.

"No, we just came down from Ohio for the summer. Why?"

"You said thank you."

"And that's, like, unusual?"

The woman eyed the partygoers. "With some folks it's apparently impossible. Ohio? Are you Cee Pinckney's folks?"

"She was my great-grandmother. I'm Mikki."

"Nice to meet you, Mikki. Ms. Pinckney was a fine lady. Sorry she's gone."

"I take it you live in Channing?"

"All my life, but just not the postcard part."

"What?"

"You know the part you see on postcards? I live in the area tourists never see. We can't afford the pretty ocean views."

"Would that be Sweat Town?"

"So you've heard of it?"

"Somebody told me. Sounds like where we lived in Cleveland. What's your name?"

"Folks call me Fran."

"It was nice talking to you, Fran."

"Same here, honey."

She turned away to serve someone else.

Troubled by what Fran had told her, Mikki strolled around the pockets of people, many of whom were already wasted. The boys looked at her with lust, the girls with hostility.

Why did I come?

"Well, look who we have here."

Inwardly groaning, Mikki closed her eyes and then opened them. Things were about to get worse.

Tiffany stood in front of her, swaying slightly, plastic cup filled with beer in hand. She had on a string-bikini bottom with a mesh cutoff jersey that barely covered her chest. "What's your name again?"

Between gritted teeth she said, "Mikki."

"Oh, like Mickey Mouse." Tiffany giggled and looked around at the others and made an exaggerated bow.

"Mickey Mouse, people." Laughter swept through the ranks of the partiers. A nervous-looking Blake ran up and put his arm around Tiffany's bare waist. "Hey, Tiff, let's go get something to eat."

"Not hungry," said Tiffany with a pout. Mikki could sense this was her method of getting what she wanted. Putting her thick lips together and acting like a two-year-old.

Mikki looked at the beer and then eyed Tiffany's red convertible parked by the catering truck. "Hope you're not the designated driver."

"I can be anything I want," Tiffany replied, a coy smile on her face.

Blake pulled on her arm. "Come on, Tiff, let's get some food. You don't want to piss off your dad again, remember?"

"Shut up!" snapped Tiffany. She looked at Mikki. "I hear you and Blake have been running together on the beach."

"Yeah, so?"

"I was just surprised."

"Why's that?" Mikki asked, a hard edge to her voice.

"I didn't think he liked hanging out with freaks."

Mikki eyed the other girl's scant clothing. "You know, next time you might want to consider something that actually comes close to covering your big butt."

"Shut up!"

"Okay, I'm leaving now." Mikki turned to walk away.

"Hey, I'm talking to you."

Tiffany grabbed her shoulder. Mikki's arms and legs seemed to move of their own accord. Her hand clamped like a vise on the other girl's wrist. Mikki spun the arm behind Tiffany's back, jerked upward, angled one of her feet in front of Tiffany's legs, and gave a hard shove from behind. The next moment Tiffany was lying facedown in the sand, her mesh top up around her head.

Blake looked at her in amazement. "How'd you do that?" he asked Mikki.

Mikki looked down at her hands as if they belonged to someone else. "My . . . my dad taught me."

They both looked down at Tiffany, who was spitting out sand and crying. Other people were walking toward them.

"I'm outta here," said a panicked Mikki.

She turned, pushed past some folks, and raced off. As she passed by Fran, the woman winked at Mikki and raised a serving spoon in silent salute.

40

Hurrying down the beach, Mikki collided with someone who appeared, ghostlike, out of the darkness.

"Liam?"

The tall, gangly Liam had on a hoodie and sweatpants.

"What are you doing here?" she asked breathlessly.

"Walking. What about you?" He looked over her shoulder in the direction of the party Mikki had just left. "Tiffany's party? Don't tell me you've gone over to the dark side?" he said with a grin.

"It was stupid," admitted Mikki.

"Well, if you want to come with me, I'll show you a much better party."

"What?"

"But I have to warn you, they don't have caterers."

"How'd you know Tiffany's party was catered?"

"Because my mom did it for a couple years until little

Tiffany demanded alcohol be served. Then my mom told old man Murdoch where to stick it."

"Good for her."

"Yeah, funny, for some reason, after that, I never got invited to her little shindig. Well, enough about the rich and the spoiled. Let's get going."

He started to walk off, and Mikki hurried after him. "Where to?"

"Like I said, a better party."

The breakers crashed on the beach, providing a slow, melodious chorus to their footsteps slapping against the hard, wet sand. The sounds and the lights reached them about a quarter of a mile down the beach.

"Is that the better party?" she asked.

"Yep."

As they drew closer, the scene became clearer. The bonfire was full and the flames high. Girls and guys sat around the fire holding out sticks with hot dogs and marshmallows riding on their points. Mikki could hear a guitar strumming and sticks popping on a drum pad. Laughter and whoops amid the crash of waves. There were a few couples making out, but most were just hanging out, talking and dancing.

"Hey, Liam," said one guy as he approached them. "Everyone was hoping you'd make it." He handed them each a long stick. "Dogs are cooking." They joined the crowd. Mikki could see a few football jerseys, but most were dressed in jeans and T-shirts. There were no designer labels in sight. Everyone greeted Liam with high fives, chest bumps, and knuckle smacks.

"Pretty popular guy," Mikki remarked.

"Nah, the guys think my mom is hot, and the girls want jobs at the Little Bit. They're just looking to use me."

Mikki laughed. "So do all of you go to high school together?"

"Yeah. But most of these kids are from Sweat Town, which I find a lot more palatable than Tiffany's mansion crowd." Liam eyed the two guys playing the guitar and the drum pad. He looked at Mikki. "Want to really get this party cooking?"

She instantly got his meaning. "Oh, let's *so* do it."

They played for nearly thirty minutes while the crowd whooped and cheered.

Mikki sang parts of a song she was working on and that the crowd really got into, even chanting back parts of the lyrics. Then Mikki grabbed the drumsticks and showed herself to be nearly as adept at drums as she was at guitar. Even Liam looked at her in amazement when she finished her set. She explained, "When I formed my band, I learned every instrument. I'm sort of a control freak."

Afterward they roasted some hot dogs. When someone started playing tunes off a portable CD player, Liam said, "Hey, you want to do some sand dancing?"

"What's that?"

"Uh, it's really complicated. It's dancing in the sand in your bare feet."

She smiled. "I think I can manage that."

He put both arms around her waist, and she put her hands on his shoulders. They moved slowly over the beach.

"Feels sort of cool," Mikki said. "On the feet," she added quickly.

"Me too," he said, grinning. "Okay, now it's time for the old tradition of sand angels. Now, that's—"

"Let me guess." She plopped down on her back in the sand and moved her arms and legs up and down.

Liam joined her. "Wow, brains and beauty."

As the music played on, they danced and grew closer.

"This is really nice, Liam."

"Yeah, it is."

She cupped his chin with her hand.

"Mikki?" he said questioningly.

She kissed him and then stepped back. "I had a great time, Liam. Thanks for bringing me."

"Any time. I'm working the late shift this coming week at the Little Bit. Come on down, and I can get you anything you want for free."

"How can you do that?"

"I'm the cook. Ain't nothing happening without me."

Mikki laughed.

"You need a way home?" he asked.

"I actually rode a bike I found at the house. Left it up on the street. It's not that far."

"I've got a bike too. I'll ride with you. It's on my way."

"You don't have to do that."

"I know. I want to." He paused, looking embarrassed. "I mean..."

"I know what you mean," she said softly.

He saw her safely to her house, waved, and rode off.

When she walked in the house, her dad called out to her from the darkened front room.

"So?" he said.

She came forward, squinting in the poor light to see him. He was on the couch looking at her.

"So what?"

"Have fun?"

"Yeah, just at a different party."

She told her dad about the evening.

"Sounds like you made the right choice."

She sat down next to him. "So how's the lighthouse coming? You've really been spending a lot of time on it."

He looked down. "I know it must seem strange."

"Dad, it doesn't seem strange. Okay, maybe a little," she amended with a smile. "But you said the reason we came down here was so you could spend more time with us. Remember? But you and Sammy work all the time, and I'm stuck watching Cory and Jackie."

Jack's head dropped lower with this comment. "It's just . . . I don't know. It's complicated, Mikki. Really complicated."

Mikki rose. In a disappointed tone she said, "Yeah, I guess it is."

"But I'll try to get better. Maybe we can do something next weekend?"

She brightened. "Like what?"

Jack said lamely, "Um, I haven't thought of it yet."

Her face fell. "Right. Sure. Good night."

As she headed up the stairs to bed, Jack started to call after her, but then he stopped and just sat there in the dark.

Neither one of them noticed Sammy standing at his bedroom door listening to their exchange. The former Delta Force member went into his room, picked up his cell phone, and made a call.

41

As Mikki was running on the beach a few days later, Blake joined her.

He said immediately, "Look, I'm sorry about what happened at the party. Tiff was wasted."

"Gee, really?"

"She's usually not that obnoxious."

"Give me a break. She's a fricking nightmare in a G-string."

"Okay, maybe she is. Where'd you end up?"

"Another party on the beach."

"What party?"

"One Liam Fontaine took me to. And most of the people there were from Sweat Town. Heard of it?"

"Mikki, I live in Sweat Town."

This stunned her so much she stopped running. "What?"

"My mom works as the housekeeper for the Murdochs."

"Then why do you hang out with Tiffany?"

"Like I said, my mom works for them."

"And what, that obligates you to do her bidding?"

Blake laughed nervously. "I don't do her bidding. I just hang out with her sometimes."

They started running again. "Well, good for you. Who you hang out with says a lot about a person."

"Hey, what's wrong with me being friends with her? Are you saying poor people can only hang out with other poor people?"

"No, of course I'm not saying that."

"I have a lot of friends in Sweat Town. I play football with a bunch of them. And I go to Tiffany's and she has cool stuff and I have fun with her. So what?"

"Look, do what you want."

"Well, what I want is to go out with you." This time Blake stopped running, forcing Mikki to do the same. "So how about it? Will you go out with me?"

"Why?"

"Why? Because I like you."

"You don't really know me."

"Which is a perfect reason to go out. To get to know each other better. But hey, if you're not interested, forget it. Have a good one, and I'm sorry I don't fit your idea of a perfect person. Maybe Liam does." He started to jog off in the other direction.

"Wait a minute."

He stopped as she walked over to him. "What exactly do you want to do on this date?"

"What?"

"The plan, Blake. I need to know the parameters of what you're talking about. I'm not looking to run into a crowd of rich people again and have to kick somebody's butt." She added, "Unless it's Tiffany's. I actually enjoyed that."

"It's nothing like that. There's a coffee bar in town. They play music at night. Nothing live, but they have a DJ who's really good. I thought we could go and listen to some tunes, dance, and chill out. That's all."

She considered this. "That sounds okay. But just dancing and listening to tunes."

He eyed her closely. "Why? You got something else going?"

"No, I just—"

"Liam?"

"That's none of your business," she said hotly.

"Okay, okay. You're right. Look, I've got my license. I can pick you up tomorrow night around seven?"

"I'll check with my dad, but I think that'll be okay."

"Good," said Blake. "Glad we got that settled. Want to finish the run?"

She grinned and pushed him backward over a bump in the sand. He fell sprawling on his backside. "Catch me if you can," she called out as she sprinted off laughing.

He jumped up and raced after her.

42

"I'm hungry, Jack, so let's go."

They were parked on the street in Channing. Sammy was eyeing Jenna's restaurant, but Jack didn't seem to want to budge.

"It's not like this is the only place to eat in town, Sammy."

Sammy opened his door. "You just need to get over it."

"Over what?"

Sammy snapped, "She's just a nice lady who's trying to be friends with you, and you won't give her the time of day because you feel guilty about Lizzie."

"I don't know what the hell you're talking about! I'm nice to her."

"Great. If that's the way you want it. I'm going to eat. Stay here if you want."

Sammy slammed the truck door and went inside A Little Bit of Love.

Jack sat there brooding, his fingers tapping against the steering wheel. Finally, he climbed out of the truck and followed Sammy inside. His friend was tucked in a corner, already studying his menu. Jenna wasn't at the hostess stand, so Jack wandered back and sat down across from Sammy. The older man handed him a menu. "Figured your empty belly would bring you to your senses."

Jack took the menu, glanced at it, and then dropped it on the table. "I don't know what you expect from me."

"I don't expect anything from you."

"Well, something's clearly bugging the crap out of you."

Sammy dropped his menu too. "Okay, man, let's hash this out. When's the last time you played with Jackie? Or Cory? Or said two words to Mikki?"

"I talked to Mikki about stuff just the other night."

"I know you did because I was there listening. But what exactly has changed? You work all day, and then you work on that damn lighthouse all night. It's not healthy, Jack. You planning on having any fun ever again?"

Jack stared hard at his friend. "What makes you think I deserve to have any fun ever again?"

"You half killed yourself clawing your way back from a death sentence. And for what? To be miserable the rest of your life?"

Jack picked up the menu. "You're making it way too simple."

"And you're making it way too complicated. You got kids, Jack. They need you."

"I'm busting my ass to support them."

"Is that all?"

"What do you mean?"

"The only reason you're busting your ass? Because of them?"

"I know I haven't exactly been the perfect father. My daughter has already reminded me of that."

"She does that because she cares about you. And, hell, she's damn near sixteen. She probably wants to spend her time down here doing something other than watching her two kid brothers all day."

"She went to a party on the beach. She plays music with that Liam kid."

"Okay, fine, excuse me for giving a damn."

Jack's anger evaporated with this last comment. "You're right. It's not enough to support my kids. I have to be there for them."

Sammy looked surprised and relieved. "Well, hallelujah. Maybe after all that work on the lighthouse, you're finally seeing it."

"What?"

"The damn light."

But Jack wasn't listening to him anymore. He was thinking about something else Sammy had said.

She's damn near sixteen.

The date popped into Jack's head. Her birthday. Coming up fast. And it was a big one.

"You guys ready to order?"

Jack looked up to see a waitress standing next to their table. "What?"

The woman smiled and tapped the menu. "This is a restaurant. And that's a menu. I just took it on faith that you might want to order some food."

"I'll take care of these two, Sally," said a voice. Jenna

walked up. "They could be trouble," she added with a coy smile.

"Okay, boss." Sally walked off.

Sammy looked at her and grinned. "So tell me the specials."

"Now, Mr. Duvall, you know that everything on the menu is special, and you've eaten most of it."

Jack looked at Sammy in surprise. "You have?"

Sammy said defensively, "I get hungry. Just because you don't eat doesn't mean I have to do the same."

"How about our famous pork barbecue sandwich with fried onion rings and slaw on top? It's hell on the arteries, but you're guaranteed to die with a smile on your face."

"Sounds good," said Sammy. He stared at Jack. "Make it two. And make sure you put a smiley face on his; might improve the man's mood." He winked at Jenna.

She said, "Well, I wanted to talk to you about something anyway, Jack. Let me put your order in, and I'll be right back."

She walked off and returned a minute later, drawing up a chair.

"I'll get to the point. Your daughter would like to waitress here. And I want to hire her."

"What?" said Jack. "She didn't tell me about it."

Sammy said testily, "She wanted to, but it's not like you've been around."

Jack ignored this and looked at Jenna. "Waitress?"

"It's an honest profession, and I pay a fair wage."

Jack glanced at Sammy. "I'll have to get someone to watch the boys."

Jenna said, "I actually thought of that. The lady you're

doing work for, Anne Bethune? She runs a summer camp at her place. It's right on the beach. The boys could go there. They'd have a great time."

Sammy said, "I've gotten to know Anne, and I saw how the camp was set up. They'll love it."

"But *I* don't really know the woman."

"She's the principal at the local elementary school, Jack," said Jenna. "She has two kids of her own. In fact, when I first moved here, I put Liam in the camp and he had a blast. She has qualified people helping her too."

Sammy added, "So that way Mikki can work here during the day. Earn some money, get out of the house. Have a life."

Jenna added, "And she gets her meals free. I think it'll be good for her."

"How much does the camp cost?"

"Now, that's the interesting thing," said Sammy. "I'm doing some extra work for her on the side, and Anne agreed to let the boys come there in exchange for it."

"Sammy, you didn't have to do that."

"Like hell I didn't. They need to have some fun too."

Jack looked between Jenna and Sammy. "Why do I sense this was all planned out?"

Sammy snapped, "You got a good reason not to do it?"

"Well, no. It actually sounds like a great idea."

"Okay, then. So what's the problem?"

Jack locked gazes with Sammy for a long moment before finally looking away. "Okay, fine."

Sammy slapped the table. "There you go. That wasn't too hard, was it? Now, Jenna, can you add two beers to our order? I feel the need to celebrate."

Jenna went off to do this while Jack pretended to go to

the restroom. Instead he followed Jenna. "Can I talk to you about something?"

She looked at him in surprise. "Is everything okay?"

"Yeah," he said quickly. "I just need to ask you about something."

"Look, Jack, I know it seemed like we ganged up on you about the camp and Mikki working here, but—"

He smiled. "I actually really appreciate what you're doing."

"Thank Sammy. It was his idea. You got a good friend in that man."

"You're right. I do." He looked at her. "And a good friend in you too."

This comment seemed to catch Jenna off guard.

"I'm just... It's not that..."

She stopped in midsentence and looked away, flustered.

Jack said, "I know I've been a little unfriendly with you, and I'm sorry."

She quickly looked back at him. "You don't have to apologize, Jack. In my book you've done nothing wrong. So what did you want to ask me?"

"I don't want to do it now. What time would be good later?"

"I can get away from here around nine."

"I can pick you up here. Drive you home."

"That's fine. Liam has his license. He can drive the car back."

"I'll see you then."

43

The café was crowded, and Blake and Mikki got as close to the DJ as possible. The tunes were already blasting, and people were dancing. Blake and Mikki got Cokes from the bar and settled into a corner to watch and listen.

"You look really good," Blake said.

Mikki had on jean shorts, flip-flops, a white sleeveless blouse, and a pair of earrings her mother had given her for her fourteenth birthday. Her hair was tied back in a ponytail, and she'd washed the latest color out of the strands. Her skin had tanned, and her face glowed.

Blake had on jeans and a long-sleeve shirt worn out with the sleeves rolled up. She eyed him. "You don't look so bad either."

He laughed. "Thanks a lot. Want'a dance?"

"Okay."

They hit the dance floor and spent a half hour getting sweaty and out of breath, as they jostled next to kids doing the same thing. After another couple hours of listening to the music, things started to wind down. Blake said, "How about a walk on the beach? Nice night."

"Okay, but remember what I did to Tiffany." She held up her hands in a pseudo–martial arts pose.

Blake laughed. "I'm not messing with you. Or your dad."

They strolled along the sand. Mikki took her flip-flops off and carried them in one hand. Her free hand touched Blake's, and he wrapped one of his fingers around one of hers. At first she pulled back, but a moment later they were holding hands.

They reached an isolated section of beach where tall dunes were covered with lush, tangled vegetation.

Blake said, "I guess we better head on back."

"Okay."

He turned to her. She faced him.

"This was nice," she said.

"Not just saying that?"

"No, I'm not."

"Most girls are easy to read. But not you."

"I get that a lot."

He grinned, cupped her chin with his hand. He dipped his head to hers.

She pulled back.

He looked annoyed. "What's wrong? You've kissed before, right?"

"Of course I have," she said heatedly. "I'm almost sixteen."

"So what's the problem?"

"There's no problem." She grabbed him by the neck and planted a kiss on him. When they pulled apart, he exclaimed, "Wow. Okay, that was cool."

However, from Mikki's look, the kiss had not had the same effect on her. In fact, she looked a little guilty.

"Let's get back," she said hurriedly.

They'd only walked a few feet when Blake said, "What was that?" He turned around and stared at the dunes.

"What was what?" said Mikki.

Then the sound came again. Something was moving through the dunes.

"What is it?" Mikki asked, her fingers closing around Blake's wrist.

"I don't know. But something's up there."

"Maybe a dog or a cat?"

Another sound.

Mikki said, "That's not a dog or cat. That was someone talking. Blake, let's just get out of here."

"Hold on, there's something weird going on here. I think I recognize that voice." He called out, "Dukie? Dukie, is that you?"

"Who's Dukie?"

"Left tackle on the football team. Big and dumb. I don't know what he'd be doing here." He looked around. "Look, just hang here a sec; I'll be right back."

"Blake, don't go up there."

"Just hang on; I'll be right back."

He scooted toward the mounds of sand and quickly disappeared into the darkness. Mikki stood there looking anxiously around. There was no moon tonight, and it was hard to tell where the water ended and the land began.

"Blake?" she whispered harshly, but there was no answer. She moved closer to the dunes. "Blake?"

Hands came out of nowhere and grabbed her. She tried to scream, but something clamped over her mouth. As she looked frantically around, she saw that all the people around her were wearing Halloween masks, dark, gruesome ones.

Somebody put duct tape across her mouth. Another bound her hands behind her back. She jerked and pulled and fell down. Hands held her against the sand. Something was poured over her hair. Someone covered her eyes, and she felt something being sprayed on her clothes. She kept jerking and trying to scream. Tears poured down her face.

Someone yelled, and then there was a loud grunt.

Suddenly, whoever was holding her down fell over hard. The crowd abruptly moved away from her. Mikki sat up and struggled to see what was going on. As her eyes focused, she saw Liam hitting one of the masked people, and the person crumpled. Someone jumped on Liam's back, but he whirled around and threw the attacker off. As the person hit the sand, the mask popped off and Mikki saw Tiffany Murdoch staring at her. Mikki managed to get the rope off her hands and tore the duct tape off her mouth as another, larger person in a mask hit Liam and knocked him down. Two others jumped on top of him. Then another guy roughly pulled those two off and straddled Liam. Mikki leapt up, raced across the sand, and jumped on top of the guy, pulling his head backward, her nails raking his face.

He yelled something and pushed her off as he twisted away and fell down. Then he jumped to his feet, his mask askew. Sitting on her butt in the sand, Mikki looked up in disbelief.

"Blake?"

He rubbed the scratch marks on his face, turned, and ran. Mikki saw him grab Tiffany's hand, and they raced off toward the dunes. Mikki tore her gaze away from them in time to see the remaining guy drive his foot into Liam's stomach. She scooped up some sand, jumped up, ripped off the guy's mask, and threw the sand in his eyes. He yelled and started jumping around, clawing at his eyes. She pushed him backward, and he fell, then picked himself up and staggered after the others.

Mikki raced over to Liam, who lay facedown in the sand holding his stomach.

"Oh my God, Liam, are you okay?"

He slowly sat up, breathing hard. She wiped the sand off his face and clothes.

"Wow, you really know how to party," he said, grinning weakly.

"What are you doing here?" she asked.

"Just got off work. Was taking a stroll to wind down before I drove home. Then I heard some weird stuff and saw some people behind that dune. Then you two came walking by. When they jumped you I came flying in."

"You . . . you were watching us? Then you saw . . . ?"

"Hey, no big deal. I'm just glad you're okay." He rose gingerly. "Come on. I'll drive you home."

Mikki didn't move. "I'm sorry, Liam."

"Sorry for what?"

"It wasn't nearly as cool as when you and I kissed."

He looked down, his fingers clenching as though looking for the comfort of his drumsticks. "Really?"

"Absolutely, really."

She stood. "You were really brave to do that. You saved me."

"Jerks." He looked at her and drew in a quick breath. "Damn."

"What?"

"Your hair and your clothes."

She looked down at her clothes. They were spray painted red along with her exposed skin. She touched her hair; it was sticky and clumped and smelled like rotten eggs.

"Jerks," she said. She looked in the direction of the dunes. "Blake was part of it. I can't believe I was that stupid."

"So were you on a date with him? I mean, that's cool. He's the quarterback, not a bad-looking guy either."

"It was a mistake," she said, gripping his arm. "For a lot of reasons. And he set me up. I bet it had to do with me beating up Tiffany at the beach party."

Liam looked shocked. "You beat up Tiffany? You didn't tell me that."

"Well, she had it coming."

He laughed and then grabbed his ribs.

"Are you sure you're okay?" she said worriedly as she put a hand around his waist to support him.

As their bodies touched, they looked at each other.

She said, "I'm really gross right now, Liam."

"No, you're not; you're beautiful."

Mikki went up on her tiptoes even as the tall Liam bent down to her. They kissed, this time far longer than they had the first time.

As they drew apart and opened their eyes, she said, "You're my knight in"—she looked at his dark clothes and smiled—"black shining armor and hiking boots."

He touched her cheek and grinned. "And you're my fair maiden in flaming red with stinky stuff in her hair."

"Liam, we can't tell our parents. My dad will go after all of them and probably end up in jail."

"But what about your clothes and hair?"

"I'll clean up before I sneak in the house."

Liam said, "So we're not going to get back at Tiffany and her friends?"

"Oh, I didn't say that. We're going to get back at them, but we're going to do it the right way, not the stupid way they tried to do it."

"So how, then?"

"You'll see."

She plopped down in the ocean water and started to scrub.

44

Jack was waiting outside the restaurant when Jenna came out promptly at nine. She climbed in the VW van, and he pulled off.

"This looks like a vintage ride," she said.

"Sammy's. He likes to tinker with cars."

"That's not all he likes to tinker with."

He glanced at her. "Meaning what?"

"Meaning he and Anne Bethune are seeing each other."

"What? Why am I always the last to know?"

She squeezed his shoulder. "You just need to get out more, honey."

"When did it start?"

"Oh, about the time they laid eyes on each other; at least that was how Anne described it. In fact, that's where he was the day you beat up those guys. They went for a ride on his Harley." Jenna bent down and took off her shoes and started rubbing her feet. "Sorry, after ten hours these puppies are screaming." She rolled down the window and breathed in the crisp evening air. "God, I remember in college, a guy I dated had a Harley. One time when Liam was staying with my mom we rode it all over the Blue Ridge Parkway. It was so much fun."

"Were you away from Liam a lot back then?"

She rolled the window back up. "Hardly ever, actually. I went to college close to home so I could stay there. My mom was divorced and ran a business out of her house. She would watch Liam for me when I was at class or working."

"Working?"

"Only way to pay for school. No silver spoons in my neighborhood. I knew I wanted to go to college, and then law school. And then work at a big firm in a big city."

"Sounds like you had it all mapped out."

"Well, I didn't have Liam mapped out. He just happened. Two stupid teenagers." Her features grew solemn. "But I don't know what I'd do without him in my life. He's a great kid. And he and Mikki really seem to have hit it off. When I told him she was going to be working at the Little Bit, he was really psyched."

"Well, that's actually the reason I wanted to talk to you. About Liam."

"What about him?"

Jack told her his plan.

She was smiling and nodding as he finished. "Okay, that sounds terrific. In fact, I'm real proud of you, *Dad*. But in return you have to do one thing for me."

He looked at her warily. "What?"

"Can you take me for a ride on the Harley?"

Jack drove to the Palace, got Sammy's permission, and fired up the Harley. Jenna got on back, and they drove off, paralleling the ocean on the long, winding road. As the wind whipped across their faces, Jenna said, "Boy does this bring back memories."

"Having fun, then?"

"You know it." She squeezed his middle as they leaned into turn after turn. After thirty minutes he drove her home.

"Liam's not here yet. Would you like to come in for some tea or coffee, or something stronger?"

They sat out on the rear deck sipping glasses of Chardonnay Jenna had poured them. After going over the details of Jack's plan in more depth, Jenna said, "How's the lighthouse coming?"

He put down his glass. "Good. Stairs are coming along, and Charles found the parts to repair the light."

"I bet it'll be something to see it fired up again."

"Yeah, I think it will," Jack said absently.

"And why do I think that's not why you're really doing it?"

He glanced up at her. "I fix things. That's what I do."

"Some things can't be fixed with a hammer and a set of plans."

He drained the rest of his glass. "I better get going." He rose.

"Jack?"

"Yeah?" His voice seemed defensive.

"Let me know when you get the lighthouse working. I'd really love to see it."

Taken aback by her obvious sincerity, he said, "I will, Jenna."

"And thanks for the ride. Most fun I've had in a long time."

Before he realized, Jack had already said it.

"Me too."

45

The next morning at the breakfast table Jack said, "I didn't hear you come in last night, Mik."

"I actually got in early," Mikki lied as she poured out a glass of OJ.

"So how was the date?"

"It was okay. But we're just not that compatible."

"It happens."

"Yeah, it does. Hey, Dad, I'm going into town today."

"Why?"

"Just an errand to run. Liam's going with me. I won't be long. Sammy said he'd watch Jackie for me."

"When do you start working at the restaurant?"

"Tomorrow. That's when Cory and Jackie start camp."

"You know, you could have come to me with all that."

She put a hand on her hip and said, "Could I have, Dad? Really?"

He looked away. "So how are you getting to town? Want a lift?"

"Liam's picking me up."

"Look, Mikki, I want you to be able to talk to me about stuff. If we can't do that, then we've got no shot at this father-daughter thing."

"You really mean that?"

"Yeah, I do."

"Well, it would be a nice start if you didn't work all day and then go to the lighthouse all night."

"But I've almost got it finished."

"Okay, Dad, whatever. We can talk when you're done with it."

Mikki walked out to the street, where Liam was waiting for her in his car.

Liam grinned. "When you called this morning with your plan, I have to admit I was really intrigued. Now I'm downright fired up."

"Good, because so am I."

They arrived in downtown Channing and parked in front of the Play House. There were a number of cars sitting at the curb, including Tiffany's red convertible. The marquee read, CHANNING TALENT COMPETITION APPLICATIONS TODAY.

Mikki grinned. "When I saw that sign last night, I really didn't think anything of it. You know, who cares? But now—now the timing couldn't be more perfect."

"Let's do it," said Liam.

They walked inside the lobby and joined a line of people standing in front of a long table behind which sat a number of ladies with hair styled to the max and wearing clothes that probably cost more than some automobiles. One of them, an attractive blond woman in a formfitting dress, seemed to be in charge.

"Let me guess," Mikki whispered to Liam as she pointed at the woman. "Tiffany's mom?"

Liam nodded. "How'd you know?"

"I just flash-forwarded Tiffany twenty-five years."

"Chelsea Murdoch. I heard my mom once say she was even worse than her daughter."

"Wow, now, that's a lady I have got to tangle with."

When Liam and Mikki reached the table, Chelsea Murdoch looked up at them with such a haughty expression that Mikki just wanted to slap her. "Yes?"

"We'd like to enter the competition," said Mikki politely.

Murdoch glanced at Liam and looked confused. "Both of you?"

"That's right. Together."

"Liam Fontaine, right?" she said.

"The one and only."

The woman smirked, and then her gaze swiveled to Mikki. "And you are?"

"Michelle Armstrong. We're down here from Cleveland for the summer."

The woman looked amused. "Cleveland?"

"Yes, it's the largest city in Ohio. Did you know that?" Mikki said innocently.

"No, I never saw a good reason to find out," she replied dryly and then bumped elbows with the woman sitting next to her, who chuckled. Mrs. Murdoch pushed a paper toward them. "Fill this out. And there's a ten-dollar processing fee. What are you going to do for your act?"

"Music," said Mikki. "Drums, keyboard, and guitar."

Murdoch looked at her coolly. "Pretty ambitious."

"I'd like to think so," Mikki replied sweetly. "I'm sure the competition is pretty tough."

"It is. In fact, one young lady has won it three years in a row and is looking to make it four."

"Would that be Tiffany?"

"Yes. She's my daughter."

"Of course. But I already knew she'd won it three times in a row."

"How?"

Mikki pointed to the mammoth banner on the wall behind them, which had a large picture of Tiffany holding up three trophies with the words TRIPLE CROWN stenciled over her head. "That was, like, sort of the first clue."

Mikki returned Murdoch's scowl with a smile.

"Just put the form in the box over there and give your money to the lady in the blue dress," she snapped.

"Great. Thanks for all your help, Mrs. Murdoch," Mikki said in her most polite schoolgirl voice.

Mikki could feel the woman firing laser eye darts at her as they walked off. She filled out the form and gave it and their entry fee to the woman in the blue dress.

"Okay, step one is done," Liam said.

"And here comes step two."

Tiffany and some of her friends had just walked into the lobby of the theater.

When Mikki marched up to them, Tiffany stiffened.

"Hey, Tiff."

Tiffany looked puzzled, and then glanced at her friends and back at Mikki. "Hi," Tiffany said coolly.

"I wanted to thank you for the great time on the beach. It was really memorable."

Tiffany snorted, and the other girls laughed. "Uh, okay," said a grinning Tiffany.

Mikki leaned closer. "And just so we're straight, we're, like, so going to kick your ass in the talent competition."

The smile vanished from Tiffany's face, and her friends stopped laughing.

Mikki drew even closer. "Oh, one more thing. You ever lay another finger on me, they won't be able to find all the pieces to put you back together again, sweetie." She'd unconsciously used the same threat she'd overheard her dad invoke back in Cleveland.

Tiffany blinked and took a step back. "You think you're so tough?"

Mikki put her face an inch from the other girl's. "I'm from Cleveland. It's sort of a requirement."

Outside, as they passed Tiffany's red convertible, Liam glanced around to make sure no one was watching, then reached in his pocket and pulled out a white tube. Pretending to be picking up something, he squirted the clear liquid from the tube onto the convertible's driver's seat. It was invisible against the leather.

"What's that?" Mikki asked.

"After what they did to you, I think Super Glue is in order."

"Liam, I'm so liking your style, dude."

46

"Okay, so what's the conspiracy?"

Jenna had come into the kitchen at the Little Bit to find Liam and Mikki using their break to huddle in one corner.

"Nothing, Mom," Liam said a little too innocently.

"Son, you forget I was a lawyer. My lie detector is well oiled."

He looked sheepish and glanced at Mikki. "You want to tell her?"

Mikki said, "We entered the talent competition as a musical act."

"Well, that's great. Why keep it a secret?"

Liam answered. "We'll be going up against Tiffany, and I know her family is an important player in town. We beat her out of winning for the fourth year in a row, the Murdochs might mess with you."

"They can try and mess with me, but I don't think it'll do much good. The Little Bit is pretty much here to stay."

She looked at both of them curiously. "So why this sudden interest in beating Tiffany Murdoch?"

The two teens looked at each other.

Sensing they were holding something significant back, Jenna said, "Okay, both of you, I happen to be the boss. And I want the truth. Right now."

Between them, Mikki and Liam told her what had happened on the beach.

When they'd finished, the look on Jenna's features was very dark. "That was a criminal assault on you, Mikki. And you too, Liam. You two could have been really hurt."

"It was no big deal, Mom," said Liam.

"It was a very big deal. Those kids need to be held accountable for what they did. Otherwise, they might do it again."

"Mom, please don't do anything. We want to handle this in our own way."

Mikki added, "And if my dad finds out, he'll beat them all up and probably end up in jail. I know my dad. He's really overprotective. They were just teenagers, and he's an ex–army ranger. You saw what he did to those two big guys. He can be like a SWAT team all by himself when he needs to be. They'd throw the book at him. So please don't say anything, Jenna. Please."

Jenna's features finally lightened. "Okay, I see your logic. But does your dad know you're entering the talent competition?"

"Not yet."

"Well, I think the sooner he knows, the better."

Mikki gazed at her. "Would you mind telling him?"

"Me? Why?"

"It might be better coming from another parent. I don't

think he'll mind, but he's been a little preoccupied lately. And we've already entered. I can't pull out now."

Jenna thought about this for a few seconds. "Okay, I'll talk to him." She checked her watch and smiled. "Break time's over. We run a real sweatshop here. So get to it."

Mikki gave her a quick hug. "Thanks. You're a lifesaver. So when do you think you'll talk to him?"

"I think I know where to find him at the right time."

At a little past midnight, Jack stood on the catwalk of the lighthouse, staring out at a clear sky. After his conversation with Mikki and the disappointment so evident on her face, he had really tried to not come out here, but something made his legs move, and here he was.

He'd worked all day with Sammy on Anne Bethune's project, which had also given him time to see her camp. He had to admit that Jackie and Cory were having a wonderful time, and they were learning things too. Anne had an instructor who took the kids down to the water and showed them about marine life and other science subjects appropriate for younger kids. Cory was in his element with painting and acting out scenes that he had written in a performance art workshop the camp also offered. It was exactly the sort of experience Jack had hoped for when they came down here for the summer. However, Jack was trying not to focus on the fact that he wasn't an integral part of that experience, that it was being done through what amounted to surrogates.

If I can just finish the lighthouse.

He walked back inside the structure and gazed down at the new stairs. He'd just driven in the last nail a few minutes ago. Work still needed to be done on them, mostly finishing items, but they were safe to walk on and would last a long time. He planned to start disassembling the scaffolding tomorrow night and return it to the hardware store. He picked up Lizzie's doll and went back out on the catwalk. Sweaty from all the hard work in the confines of the lighthouse, he took off his shirt and let the cool breeze flow over him.

He looked at the doll and then gazed up at the sky. Heaven was somewhere up there. He'd been thinking about where a precocious little girl would have thought it was located. He looked at discrete grids of the sky, much like he'd compartmentalized and studied the desert in the Middle East when he was fighting in a war there. Which spot was most likely to hold an IED or a sniper?

Only now he was looking for angels and saints.

And Lizzie.

He set the doll down and took the letter from his shirt pocket. Now that he'd finished the stairs, he told himself it was time to read the next one. The envelope had the number four written on it. He slipped the letter out. It was dated December twenty-first. He leaned against the railing and read it.

Dear Lizzie,

Christmas is almost here, and I promise that I will make it. It will be a great day. Seeing the kids' faces when they open their presents will be better for me than all the medications in the world. I know this has been hard on everyone, especially you and the kids. But I know that your mom and dad have really been a tremendous help to you. I've never gotten to know them as well as I would have liked. Sometimes I feel that your mom thinks you might have married someone better suited to you, more successful. But I know deep down that she cares about me, and I know she loves you and the kids with all her heart. It is a blessing to have someone like that to support you. My father died, as you know, when I was still just a kid. And you know about my mom. But your parents have always been there for me, especially Bonnie, and in many ways, I see her as more of a mom to me than my own mother. It's action, not words, that really counts. That's what it really means to love someone. Please tell them that I always had the greatest respect for her and Fred. They are good people. And I hope that one day she will feel that I was a good father who tried to do the right thing. And that maybe I was worthy of you.

Love,
Jack

47

"Am I interrupting something?"

Jack turned to see Jenna standing there on the catwalk, a bottle of wine and two glasses in hand. She saw the letter in his hand but said nothing as he thrust it in his jeans pocket and quickly pulled his shirt on, his fingers struggling to button it up as fast as possible.

"What are you doing here?" he said a little harshly.

She took a step back. "I'm sorry if I snuck up on you."

"Well, you did."

"Look, I'll just leave."

She turned to go when he said, "No, it's okay. I'm sorry. I didn't mean to snap at you. I just wasn't expecting anyone."

She smiled. "I wonder why? It's after midnight and you're standing on your own property at the top of a lighthouse. I would've thought there'd have been hundreds of people through here by now."

His anger faded, and a grin crept across Jack's face. "Dozens maybe, but not hundreds." He eyed the wine. "Coming from a party?"

She looked around and set the glasses on an old crate while she uncorked the wine. "No, hoping I was coming *to* one."

"What?"

She poured out the wine and handed him a glass, then clinked hers against his. "Cheers." She took a sip and let it go down slowly as she gazed out over the broad view. "God, it's beautiful up here."

"Yeah, it is."

"So you finished the stairs, I see."

"Still need to do some work, but the heavy lifting's done."

"I guess you're wondering what the heck I'm doing here?"

"Honestly? Yeah, I am."

She told him about Liam and Mikki entering the talent competition but withheld the reason why.

"Hey, that's great. I bet they have a good chance to win."

"They do, actually. I'm no expert, but I'd pay money to hear them."

Jack swallowed some of his wine. "But why didn't Mikki just come and tell me?"

"I'm not really sure. She asked me to, and I agreed. Maybe you should ask her."

Jack slowly nodded. "I know I've gotten my priorities screwed up."

"Well, realizing the problem is a good first step to fixing it. And like you said, you fix things."

"Yeah, well, lighthouses are easier than relationships."

"I would imagine anything is easier than that. But that doesn't mean you can ignore it."

"I'm starting to see that."

"I know what you told me before, but why is this so important to you, Jack?"

He put his wineglass down. "This feels like the place I can be closest to her," he said slowly. He glanced over to find Jenna staring at him with a concerned expression. "Look, I'm not losing touch with reality."

"I didn't think you were," she said quickly.

"But it's still crazy, right?"

"If you feel it, it's not crazy, Jack. You've been through a lot."

"The Miracle Man," he said softly.

Jenna gazed at him but said nothing, waiting for him to speak.

"I wasn't supposed to be here, Jenna. I mean living. I was just hanging on 'til Christmas, for the kids. For Lizzie."

She touched his shoulder. "I shouldn't have asked. You don't owe me an explanation about anything."

"No, it's okay. I need to get this out." He paused, drawing a long breath, seeming to marshal his thoughts. "I spent half our marriage in the army, most of it away from home." He stopped, glanced at the dark sky. "I was crazy in love with my wife. I mean, they say absence makes the heart grow fonder? I could be in the next room and miss Lizzie, much less halfway around the world."

A tear trickled from Jack's right eye, and Jenna's mouth quivered. She swallowed with difficulty.

"I always saw Lizzie and me as one person whose

halves got separated somehow, but they found each other again. That's how lucky I was."

Jenna said quietly, "Most people never have that, Jack. You were truly blessed."

"The last night we were together she told me she wanted to come back here for the summer. I could tell she wanted to believe that I would be alive to come with her. She even talked about me fixing up the place. This lighthouse. I never thought I'd have the chance."

"So you're fulfilling Lizzie's last wish?"

"I guess." He turned to look back out to sea. "Because she never got the chance to come back."

Jenna said, "And then you got better?"

He glanced at her, his eyes red. "But do you know why I got better? Because Lizzie was right there with me every step of the way. She wouldn't let me die."

"Why are you telling me all this?"

"Because if I don't tell someone, I think I'm going to...to...I don't know. And you seemed like someone who would understand."

A gentle rain began to fall as they stood there. Jenna put down her glass, gripped Jack's shoulders, turned him to her, and put her arms around him.

As the rain continued to come down, they stood there in the darkness slowly swaying from side to side.

"I do understand, Jack. I really do."

48

"Jenna, you really don't have to do this," said Mikki.

They were at a women's clothing store in downtown Channing during a break from working at the restaurant.

She continued, "It's no big deal. I mean it's only dinner out with my family. Dad and Sammy and certainly Cory and Jackie aren't going to care what I have on."

"But it's also your sixteenth birthday, honey, and that only happens once in your life."

Together, they'd selected a half dozen outfits, and Mikki was trying them on. After Mikki decided on a dark sleeveless dress, Jenna helped her pick out shoes, a purse, and other accessories.

"Thanks, Jenna. I can't exactly go bra shopping with my dad."

"No, I guess you really can't." She smiled mischievously. "Though it might be kind of fun if you did. Just to see the former tough-as-nails army ranger squirm over cup sizes."

Mikki was looking down at all the items and mentally calculating the prices. Her face turned red. "Uh, I'm going to have to put some of these things back."

"Why?"

"I... I don't have enough money."

"Sure you do; I just gave you an advance on your salary."

"What?"

"I do it with all my new employees, or at least the ones turning sixteen who want something new to wear."

"I'm not looking for a freebie."

"And I'm not giving it. This will be deducted from your paycheck in equal installments over the next sixty years, young lady."

Mikki laughed. "Are you sure?"

"Absolutely. Seriously, you're a really good waitress and a hard worker. That should be rewarded."

After they left the shop, Jenna said, "How about an ice cream? I've got something I want to talk to you about."

They sat outside on a street bench with their cones.

"First things first. I spoke with your dad about the talent competition, and he's completely fine with you entering."

"Wow, that's great."

"Although he did wonder why you didn't just come and ask him directly about it."

"And what did you tell him?"

"I played dumb and basically dodged the question." She licked her cone and seemed to be choosing her next words carefully. "The lighthouse?"

Mikki sighed. “What about it?”

“Your dad spends a lot of time out there.”

“How did you know that?”

“Well, aside from your miserable expression, I just know; let’s leave it at that. Now, have you ever been out there with him?”

“No.”

“Why?”

“I just don’t; no reason.”

“You resent it?”

“Resent a stupid building? That’s a dumb question,” she said irritably.

“Is it?”

Mikki finished her ice cream, wiped off her fingers, and threw the trash in a bin next to the bench. “Look, if he chooses to be out there instead of with his family, who am I to rock the boat?”

“I think you just answered my question. You know that was your mom’s lighthouse?”

Mikki scowled. “Yeah, my mom when she was a little girl.”

“So you think it’s odd he seems so . . .”

“Obsessed? Yeah, a little. What would you think?”

“Hard to say. Now, tell me about what those jerks were yelling at your dad on the street that day. Miracle Man?”

Mikki looked uncomfortable and drew a long breath. “I don’t really want to talk about that.”

“Please, Mikki. I really do want to help. But I need to know.”

Mikki took the next few minutes to fill her in.

Jenna looked thoughtful. “So basically the tabloid made everything up?”

"Well, that's what my dad says."

"And you believe a newspaper that makes millions selling lies over your father? How does that make sense?"

Mikki refused to look at her. She said, "Where there's smoke, there's fire."

"That makes even less sense."

"Easy for you to say. It wasn't your family getting destroyed."

"No, but let me put on my lawyer hat for a minute and analyze this." She paused, but only for a moment. "Your dad loses the woman he loves in a tragedy that was really no one's fault. Then he loses the rest of his family and is left to die alone. Instead, he somehow finds the strength to beat a certain death sentence, brings his family back together, and tries to make a go of it as a single parent. And then a bunch of gut-wrenching lies get spread all over the news and people are calling him terrible things based on those lies, and he has to just stand there and take it." She stopped. "What an evil guy your dad is."

Jenna looked over to find Mikki staring down at her feet, a stunned expression on her face.

"I guess I never looked at it that way," she said after a long silence. "I can see why you were a lawyer."

"It's the hardest thing in the world to put yourself in someone else's place, try to really feel what they feel, figure out why they do the things they do. Especially when it's easier to stick a label on something. Or someone."

"And the lighthouse?"

"Lizzie loved it at some point in her life. It was important to her. She wanted to see it work again. That's good enough for your father. He'll work himself to the bone to try and fix it."

"For her?"

"Your dad isn't crazy. He knows she's gone, Mikki. He's doing this for her memory. At least partly. This is all part of the healing process; that's all. Everyone does it differently, but this is just your father's way."

"So what do you think I should do?"

"At some point, find the courage to talk to him."

"About what?"

"I think you'll figure it out."

Mikki laid her hand on Jenna's arm. "Thanks for the ice cream. And the advice."

"You're very welcome to both, sweetie."

49

On Saturday night Jenna helped Mikki get dressed in her new clothes and did her hair. She pinned most of it back but let a few strands trickle down Mikki's long, slender neck.

Cory and Jackie were sitting on the couch together watching TV. They both stared wide-eyed at their sister when she came down the stairs followed by a proud-looking Jenna.

"Mikki bootiful," said Jackie.

Cory didn't say anything; he just kept staring, like this was the first time he'd realized his sister was a girl.

Sammy came out of the kitchen, saw her, and said, "Wow. Okay, people, heartbreaker coming through, make room. Make room."

Mikki blushed deeply and said, "Sammy, knock it off!"

"Honey, take the compliments from the men when you can," advised Jenna.

Sammy yelled, "Jack, get your butt in here. There's big trouble."

Jack walked in from the kitchen and froze when he saw her.

Mikki took in all the males staring at her and finally said, "What?"

"Nothing, sweetie," said Jack. "You look terrific."

"Jenna helped me."

Jack flashed her an appreciative look. "Good thing. I'm not really all that great with hair and makeup."

Jenna chuckled. "Gee, don't they teach that in the army?"

"So where are we going?" asked Mikki.

"Like I said, dinner with the family. To celebrate your sweet sixteen."

She looked at Cory and Jackie watching cartoons and munching on cheese curls. Jackie's face and hands were totally orange and sticky. Cory let out a loud belch. "Great," she said, trying to sound enthusiastic.

Sammy looked at Jack. "Hold on a sec. You said we had to finish that job tonight. Promised the lady. Remember?"

"Oh, damn, that's right. What was I thinking?" Jack slapped his forehead in frustration.

Mikki scowled, "Tonight? What job?"

Jack looked stricken. "A big one. I forgot, honey."

Mikki's face flushed and her eyes glistened. "Dad, it's my *sixteenth* birthday."

"I know, sweetie, I know. Thank goodness I had a backup plan."

"What?"

He opened the front door, and Mikki gasped.

Liam was standing there dressed in pressed chinos and a white button-down shirt. His face was scrubbed pink, and he'd even combed his long hair. In his hand was a bouquet of flowers.

Mikki looked from him to her dad. "Uh, what is going on?"

Jack grinned. "Like you really wanted to go out on your sixteenth birthday with your old man and two little brothers? Give me a break."

"That would've been fine," she said, trying to keep a straight face.

"Yeah, right," scoffed Sammy. He turned to Liam, who hadn't budged an inch. "Well, get in here, son, and deliver the flowers to the lady." He grabbed Liam's arm and propelled him into the room.

Liam handed the bouquet to Mikki. "You really look great," he said shyly.

"Pretty slick yourself." She eyed her dad. "How did you possibly manage this without Cory or Jackie squealing?"

"That's easy. I didn't tell them. But Jenna was a major co-conspirator."

Jenna did a mock curtsy. "Guilty as charged."

"So, what's the plan?" Mikki asked.

"Like I said, dinner. For two. Reservations have already been made."

Jenna amended, "Not the Little Bit. At the fancy restaurant in town. I know the owners really well. They've got a great table picked out for you and a special menu."

"Wow, I can't believe this is happening. I feel like Cinderella."

Jack put his arm around his daughter. "Nice to know I can still surprise you."

"Thanks, Dad. Well, I guess we better go," she said.

"Wait a sec," Jack said. "Close your eyes."

"Dad!"

"Please, just do it."

Sighing heavily, she closed her eyes. Jack slipped the necklace from his pocket and affixed it around her neck. "Okay."

She looked down and gasped. She rushed to a mirror hanging on the wall.

"This was Mom's necklace," she said in a hushed tone.

Jack nodded. "I gave it to her on our first wedding anniversary."

Mikki turned to look at him, tears glimmering in her eyes.

"Happy birthday, baby."

Father and daughter shared a lingering hug.

After Liam and Mikki had gone off on their date, Jack stood on the front porch staring at the sandy yard. Jenna joined him there. Jack's eyes were moist, and he wouldn't look at her.

"You okay, *Dad*?" she asked.

"They grow up fast, Jenna."

"Yes, they do. But growing up is okay. What we don't want them to do is grow *away* from us."

"You're pretty good at this parenting thing."

"You do something solo long enough, I guess you either get good at it or you crash."

"So there's hope for me?"

"I'd say definitely." She slid her arm through his. "She's a great kid, Jack."

"Because of Lizzie."

"Give yourself some of the credit. You did good tonight, Jack Armstrong."

"You really think so?"

"Yeah, I really do."

50

Mikki and Liam had just finished dinner when he excused himself to go to the restroom. A few seconds later, Mikki was stunned to see Blake Saunders walk up to her table.

"What are you doing here, you weasel?" she snarled.

"I work here."

"You work here?"

"Busing tables. Sweat Town, like I said."

"Gee, doesn't sweet little Tiffany give you an allowance?"

"Look, I know you're upset, and you have every right to be."

"You're wrong, Blake. If I were upset, that would mean I cared, and I don't. You had your stupid fun, but Liam could have really gotten hurt."

"I pulled those two idiots off him, in case you didn't notice. I was on top of him to protect him. Nobody was supposed to get hurt. But then you jumped on my back and basically scratched my face off."

"Hey, let's not forget that none of it would've happened if you hadn't set me up. And why exactly did you do that?"

Blake looked down. "Because of what you did to Tiff. She was upset. She wanted to get back at you."

"And you do whatever Tiff tells you to? That's beyond pathetic."

"Yeah, I guess it is," Blake admitted.

"Look, you're not going to fool me with your 'I'm all sorry' act. Okay? So just save your breath."

"Did you put the glue in her car seat?"

"Don't know what you're talking about."

"Well, in case you were wondering, she was pissed. She had to take off her pants to get out of the car. And she hadn't bothered to put on underwear. She had to run up the steps to her house. But she slipped and fell over into the bushes, scratched her rear end up good. At least that's what my mom said. Guess all the hired help got a good laugh about that later."

Hearing this, Mikki could not suppress a grin. "It's nice to know that bad things do happen to bad people."

"I heard you entered the talent competition."

"That's right. Me and Liam. I'm sure you'll be there to root on precious Tiff."

"Actually, I hope you kick her butt."

He turned and walked away.

After leaving the restaurant, Liam and Mikki drove to the beach, parked, took off their shoes, and walked along the sand.

"I never saw the ocean before coming here," said Mikki as she drew close enough to the water to let it cover her feet.

"Mom and I have always been close to the water. Well, pretty close."

"I really like it here. I didn't think I would after living in the city all my life, but I do."

"It took some adjustment on my part, but it can be cool."

"Blake Saunders came up to me at the restaurant while you were in the bathroom."

Liam did not seem annoyed by this, only curious. "Really? What did he want?"

"To apologize for helping Tiffany get the jump on me. He said he was trying to protect you, not hurt you."

"Yeah, I actually believe him."

"You do?"

"Blake is not your typical bully jock, Mikki. He's actually a nice guy. Okay, he runs around with Tiffany too much, but I've never had a problem with him. In school he's been cool with me. We even hang out and stuff sometimes."

"I didn't know that."

"Yeah."

It started to rain, and they ran toward an old lifeguard shack and took cover under the roof overhang.

"Your mom is really cool, Liam."

"I don't even remember my dad. He was gone right after I was born."

"That must've been hard."

"I guess it could've been. But my mom loves me enough for two parents," Liam said firmly.

"I really miss my mom."

Liam put an arm around her. "That's completely normal, Mikki. You should miss her. She was your mom. She helped raise you. She loved you, and you loved her."

"Pretty sensitive stuff coming from a guy."

He smiled. "I'm a musician. It's in our blood."

He put his arms around her, and they kissed as the rain and wind picked up and the breakers started to roll and crash with more intensity.

Mikki said, "Your mom talked to me the other day about my dad. It made me really start to think about things."

"What do you mean?"

"I didn't handle things really well when my dad was sick. In fact, I pretty much screwed it up."

"How?"

"When people are in trouble and they reach out, you can either reach out to them or pull back. I pulled back. I was a bitch to my mom. I was no help to my dad. In fact, I avoided him. I was rebellious, pushed the envelope, did all sorts of crap that made things harder for them." Tears trickled down her cheeks. "And do you know why I did all that?"

Liam looked at her. "Because you were scared?"

She stared back. "I was terrified watching my dad die. And instead of trying to make the time he had left pleasant, I just ran the other way. I couldn't deal with it. I didn't want to lose him, and a part of me hated him for leaving us. For leaving *me*." She let out a sob. "And it's just killing me now that my mom died and all I can think is that I made her life miserable at the end. Just *miserable*."

As she started to cry, Liam held her and then undid his cuff button and held his sleeve out for her to use as a handkerchief. When she finally stopped crying, she rubbed her eyes with his sleeve. "Thanks."

"It's okay, Mikki. This stuff is hard. No easy answers.

It's not like music. The notes are all there. You just play, have a good time. Families are really hard."

"Your mom said I needed to talk to him."

"I think she's right. You do."

The rain began to let up, and they made a run for the car. Liam drove her home. As she got out of the car, she said, "Thanks for a great sixteenth birthday."

"Hey, you made it easy."

"Right, crying on your shoulder, real easy."

"I always thought that was part of being a friend."

She leaned back in and kissed him. "It is. And you are."

51

Jack lay on his back in the room of the lighthouse that contained the lighting machinery. His hands were greasy, he was hot and sweaty, there was dust in his throat, and he was not making much progress. He'd followed the schematic detailing of the electrical and operational guts of the machinery to the letter, but still something was off. He angled his work light into a narrow gap between two metal plates.

"Dad?"

He jerked up and hit his head on a piece of metal. Rubbing the injured spot, he pulled himself out from the confined space and looked over at the opening to the area below. Mikki, her hair plastered back on her head, was staring back up at him.

"Mik, are you okay?"

"I'm fine, Dad."

He scrutinized her. "You're wet."

"It's raining."

He looked out the window. "Oh. I guess I came out here before it started."

"Can I come up?"

He gave her a hand and pulled her into the small space.

As she drew closer, he said, "It looks like you've been crying. Liam didn't—"

"No, Dad. It has nothing to do with him. Liam was great. We had an awesome date. I...I really like him. A lot."

Jack relaxed. "Okay, but then why...?"

She took her dad's hand and drew him over to a narrow ledge that ran the length of the room under the window. They sat.

"We need to talk."

"What about?" he said warily.

"What happened with Mom, you, me. Everything, basically."

"Now?"

"I think so, yeah."

Jack wiped his hands with a rag and tossed it down.

"Look, I know you guys think it's crazy what I'm doing out here. And hell, maybe it is."

She put a hand on his arm to forestall him. "No, Dad, I don't think it's crazy." She paused. "Jenna talked to me about some things."

"What things?" Jack said abruptly.

"Like how you've basically been through hell and we all need to cut you some slack and that everybody grieves in their own way."

"Oh." Jack looked over at the lighting apparatus and then back at her. "I'm trying to get through this, Mikki; I really am. It's just not easy. Some days I feel okay; some days I feel completely lost."

Mikki's face crumpled, and she began to sob as she poured her heart out. "Dad, I was just so scared when you were sick. I didn't know how to handle it. So I just thought if I ran away from it all, I wouldn't have to deal with it. It was selfish. I'm so sorry."

He put his arm around her heaving shoulders and let her cry. When she was done, he handed her a clean rag to wipe her eyes.

"Mikki, you are one smart kid, but you're also only sixteen. You're not supposed to have all the answers. I'm thirty-five and I don't have all the answers either. I think people need to cut you some slack too."

"But I still should have known," she said, another sob hiccuping out of her.

He stroked her hair. "Let me tell you something. When my dad was dying, I did pretty much the same thing. At first I was sad, and then I was scared. I would go to bed at night scared and wake up scared. I would see him walking around in his pajamas in the middle of the day. He was just waiting to die. No hope. And this was a big strong guy I'd always looked up to. And now he was all weak and helpless. And I didn't want to remember my dad like that. So I just pushed everything inside. And I tuned everyone out. Even him. I was selfish too. I was a coward. Maybe that's why I went into the military. To prove that I actually had some courage."

She looked at him with wide, dry eyes. "You did, honest?"

"Yeah."

"Life really sucks sometimes," Mikki said, as she sat back and wiped her nose.

"Yeah, sometimes it really does. But then sometimes it's wonderful and you forget all about the bad stuff."

She looked down, nervously twisting her fingers.

"Mik, is there something else you need to tell me?"

"Will you promise not to get mad?"

Jack sighed. "Is that a condition of you telling me?"

"I guess not, but I was only hoping."

"You can tell me anything."

She turned to face him and drew a long breath. "I was the one who talked to that gossip paper."

Jack gaped at her. "You?"

Fresh tears spilled down Mikki's cheeks. "I know it was so stupid. And it got completely out of hand. Most of the junk he wrote he just made up."

"But how did you know about any of it?"

"I overheard you and Mom talking the night she died. And I saw what that jerk Bill Miller did."

"But why would you talk to a tabloid? You know what those papers do. It made your mom look..."

"I know. I'm so sorry, Dad. It was so totally stupid. I... I don't know why I did it. I was confused and angry. And I know you probably hate me. And I don't blame you. I hate myself for doing it." All of this came out in a rush that left her so out of breath she nearly gagged.

Jack put his arms around her and drew her to him. "Just calm down. It doesn't matter anymore. You messed up. And you admitted to it. That took a lot of courage."

Mikki was shaking. "I don't feel brave. I feel like a shit. I know you hate me. Don't you?"

"It's actually against the law for a dad to hate his daughter."

"I'm just really, really sorry, Dad. Now that my

head's on right about things, it just seems so stupid what I did."

"I don't think either of us was thinking too clearly for a while."

"Will you ever be able to forgive me? To trust me again?"

"I do, on both counts."

"Just like that?"

He touched her cheek. "Just like that."

"Why?"

"Something called unconditional love, honey."

52

Jenna looked up from the counter at the Little Bit to see Jack standing there.

She smiled. "I heard the kids had a fabulous time."

"Yeah, Mikki's still gushing about it."

"You want something to eat? Steak sandwich is the special."

"No, I'm good. Look, I was wondering if you had time tonight for some dinner."

Jenna came from behind the counter to stand next to him.

"Dinner? Sure. What did you have in mind? Not here. Even I get sick of the menu." She smiled and then turned serious. "Hey, I can cook for you."

"I don't want you to have to do that."

"I love to cook. It's actually therapeutic. But you'll have to be my sous chef."

"What does that mean?"

"Slicing and dicing mostly."

"I can do that. But can you get away from this place?"

"For one night, yes. Practically runs itself these days, and my number one son will be here, along with your daughter. I don't think they even need me anymore. Say around seven thirty?"

"Okay, great."

"Anything in particular you want to talk about?"

"A lot of things."

When Jack got to Jenna's house that night, music was on, wine was poured, and scented candles were lit.

"Don't be freaked out by any of this," she said as she ushered him in. "I just like to be comfortable. I'm not going all *Sex and the City* on you." She eyed him. "You look nice."

He looked down at his new pair of jeans, his pressed white collared shirt, and a pair of pristine loafers that were pinching his feet. Then he looked at her. She had on a yellow sundress with a scalloped front and was barefoot.

"Not as nice as you," he replied. "And can I go barefoot too? These new shoes are killing me."

When he looked at her feet, she smiled. "You go for it. When I was a kid, my mom had to force me to wear shoes. Loved the feel of the grass on my feet. I think one reason I moved to the Deep South is because not many people wear shoes down here."

She led him into the kitchen and pointed to a cutting board and a pile of vegetables and tomatoes next to it. "Your work awaits."

Jack chopped and sliced while Jenna moved around the kitchen preparing the rest of the meal.

"So you like to cook?"

"I actually wanted to do it professionally."

"But you became a lawyer instead?"

"Yep, it was one of those crazy zigzags that life takes. When Liam was older, I took culinary classes. Then when I was thinking about changing careers, running a restaurant seemed a nice fit. The Little Bit's menu is limited, but I've made every dish on it." She slid a pan of chicken into the oven. "And at home is where I really get to impress people."

"I'm looking forward to being impressed, then."

An hour later they sat down to eat. After a few bites, Jack raised his glass of wine in tribute to her skills in the kitchen. "I'm not exactly an expert, but this is great."

She clinked her glass against his. "I'm sure it was all due to how you sliced and diced the veggies."

"Yeah, right."

She put her glass down and eyed him. "Okay, do we talk about things now or with dessert and coffee?"

"How about *after* dessert and coffee?"

"Why?"

He looked sheepish. "Because I'm having a great time."

"And you think what you want to say will spoil that?" she said with a bit of alarm.

"No, nothing like that. But it will change it."

They walked on the beach after the cake and coffee were consumed. Jack ambled slowly, and Jenna matched his stride.

"Mikki said you and she talked."

"She's a really smart kid. She gets it, Jack. She really does."

"We talked after she came back from her date. She said you had basically told her to see things from my perspective."

"I thought that was important."

"I can understand why she was upset." He stopped and kicked at the wet sand. "After I got the kids back, I fell into my old routine. And Mikki jumped on that."

"On what?"

"That I didn't have a clue how to run a family."

"Who does? We all just wing it."

"That's nice of you to say, Jenna. But it's giving me credit I don't really deserve."

"You really put a lot pressure on yourself. Bet you did that in the army too."

"Only way you survive. You practice perfection. You have a mission, you prep the crap out of it, and you execute that prep. Same with building stuff. You have a plan, you get your materials, and you build it according to the plans."

"Okay, but did every mission and every building project go according to plan?"

"Well, no. They never do."

"Then what did you do?"

"You improvise. Fly by the seat of your pants."

"I think you just defined parenting in a nutshell."

"You really believe that?"

"Belief isn't a strong enough word. I basically *live* that."

"You'd think I'd know that by now, having three kids."

"All kids are different. It's not like one size or model fits all. I only have Liam, but I have five siblings. We drove my parents nuts, all in different ways. It's not smooth, it doesn't make sense half the time, and it's the hardest, most exasperating job you can ever have. But the payoff is also the biggest."

"Does it get easier?"

"Truthfully, some parts of it do, only to be replaced by other parts that are actually harder." Jenna gripped his shoulder. "Time, Jack. Time. And little steps. You nearly died. You lost the woman you love. You've moved to a different town. That's a lot."

"Thanks, Jenna. I needed to hear all this."

"Always ready to give advice, even if most of it is wrong."

"I think most of it is right, at least for me."

She slowly pulled her hand away. "Things get complicated, Jack, awfully fast. I'm a big believer in taking your time."

"I think I'm beginning to see that. Thanks for dinner."

She pecked him on the cheek. "Thanks for asking. But why did you think this was going to change things between you and me? I think you just wanted some assurance, maybe some comfort."

"But those are big deals for me. I don't go to people with things like that. I'm more of a loner. When Lizzie was alive, I'd go to her."

"Your soul mate?"

"And my best friend. There was nothing we couldn't talk about."

Jenna sighed resignedly. "You just described my image—no, my *dream*—of the perfect relationship."

"It wasn't all perfect. We had our problems."

"But you worked them out together?"

"Well, yeah. That's what a marriage is, right?"

"It's supposed to be that way. But more and more I don't think it is. People seem to give up on each other way too easily. Grass is greener crap."

"I'm surprised you never got married again. I'm sure it wasn't for lack of offers."

"It wasn't," she admitted. "But like I said before, I guess the right offer never came along."

As they headed back to the house, she asked, "So how's the lighthouse coming?"

"Not great," he admitted. "I guess I'll die trying to get it to work again."

As he drove off later, Jenna watched from the front porch, a worried look on her face.

53

A week later Jack turned the wrench one more time, taped over an electrical connection, spun the operating dial to the appropriate setting, and stepped back. It had been a week since he'd had dinner with Jenna. And every night he'd been out here working until the wee hours of the morning on the lighthouse. He felt like a marathoner near the end of the run. Three times he thought he had it right. Three times he turned out to be wrong. And his anger and frustration had grown with each disappointment. He'd snapped at Sammy and at all three kids over the last few days. He'd even made Jackie cry one time and felt awful about it for days afterward. Yet still, here he was.

"Come on," he said, looking at the guts of the light. "Come on. Everything checks out. Down to the smallest detail. There is no good reason you won't work."

He stood back and reached for the switch that powered the system. He counted to three, made a wish, took a breath, held it, and hit the switch.

Nothing happened. The light remained as dark as it had been for years.

Instead of another intense sense of disappointment, something seemed to snap in Jack's head. All the misery, all the frustration, all the loss bottled up inside of him was suddenly released. He grabbed his wrench and threw it at the machinery. It struck the wall, ricocheted off, and cracked the window. Then he ran down the steps, grabbed a crate at the bottom of the lighthouse, carried it out to the rocks, and hurled it as far as he could. It crashed down, and the contents exploded over the wet rocks. With another cry of rage, he ran down to the beach, yelling and cursing, spinning around uncontrollably before he dropped down into the sand and sat there, rocking back and forth, his face in his hands, tears trickling between his clenched fingers.

"I'm sorry, Lizzie. I'm sorry. I tried. I really tried. I just can't make it *work*. I can't make it work," he said again in a quieter voice. "I can't accept that you're gone. I can't! You should be here, not me. Not me!"

His breathing slowed. His mind cleared. The longer he sat there, the greater his calm grew. He looked out to the darkened ocean. He saw the usual distant pinpoints of light representing far-off ships making their way up or down the Atlantic. They were like earthbound stars, thought Jack. So close, but so far away.

He looked skyward toward Lizzie's little patch of Heaven...somewhere. He'd never found it. *It just swallows you up. It's so big and we're so small,* thought Jack.

Now he could fully realize how a little girl could

become obsessed over a lighthouse. He was a grown man and it had happened to him. The mind, it seemed, was a vastly unpredictable thing.

"Dad?"

Jack turned to see Mikki standing behind him. She was in pajama bottoms and a T-shirt, with a scared look on her face.

"Are you okay?" she said breathlessly. "I . . . I heard you yelling." She wrapped her arms around his burly shoulders. "Dad, are you okay?" she asked again.

He drew a long breath. "I'm just trying to understand things that I don't think there's any way to understand."

"Okay," she said in a halting voice.

He looked back at the Palace. "I moved all of us here for a really selfish reason. I wanted to be close to your mom again. She grew up here. Place was filled with stuff that belonged to her. Every day I'd find something else that she had touched."

"I can understand that. I didn't want to come here at first. But now I'm glad I did." She touched his arm. "I look at that photo of Mom you gave me every day. It makes me cry, but it also feels so good."

He pointed to the lighthouse. "Do you want to know why I've been busting my butt trying to get that damn thing to work?"

She sat down next to him. "Because Mom loved it?" she said cautiously. "And she wanted you to repair it?"

"At first I thought that too. But it finally just occurred to me when I saw you standing there. It was like a fog lifted from my brain." He paused and wiped his face with his sleeve. "I realized I just wanted to fix something, anything. I wanted to go down a list, do what I was supposed to do, and the end result would be, presto, it works. Then everything would be okay again."

"But it didn't happen?"

"No, it didn't. And you know why?"

Mikki shook her head.

"Because life doesn't work that way. You can do everything perfectly. Do everything that you think you're supposed to be doing. Fulfill every expectation that other people may have. And you still won't get the results you think you deserve. Life is crazy and maddening and often makes no sense." Jack paused and looked at his daughter. "People who shouldn't be here are, and someone who should be here isn't. And there's nothing you can do about it. You can't change it. No matter how much you may want to. It has nothing to do with desire, and everything to do with reality, which often makes no sense at all." He grew silent and looked out to the black ocean.

Mikki leaned against him and gripped his hand.

"We're here for you, Dad. *I'm* here for you. *I'm* part of your reality."

He smiled. And with that smile her look of fear finally was vanquished. "I know you are, baby." He hugged her. "You know I told you I was scared when my dad was dying, that I withdrew from everybody?"

"Yeah."

"Well, when my mom left me, I pulled back even more. If it wasn't for your mother, I think I would've just kept pulling back until I disappeared. I played sports and all, but I didn't have many friends, I guess because I didn't want them. Then we got married and I went off to the military. Then when I got home I picked a job that required a lot of hours and a lot of sweat."

"You had to support your family."

"Yeah, but in a way I think I was still retreating. Still trying to hide."

"Dad, you were there for us."

"I missed a lot of things I shouldn't have. I know it, and so do you."

She squeezed his arm. "There's still a lot more to see," Mikki said quietly.

He nodded. "There is a lot more to see, honey. A lifetime more."

She shivered. He put his arm around her. "Come on. Let's go in."

As they walked past the lighthouse, Mikki glanced at it and said, "Are you sure?"

Jack didn't even look at it. "I'm very sure, Mikki. Very sure."

54

After Jack got back to his room, he dropped, exhausted, onto the bed, but he didn't go to sleep. He lay there for a while, staring at the ceiling. Life was often unfair, insane, damaging. And yet the alternative to living in that world was not living in it. Jack had been given a miracle. He had already squandered large parts of it. That was going to stop. Now.

He opened his nightstand and pulled out the stack of letters. He selected the envelope with the number five on it, slid out the letter, and flicked on the light. What he'd just told Mikki, he firmly believed, because he'd once written down these same sentiments. He had just forgotten or, more likely, ignored them in his quest for the impossible. He began to read.

Dear Lizzie,

As I've watched things from my bed, I have a confession to make to you. And an apology. I haven't been a very good husband or father. Half our marriage I was fighting a war, and the other half I was working too hard. I heard once that no one would like to have on their tombstone that they wished they'd spent more time at work. I guess I fall into that category, but it's too late for me to change now. I had my chance. When I see the kids coming and going, I realize how much I missed. Mikki already is grown up with her own life. Cory is complex and quiet. Even Jackie has his own personality. And I missed most of it. My greatest regret in life will be leaving you long before I should. My second greatest regret is not being more involved in my children's lives. I guess I thought I would have more time to make up for it, but that's not really an excuse. It's sad when you realize the most important things in life too late to do anything about them. They say Christmas is the season of second chances. My hope is to make these last few days my second chance to do the right thing for the people that I love the most.

Love,
Jack

Jack slowly folded the letter and put it away. These letters, when he was writing them, were the only things he had left, really. They represented the outpouring from his heart, the sort of things you think about when the trivial issues of life are no longer important because you have precious little time left. If everyone could live as though they were in jeopardy of shortly dying, Jack thought, the world would be a much better place. But in the end they were only letters. Lizzie would have read them, and perhaps they would have made her feel better, but they were still just words. Now was the time for action. He knew what he had to do.

Be a father for my children. Repair that part of my life.

Jack rose and went from room to room, checking on his kids. He sat next to Jackie as the little boy slept peacefully, his hand curled around his monster truck. Cory slept on his stomach, his arms coiled under him. A tiny snore escaped his lips. Next, Jack stood in the doorway of Mikki's room, watching the rise and fall of her chest, the gentle sound of her breathing.

He closed her door and went downstairs and onto the rear screened porch. From here he could see the lighthouse soaring into the sky. He had built it into some mythical symbol, but it was only a pile of bricks and cinder blocks and metal guts. It wasn't Lizzie. It had no heart. Not like the trio beating in the bedrooms above. Three people who needed him to be their father.

In this last letter he had been lamenting that there were no second chances left to him. Yet that insane, unfair world that he had sometimes railed against had done something remarkable. It had given him another shot at life.

I'm done running.

Jack went back to bed and slept through the night for the first time in a long time.

55

Beginning the next day, Jack literally hung up his tool belt for the rest of the summer. Instead of going to work, he drove Jackie and Cory to Anne Bethune's camp. And he didn't just drop them off and leave. He stayed. He sat and drew pictures and built intricate Lego structures with Jackie, and then, laughing, helped his son knock them down. He instructed Jackie on how to tie his shoes and cut up his food. He helped construct the sets for a play that Cory was going to be in. He also helped his oldest son with his lines.

After camp they would go to the beach, swim, build sand castles, and throw the ball or the Frisbee. Jack got some kites and taught the boys how to make them do loops and twisters. They found some fishing tackle under the deck at the Palace and did some surf fishing. They never caught anything but had great fun in their abject failure to hook a single fish.

Jenna and Liam came by regularly. Sometimes Liam would bring his drums, and he and Mikki would practice for the talent competition. Since the Palace wasn't soundproofed, the pair would go up to the top of the lighthouse. That high up, their powerful sound was dissipated, although the seagulls were probably entertained.

At least the lighthouse was good for something, thought Jack.

He and Mikki took long walks on the beach, talking about things they had never talked about before. About Lizzie—and high school and boys and music and what she wanted to do with her life.

Mikki continued to waitress at the Little Bit. Jack and Sammy dropped in to eat frequently. And they also did some repairs for Jenna, but only because she refused to charge them for their meals. Charles Pinckney visited them at the Palace. He would tell them stories of the past, of when Lizzie was a little girl about Jackie's age. And all of them would sit and listen in rapt attention, especially Jack.

Jack took Jenna for rides on the Harley, and they were over at each other's homes for meals. They would take walks on the beach and talk. They laughed a lot and occasionally drew close, and arms and fingers touched and grazed, but that was all.

They were friends.

The summer was finally going as Jack had hoped it would. He would lie awake at night, listening to the sounds in the darkness, trying to differentiate among his children's breathing. He got pretty good at it. Sometimes Jackie would have a nightmare and would bump open his dad's door and climb into bed with him. The little boy would lay tight against his dad, and Jack would gently stroke his son's hair until he fell asleep again.

One evening he and Sammy were drinking beers out on the screen porch. Mikki and Liam were at the top of the lighthouse having one last practice before the competition. The two boys were down on the beach building the last sand castle of the day. The sun had just begun its descent, flaming the sky red and burning parts of it orange.

Sammy looked over at his friend. "Life good?"

Jack nodded. "Life is definitely good."

"Summer's almost over."

"I know."

"Plans?"

"Still thinking about it." Jack gazed at him. "You?"

"Still thinking about it."

They both turned when someone knocked on the door to the porch. It was Jenna.

"I came to pick up Liam and all his drum stuff," she said, joining them. "Big day tomorrow. They need to get their rest."

Sammy said, "I'll go help him."

Before either of them could say anything, he headed on down, leaving Jack and Jenna alone.

"So what happened?" she asked.

Jack looked over at her. "What?"

"You're a changed man, Jack Armstrong. I was just wondering why."

He finished his beer. "This will sound really corny, but sometimes when a person opens their eyes, they can actually see," he said.

"I'm happy for you; I really am."

"You were a big part of it, Jenna."

She waved this off. "You would've figured it out on your own."

"I don't know about that. I hadn't figured it out for a long time." They both looked out to the ocean and then to the lighthouse.

"Never got it to work," he said.

"Sometimes things don't seem to work unless you really need them to."

He nodded slowly. "Going to the competition tomorrow?"

"Are you kidding? Of course."

"Why don't you drive over with us? Sammy's taking their stuff over in the truck, and we can all ride in the VW."

"Sounds like a plan."

Jenna left with Liam, and the Palace settled down for the night.

Jack knocked on Mikki's door and went in.

She was sitting on her bed going over the program she and Liam were going to perform. Jack perched on the edge of her bed.

"You know that stuff by heart," he said.

"Can never be too prepared."

"Now you're starting to sound like your old man."

"And is that a bad thing?"

He gave her a lopsided grin. "I hope not. Look, you're going to do great tomorrow. Win or not."

She stared at him over the top of her musical sheets. "Oh, Dad, we're, like, so going to win."

"Nothing wrong with confidence. But don't get cocky."

"It's not that. I've checked out all the other acts. I even

saw a video of Tiffany's little baton twirl from last year. She's mediocre at best. I have no idea how she won three years in a row. Well, I do have an idea. Her mother runs the show. But nobody has worked as hard as Liam and I have."

"Well, whatever happens, I'll be out there in the audience cheering for you." He rose to go. "But you do need a good night's sleep. So not up too late, okay?"

He turned to the door.

"Dad?"

He turned back to her. "Yeah, Mik?"

She got off the bed, wrapped her arms around him, and squeezed.

"Thank you, Daddy."

Jack wrapped his arms around her. "For what, baby?"

She looked up at him. "For coming back to us."

56

"Okay, we're on next to last," said Mikki, coming backstage at the Play House.

Liam looked at her. "Who's last?"

Mikki made a face. "Who do you think? Ms. Reigning Champion. That way she gets a look at all the competition and her performance is the clearest in the judges' minds."

Liam shrugged. "I don't think it'll matter. I've seen the judges. They're all cronies of her mom's."

"Keep the faith. We've worked our butts off, and we've got a terrific act."

"How's the crowd?"

"Big. With our families smack in the middle."

When Mikki turned back around, Tiffany stood there wearing a short white robe.

Mikki eyed her. "Saving the debut of the skimpy for the crowd?"

"My daddy always said you don't give it away for free,

sweetie." She looked Mikki up and down. "But then if you don't have anything somebody wants, I guess you *have* to give it away."

Mikki smirked. "Wow, that's really deep. So do you do flaming batons?"

Tiffany looked at her like she was insane. "No. Why would I? That stuff is dangerous."

"Well, to beat us you're going to have to get out of your comfort zone. 'Cause the level of competition just got stepped up, big-time. *Sweetie.*"

Tiffany laughed, but Mikki could tell by the sudden look of uncertainty in the girl's eye that she had done what she'd intended to do.

Freeze her opponent.

Before the competition began, she and Liam went out to the audience to see their families.

The Armstrongs, Sammy, Charles Pinckney, and Jenna were all sitting together.

Jenna smiled and gave Mikki and her son hugs. "I'm really proud of you two."

"Knock 'em dead," called out Cory.

"Yeah, dead," yelled Jackie.

Chelsea Murdoch walked by with her entourage. Her dress was too tight and too short and her heels too high for her age. She looked like what she was: her daughter, only a quarter century older.

She eyed Jenna. "Haven't seen you here before."

"Never had a reason to come before, Chelsea," said Jenna. "This is Liam's first time competing."

Murdoch smiled condescendingly. "Tiffany's going for four straight. Crowd always loves her routine. She's thinking of carrying on baton in college," she added loftily.

"Well, good for her," piped in Mikki. "It's always nice to have a career plan."

Before Murdoch could say anything, Mikki added, "Okay, we gotta go. Show's about to start."

"Good luck, Mik," said Jack.

Looking dead at Tiffany's mom, she said, "It won't be about luck, Dad. Like the sign says, it's a *talent* competition."

There were twenty-one acts, mostly younger people, but there was an older barbershop quartet that was pretty good. Mikki watched from the side of the stage, mentally calculating where the serious competition was. Liam just stayed backstage chilling and idly tapping his sticks together. She came back to him and strapped on her guitar.

"It's showtime, big guy."

"Cool. I was about to fall asleep."

"Now, that's exactly what I need: a drummer with ice in his veins."

Liam smiled. "Let's rock this sleepy little town."

"Oh, yeah," said Mikki.

57

At first the beat was mellow. Still, the crowd whooped and clapped. Sensing the rising energy, Mikki gave Liam the cue they'd practiced. She cranked her amp and stomped on her wah-wah pedal, and her hand started flying across the face of the Fender guitar. They dove right into a classic Queen roof blaster, with Liam moving so fast he appeared to be two people, alternating between drums and keyboard. The crowd was on its feet singing the lyrics.

Mikki knew that once you had the crowd right where you wanted them, and they thought you'd already given everything that was in your tank, you did something special.

You gave them more.

She unplugged her amp and pulled off her guitar. She actually pitched it across the stage. At the same moment, Liam tossed his stick in the other direction. She snagged the sticks, he caught the Fender, and they exchanged positions. Liam plugged in the amp and became the guitarist, his long fingers expertly traversing the Fender. Mikki perched on the stool and hammered away at the full array of the drum set.

The finale was a dual one, with a solo each. Mikki rocked the house with a six-minute broadside and finished up with a mighty crescendo, her hands moving so fast there appeared to be six pairs of them. And when the audience didn't have any breath left and their palms were raw from clapping, Liam performed a guitar solo that would have made Jimmy Page and Santana proud. He held the last chord for a full minute, the amp-powered beat shaking the Channing Play House like cannon fire.

And then there was silence. But only for a few seconds as the crowd caught its collective breath, and then the applause and screams and cheers came in waves. Mikki held hands with Liam and took bow after bow. They finally had to motion for the people to sit down and stop applauding.

As they went backstage, the other performers rushed up to congratulate them.

"You rock," said the fiftyish baritone in the barbershop quartet. "You took me back to my Three Dog Night days."

Breathless and wearing wide grins, Liam and Mikki moved off to the side. Tiffany passed by them, not saying a word. She loosened her robe and let it fall off. The outfit underneath did not leave much, if anything, to the imagination. She turned to them and, using her fingers, formed an *L* on her forehead.

Mikki pointed to the stage. "You're not a loser *yet*. That comes later, *sweetie*."

Other than stumbling twice and nearly dropping her

baton, Tiffany did okay. The applause was polite except for the section led by her mother, which lasted so long that finally some people turned in their seats to see who was still applauding what had been a fairly mediocre performance.

A few minutes later, all the contestants were called to the stage in a single group.

Mikki found her dad in the crowd and gave a thumbs-up. Jack gave her two thumbs-up back while Sammy extended a crisp salute. Cory did an elaborate bow to his sister's dominance on the stage, and Jackie copied him.

Jenna caught Liam's eye and blew him a kiss.

The head judge stood and cleared her throat. "We have reached our decisions. But first I would like to thank all the contestants for their fine performances."

This statement was followed by polite applause.

"Now, in third place, Judy Ringer for her sterling dance performance of *The Nutcracker*."

Judy, a skinny fourteen-year-old, ran out to get her trophy and a bouquet of flowers.

"Thank you, Judy. Now, in second place, we have Dickie Dean and his Barbershop Four."

The man who had lauded Mikki and Liam's performance hustled out and received the award for his group as the crowd clapped.

"And now for the first-place champion."

The crowd held its collective breath.

The judge cleared her throat one more time. "For the fourth year in a row, Tiffany Murdoch and her fabulous baton routine."

Tiffany stepped forward, all smiles, and whisked over

to get her trophy, hundred-dollar check, and flowers, while her mother beamed. Trophy and flowers in hand, Tiffany strode to the microphone. "I'm truly overwhelmed with gratitude. Four years in a row. Who would have thought it possible? Now I'd like to thank the judges and—"

"That's a load of crap," bellowed a voice.

All heads turned, including Jack's and Jenna's, to see Cory standing up on his seat and pointing an accusing finger at the head judge.

"This sucks!" roared Cory.

"This sucks!" repeated Jackie, who was standing on his chair and pointing his finger too.

"Cor," snapped Jack. "Jackie, get down and be quiet."

But Jenna put a hand on his arm. "No. You know what? They're right." She stood and yelled, "This stinks."

Jack shrugged, stood, and called out, "Are you telling me that Mikki and Liam didn't even make the top three? You people are nuts."

The head judge and Chelsea Murdoch scowled back at them.

Another chorus came from farther back in the theater.

Mikki craned her neck to see. It was Blake and some of the other people from Sweat Town, including Fran, the woman who'd worked as a caterer at Tiffany's party.

"Recount," demanded Blake. "Recount."

Mikki grinned at him.

"Recount! Recount!" chanted the crowd.

Tiffany stood in the center of the stage trying to pretend she was oblivious to all of the criticism. She held her trophy and posed for pictures for a photographer from the local paper.

Then the crowd started chanting, "Encore! Encore!"

Mikki looked at Liam. He said, "What the heck, let's give 'em the Purple."

She nodded, picked up her guitar, cranked her amp, poised her foot on top of her wah-wah pedal, and struck a chord so powerfully amplified that Tiffany screamed and almost fell off the stage. Mikki looked over at Liam and nodded. A moment later the heart-pumping sound of "Smoke on the Water" by Deep Purple roared across the theater.

Minutes later, as the last note of the song died away, Liam and Mikki, their arms around each other, took a bow together. This was a trigger for the ecstatic, cheering crowd to rush the stage. Tiffany had to run to get out of the way of the stampede. The news photographer and reporter joined the crowd, leaving the baton twirler all alone. Tiffany stormed off the stage and threw her trophy in the trash, while her mother followed her out of the theater, trying to soothe her furious daughter.

Later, on the drive home, Mikki and Liam sat in the back of the VW bus. The two teens glowed both with the sweat of their musical exertions and also with sheer excitement.

Liam said, "This is like the greatest day of my life. I mean I've *never* felt this good about losing before."

Jack looked in the rearview mirror at his daughter. "So what happened to alternative edgy beats with a nontraditional mix of instrumentals?"

She grinned. "Wow—you *were* listening. I'm impressed. Anyway, sometimes you just can't beat good old rock and roll, Dad."

"The best part," said Cory, "was watching Tiffany storming off."

Jenna looked in the back of the van and tapped Jack on the arm, motioning with her eyes. He gazed into the rear-view mirror to see Liam and Mikki sneak a kiss.

She whispered, "I think, for them, that's the best part."

58

"Hey!" Jack yelled.

He and Sammy had just come out of the grocery store in downtown Channing when Jack saw a guy grab his tool belt out of the truck's cargo bay and run off. Jack and Sammy raced after him, Jack a few paces in front. He saw the guy duck down a side street. He turned the corner and accelerated, Sammy right behind him. The side street turned into an alley. Then they left the alley and entered a wider space. But it was a dead end; a blank brick wall faced them. They pulled up, puffing.

Jack realized what was going on about the same time Sammy did.

"Trap," Jack said.

"And we just ran into it like a couple of high school knuckleheads."

They looked behind them as five large men holding baseball bats came out of hiding behind a Dumpster. Jack could see that the man in the lead was the same one he'd thrown headfirst into the side of the pickup truck shortly after they'd arrived in Channing.

The men moved forward as Jack and Sammy fell back until they were against the brick wall. Jack slipped off his belt, coiled it partially around his hand, and stood ready. Sammy rolled up the sleeves of his work shirt and assumed a defensive stance. He beckoned them on with a wave of his hand.

"Okay, who wants to go to the hospital first?" he said.

With a yell, the biggest man ran forward and raised his bat. Jack whipped his belt, and the metal tip caught the man right on the arm, cutting it open. He screamed and dropped the bat. Sammy drilled a foot into his gut, sending him to his knees. Next, Sammy clamped an iron grip around the big man's neck.

"I don't waste my A game on the JV." Sammy crushed the man's jaw with a sledgehammer right hand that sent him to the asphalt. Sammy looked back up. "One down, four to go. Who's the next victim?"

Two more men, including the one whom Jack had beaten up before, yelled and ran forward. Jack grabbed the man's bat, pivoted his hips, and pulled hard. The man sailed past him and hit the wall, bouncing off. Groggy, he rose in time to be put back down by Jack's fist slamming into his face.

The other guy had his feet kicked out from under him by Sammy. He ripped the bat out of the guy's hands and bopped him on the head with it, knocking him out. When Jack and Sammy looked up, the other men had disappeared.

"Okay, that was fun," said Sammy.

His smile vanished a minute later when Sheriff Tammie hustled into the alley with a skinny deputy in tow.

Tammie took one look at the men lying on the ground and Jack and Sammy holding bats, and he pulled his gun, his face dark and furious.

"Put those bats down now. You're both under arrest."

"They attacked us!" exclaimed Jack as he and Sammy dropped the bats.

"Then how come they're knocked out and you two had the bats?"

"Because they were crappy fighters," said Sammy. "Is that our fault?"

Jack pointed at one of the men on the pavement. "Look, he's the same one I fought with before. He and a bunch of his guys came after us to settle the score. We were just defending ourselves."

"That's for a court to decide."

"You're really charging us?" said Jack. "What about the other guys?"

"Their butts are going to jail too."

"Well, at least that's some justice," snapped Sammy.

"And we got to let the wheels of justice do their thing. Just the way it has to be," said Tammie.

Jack and Sammy were cuffed, loaded into the sheriff's cruiser, and transported to the jail. Jack slumped down on a bench at the back of the cell, but Sammy said, "Hey, we get a lawyer, right?"

"That's what I said when I read you the Miranda card," replied Tammie.

Tammie let Jack make a call.

He said, "Jenna, it's Jack. Uh, I'm in a little bit of trouble."

Ten minutes later, Jenna and Charles Pinckney hurried into the sheriff's office and were escorted back to see the prisoners.

"My God, Jack, what happened?" she said.

He explained everything that had happened in the alleyway.

"I've talked the sheriff into releasing you on your own recognizance," she said.

"So we can go?"

"For now, yes, but it looks like the men are pressing charges, at least according to Tammie."

"But isn't it our word against theirs?" said Sammy.

"Still have to go to court."

"But we didn't do anything wrong."

"I'm sorry, Jack," said Jenna. "I'm doing the best I can."

His anger faded. "I know. And I appreciate you getting down here so fast. Didn't know anyone else to call."

"Well, for now, you're free to go. I'll get the sheriff."

Two days later, a man in a suit knocked on the door of the Palace.

Jack answered it.

"Jack Armstrong?"

"Yeah. Who are you?"

The man stuffed some papers into Jack's hand. "Consider yourself served."

The man walked off as Sammy joined Jack at the door.

"What is it?" he asked him. "Served with what? Those jerks from the alley really suing us?"

Jack read quickly through the legal documents.

When he looked up, his eyes held both anger and fear.

"No, it's a lot worse. Bonnie is suing for custody of the kids."

59

"I can't believe Grandma is doing this," said Mikki. "Why would she?"

The Armstrongs were arrayed on the couch and floor at the Palace. Sammy was there, and so were Liam and Jenna. Jack had shown Jenna the documents, and she had read them carefully with her lawyer's eye.

"I don't know," said Jack, though he actually had a pretty good idea.

Jenna looked up from the papers. "She's requested an expedited hearing to get temporary custody pending a full hearing. In non-legalese, that means she wants to get in front of a judge fast to get the kids now and then worry about the rest later."

"She can do that?" said Sammy.

"The courthouse is open to everyone. But she has to prove her case. It's difficult to have children taken away from a parent."

Jack asked, "Exactly when and where is all this going to happen?"

"In two days. In family court in Charleston."

"But we live in Ohio."

"But you have property in South Carolina and you're living here now, if only for the summer. However, I can argue that the South Carolina court lacks jurisdiction."

"*You* can argue?" said Jack.

"Do you have anyone else in mind to represent you? I've got a license to practice in South Carolina, and I've kept everything current."

"Did you practice family law?" asked Mikki.

"I've done some of it, yes. And I know my way around a courtroom." She held up the documents. "But we don't have much time to prepare."

"Jenna, you don't have time to do this. You've got a business to run."

Before she could respond, Liam said, "I can do that. Mom taught me everything about the business. It'll be fine."

Jenna smiled. "See?"

"Are you sure?"

"Heck, nice change of pace. You can only bake so many pies before you feel the need to punch somebody. Going to court gives me a chance to whack some idiots—not literally, of course, but you get the point."

"All right, but you're going to bill me for your time."

"We'll work something out."

Mikki said, "What exactly is she saying that would make a court take us from Dad?"

Jenna's face grew serious and she looked at Jack questioningly. He nodded, "You can tell them."

"Basically that your father is unfit to be your guardian. That he's a danger to himself and others."

"That's stupid," said Cory, jumping to his feet.

"Yeah, stupid," said Jackie, though, in an act of surprising independence from his brother, he remained seated, his arms folded defiantly over his little chest.

"I'm not agreeing with her, just telling you what she's alleging."

"Does she have any proof of that?" said Mikki heatedly. "Of course not, because it's not true."

"She'll be able to show any proof she has at the hearing," Jenna explained. She looked at Jack again. "And we have to show proof that you are fit."

"How do we do that?"

"You can testify. So can Mikki and Cory. Jackie's too young, of course. I can get Charles to be a character witness. And Sammy here. They can all attest to your fitness. I have no idea what angle she's using, but I can't imagine she'll be able to show the level of proof required to take children away from their surviving parent."

Later, Jack walked Jenna out to her car.

"Jack, there is one thing I didn't want to say in front of the kids."

"What?"

"I don't think the timing on Bonnie's action is coincidence. I think it's tied to your arrest for assault. She could've easily found out. And I can guarantee they'll use that to prove their case."

"But I'm innocent."

"Doesn't matter. It's all perception. And if they can convince the judge you're violent? Not good."

"Great. Guilty until proven innocent."

"Jack, if there's anything to tell me about this, now would be a good time."

"What do you mean?"

"I mean why you think your mother-in-law is doing this."

"She blames me for Lizzie's death. She came here pretending to want to reconcile, but I turned down her offer of moving in with her in Arizona. And she only came by *once* to see the kids this summer. Some grandparent she is."

"Uh, that's actually not right, Dad."

They turned to see Mikki standing behind them.

"What?" said Jack.

"Grandma came by like six times while you were out working."

"You never told me that."

"She asked us not to. Said you might get mad."

"I told her to come and visit. I wouldn't have gotten mad."

"Well, that's not what she said."

Jenna looked at her. "What did you talk about?"

Mikki shrugged. "Stuff."

"Did she ever ask about your dad?"

"Yeah," Mikki said nervously.

"Mikki, you need to tell us everything. We can't be surprised in court."

Mikki started to tear up. "It was when Dad was working so hard and he was out in the lighthouse all the time."

Jack said gently, "It's okay, sweetie; I understand. Just tell us what you told her."

Mikki calmed. "She asked what your mood was, if you were doing anything strange. If you didn't seem to be feeling well."

"And you told her about the lighthouse and... things?" said Jack.

Mikki nodded, a miserable expression on her face. "I'm sorry, Daddy. I didn't know she was going to sue you."

"It's not your fault. It'll be okay."

"Are you sure?"

"Absolutely." He looked at Jenna. "I've got a great lawyer. Now, go back in the house, Mik. Jackie's probably attempting somersaults from one of the ceiling fans."

After she left, Jack looked at Jenna. "I lost the kids once. I can't lose them again."

She put her hand over his. "Listen to me, Jack. You're not going to lose them, okay? Now, I've got to go. Lots of stuff to prepare."

She drove off, leaving Jack standing in the front yard of the Palace, looking at the ground and wondering if his second chance was coming to a premature end.

60

The kids were scrubbed and dressed in their best clothes. Jack and Sammy had bought jackets and dress slacks for the courtroom appearance. Jenna was dressed in a black skirt and jacket, heels and hose. Liam had taken time off work to join them for moral support. He and Mikki sat holding hands in the front row.

The courtroom was surprisingly small, and Jack felt immediately claustrophobic as he stepped inside. And it was very quiet. Jack didn't like such quiet. He had sensed it on the battlefield many times. It usually heralded an ambush.

The judge was not on the bench yet, but the uniformed bailiff was standing ready. Bonnie's lawyer was already seated at his table. Jack jerked when he saw Bonnie and Fred sitting behind him. Fred was studying his hands, while Bonnie was actively engaged in discussion with her lawyer, and also with another man in a suit. Other than that, the courtroom was empty.

As Jack looked at the young man, he suddenly remembered where he'd seen him before. In a car with Bonnie parked on the streets of Channing.

Jenna walked over and spoke with the bailiff for a minute or so before approaching Bonnie's lawyer. They went off to a corner to speak in private, while Bonnie stayed sitting and talking to the other man, who was showing her something on a laptop computer.

Jack watched as Bonnie's lawyer handed Jenna a packet of documents. She frowned and asked him something, but he shook his head. She said something else to him that Jack couldn't hear, but it made the other man turn red and scowl. She whipped around and marched back over to Jack. She sat down and pulled her chair closer to him and the kids.

At that moment, Sammy walked in with Charles Pinckney. Pinckney greeted Jack, Jenna, and the kids. Then he eyed Bonnie. He surprised Jack by walking over to her.

"Fred," he said. "How are you?"

Fred O'Toole looked up and seemed surprised to see Pinckney standing there. He took the other man's extended hand. "Fine, Charles, you?"

"I've been better, actually, but thank you for asking." He turned to Bonnie, who was gazing steadily at him. "Hello, Bonnie."

She nodded curtly. "Charles."

"Let's just be thankful Lizzie and Cee aren't alive to see this god-awful spectacle," he said in a tight voice.

Bonnie looked like she had been slapped. But Charles had already turned away.

Jenna held up the stack of documents and whispered to Jack. "Opposing counsel just now gave me these documents. I asked him if he would not contest an extension on the hearing date, but he refused."

"What's in those documents?" Jack asked.

"I haven't had a chance to read them, but I've glanced at a few pages. Your mother-in-law apparently has had a private detective follow you this summer." She pointed to the other man holding the laptop. "That guy."

"What?" said a shocked Jack.

"That is, like, totally insane," added Mikki.

Jack gazed nervously at him. "What's he got on the laptop?"

"Apparently some video they intend to show the judge."

"Video? Of what?"

"I don't know."

"I didn't think they could do stuff like this," said Sammy. "Surprise the other side with crap."

"Normally they can't. But this is family court. The rules are different. Everything is supposed to be done with the best interests of the children in mind. That sometimes trumps official procedures. And they're alleging that the children are in an unsafe and even dangerous environment."

"That's poppycock," said Charles.

"And we'll show it," promised Jenna. She had previously gone over with them the questions she would ask and what questions to expect the other side to throw at them.

A moment later, the bailiff announced the entrance of the judge. He turned out to be a small, thin, balding man, with thick spectacles, named Leroy Grubbs.

They rose on his entrance and then took their seats. The case was called, and Bonnie's lawyer, Bob Paterson, rose. But Jenna cut him off and asked the court for an extension, citing the late delivery of crucial documents. This was denied by Grubbs almost before Jenna finished speaking.

Paterson made his opening statement.

"Fine. Call your witnesses," said Grubbs.

The lawyer said, "Bonnie O'Toole."

61

Bonnie was sworn in and sat down in the witness box.

"You're the children's grandmother?" asked Paterson.

"Yes."

"Can you lead us through the series of events leading up to your filing this legal action?"

Bonnie spoke about Jack's illness, her daughter's death, Jack being in hospice, the children living with relatives, and Jack's recovery and his taking the children back. And, finally, she described her offer to have them all live with her because of her concerns, after consulting with doctors, that Jack's illness would most assuredly come back with fatal results.

"And what was Mr. Armstrong's response to your offer?"

"He categorically refused it."

"And what specific event prompted you to have your son-in-law put under surveillance?"

"I saw Jack beating up two men on the street in Channing, South Carolina, in broad daylight while his children were with him. The youngest, Jackie, was bawling his eyes out. It was awful. It was like Jack had lost his mind. I don't know if it was a symptom of the disease coming back or not, but I was terrified and I could tell the children were too."

The lawyer finished with Bonnie, and Jenna rose.

"Mrs. O'Toole, do you love your grandchildren?"

"Of course I do."

"And yet you seek to separate them from their father?"

"For their own good."

"And not to punish Mr. Armstrong?"

"No, of course not."

"So you're not angry with your son-in-law? You don't blame him for your daughter's death?"

"I've never blamed him. I told him that I knew it was an accident."

"But did you really believe that? Didn't you tell Mr. Armstrong that you thought he should be dead and not your daughter?"

Bonnie pursed her lips and remained silent.

"Mrs. O'Toole?"

"I've tried to move past that."

"But you still harbor resentment toward him?"

"I don't think so, no."

"And that is partly the reason you're filing for custody, for revenge?"

"Objection," said Paterson. "The witness has said she harbors no resentment."

"Withdrawn," said Jenna. "No more questions."

"Next witness," said Grubbs.

Jack and the others were surprised to see Sheriff Nathan Tammie amble into the courtroom, not looking too happy about being there. He was sworn in, and Paterson took him through his paces as a witness.

"So you warned Mr. Armstrong on the occasion of the first assault he was involved in?"

"Yes, although I warned the other guys too. Apparently Mr. Armstrong was provoked."

"And there was a second, more recent, assault involving Mr. Armstrong, was there not?"

"Yes."

"Can you tell us the circumstances?"

Tammie sighed, glanced at Jack, and explained the altercation in the alley.

"So, to sum up your testimony, Mr. Armstrong and Mr. Duvall were holding baseball bats in an alley, and three unconscious men were lying at their feet?" The lawyer glanced at the judge, presumably to gauge the man's reaction. The judge was following the line of questioning very closely. "So you arrested Mr. Armstrong and his companion, Mr. Duvall?"

"Yes. But I arrested the other guys too."

"But Mr. Armstrong will be going to court on these charges?"

"Yes."

"Could he receive prison time?"

"I really doubt that—"

"Could he?"

"Well, yes."

"No further questions."

Jenna rose. "Sheriff Tammie, why didn't you charge Mr. Armstrong on the first altercation?"

"Well, from the witness statements it was clear that he was provoked."

Jenna glanced at Bonnie. "Provoked how?"

Tammie took out his notebook. "Three witnesses said that one of the guys Mr. Armstrong went after had yelled out something about him being the miracle man and they were willing to pay him five dollars to perform a miracle on him. And he said other stuff, trying to get Mr. Armstrong's goat, I guess."

"All directed at Mr. Armstrong personally?"

"Yes."

"Did Mr. Armstrong attack at that point, when he was the subject of these statements?"

"No. He just kept walking along with his kids."

"Go on."

Tammie looked at his notes. "Then the same guy said, 'Hey, Miracle, was it true your slutty wife was cheating on you? That why you came back from the dead?' "

Jenna turned to look at Bonnie in time to see her glance sharply at Jack.

"And is that when Mr. Armstrong went after them? Because they insulted his deceased wife?"

"Yes."

"So he exercised admirable restraint when the insults were only directed to him?"

"Probably more restraint than I would have exercised if it'd been me."

"And the alleged second assault? Is it true that one of the men engaged in this assault was also the same man who was involved in the first altercation?"

"Yes."

"So it could have been that these men attacked Mr.

Armstrong in that alley and he was merely defending himself?"

"Objection," said Paterson. "Calls for a conclusion that the witness is not qualified to give."

"Sustained," said Grubbs, but he looked curiously at Tammie and then over at Jack.

Jenna said, "No further questions."

Paterson said, "I call Michelle Armstrong to the stand."

As Mikki rose and moved forward, she stopped next to her dad. He gave her a reassuring smile and gripped her hand. "Just tell the truth, sweetie," he said.

62

"Ms. Armstrong?" said Paterson politely. "You had a number of conversations with your grandmother this summer, didn't you?"

Mikki looked at her father, but the lawyer moved to block her view. "You must answer my questions truthfully and not look to your father for instruction."

Mikki took a deep breath. "Yes, I spoke with Grandma."

"And what did you tell her about your father's . . . um . . . actions during the summer?"

"I don't understand the question."

"All right. I mean with regards to the lighthouse, for instance."

"Lighthouse?" said the judge.

Paterson addressed him. "It was apparently Mr. Armstrong's deceased wife's favorite place as a child, and he was spending most of the nights there."

Jenna rose. "Objection. Mr. Paterson has not been sworn in as a witness, Your Honor, and has no personal knowledge of the situation."

"All right," said Grubbs. "Sustained."

Paterson turned back to Mikki. "Your statements about the lighthouse? Can you tell the court, please?"

Mikki fidgeted. "I just told her that Dad was working on the lighthouse, that's all. It was no big deal."

"Would he work out there late at night?"

"Yes."

"With Mr. Duvall?"

"Yes."

"Leaving you three children alone in the house?"

Mikki's face grew hot. "I'm *not* a child. I'm sixteen."

"All right, leaving you and your younger brothers alone in the house?"

"Sometimes, but nothing happened."

"On the contrary, did you not tell your grandmother on at least three occasions that your younger brother, Jack Jr., got out of bed and once fell down the stairs?"

Jack looked shocked. He stared at Mikki. She swallowed hard. "But he was okay. Just a bruise on his back."

"And on another occasion Jack Jr. wandered out of the house and you couldn't find him for at least an hour? And he turned up walking down the street?"

Jack slumped back in his chair, totally flummoxed.

"Yes. But he was okay."

"And did you tell your father about these incidents?"

"No."

"Why not?"

"I... I didn't want him to get upset."

"Does he get upset often?"

"Well, I mean, no; no, he doesn't."

"Did you also tell your grandmother that your dad was obsessed with the house and the lighthouse because your deceased mother loved it so much there and he was trying to reconnect somehow with her?"

Mikki flushed a deep red and started breathing quickly. Tears trickled from her eyes. "I was mad at him; that's why I said those things."

"So they weren't true? Remember you are under oath."

Jenna rose. "Your Honor, counsel is badgering. I request a recess so the witness can compose herself."

Grubbs looked at Mikki. "Are you all right?"

Mikki drew in a deep breath, wiped her eyes, and nodded. "I'm okay."

"Proceed."

Paterson continued. "And did you also tell your grandmother that your father had no clue how to run a family and didn't seem to care about you and your brothers?"

Jack looked down.

Mikki teared up again. "That was before he changed."

"Changed?"

Obviously flustered, Mikki started speaking too fast. "Yes, I mean he was like that before. No, I mean, not bad. He did love us. I mean he *does* love us. He takes great care of us."

"But didn't you also tell your grandmother that you were worried about your dad's mental state?"

In a hushed voice Mikki said, "No, I don't remember saying that."

"So you've never seen your dad acting irrationally or even in a fit of rage?"

"No, never."

Paterson turned to the man in the suit sitting next to Bonnie. "Mr. Drake, if you would?" The man rose and wheeled forward a TV on a rolling stand and slid a DVD into a player underneath the TV.

Paterson said to the judge, "Your Honor, Mr. Drake is a licensed private investigator hired by Mrs. O'Toole to keep watch over the Armstrong children. The video you're about to see represents one of the results of this surveillance."

The TV screen came to life, and they all watched as Jack came running out of the lighthouse carrying the crate. He smashed it on the rocks and then raced down to the beach, twisting and turning in what looked unmistakably like a fit of insane rage. Then he dropped to the sand and wept. The next image was Mikki creeping up to her father.

On Paterson's cue the DVD was stopped, and he turned back to Mikki.

"You obviously saw your father that night?"

Mikki nodded.

"And you wouldn't describe that behavior as irrational or even a fit of rage?"

"He was upset, but he got better."

"So in your mind he was . . . sick?"

"No, that's not what I meant." She stood. "You're putting words in my mouth," she cried out.

Grubbs said, "Young lady, I understand that this is very stressful, but please try to keep your emotions under control. This is a court of law."

Mikki sniffled and settled back in her chair.

"If your father were to fall ill again while you were living with him, who would take care of the family?"

"I would."

Paterson smiled. "You may not be a child, but you're also not of legal age to live alone with your brothers."

Mikki looked furious. "And Sammy. He's my dad's best friend."

"Ah, Mr. Duvall. Yes." Paterson glanced at some notes. "Did you know that after he returned from Vietnam, Mr. Duvall underwent psychiatric counseling and that he also received two drunk-driving citations?"

Sammy erupted from his chair. "My whole damn unit was ordered to undergo that counseling because we'd done two tours in 'Nam and seen atrocities you never will, slick. And those DUIs were over thirty years ago. Never had a damn one since."

The judge smashed his gavel down. "Another outburst like that, sir, and you will be removed from this courtroom."

Paterson turned back to Mikki. "So, Mr. Duvall will look after you?"

"Yes," Mikki said stubbornly.

He turned to Drake again and nodded. The TV screen came to life. They watched first as Sammy drove his Harley way too fast and without a helmet. The second scene was Sammy dozing on the beach with a couple of empty beer cans lying next to him as Jackie and Cory played very close to the water.

"Quite a responsible caretaker," said Paterson dryly. "Now, Ms. Armstrong, can you tell us what you think your mother's death did to your father?"

Jenna jumped to her feet. "Relevance?"

"We're trying to determine the conditions of the children's environment, Your Honor. The state of mind of the surviving parent is highly relevant."

"Go ahead."

"Ms. Armstrong, please answer the question."

"He was devastated. We all were."

"Is he still devastated?"

"What do you mean?"

"Your father has been involved in two fights and been arrested for an assault for which he could go to prison. You saw the video of him throwing things and jumping around in a state of fury, and of your two brothers being left in the care of Mr. Duvall while he was apparently either drunk or asleep. You've given testimony that he neglected his three children to work on a lighthouse, resulting in injury to your younger brother. Do you believe those to be the acts of a rational person?"

"But I told you he's better now."

"So he was worse at some point?"

"Look, I know what you're trying to do, but my dad is not crazy, okay? He's not."

"But you're not qualified to make that judgment, are you? It really is for this court to decide if your father is fit to have custody of his children."

Mikki stood again, tears streaming down her face. "My dad is not crazy. He loves us. He is a great dad."

Paterson gave her a weak smile. "I'm sure you love your dad."

"I do," Mikki said fiercely.

"And you'd say anything to protect him."

"Yes, I would. I . . ." Mikki realized her mistake too late.

"No further questions."

As Paterson walked away, Mikki looked at her dad. "I'm sorry, Dad. I'm really sorry."

Jack said quietly, "It's okay, sweetie." When Jenna rose to question Mikki, Jack put a hand on her arm and shook his head. "No, Jenna, she's been through enough."

"But Jack—"

"Enough," said Jack firmly.

Jenna turned to the judge. "No questions," she said reluctantly.

Grubbs looked at Paterson. "Any more witnesses?"

"Just one, Your Honor, before we rest our case." Paterson turned toward the table where Jenna was sitting. "We call Jack Armstrong."

63

Jack was sworn in and settled uncomfortably into the witness box, hitching his suit jacket around him.

Paterson approached. "Mr. Armstrong, did you know that your illness can cause severe depression and even mental instability?"

"I don't have an illness."

"Excuse me?"

"I was given a clean bill of health. Look at me. Does it seem to you like I'm dying?"

Paterson picked up some documents and handed them to the bailiff. "These are opinions from three doctors, all world-class physicians, who state categorically that there is no cure for your illness and that it is fatal one hundred percent of the time."

"Then they'll have to change that to 99.9 percent, won't they?"

"Do you blame yourself for your wife's death, Mr. Armstrong?"

"A person will always blame themselves, even if they could do nothing to prevent it. It's just the way we are."

"So is that a yes?"

"Yes."

"That must be emotionally devastating."

"It's not easy."

"Talk to me about your obsession with the lighthouse."

Jenna said, "Objection. Drawing a conclusion."

"Sustained."

"Tell us about your reasons for working so long and hard on the lighthouse, Mr. Armstrong."

Jack furrowed his brow and hunched forward. "It's complicated."

"Do your best," said Paterson politely.

"It was her special place," Jack said simply. "That's where she'd go when she was a kid. I found some of her things there—a doll, a sign that she'd made that said, 'Lizzie's Lighthouse,' and some other things. And when she was alive she said she wanted to come back to the Palace. I guess me going there instead and fixing it up was a way to show respect for her wishes."

"All right. What else?"

Jack smiled. "Lizzie thought she could see Heaven from the top of the lighthouse."

"Heaven?"

"Yes," Jack said. "She believed that when she was a little girl," he added quickly.

"But you're an adult. So you didn't believe that, or did you?"

Jack hesitated. Jenna glanced at the judge and saw his eyebrows rise higher the longer Jack waited to answer.

"No, I didn't. But..." Jack shook his head and stopped talking.

The lawyer let this silence linger for a bit as he and the judge exchanged a glance.

"So you wanted to fix up the place?"

"Yes. The stairs to the lighthouse fell in, and I wanted to repair them. And the light too."

"Fix the light? It's my understanding that the lighthouse in question is no longer registered as a navigational aid."

"It's not. But it stopped working while Lizzie was still there. So I decided to try and repair it."

"So let me get this straight, if I can," said Paterson in a skeptical tone. "You neglected your family so that you could repair a lighthouse that is no longer used as a navigational aid, solely because your wife as a child thought she could see Heaven from there? Let me ask the question again: Did you think you could see Heaven from there?" he asked in a chiding tone.

"No, I didn't," said Jack firmly.

"We have one more video to show, Your Honor."

"All right."

Paterson turned to Drake, who worked the controls, and the image appeared on the TV of Jack standing on the catwalk around the lighthouse reading one of his letters to Lizzie.

"Could you tell us what you're doing in that picture, Mr. Armstrong?"

"None of your business," snapped Jack, who was staring at the TV.

Jenna stood. "Your Honor, relevance?"

"Again, state of mind," replied Paterson.

"Answer the question," instructed the judge.

"It's a letter," said Jack.

"A letter? To whom?"

"My wife."

"But your wife is deceased."

"I wrote the letters to her before she... before she died. I wrote them when I was sick. I wanted her to have them after... I was gone."

"But she can't read them now. So why were you reading them? You obviously knew what was in them."

"There's nothing wrong with reading old letters. I'm pretty sure people do it all the time."

"Perhaps, but not in the middle of the night on top of a lighthouse while small children are alone in the house."

"Argumentative," snapped Jenna.

"Sustained," said Grubbs.

Jack looked at Paterson and said, "I know you're trying to make it look like I'm nuts. But I'm not. And I'm not unfit to care for my children."

"That's for this court to decide, *not* you."

Jack sat there for a few seconds. The walls of the courtroom seemed to be closing in on him, cutting off his oxygen. His anger, always near the surface ever since Bonnie had filed her lawsuit, now burst to the surface. He looked at Paterson. "Have you ever lost anyone you loved?"

Paterson looked taken aback but quickly recovered. "I'm asking the questions."

Jack now looked directly at Bonnie. "You know how much I loved Lizzie."

Paterson said, "Mr. Armstrong, you're not allowed to do that."

Jack ignored him. He stood, his eyes burning into his mother-in-law's. "I would've gladly given my life so that she could have lived. You know that."

"Mr. Armstrong," cautioned the judge.

"She meant everything to me. But she died."

"Mr. Armstrong, sit down!" snapped Grubbs as he smacked his gavel.

Jack pointed a finger at Bonnie and cried out, "No one feels worse than I do about what happened. No one! It is a living hell for me every day. I lost the only woman I have ever loved. The only person I wanted to share my life with. The best friend I will ever have!" The tears were sliding down Jack's anguished face.

The judge barked, "Bailiff!"

Jack said, "The best things that Lizzie and I ever created were our kids. *Our* kids. So how dare you try to take away the only parent they have left just because you're mad at me. How *dare* you."

The bailiff forcibly removed Jack from the courtroom while Bonnie looked on, obviously shocked by his outburst.

Paterson said, "Nothing further, Your Honor." He walked back to his chair, barely able to conceal his smile.

The judge looked critically at Jenna. "Do you have anything to add, counselor?"

Jenna looked at the distraught kids and then at the judge. "No, Your Honor."

The judge said, "I'll render my judgment on the motion this afternoon."

Jack was released from the bailiff's custody a few

minutes later. They didn't wait at the courthouse but drove back in silence to Channing. They waited in a small room at the back of the Little Bit. They all jumped when Jenna's cell phone buzzed. She answered the call and listened, and her expression told Jack all he needed to know.

"The judge granted the motion for temporary custody," she said.

And it's my fault, thought Jack. *I've lost my family. Again.*

64

Jack sat on his bed at the Palace holding letter number six in his hand. He hadn't read it yet. He was thinking about other things.

No matter what you do, no matter how hard you fight, life sometimes just doesn't make sense.

Bonnie and representatives from Social Services were coming this evening to take the kids away from Jack, perhaps forever. He looked down at the letter, then balled it up and threw it down on the bed next to the other five. As he looked out the window, three cars pulled into the driveway of the Palace, including Sheriff Tammie in his police cruiser. Though it was only seven in the evening, the sky was as dark as midnight. A tropical storm was just off the coast, and the wind was beginning to slam the low country with a fury. That was the major reason they were coming tonight. To move the kids farther inland. Jack had put up no fight, principally because he wanted his kids to be safe. The lights kept flickering on and off in the house.

Someone tapped on his door.

"Yeah?"

It was Jenna. "They're here, Jack," she said quietly.

"I know."

As Jack came downstairs, he stared at the three packed bags standing next to the front door. Then he looked over at the kids. Cory and Mikki were on the couch crying, and Jackie, not understanding what was going on, was crying too. He clutched his monster truck in one hand and hugged his siblings with the other, his little body quaking.

Liam simply stood by, not knowing what to do. His big hands clenched and unclenched in his anxiety. Jack went over to his kids and started whispering to them. "It's going to be okay, I promise. This is only temporary."

Jack and Jenna both answered the door. Bonnie, Fred, and the Social Services people stood there with umbrellas in hand.

"Are the children ready?" one of the Social Services folks asked Jack.

He nodded, his gaze squarely on Bonnie.

"Bonnie?" She looked at him, her face flushed. "Do we have to do it this way?"

"I'm only thinking of the children, Jack."

"Are you sure about that?"

"I'm very sure."

Sammy, Liam, Jackie, and Cory had joined them on the front porch.

Cory said, "Grandma, please don't do this. Please. We want to stay with Dad."

One of the Social Services people, a woman, stepped

in and said, "This is not the time or place to discuss this. The judge has ruled." She looked at Jack. "We really want this to go smoothly. And I'm sure you do too, for the sake of the kids." The woman glanced over her shoulder at Sheriff Tammie, who stood outside his cruiser looking very uncomfortable.

Sammy eyed Jack, but it was Jenna who stepped forward and said, "We do." Sammy took a step back, and Jack looked at his two kids. "Okay, guys, you're going to be back here faster than you can say Jack Rabbit."

Cory nodded, but the tears still slid down his face. Jackie looked at Cory and started to tear up again. Jack hugged both of them. "It's going to be okay," he said. "We're a family. We'll always be a family, right?" They both nodded. "We'll get your bags. Liam, go get Mikki. I'm sure you want to say good-bye to her. They need to get on the road before the storm gets any worse."

Sammy and Jack carried the bags out to the car, and Jack strapped Jackie in while Cory buckled up next to him. When Jack looked back up at the porch, he knew something was wrong. Liam was standing there, his face pale and his expression wild.

Bonnie had seen this too. Despite the wind and rain, she got out of the car.

"What is it?" said Jack as he ran up to Liam.

"I can't find Mikki."

Jack and the others raced into the house. It took only ten minutes to search the place. His daughter was gone.

A quarter mile down the beach, Mikki was stumbling along, crying hard. The wind and rain battered her, but she kept going, leaning into the gusts swarming off the ocean. She kept weaving away from the waterline as the storm pushed the Atlantic farther landward. As upset as she was, Mikki didn't see the palmetto tree toppling over until it was almost too late. At the last possible instant, she lunged out of the way, but dodging the tree carried her too close to the waterline and in the path of a huge wave that crashed over her. Mikki didn't even have time to scream before the receding wave swept her out.

65

Jack stared out at the darkened sky from the front room of the Palace. The rain was coming down even harder. Liam had quickly driven home to see if Mikki had gone there, but he'd called to say she wasn't at his house.

Bonnie said, "Jack, what do we do? What do we do?" Her voice was hysterical.

Jack turned to her and said sharply, "The first thing we do is not panic."

One of the Social Services personnel said, "We should call the police. The sheriff drove off before this happened, but I'm sure we can get him back."

Jack shook his head and said in a crisp, take-charge manner, "There's only Tammie and one deputy, and they'll be preoccupied with the storm. We can call them, but we can't just sit around and wait for them to start looking for her. We have to start searching the area. We need to split up. Search by street and also the beach."

He pointed to Fred. "Fred, you and Bonnie drive west in your car. Go slow, look for Mikki that way." He turned to the pair from Social Services. "You go east in your car and do the same thing. Let's exchange cell phone numbers. Whoever finds her calls the others. Sammy and I will take opposite directions on the beach." He turned to Cory. "Cor, can you be a real big guy for me and stay here with Jackie? Go to the lower level and stay away from the windows."

Cory swallowed and looked terrified at his dad. "Mikki's coming back, right?"

"She absolutely is. I bet she shows up here any minute. And we need someone to be here when she does, okay?"

"Okay, Dad."

Jack headed right on the beach while Sammy went left. The rain was being pushed nearly sideways by the wind, and most of the sand was underwater. Jack swung his flashlight in wide arcs, but it barely penetrated the darkness. It finally caught on one object, and when Jack saw what it was, his heart thudded in his chest and a cold dread settled over him.

It was Mikki's sneaker floating in a pool of shallow water. He looked in all directions for his daughter but could see nothing. He called out her name, but the only thing he heard in response was the scream of the wind. He raced on to check backyards and behind dunes, but found nothing.

"I can't see a damn thing," he said to himself. He stared out at the angry ocean, engorged and rendered infinitely more dangerous by the strength of the storm pushing it against the coast. He turned and jogged back, his gaze toggling between land and sea. He had to bend forward to keep from being blown back by the powerful winds. Every ten seconds he screamed out her name. Near the Palace he met Sammy, who reported similar failure.

Jack showed him the sneaker.

"That is not good, Jack," said Sammy.

"We're running out of time. The storm is just about to really hit."

"What do you want to do?"

"We need to be able to see a big swath of land and water."

"No way you can get a chopper with a searchlight up in these conditions."

At this remark, Jack started and looked up at the lighthouse. He turned and ran toward it, Sammy on his heels. He kicked open the lower door and took the steps two at a time. He reached the top and hoisted himself through the access door. Sammy poked his head through a few seconds later, breathing hard.

"What the hell are you doing?"

"Getting a light."

"Jack, this damn thing doesn't work."

"It's going to work tonight! Because I'm going to find my daughter," Jack shouted back at him. He ripped open his toolbox, which he'd left in the corner, snatched some wrenches, grabbed the old schematic, and began to analyze it, his gaze flitting up and down its complex drawings. While Sammy held the paper, Jack worked on section after section of the mechanism, his ability to repair it having assumed a whole new level of urgency.

As Sammy watched him work, he said, "But we need a searchlight, not something that's going to—"

"There's a manual feature," Jack snapped as he squeezed his body into a narrow crevice to check the wiring there. "The light path can be manipulated by hand."

He pulled himself out of the space and hit the power switch.

"Damn it!" Jack flung his wrench down.

He peered out into the darkness, where his little girl was... somewhere.

He involuntarily shuddered.

No. I will not lose my daughter.

A burst of lightning that speared the water was followed by a boom of thunder as the storm reached its peak. Footsteps came from below, and first Jenna's and then Liam's faces appeared at the opening to the room. They were both soaked through.

"We've been searching the street and beach on our end, but there's no sign of Mikki," Jenna said to Sammy as she looked at Jack's back.

"We were trying to power up the light," Sammy explained, "but no luck."

Sammy said, "Bonnie called. And so did the other people. They found nothing either." He held up Mikki's soaked shoe. Jenna and Liam paled when they saw it. All three instinctively looked out to the frothing ocean.

Jack remained frozen against the glass, staring out into the darkness. The electricity to the lighthouse flickered, went out, and then sputtered back on. Jack was still staring at the darkness when he saw it. At first he thought it was another bolt of lightning lancing into the water, but there was no boom of thunder following it. Yet it had been a jagged edge of current; he'd seen it! Jack suddenly realized that in that second of darkness, what he'd seen had been reflected in the glass, only to become invisible when the power came back on and the lights were restored.

He whirled around and leapt toward the machinery. "Turn the light off, Sammy," he screamed.

"What?"

"Turn it off. Off!"

Sammy hit the switch, plunging them all into darkness.

Jack, his chest heaving with dread because he knew this was his last chance, stared at the machinery with an intensity he didn't know he even had. He could hear nothing, not the storm, not Sammy's or Jenna's or Liam's breathing, not even his own. There was nothing else in the world; only him and this metal beast that had confounded him all summer. And if he couldn't figure it out right now, his daughter was lost to him.

"Turn the lights back on."

Sammy hit the switch.

And Jack saw the beautiful arc of electrical current nearly buried between two pieces of metal in a gap so narrow he didn't even know it was there. *That* was what had been reflected in the window.

He dropped to his knees, scuttled forward, and hit the gap with his flashlight. Two wires were revealed. They were less than a centimeter apart, but not touching.

"Sammy, get me electrical tape and a wire nut and then turn the main power off."

Sammy grabbed the tape from the box, tossed the roll and red wire nut to Jack, and then turned off the power. While Jenna held the flashlight for him, he slid his hands in the gap, pieced the two wires together using the wire nut, and then wound tape around it.

Jack stood and called out, "Turn the power back on, and then hit the switch. Everyone look away from the light."

Sammy turned on the power and flicked the switch. At first nothing happened. Then, as if it was awakening from years of sleep, the light began to come on, building in energy until, with a burst of power, it came fully to life. If Jack hadn't told them to look away, they would have been blinded. The powerful beam illuminated the beach and ocean to an astonishing degree as it started to whirl around the top of the lighthouse.

Jack raced around to the back of the equipment, hit a button, and grabbed a slide lever. The light immediately stopped swirling across the landscape and became a focused beam that he could maneuver.

"Sammy, take control of this. Start from the north and move it slowly southward in three-second stages."

While Sammy guided the light, Liam, Jack, and Jenna stayed glued to the window, looking at the suddenly lightened nightscape.

Jenna spotted her first. "There! There!"

"Steady on the beam, Sammy," screamed Jack. "Hold right there."

Jack threw himself through the opening and took the steps three at a time. He nearly flattened Bonnie, who was coming up the stairs.

"What is—"

Jack didn't bother to answer.

He ran on.

The light had revealed Mikki's location. She was in

deep water, clinging to a piece of driftwood as ten-foot-high waves pounded her. She looked to be caught in the seesaw grip of the storm. She might have only a few minutes left to live.

Then so do I, thought Jack.

66

Jack Armstrong ran that night like he had never run before. Not on the football field, and not even on the battlefield when his very life depended on sheer speed. He high-stepped through four-foot waves that were nearly up to the rocks the lighthouse was perched on. A towering breaker ripped out of the darkness and knocked him down. He struck his head on a piece of timber thrown up on the sand by the storm. Dazed, he struggled to his feet and kept slogging on. He saw the light, a pinpoint beam. But he couldn't see Mikki. Frantic, he ran toward the illumination.

"Mikki! Mikki!"

Another wave crushed him. He got back up, vomiting salt water driven deeply down his throat. He ran on, fighting rain driven so hard by turbocharged wind that it felt like the sting of a million yellow jackets.

"Mikki!"

"Daddy!"

It was faint, but Jack saw the light shift to the left. And then he saw it: a head bobbing in even deeper water. Mikki was being pulled inexorably out to sea.

"Daddy. Help me."

Like a charging rhino, Jack ran headlong toward the brunt of the storm. An oncoming wave rose up far taller than he was, but he avoided most of its energy by diving under it at the last possible second. He emerged in water over his head. The normal riptide was multiplied tenfold by the power of the storm, but Jack fought through it, going under and coming up and yelling, "Mikki." Each time she called back, and Jack swam with all his might toward the sound of her voice.

The lightning and thunder blasted and boomed above them. A spear of lightning hit so close that Jack felt the hairs on his arms and neck stand. He snatched a breath and went under again as another foaming wave crashed down on him. He came up. "Mikki!"

This time there was no answer.

"Mikki!"

Nothing.

"Michelle!"

A second later he heard a faint "Daddy."

Jack redoubled his efforts. She was getting weak. It was a miracle she was still alive. If that piece of driftwood got ripped from her, it would all be over. And then he saw her. The sturdy beam of light was tethered to the teenager like a golden string. Mikki was managing to stay afloat by using the driftwood she'd snagged somehow, but there was no way she could keep that up much longer. Jack swam as hard as he could, fighting through wave after wave and cursing when one threw him off course, costing him precious seconds. But the whole time he kept his eyes on his daughter.

And yet he realized that as each second passed, she was moving farther from him. It was the storm, the rip-tide, the wind, everything. He swam harder. But now he was fifty feet away instead of forty. He took a deep breath and slid under the water to see if he could make better time. But it was pitch-dark even just below the surface, and the current was just as strong.

When he came back up, he couldn't see her and cursed himself for taking his eyes off his daughter. His limbs and lungs were so heavy. Jack looked to the shore and then at the angry sky. He was being pulled out too now. And he wasn't sure he had the strength to get back in. It didn't matter.

I'm not going back without her.

Jack treaded water, looking in all directions as the storm bore down with all its weight on the South Carolina coast.

He shook with anger and fear and . . . loss.

I'm sorry, Lizzie. I'm so sorry.

What if I just stop swimming? What if I just stop?

He would sink to the bottom. He looked at the shore. He could see the lights. His family—what was left of it—was there. Bonnie would raise the boys. He and Mikki would go to join Lizzie.

He looked to the sky again. When a bolt of lightning speared down and lighted the sky, he thought he could see Lizzie's face, her hand reaching out, beckoning to him. He could just stop swimming right now. Right now.

"Daddy!"

Jack turned in the water.

Mikki was barely twenty feet from him. This time the movement of the water had carried him toward her.

Finding a reserve of strength he didn't think he had, Jack exploded through the water. The ocean pushed back at him, throwing up wall after wall of frothing sea to keep him from her. He swam harder and harder, his arms slicing through the water as he fought every counterattack the storm threw at him.

A yard. A foot. Six inches. Every muscle Jack had was screaming in exhaustion, but he fought through the pain.

"Daddy!" She reached out to him.

"Mikki!"

He lunged so hard he nearly came fully out of the water. His hand closed like a vise around her wrist, and he pulled his daughter to him.

She hugged him. "I'm sorry, Daddy, I'm so sorry."

"It's okay, baby. I've got you. Just lie on your back."

She did so, and he put his arms under hers and kicked off toward land.

Now all I've got to do is get us back, thought Jack.

The problem was that when Jack tried to ride a wave in, the undertow snatched him back before he could gain traction on the shore. Then a huge wave forced them both underwater, before Jack brought them back, coughing and half-strangled. Jack was very strong, and as a ranger he'd swum miles in all sorts of awful conditions. But not in the middle of what was now likely a category 1 hurricane with someone else hanging on to him. He was caught in a pendulum, and he couldn't keep it up much longer. He might be able to get to shore by himself, but he was prepared to die with his daughter.

"Jack!"

He looked toward the beach. Liam and Sammy were standing there with a long coil of rope and screaming at him. Tied to the end of the rope was a red buoy. He nodded to show he understood. Sammy wound up and tossed the rope. It fell far short. He pulled it back and tried again. Closer, but still not close enough.

"Sammy," he screamed. "Wait until the waves push us toward the beach, and then toss it."

Sammy nodded, timed it, and threw the rope. Just a few feet short now. One more time. Jack lunged for the buoy and snagged it. But a monster wave crashed down on them, and Mikki was ripped from him.

He caught a mouthful of water and spit it out. As he looked down, he felt Mikki sliding past him and away from shore, out to sea. Everything was moving in slow motion, reduced to milliseconds of passing time.

"No!" screamed Jack.

He shot his hand down and grabbed his daughter's hair an instant before she was past him and gone forever. Sammy and Liam pulled with all their strength on the rope. Slowly, father and daughter were pulled to shore.

As soon as he hit solid earth, Jack carried Mikki well away from the pounding waves. His daughter was completely limp, her eyes closed.

As Jack bent down, he could see that Mikki was also not breathing. He immediately began to perform mouth-to-mouth resuscitation. He pinched Mikki's nose and blew air into her lungs. He flipped her over and pushed against her back, trying to expand her lungs, forcing the water out.

Sammy called 911 while Jack continued to frantically work on his daughter and was now doing CPR.

A minute later, Jack sat up, his breaths coming in jerks. He looked down at Mikki. She wasn't moving; her skin was instead turning blue. His daughter was dead.

He'd lost her. Failed her.

A crack of lightning pierced the night sky, and Jack looked up, perhaps to that solitary spot his wife had tried to find all those years ago. With a sob he screamed, "Help me, Lizzie, help me. Please."

He looked down. No more miracles left. He'd used the only one he would ever have on himself.

Liam knelt next to Mikki, tears streaming down his face. He touched Mikki's hair and then put his face in his hands and sobbed.

Suddenly Jack felt a force at the back of his neck. At first he thought that Sammy was trying to pull him away from his dead child. But the force wasn't pulling; it was *pushing* him back to her. Jack bent down, took an enormous breath, held it, put his mouth over Mikki's, and blew with all the strength he had left in his body.

As the air fell away from him and into Mikki, everything for Jack stopped, and the storm was gone. It was like he had envisioned dying to be. Quiet, peaceful, isolated, alone. As that breath rushed from him, the events of the last year also raced through his mind.

And now, this; Mikki. Gone.

Jack felt himself drifting away, as though over calm water, propelled to another place, he had no idea where. But he was alone. Lizzie and now Mikki were gone. He no longer wanted to live. It didn't matter anymore. There was peace. But there was also nothing else because he was alone.

The water hitting him in his face brought him back.

The thoughts of the past retreated, and he was once more in the present. It was still raining. But that's not what had struck him.

He looked down as Mikki gave another shudder and coughed up the water that had been buried deeply in her lungs. Her eyes opened, fluttered, opened again, and stayed that way. Her pupils focused, and she saw her dad hovering above her. Mikki put out her arms, gripped her father's neck tightly.

"Daddy?" she said in a tiny voice.

Jack sank down and held her. "I'm here, baby. I'm here."

67

The ambulance took Mikki and Jack to the hospital to be checked out. Sammy followed in his van with Liam, while Jenna stayed with the boys at the Palace. Jenna had made hot tea for Bonnie, who had watched Jack's heroic rescue of his daughter from the top of the lighthouse. Now she just sat small and stooped on the edge of the couch, a sob escaping her lips every few seconds.

Jenna had tried to comfort her, while Fred just sat in another chair and stared at his hands. When Sammy called from the hospital and told them they would be home shortly and that everyone was okay, Jenna had finally broken down and wept.

Afterward, Jenna had ventured into Jack's room; she wasn't sure why. As her gaze swept the space, it settled on the letters, which were still lying on the bed. She went over, sat down, picked them up, and started reading.

She emerged from the room ten minutes later, her

eyes red with fresh tears. She walked over to Bonnie and tapped her gently on the shoulder. When Bonnie looked up, Jenna said, "I think you need to read these, Mrs. O'Toole."

Bonnie looked confused, but she accepted the letters from Jenna, slipped on her reading glasses, and unfolded the first one.

The storm, its fury rapidly spent after fully hitting land, had largely passed by the time they returned from the hospital. An exhausted Mikki was laid in her bed with Cory and Liam watching over her like guardian angels, counting each one of her breaths.

Jack told everyone that Mikki had suffered no permanent damage and should be as good as new.

"The doctor said she was one strong lady," added Sammy.

"Like her mother," said Jack as he looked at Bonnie.

He passed through the house and went outside and up to the top of the lighthouse. He stared out now at the clearing sky, the sun coming up in the east. He bent down and saw the wires he had spliced the night before. It was a miracle that he had finally spotted the trouble that had befuddled him for so long. Yet a miracle, thought Jack, was somehow what he, however irrationally, had been counting on.

He leaned against the wall of glass and stared out at what looked to be the start of a beautiful late-summer day.

He turned when he heard her.

Bonnie, wheezing slightly, appeared at the opening for the room. He helped her through, and they stood side by side looking at each other.

"Thank God for what you did last night, Jack."

Jack turned and looked back out the window. "It was Lizzie, you know."

"What?" Bonnie moved even closer to him.

Jack said, "I'd given up. Mikki was dead. I didn't have any breath left. She was dead, Bonnie. And I asked Lizzie to help me." He turned to her. "I looked up to the sky and I asked Lizzie to help me." A sob broke from his throat. "And she did. She did. She saved Mikki, not me."

Bonnie nodded slowly. "It was both of you, Jack. You and Lizzie. The match made in Heaven. Two people meant for each other if ever there was."

He stared at her, surprised by the woman's blunt words.

From her pocket she drew out the letters. "I think these belong to you." She handed them back to him and reached out and touched his face. "Sometimes people can't see what's right in front of them, Jack. It's strange how that works. How often it happens. And how often it hurts people we're supposed to love." She paused. "I do love you, son. I guess I always have. And one thing I know for certain is that you loved my daughter. And she loved you. That should have been enough for me." She paused again. "And now, it is."

They exchanged a hug, and she turned to go.

"Bonnie?"

She looked back.

"The kids?" he said in a small voice.

"They're right where they should be, Jack. With their father."

68

When Mikki opened her eyes, the first thing she saw was her dad. Right after that she saw Liam, peering anxiously over Jack's shoulder.

"I'm really okay, guys," she said a little groggily.

Jack smiled and looked at Liam. "Give us a minute, will you?"

Liam nodded, flashed Mikki a reassuring grin, and left the room.

Jack gripped her hand, and she squeezed back. Mikki said, "Sorry for all the excitement I caused. It was really dumb."

"Yes, it was," he agreed. "But we were all under a lot of pressure."

"So the lighthouse finally worked?"

He let out a long breath. "Yeah. If it hadn't..." His voice trailed off, and father and daughter started to weep together, each clutching the other, their bodies shaking with the strain.

"I can't believe how close I came to losing you, baby."

"I know, Dad, I know," she said in a hushed voice.

They finally drew apart.

"So what now? We still go with Grandma?"

"No, you're staying right here with me."

Mikki screamed with joy and hugged him again.

"Does Liam know?" she said excitedly.

"No, I thought I'd leave that to you." He rose. "I'll go get him."

As he turned she said, "Dad?"

"Yeah?"

"No matter what happens in my life, you'll always be my hero."

He bent down and touched her cheek. "Thanks… Michelle."

Later, as he stood by the doorway watching the two teens excitedly talking and hugging, Jack first smiled, then teared up, and then smiled again. She was clearly not a little girl anymore. And Jack could easily see how fast her life, and his, would change in the next few years.

Later, as Jack walked along the beach, a voice called out, "I'm going to miss you Armstrongs when you go back to Ohio." He turned to see Jenna walking toward him.

"No, you won't," said Jack, "because we're staying right here."

She drew next to him. "Are you sure?"

He smiled. "No, but we're still staying."

She slipped an arm around him. "I'm glad things have worked out."

"I couldn't have done it without you."

"You're way too generous with your praise."

"Seriously, Jenna, you helped in a lot of ways. A lot."

"So what are we going to do about the budding romance?"

"What?" he said in a startled voice.

"Between our kids."

"Oh."

She laughed, and he grinned sheepishly.

"I think we take it one day at a time." He looked directly at her. "Does that sound okay, Jenna?"

"That sounds very okay, Jack."

Epilogue

A little over two years later, Jack sat on the beach in almost the exact spot he and Mikki had occupied the night he'd realized he had so much to live for. The house was quieter now. Mikki and Liam had just left for college. She'd aced her last two years in high school and gone out to Berkeley on a scholarship. Liam the drummer had cut off his hair and was at West Point. Though they were a continent apart, the two remained the best of friends.

Cory was working part-time at the Play House and learning the ropes of theater management from Ned Parker. Jackie had started talking full-blast one morning about a year ago and had never stopped since. Although, Jack noted with some measure of fatherly pride, his favorite toy was still the monster truck.

He got up and made his way to the top of the lighthouse. He hadn't been up here since the morning after almost losing Mikki. He stepped out onto the catwalk and looked toward the sea. His eyes gravitated to the spot where father and daughter had fought so hard for their lives. Then he looked away and up to a clear, blue summer sky.

Lizzie's Lighthouse. It worked when I needed it to.

Jack had two very important things to do today. And the first one was waiting for him down the beach. He left the lighthouse and set off along the sand. His hands rode in his pockets; the words he would say slipped through his mind. As he drew closer, Jack realized that he had just traveled over a half mile by beach and a lifetime by every other measure.

She was there waiting for him by prearrangement. He slipped his arms around Jenna and kissed her. And much like he had done two decades before, Jack knelt down and asked a woman he loved if she would do him the honor of becoming his wife.

Jenna cried and allowed him to slip the ring over her shaky finger. After that they held each other for a long time on that South Carolina beach as a gentle breeze rippled across them.

"Sammy's going to be the best man," Jack said.

"And Liam will be giving me away," Jenna replied. "I love you, Jack."

"I love you too, Jenna."

They kissed again and visited for a while, discussing plans. Then Jack walked back to the Palace. His pace this way was not quite as brisk. The distance seemed a lot longer going back. There was a reason for this.

The first trek had been to create a bridge for his future.

This trip involved him making a painful separation from the past.

He reached the beach in front of his house and sat

down in the sand. He pulled out a photo of Lizzie and held it in front of him. It was still nearly impossible for him to believe that she had been gone nearly three years. It just couldn't be. But it was.

He traced the curve of her smile with his finger while he stared into those beautiful green eyes that he always believed would be the last thing he would see in life before passing on. While Jack had just asked another woman to marry him, and this seemed fitting and right in so many ways, he knew that a significant part of him would always love Lizzie. And that this too was fitting and right in so many ways.

Bonnie had been correct about that. Lizzie and Jack had been meant to be together forever if ever two people were. Only sometimes life doesn't match what should be. It just is. And people have to accept it, no matter how hard it may be.

You should respect the past. You should never forget the past. But you can't live there.

And now he had something else to finish. Something very important.

From his windbreaker he pulled out a single piece of paper and a pen. His hand shaking slightly and the tears already sliding down his face, Jack Armstrong touched the pen to the paper and began to write.

Dear Lizzie,

A lot has happened that I need to tell you about.

An hour later he finished the letter with, as always,

Love,
Jack

He sat there for a while, allowing the sun and breeze to dry his tears because for some reason he did not want to wipe them away by hand. He folded the letter carefully and placed it in an envelope marked with the number seven. He put the envelope and the photo of Lizzie in his pocket and walked toward the house.

When he reached the grass, he turned and looked upward. His mouth eased to a smile when he realized what he was looking at. Today, he'd finally found it, after all this time searching.

Right there was the little piece of the sky that contained Heaven. He somehow knew this for certain. Ironically, like so many complexities in life, the answer had been right in front of him the whole time.

"Pop-pop!"

He turned to see Jackie flying toward him. The boy gave a leap, and Jack caught him in midair.

"Hey, buddy."

"What are you doing?"

Jack started to say something and then stopped. He turned so they were both looking out toward the ocean. He pointed to the sky. "Mommy's up there watching us, Jackie."

Jackie looked awestruck. "Mommy?" Jack nodded. Jackie waved to the sky. "Hi, Mom." He blew her a kiss.

Then Jack turned back around and carried his son toward the house. Right before he got there, he slowly looked back at that little patch of blue sky.

Good-bye, Lizzie.

For now.

Jack's Letters

Dear Lizzie,

There are things I want to say to you that I just don't have the breath for anymore. That's why I've decided to write you these letters. I want you to have them after I'm gone. They're not meant to be sad, just my chance to talk to you one more time. When I was healthy you made me happier than any person has a right to be. When I was half a world away, I knew that I was looking at the same sky you were, thinking of the same things you were, wanting to be with you and looking forward to when I could be. You gave me three beautiful children, which is a greater gift than I deserved. I tell you this, though you already know it, because sometimes people don't talk about these things enough. I want you to know that if I could've stayed with you I would have. I fought as hard as I could. I will never understand why I had to be taken from you so soon, but I have accepted it. Yet I want you to know that there is nothing more important to me than you. I loved you from the moment I saw you. And the happiest day of my life was when you agreed to share your life with mine. I promised that I would always be there for you. And my love for you is so strong that even though I won't be there physically, I will be there in every other way. I will watch over you. I will be there if you need to talk. I will never stop loving you. Not even death is powerful enough to overcome my feelings for you. My love for you, Lizzie, is stronger than anything.

Love,
Jack

Dear Lizzie,

Christmas will be here in five days, and I promise that I will make it. I've never broken a promise to you, and I never will. It's hard to say good-bye, but sometimes you have to do things you don't want to. Jackie came to see me a little while ago, and we talked. Well, he talked in Jackie language and I listened. I like to listen to him because I know one day very soon I won't be able to. He's growing up so fast, and I know he probably won't remember his dad, but I know I will live on in your memories. Tell him his dad loved him and wanted the best for him. And I wish I could have thrown the football to him and watched him play baseball. I know he will have a great life.

Cory is a special little boy. He has your sensitivity, your compassion. I know what's happening to me is probably affecting him the most of all the kids. He came and got into bed with me last night. He asked me if it hurt very much. I told him it didn't. He told me to say hello to God when I saw him. And I promised that I would.

And Mikki.

Mikki is the most complicated of all. Not a little girl anymore but not yet an adult either. She is a good kid, though I know you've had your moments with her. She is smart and caring and she loves her brothers. She loves you, though she sometimes doesn't like to show it. My greatest regret with my daughter is letting her grow away from me. It was my fault, not hers. I see that clearly now. I only wish I had seen it that clearly while I still had a chance to do something about it. After I'm gone, please tell her the first time I ever saw her, when I got back from Afghanistan and was still in uniform, there was no prouder father who ever lived. Looking down at her tiny face, I felt the purest joy a human could possibly feel. And I wanted to protect her and never let anything bad ever happen to her. Life doesn't work that way, of course. But tell her that her dad was her biggest fan. And that whatever she does in life, I will always be her biggest fan.

Love,

Jack

Dear Lizzie,

Christmas is five days away and it's a good time to reflect on life. Your life. This will be hard. Hard for me to write and hard for you to read, but it needs to be said. You're young and you have many years ahead of you. Cory and Jackie will be with you for many more years. And even Mikki will benefit. I'm talking about you finding someone else, Lizzie.

I know you won't want to at first. You'll even feel guilty about thinking about another man in your life, but, Lizzie, it has to be that way. I cannot allow you to go through the rest of your life alone. It's not fair to you, and it has nothing to do with the love we have for each other. It will not change that at all. It can't. Our love is too strong. It will last forever. But there are many kinds of love, and people have the capacity to love many different people. You are a wonderful person, Lizzie, and you can make someone else's life wonderful. Love is to be shared, not hidden, not hoarded.

And you have much love to share. It doesn't mean you love me any less. And I certainly could never love you more than I already do. But in your heart you will find more love for someone else. And you will make him happy. And he will make you happy. And Jackie especially will have a father to help him grow into a good man. Our son deserves that. Believe me, Lizzie, if it could be any other way, I would make it so. But you have to deal with life as it comes. And I'm trying my best to do just that. I love you too much to accept anything less than your complete and total happiness.

Love,
Jack

Dear Lizzie,

Christmas is almost here, and I promise that I will make it. It will be a great day. Seeing the kids' faces when they open their presents will be better for me than all the medications in the world. I know this has been hard on everyone, especially you and the kids. But I know that your mom and dad have really been a tremendous help to you. I've never gotten to know them as well as I would have liked. Sometimes I feel that your mom thinks you might have married someone better suited to you, more successful. But I know deep down that she cares about me, and I know she loves you and the kids with all her heart. It is a blessing to have someone like that to support you. My father died, as you know, when I was still just a kid. And you know about my mom. But your parents have always been there for me, especially Bonnie, and in many ways, I see her as more of a mom to me than my own mother. It's action, not words, that really counts. That's what it really means to love someone. Please tell them that I always had the greatest respect for her and Fred. They are good people. And I hope that one day she will feel that I was a good father who tried to do the right thing. And that maybe I was worthy of you.

Love,
Jack

Dear Lizzie,

As I've watched things from my bed, I have a confession to make to you. And an apology. I haven't been a very good husband or father. Half our marriage I was fighting a war, and the other half I was working too hard. I heard once that no one would like to have on their tombstone that they wished they'd spent more time at work. I guess I fall into that category, but it's too late for me to change now. I had my chance. When I see the kids coming and going, I realize how much I missed. Mikki already is grown up with her own life. Cory is complex and quiet. Even Jackie has his own personality. And I missed most of it. My greatest regret in life will be leaving you long before I should. My second greatest regret is not being more involved in my children's lives. I guess I thought I would have more time to make up for it, but that's not really an excuse. It's sad when you realize the most important things in life too late to do anything about them. They say Christmas is the season of second chances. My hope is to make these last few days my second chance to do the right thing for the people that I love the most.

Love,
Jack

Dear Lizzie,

A lot has happened that I need to tell you about.

Love,

Jack

Acknowledgments

To Michelle, for taking the journey with me.

To Mitch Hoffman, for readily jumping in with both feet on something so different.

To David Young and Jamie Raab, for allowing me to stretch.

To Emi Battaglia, Jennifer Romanello, Chris Barba, Karen Torres, Tom Maciag, Maja Thomas, Martha Otis, Anthony Goff, Michele McGonigle and Kim Hoffman, and all others at Grand Central, for their unparalleled support.

To Aaron and Arleen Priest, Lucy Child, Lisa Erbach Vance, Nicole James, Frances Jalet-Miller, and John Richmond, for carrying the laboring oar so much.

To Maria Rejt, Trisha Jackson, and Katie James at Pan Macmillan, for so successfully building my career across the waters.

To Eileen Chetti, for a superb copyediting job.

To Grace McQuade and Lynn Goldberg, for doing what you do so damn well.

To Lynette and Natasha, for keeping the home fires well lit and burning robustly.

When a professional assassin goes rogue, the government calls on Will Robie to stop one of their own—but this time, he may have met his match . . .

Please turn this page for a preview of

The Hit.

1

Feeling energized by the death that was about to happen, Doug Jacobs adjusted his headset and brightened his computer screen. The picture was now crystal clear, almost as if he were there.

But he thanked God he wasn't.

There was thousands of miles away, but one couldn't tell that by looking at the screen. They couldn't pay him enough to be *there*. Besides, many people were far better suited for that job. He would be communicating shortly with one of them.

Jacobs briefly glanced around the four walls and the one window of his office in the sunny Washington, D.C., neighborhood. It was an ordinary-looking low-rise brick building set in a mixed-use neighborhood that also contained historical homes in various states of either decay or restoration. But some parts of Jacobs's building were not ordinary at all. These elements included a heavy-gauge steel gate out front with a high fence around the perimeter of the property. Armed sentries patrolled the interior halls and surveillance cameras monitored the exterior. But there was nothing on the outside to clue anyone in to what was happening on the inside.

And a lot was happening on the inside.

Jacobs picked up his mug of fresh coffee, into which he had just poured three sugar packets. Watching the screen required intense concentration. Sugar and caffeine helped him do that. It would match the emotional buzz he would have in just a few minutes.

He spoke into the headset. "Alpha One, confirm location," he said crisply. It occurred to him that he sounded like an air traffic controller trying to keep the skies safe.

Well, in a way that's exactly what I am. Only our goal is death on every trip.

The response was nearly immediate. "Alpha One location seven hundred meters west of target. Sixth floor of the apartment building's east face, fourth window over from the left. You should just be able to make out the end of my rifle muzzle on a zoom-in."

Jacobs leaned forward and moved his mouse, zooming in on the real-time satellite feed from this distant city that was home to many enemies of the United States. Hovering over the edge of the windowsill, he saw just the tip of a long suppressor can screwed onto a rifle's muzzle. The rifle was a customized piece of weaponry that could kill at long distances—well, so long as a skilled hand and eye were operating it.

And right now that was the case.

"Roger that, Alpha One. Cocked and locked?"

"Affirmative. All factors dialed in on scope. Crosshairs

on terminal spot. Tuned frequency-shifting suppressor. Setting sun behind me and in their faces. No optics reflect. Good to go."

"Copy that, Alpha One."

Jacobs checked his watch. "Local time there seventeen hundred?"

"On the dot. Intel update?"

Jacobs brought this information up on a subscreen. "All on schedule. Target will be arriving in five minutes. He'll exit the limo on the curbside. He's scheduled to take a minute of questions on the curb and then it's a ten-second walk into the building."

"Ten-second walk into the building confirmed?"

"Confirmed," said Jacobs. "But the minute of interview may go longer. You play it as it goes."

"Copy that."

Jacobs refocused on the screen for a few minutes until he saw it. "Okay, motorcade is approaching."

"I see it. I've got my sight line on the straight and narrow. No obstructions."

"The crowd?"

"I've been watching the patterns of the people for the last hour. Security has roped them off. They've outlined the path he'll take for me, like a lighted runway."

"Right. I can see that now."

Jacobs loved being ringside for these things, without actually being in the danger zone. He was compensated more generously than the person on the other end of the line. At a certain level this made no sense at all.

The shooter's ass was out there, and if the shot wasn't successful or the exit cues made swiftly, the gunner was dead. Back here, there would be no acknowledgment of affiliation, only a blanket denial. The shooter had no documents, no creds, no ID that would prove otherwise. The shooter would be left to hang. And in the country where this particular hit was taking place, hanging would be the shooter's fate. Or perhaps beheading.

All the while, Jacobs sat here safe and drew bigger money.

But he thought, *Lots of folks can shoot straight and get away. I'm the one doing the geopolitical wrangling on these suckers. It's all in the prep. And I'm worth every dollar.*

Jacobs again spoke into his headset. "Approach is right on target. Limo is about to stop."

"Copy that."

"Give me a sixty-second buffer before you're about to fire. We'll go silent."

"Roger that."

Jacobs tightened the grip on his mouse, as though it were a trigger. During drone attacks he had actually clicked his mouse and watched a target disappear in a flame ball. The computer hardware manufacturer had probably never envisioned its devices being used for *that.*

His breathing accelerated even as he knew the shooter's respiration was heading the other way, achieving cold zero, which was what one needed to make a long-range shot like this. There was no margin of error at all. The shot had to hit and kill the target. It was that simple.

The limo stopped. The security team opened the door. Bulky, sweaty men with guns and earwigs looked everywhere for danger. They were pretty good. But pretty good did not cut it when you were up against outstanding.

And every asset Jacobs sent out was outstanding.

The man stepped onto the sidewalk and squinted against the sun's dying glare. He was a megalomaniac named Ferat Ahmadi who desired to lead a troubled, violent nation down an even darker road. That could not be allowed to happen.

Thus it was time to nip this little problem in the bud. There were others in his country ready to take over. They were less evil than he was, and capable of being manipulated by more civilized nations. In today's overly complex world, where allies and foes seemed to change on a weekly basis, that was as good as it got.

But that was not Jacobs's concern. He was here simply to execute an assignment, with emphasis on the "execute" part.

Then over his headset came two words: "Sixty seconds."

"Copy that, Alpha One," said Jacobs. He didn't say anything as stupid as "good luck." Luck had nothing to do with it.

He engaged a countdown clock on his computer screen.

He eyed the target and then the clock.

Jacobs watched Ahmadi talk to the reporters. He took a sip of coffee, set it down, and continued to watch as Ahmadi finished with his prearranged questions. The man took a step away from the reporters. The security team held them back.

The chosen path was revealed. For the photo op it would present, Ahmadi was going to walk it alone. It was designed to show his leadership and his courage.

It was also a security breach that looked trivial at ground level. But with a trained sniper at an elevated position it was like a fifty-yard gash in the side of a ship with a billion-candlepower beacon lighting it.

Twenty seconds became ten.

Jacobs started counting the last moments in his head, his eyes glued to the screen.

Dead man arriving, he thought.

Almost there. Mission nearly complete, and then it was on to the next target.

That is, after a steak dinner and a favorite cocktail and trumpeting this latest victory to his coworkers.

Three seconds became one.

Jacobs saw nothing except the screen. He was totally focused, as though he were going to deliver the kill shot himself.

The window shattered.

The round entered Jacobs's back after slicing through his ergonomic chair. It cleared his body and thundered out of his chest. It ended up cracking the computer screen as Ferat Ahmadi walked into the building unharmed.

Doug Jacobs, on the other hand, slumped to the floor.

No steak dinner. No favorite cocktail. No bragging rights ever again.

Dead man arrived.

2

He jogged along the park trail with a backpack over his shoulders. It was nearly seven at night. The air was crisp and the sun was almost down. The taxis were honking. The pedestrians were marching home from a long day's work.

Horse-drawn carriages were lined up across from the Ritz-Carlton. Irishmen in shabby top hats were awaiting their next fares as the light grew fainter. Their horses pawed the pavement and their big heads dipped into feed buckets.

It was midtown Manhattan in all its glory, the contemporary and the past mingling like coy strangers at a party.

Will Robie looked neither right nor left. He had been to New York many times. He had been to Central Park many times.

He was not here as a tourist.

He never went anywhere as a tourist.

The hoodie was drawn up and tied tight in front so his face was not visible. Central Park had lots of surveillance cameras. He didn't want to end up on any of them.

The bridge was up ahead. He reached it, stopped, and jogged in place, cooling down.

The door was built into the rock. It was locked.

He had a pick gun and then the door was no longer locked.

He slipped inside and secured the door behind him. This was a combination storage and electrical power room used by city workers who kept Central Park clean and lighted. They had gone home for the day and would not be back until eight the next morning.

That would be more than enough time to do what needed doing.

Robie slipped off the knapsack and opened it. Inside were all the things he required to do his work.

Robie had recently turned forty. He was about six-one, a buck eighty, with far more muscle than fat. It was wiry muscle. Big muscles were of no help whatsoever. They only slowed him down when speed was almost as essential as accuracy.

There were a number of pieces of equipment in the knapsack. Over the course of two minutes he turned three of those pieces into one with a highly specialized purpose.

A sniper rifle.

The fourth piece of equipment was just as valuable to him.

His scope.

He attached it to the Picatinny rail riding on the top of his rifle.

He went through every detail of the plan in his head

twenty times, both the shot he had to make and his safe exit that would hopefully follow. He had already memorized everything, but he wanted to arrive at the point where he no longer had to think, just act. That would save precious seconds.

This all took about ninety minutes.

Then he ate dinner. A bottle of G2 and a protein bar.

This was Will Robie's version of a Friday night date with himself.

He lay down on the cement floor of the storage room, folded his knapsack under his head, and went to sleep.

In ten hours and eleven minutes it would be time to go to work.

While other people his age were either going home to spouses and kids or going out with coworkers or maybe on a date, Robie was sitting alone in a glorified closet in Central Park waiting for someone to appear so Robie could kill him.

He could dwell on the current state of his life and arrive at nothing satisfactory in the way of an answer, or he could simply ignore it. He chose to ignore it. But perhaps not as easily as he once had.

Still, he had no trouble falling asleep.

And he would have no trouble waking up.

And he did, nine hours later.

It was morning. Barely past six a.m.

Now came the next important step. Robie's sight line. In fact, it was the most critical of all.

Inside the storage room, he was staring at a blank stone wall with wide mortar seams. But if one looked more closely, there were two holes in the seams, which had been placed at precise locations to allow one to see outside. However, the holes had been filled back in with a pliable material tinted to look like mortar. This had all been done a week ago by a team posing as a repair crew in the park.

Robie used a pincers to grip one end of the substance and pull it out. He did this one more time and the two holes were now revealed.

Robie slid his rifle muzzle through the lower hole, stopping it before it reached the end of the hole. This configuration would severely restrict his angle of aim, but he could do nothing about that. It was what it was. He never operated in perfect conditions.

His scope lined up precisely with the top hole, its leading edge resting firmly on the mortar seam. Now he could see what he was shooting at.

Robie sighted through it, dialing in all factors both environmental and otherwise that would affect his task.

His suppressor jacket was customized to fit the muzzle and the ordnance he was chambering. The jacket would reduce the muzzle blast and sonic signature, and it would physically reflect back toward the gun's stock to minimize the suppressor's length.

He checked his watch. Ten minutes to go.

He put in his earwig and clipped the power pack to his belt. His comm set was now up and running.

He sighted through the scope again. His crosshairs were suspended over one particular spot in the park.

Because he couldn't move his rifle barrel, Robie would have a millisecond's glimpse of his target and then his finger would pull the trigger.

If he was late by a millisecond, the target would survive.

If he was early by a millisecond, the target would survive.

Robie took this margin of error in stride. He had had easier assignments, to be sure. And also tougher ones.

He took a breath, and relaxed his muscles. Normally he would have someone acting as a long-distance spotter. However, Robie's recent experiences with partners in the field had been disastrous, and he had demanded to go solo on this one. If the target didn't show, or changed course, Robie would get a stand-down signal over his comm pack.

He looked around the small space. It would be his home for a few minutes more and then he would never see it again. Or if he screwed up, this might be the last place he ever saw.

He checked his watch again. Two minutes to go. He didn't return to his rifle just yet. Taking up his weapon too early could make his muscles rigid and his reflexes too brittle, when flexibility and fluidity were needed.

At forty-five seconds to target, he knelt and pressed his eye to the scope and his finger to the trigger guard. His earwig had remained silent. That meant his target was on the way. The mission was a go.

He wouldn't look at his watch again. His internal clock was now as accurate as any Swiss timepiece. He focused on his optics.

Scopes were great, but they were also finicky. A target could be lost in a heartbeat and precious seconds could pass before it was reacquired, which guaranteed failure. He had his own way of dealing with that possibility. At thirty seconds to target he started exhaling longer breaths, walking his respiration and heart rate down notch by notch, breath by elongated breath. Cold zero was what he was looking for, that sweet spot for trigger pulls that almost always ensured the kill would happen. No finger tremble, no jerk of the hand, no wavering of the eye.

Robie couldn't hear his target. He couldn't yet see him.

But in ten seconds he would both hear and see him.

And then he would have a bare moment to acquire the target and fire.

The last second popped up on his internal counter.

His finger dropped to the trigger.

In Will Robie's world once that happened there was no going back.

3

The man jogging along did not worry about his security. He paid others to worry for him. Perhaps a wiser man would have realized that no one valued a specific life more than its owner. But he was not the wisest of men. He was a man who had run afoul of powerful political enemies, and the price for that was just about to come due.

He jogged along, his lean frame moving up and down with each thrust of hip and leg. Around him were four men, two slightly in front and two slightly behind him. They were fit and active, and all four had to slow down their normal pace a bit to match his.

The five men were of similar height and build and wearing matching black running suits. This was by design because it resulted in five potential targets instead of one. Arms and legs swinging in unison, feet pounding the trail, heads and torsos moving at steady but still slightly different angles. It all added up to a nightmare for someone looking to take a long-distance shot.

In addition, the man in the center of the group wore lightweight body armor that would stop most rifle rounds. Only a head shot would be guaranteed lethal, and a head shot here over any distance beyond the unaided eye was problematic. There were too many physical obstacles. And they had spies in the park; anyone looking suspicious or carrying anything that might be out of the ordinary would be tagged and sat on until the man had passed. There had been two of those so far and no more.

And yet the four men were professional, and they anticipated that despite their best efforts, someone might still be out there. They kept their gazes swiveling, their reflexes primed to move into accelerated action if necessary.

The curve coming up was good in a way. It broke off potential sniper sight lines, and fresh ones would not pick up for another ten yards. Though they were trained not to do so, each man relaxed just a fraction.

The suppressed round was still loud enough to catapult a flock of pigeons from the ground to about a foot in the air, their wings flapping and their beaked mouths cooing in protest at this early morning disturbance.

The man in the center of the joggers pitched forward. Where his face had once been was a gaping hole.

The long-distance flight of a 7.62 round built up astonishing kinetic energy. In fact, the farther it traveled the more energy it built up. When it finally ran into a solid object like a human head the result was devastating.

The four men watched in disbelief as their protectee lay on the ground, his black running suit now mottled with blood, brain, and human tissue. They pulled their guns and looked wildly around for someone to shoot. The security chief spoke into his phone, dialing up reinforcements. They were no longer a protection detail. They were a revenge detail.

Only there was no one on whom to exact that revenge.

It had been a scope kill, and all four men wondered how that was possible, on the curve of all places.

The only people visible were other joggers or walkers. None could have a rifle concealed on them. They all had stopped and were staring in horror at the man on the ground. If they had known who he was, their horror might have turned to relief.

Will Robie did not take even a second to relish the exceptionally fine shot he had just made. The constraints on his rifle barrel and thus his shot had been enormous. It was like playing a game of Whac-A-Mole. You never knew where or when the target would pop out of the hole. Your reflexes had to be superb, your aim true.

But Robie had done it over a considerable distance with a sniper rifle and not a child's hammer. And his target wasn't a puppet. It could shoot back.

He hefted the tubes of pliable material that had been used to replace the mortar. From his knapsack he took a hardening solution from a bottle and mixed it with some powder he had in another container. He rubbed the mixture on one end and the sides of the two tubes and eased them through the open holes, lining the edges up precisely. Then he rubbed the mixture on the other end of the tubes. Within two minutes the mixture would harden and blend perfectly with the mortar, and one would be unable to slide the tubes out anymore. His sight line had, in essence, vanished, like a magician's assistant in a box.

Knapsack on his back, he was disassembling his weapon as he walked. In the center of the room was a manhole cover. Underneath Central Park were numerous tunnels, some from old subway line construction, some carrying sewage and water, and some just built for now unknown reasons and forgotten about.

Robie was about to use a complicated combination thereof to get the hell out of there.

He slid the manhole cover into place after he lowered himself into the hole. Using a flashlight, he navigated down a metal ladder and his feet hit solid earth thirty feet later. The route he had to follow was in his head. Nothing about a mission was ever written down. Things written down could be discovered if Robie ended up dead instead of his target.

Even for Robie, whose short-term memory was excellent, it had been an arduous process.

He moved methodically, neither fast nor slowly. He had plugged the barrel of his rifle with the quick-hardening solution and pitched it down one tunnel; a constant flow of fast water would carry it out to the East River, where it would sink into oblivion. And even if it were found somehow the plugged barrel would be ruined for any ballistics tests.

The stock of the weapon was dropped down another tunnel under a pile of fallen bricks that looked like they had lain there for a hundred years and probably had. Even if the stock was discovered it could not be traced back to the bullet that had just killed his target. Not without the firing pin, which Robie had already pocketed.

The smells down here were not pleasant. There were over six thousand miles of tunnels under Manhattan, remarkable for an island without a single working mine of any kind. The tunnels carried pipes that transported millions of gallons of drinking water a day to satisfy the inhabitants of America's most populous city. Other tunnels carried away the sewage made by these very same inhabitants to enormous treatment plants that would transform it into a variety of things, often turning waste into something useful.

Robie walked at the same pace for an hour. At the end of that hour he looked up and saw it. The ladder with the markings *DNE EHT.*

"The End" spelled backward. He did not smile at someone's idea of a lame joke. Killing people was as serious as it got. He had no reason to be particularly happy.

He put on the blue jumpsuit and hard hat that were hanging on a peg on the tunnel wall. Carrying his knapsack on his back, he climbed the ladder and emerged from the opening.

Robie had walked from midtown to uptown entirely underground. He actually would have preferred the subway.

He entered a work zone with barricades erected around an opening to the street. Men in blue jumpsuits just like his worked away at some project. Traffic moved around them, cabs honking. People walked up and down the sidewalks.

Life went on.

Except for the guy back at the park.

Robie didn't look at any of the workers, and not a single one of them looked at him. He walked to a white van parked next to the work zone and climbed in the passenger side. As soon as his door thunked closed, the driver put the van in gear and drove off. He knew the city well and took alternate routes to avoid most of the traffic as he worked his way out of Manhattan and onto the road to LaGuardia Airport.

Robie climbed into the back to change. When the van pulled up to the terminal's passenger drop-off, he stepped out dressed in a suit with briefcase in hand and walked into the airport terminal.

LaGuardia, unlike its equally famous cousin, JFK, was king of the short-haul flights, handling more of them than just about any other airport outside of Chicago and Atlanta. Robie's flight was very short, about forty minutes in the air to D.C.—barely enough time to stow your carry-on, get comfortable, and listen to your belly rumble because you weren't going to get anything to eat on a flight that brief.

His jet touched down thirty-eight minutes later at Reagan National.

The car was waiting for him.

He got in, picked up the *Washington Post* lying on the backseat, and scanned the headlines. It wasn't there yet, of course, although there would be news online already. He didn't care to read about it. He already knew all he needed to know.

But tomorrow the headline on every newspaper in the country would be about the man in Central Park who had gone out to jog for his health and ended up dead as dead could be.

A few would mourn the dead man, Robie knew. They would be his associates, whose opportunity to inflict pain and suffering on others would be gone, hopefully forever. The rest of the world would applaud the man's demise.

Robie had killed evil before. People were happy, thrilled that another monster had met his end. But the world went on, as screwed up as ever, and another monster—maybe even worse—would replace the fallen one.

On that clear, crisp morning in the normally serene Central Park his trigger pull would be remembered for a while. Investigations would be made. Diplomatic broadsides exchanged. More people would die in retaliation. And then life would go on.

And serving his country, Will Robie would get on a plane or train or bus or, like today, use his own two feet, and pull another trigger, or throw another knife, or strangle the life out of someone using simply his bare hands. And then another tomorrow would come and it would be as though someone had hit a giant reset button and the world would look exactly the same.

But he would continue to do it, and for only one reason. If he didn't, the world had no chance to get better. If people with some courage in their hearts stood by and did nothing, the monsters won every time. He was not going to let that happen.

The car drove through the streets, reaching the western edge of Fairfax County, Virginia. It pulled through a guarded gate. When it stopped Robie got out and walked into the building. He flashed no creds, and didn't stop to ask permission to enter.

He trudged down a short hall to a room where he would sit for a bit, send a few emails, and then go home to his apartment in D.C. Normally after a mission he would walk the streets aimlessly until the wee hours. It was just his way of handling the aftermath of what he did for a living.

Today he simply wanted to go home and sit and do nothing more exacting than stare out his window.

That was not to be.

The man came in.

The man often came in carrying another mission for Robie in the form of a USB stick.

But this time he carried nothing except a frown.

"Blue Man wants to meet with you," he said simply.

Nothing much the man could have said would have intrigued or surprised Robie.

But this did.

Robie had seen a lot of Blue Man lately. But before that—for twelve years before that, to be precise—he hadn't seen him at all.

"Blue Man?"

"Yes. The car's waiting."

4

Jessica Reel sat alone at a table in the airport lounge. She was dressed in a gray pantsuit with a white blouse. Her flat shoes were black with a single strap over the top of each foot. They were lightweight and built for speed and mobility if she had to run.

Her only nod to eccentricity was the hat that sat on the table in front of her. It was a straw-colored panama with a black silk band, ideally suited for traveling because it was collapsible. Reel had traveled much over the years, but she had never worn a hat during any of those previous trips.

Now had seemed like a good time to start.

Her gaze drifted over thousands of passengers pulling rolling luggage and carrying laptop cases over their shoulders with Starbucks cups cradled in their free hands. These travelers anxiously scanned electronic marquees for gates, cancellations, arrivals, departures. And minutes or hours or days later if the weather was particularly uncooperative, they would climb into silver tubes and be flung hundreds or thousands of miles to their destination of choice, hopefully with most of their bags and their sanity intact.

Millions of people did this same little thirty-thousand-foot-high dance every day in nearly every country on earth. Reel had done it for years. But she had always traveled light. No laptop. Enough clothes for a few days. No work went with her. It was always waiting for her when she got there. Along with all the equipment she would need to complete her designated task.

And then she would make her exit, leaving behind at least one person dead.

She fingered her phone. On the screen was her boarding pass. The name on the e-ticket was not Jessica Reel. That would have been a little inconvenient for her in these suddenly troubled times.

Her last task had not gone according to plan—at least not according to the plan of her former employer. However, it had been executed exactly as Reel had envisioned it, leaving a man named Douglas Jacobs dead.

Because of this Reel would be not only persona non grata back home, but also very much a wanted person. And the people she used to work for had an abundance of agents who could be called up to hunt her down and end her life as efficiently as she had Jacobs's.

That scenario was definitely not in Reel's grand scheme, and thus the new name, fresh documents, and panama hat. Her long hair was colored blonde from the natural brown. Tinted contacts transformed greenish eyes to gray. And she had been given a modified nose and a revised jawline courtesy of a bit of ingenious plastic surgery. She was, in all critical respects, a new woman.

And perhaps an enlightened one as well.

Her flight was called. She rose. In her flats she was five-nine—tall for a woman—but she blended in nicely with the bustling crowd. She donned her hat, purchased her Starbucks, and walked to the nearby gate. The flight left on time.

Forty somewhat bumpy minutes later it landed with a hard jolt on the runway tarmac minutes ahead of a storm's leading edge. The turbulence had not bothered Reel. She always played the odds. She could fly every day for twenty thousand years and never be involved in a crash.

Her odds of survival on the ground would not be nearly as good.

She walked off the plane, made her way to the cabstand, and waited patiently in a long line until her turn came up.

Doug Jacobs had been the first but not the last. Reel had a list in her head of those who would, hopefully, join him in the hereafter, if there was such a place for people like Jacobs.

But the list would have to wait. Reel had somewhere to go. She climbed into the next available cab and set off for the city.

The cab dropped her near Central Park. The park was always a busy place, full of people and dogs and events and workers, controlled chaos if ever there was such a thing.

Reel paid the cabbie and turned her attention to the closest entrance to the park. She walked through the opening and made her way as close as possible to where it had happened.

The police had taped off great chunks of the area so they could perform their little forensics hunt, collect their evidence, and hopefully catch a killer.

They would fail. Reel knew this even if New York's Finest didn't.

She stood shoulder to shoulder with a crowd of people just beyond the official barricades. She watched the police methodically working, covering every inch of ground around where the body had fallen.

Reel looked at the same ground and her mind started to fill in blanks that the police didn't even know existed.

The target was what it was. A monster who needed killing.

That didn't interest Reel at all. She had killed many monsters. Others took their place. That was how the world worked. All you could do was try to keep slightly ahead in the count.

She was focused on other things. Things the police could not see.

She lined up the taped outline of the body on the trail with trajectory patterns in all directions. She was sure the police had already done that, Forensics 101 after all. But soon thereafter, their deductive ability and even their imagination would reach their professional limits, and thus they would never arrive at the right answer.

For her part, Reel knew that anything was possible. So after exhausting all other possibilities and performing her own mental algorithms to figure the shooter's position, she focused on a stone wall. A seemingly impenetrable stone wall. One could not fire through such an obstacle. And the doorway into the place that was surrounded by the stone wall had no sight line to the target. And it was no doubt securely locked. Thus the police would have discounted it immediately.

Reel left the crowd and started a long sweeping walk

that angled her first to the west, then north, and finally east.

She drew out a pair of binoculars and focused them on the wall.

One would have to have two holes. One for the muzzle allowing for the greater width of the suppressor sleeve. And one for the scope.

Reel knew precisely where and how large those holes would need to be.

She worked the thumbwheel on her optics. The wall came into sharper focus. Reel looked at two areas of the wall, one higher than the other, both located in mortar seams.

The police would never see it because they would never be looking for it.

But Reel was.

There was no surveillance camera that she could see pointed at the wall. Why would there be? It was simply a wall.

Which made it perfect.

And on that wall were two patches of mortar that were a slightly different color, as though they had been more recently applied than their neighbors. And they had been, Reel knew.

As soon as the shot was fired the holes would be refilled. The hardening compound would work its magic. For some hours, even some days afterward, the coloration would be slightly, ever so slightly, different. And then it would look just like the rest.

The shot had come from there.

The escape would have also come from there.

Reel looked down at the ground.

Maintenance shed. Pipes, tunnels.

Underneath the park was a maze of tunnels—water, sewer, and abandoned subway tracks. Reel knew this for a fact. It had figured into one of her kills years ago. So many places to run and hide under America's largest city. Millions of people above were jostling for space, while down below you could be as alone as though you were on the surface of the moon.

Reel began to walk again after putting her binoculars away.

The exit would have probably been in some far-off part of the city. Then the shooter would rise up to street level. A quick ride to the airport or train station and that would be it.

The killer goes free.

The victim goes to the morgue.

The papers would cover it for a while. There might be some geopolitical retaliation somewhere, and then the story would die. Other stories would take its place. One death meant little. The world was too big. And too many people were dying violent deaths to focus for long on any one of them.

Reel walked toward a hotel where she had reserved a room. She would hit the gym to work the kinks out, sit in the steam shower, have a bit of supper, and think about things.

The jaunt to Central Park had not been without purpose.

Will Robie was one of the best, if not the best they had.

Reel had no doubt that Robie had pulled the trigger that morning in Central Park. He had covered his tracks. Made his way aboveground. Taken a plane to D.C. Checked back in at the office.

All routine, or as routine as things got in Robie's world.

In my world too. But not anymore. Not after Doug Jacobs. The only report they'll want about me now is my autopsy results.

Reel was fairly sure Robie would be summoned for another mission.

His mission will be to track me down and kill me.

You send a killer to catch another killer.

Robie versus Reel. Nice ring to it.

It sounded like the fight of the century.

And she was certain it would be.